Praise for the Culinary Mystery Series

Rocky Road

"Another fabulous installment of the Sadie Hoffmiller series. **The further I got into the story, the more complex it became** . . . definitely a rocky road of a plot!"

> —Heather Moore, author of *Heart of the Ocean* and the Timeless Romance anthologies, http://www.hbmoore.com/

Baked Alaska

"Sadie is a well-loved character with plenty of genuine issues which add depth to her personality. I love that **Josi's books are clean and well-rounded with a bit of humor, plenty of mystery, and nail-biting suspense.**"

> —Rachelle Christensen, author of *Wrong Number* and *Caller ID*, http://www.rachellejchristensen.com/

Tres Leches Cupcakes

"Kilpack is a capable writer whose works have grown and taken on a life of their own. *Tres Leches Cupcakes* **is an amusing and captivating addition to her creative compilations.**"

> —Mike Whitmer, *Deseret News*

Banana Split

"In *Banana Split*, Josi Kilpack has turned a character that we've come to love as an overzealous snoop and given her the breath of someone real so we can love her even more. **This is a story with an ocean's depth's worth of awesome!**"

> —Julie Wright, author of the Hazardous Universe series

Pumpkin Roll

"*Pumpkin Roll* is different from the other books in the series, and while the others have their tense moments, **this had me downright nervous and spooked**. During the climax, I kept shaking my head, saying, 'No way this is happening.' Five out of five stars for this one. I could not stop reading."

> —Mindy Holt, www.ldswomensbookreview.com

Blackberry Crumble

"**Josi Kilpack is an absolute master** at leading you to believe you have everything figured out, only to have the rug pulled out from under you with the turn of a page. *Blackberry Crumble* is a delightful mystery with wonderful characters and a white-knuckle ending that'll leave you begging for more."

> —Gregg Luke, author of *Blink of an Eye*

Key Lime Pie

"I had a great time following the ever-delightful Sadie as she ate and sleuthed her way through **nerve-racking twists and turns and nail-biting suspense**."

> —Melanie Jacobsen, author of *The List* and *Not My Type*,
> http://www.readandwritestuff.blogspot.com/

Devil's Food Cake

"Josi Kilpack whips up **another tasty mystery where startling twists and delightful humor mix** in a confection as delicious as Sadie Hoffmiller's devil's food cake."

> —Stephanie Black, four-time winner of the Whitney Award for Mystery/Suspense

English Trifle

"*English Trifle* is a delightful combo of mystery and gourmet cooking, highly recommended."

—*Midwest Review Journal*, October 2009

Lemon Tart

"The novel has a bit of everything. It's a mystery, a cookbook, a low-key romance and a dead-on depiction of life. . . . That may sound like a hodgepodge. It's not. It works. Kilpack blends it all together and cooks it up until it has the taste of, well . . . of a tangy lemon tart."

—Jerry Johnston, *Deseret News*

"*Lemon Tart* is an enjoyable mystery with a well-hidden culprit and an unlikely heroine in Sadie Hoffmiller. Kilpack endows Sadie with logical hidden talents that come in handy at just the right moment."

—Shelley Glodowski, *Midwest Book Review*, June 2009

FORTUNE COOKIE

OTHER BOOKS BY JOSI S. KILPACK

Her Good Name
Sheep's Clothing
Unsung Lullaby
Daisy

CULINARY MYSTERIES

Lemon Tart	*Pumpkin Roll*
English Trifle	*Banana Split*
Devil's Food Cake	*Tres Leches Cupcakes*
Key Lime Pie	*Baked Alaska*
Blackberry Crumble	*Rocky Road*

Wedding Cake (coming Fall 2014)

Fortune Cookie recipes

Download a free PDF of all the recipes in this book at
josiskilpack.com or shadowmountain.com

FORTUNE COOKIE

A CULINARY MYSTERY

JOSI S. KILPACK

SHADOW
MOUNTAIN

Library of Congress Cataloging-in-Publication Data

Kilpack, Josi S., author.
  Fortune cookie / Josi S. Kilpack.
    pages cm
  Summary: Sadie Hoffmiller is busily adding the final touches to her wedding plans, but the arrival of a mysterious letter that bears a San Francisco postmark and no return address could change everything. The only person Sadie knows in San Francisco is her older sister, Wendy, whom she hasn't seen or heard from since their mother's funeral nearly fifteen years ago.
  ISBN 978-1-60907-787-7 (paperbound)
  1. Hoffmiller, Sadie—Fiction. 2. Cooks—Fiction. 3. Weddings—Planning—Fiction. I. Title.
  PS3561.I412F67 2014
   813'.54—dc23   2013039827

Printed in the United States of America
Lake Book Manufacturing, Inc., Melrose Park, IL

10   9   8   7   6   5   4   3   2   1

To Madison
May your beautiful wings take you everywhere you want to go
but never forget their way home.

CHAPTER 1

Sadie Hoffmiller had always liked things to be just so. "A place for everything and everything in its place" was efficient, consistent, and reduced both stress and loss. Certainly the investigations she'd been involved in over the last few years had shaken up some of her confidence in being able to keep things as they should be, but for the most part, she felt the changes that the disruptions had caused were for the better. She felt more capable of recovering from difficulties, more aware of what went on around her, and increasingly confident in her ability to take life as it came and respond accordingly. Even the lingering threat on her life was something she had come to terms with, knowing she might one day face it but hoping that perhaps the threat had disappeared.

Despite her confidence at being able to fix things gone wrong, however, she still preferred order to chaos when she had any say in the matter, and of all things Sadie should be able to control, her own wedding was it. Which is why the four-by-nine-inch envelope sitting in the middle of her kitchen table terrified her.

The wedding invitations she'd spent the last two days preparing were stacked on the entry table of her living room waiting for her to take them to the post office in the morning so they would go out before the Fourth of July holiday. She hoped the post office would have a wedding-specific stamp that would be the perfect final touch. Even if the people living out of state couldn't be there, she wanted them to celebrate the occasion with her, and completing all the invitations before the festivities of the national holiday had been a goal she took great pride in accomplishing.

And yet the lone envelope on the table had been sent *to* her. Sadie had discovered it in today's mail this afternoon and had been working up the courage to open it for hours. Was it mocking her? Egging her on? Or simply staring back at her as a reminder that not everything in her life could be controlled and anticipated?

There was a return address in San Francisco along with the name Doang in the upper left-hand corner. While the name was unfamiliar, Sadie only knew one person who lived in San Francisco: her older sister, Wendy, whom she hadn't seen for years. Perhaps Doang was Wendy's current last name. Sadie worried that Wendy had somehow learned about the wedding, and though some of Sadie's chronic curiosity was certainly triggered by the unexpected letter, it hadn't been enough to overcome her reluctance to invite her sister back into her life. Especially now.

The timer on the stove buzzed, and Sadie pulled the final pan of jam bars from the oven; she'd managed to come up with a dozen tasks around the house to delay the inevitable opening of that envelope. She'd been trying not to bake after six o'clock in the evening—she had a size twelve wedding dress to fit into, after all, and at the age of fifty-eight, she couldn't simply eat salads for a week to drop a few pounds before the big day—but the letter had knocked her off the proverbial wagon, and so she got a start on the variety of cookies she'd promised for the Garrison Fourth of July bake sale. That Wendy disliked their mother's jam bar recipe was purely coincidental.

The digital time display on her microwave read 9:44 p.m. Tomorrow would be a full day of both wedding and holiday preparations now that she was home and sufficiently recovered from her vacation-turned-investigation in Utah last week. Pete's daughters and their families were coming up for the Fourth, giving Sadie the chance to continue building those relationships. The wedding was only three and a half weeks away, and there was still so much to do. *Mrs. Peter Cunningham. Wow.*

Her eyes strayed back to the envelope on the table, and now that she had nothing left to distract her, she felt ridiculous for having put this off for the better part of the day. Resolved, Sadie grabbed her letter opener from the drawer of the desk in her living room and then picked up the envelope with her other hand. The handwriting looked different from what she expected—that is, if she'd expected this at all, which she hadn't.

"Wendy," Sadie said out loud. Her sister's name sounded strange on her tongue. It was sad that they were so disconnected, and yet Sadie had little motivation to reach out to change what had always been a difficult relationship. Wendy was five years older than Sadie and the source of many frightening memories from Sadie's childhood, including broken and missing toys, finding dead spiders in her oatmeal, and on more than one occasion being locked in a closet for hours while their parents were gone.

Wendy left home at seventeen, creating a void in the lives of Sadie's parents that was never remedied. Despite all the chaos and difficulty she'd brought into the family, Wendy was still their daughter, and they'd always hoped to be a part of her life. Now and then, she'd contact them to ask for money or to throw a tantrum about one issue or another, but for the most part she stayed out of their lives.

Sadie hadn't seen Wendy since their mother's funeral almost fifteen years earlier. Wendy had only stayed in town for four hours, long enough to put her rose on the casket and rifle through Mom's jewelry box. When their father died just four years ago, Sadie had tracked her sister down—still living in San Francisco—only to have Wendy say she couldn't get away for the funeral but she'd send flowers. She didn't send any flowers, and Sadie and her brother, Jack, followed their father's casket from the church without even a whisper about Wendy's absence. After that, Sadie had stopped sending Christmas cards that had never been reciprocated, she stopped marking Wendy's birthday on her calendar at the start of each new year, and each time she thought about her sister, she forced herself to think of something else. For all intents and purposes, Sadie didn't have a sister and never really had. She hadn't even told Pete about her, other than admitting Wendy existed.

Sadie inhaled deeply, hoping to control the growing anxiety that thoughts of Wendy induced. The scent of baking in the air didn't relax her like it usually did. No doubt she would eat a dozen bars herself before finally going to bed tonight. She'd faced off with murderers and psychopaths during the last few years, but her sister could send her into a panic with just a simple letter Sadie hadn't even read yet.

Sadie slid the letter opener into the corner of the envelope. The thin blade sliced smoothly through the paper with barely a whisper. She pulled out a sheet of lined paper that revealed a newspaper article enfolded within it. Intrigued yet hesitant, she unfolded the newsprint and was a bit confused by the partial coupon for Fourth of July flower arrangements until she realized that must be the back side. She turned the article over and read the heading.

Woman found dead in Mission District apartment

Sadie's heart rate increased as she read the opening lines about a burned and badly decomposed body being found after an anonymous call to 911 about an apartment fire. Sadie clenched her eyes shut as the house seemed to shift beneath her, but when she opened them, they wouldn't focus on the rest of the words, as though they were unwilling to read more. Unable to process it, she put the article down and pushed it away from her, her head tingling. After catching her breath, she turned her attention to the lined paper she still held in her shaky hand.

Ms. Hoffmiller,

My name is Ji Edward Doang. My natural mother was your sister, Wendy Wright Penrose, and I found your address among her possessions. Her body was found in her apartment June 25th, and I thought you would want to know. I am working to clear her apartment before the tenth of the month and determine what to do with her remains when the autopsy is complete. If you are available, I would appreciate your help as it is a big job and I am quite busy with family and work. If I don't hear from you, I will understand. I was not close with her either.

Wonderful Jam Bars

Crust
1½ cups flour
½ cup quick-cooking oats, uncooked
½ cup sugar
¾ cup butter or margarine, softened
½ teaspoon baking soda

Topping
¾ cup flaked coconut
¾ cup chopped nuts (walnuts work best)
¼ cup flour
¼ cup packed brown sugar
2 tablespoons butter or margarine, softened
½ teaspoon cinnamon
1 to 1½ cups strawberry, raspberry, or apricot jam

Preheat oven to 350 degrees. Grease the bottom and sides of a 9x13-inch baking dish.

Combine all crust ingredients in a large mixing bowl. Using an electric mixer, beat on low speed 1 to 2 minutes, scraping the bowl often until mixture is crumbly. Using your hands, press mixture into the bottom of greased pan. Bake for 18 to 20 minutes or until edges are lightly browned.

While crust is baking, combine coconut, nuts, flour, brown sugar, butter, and cinnamon in a mixing bowl. Beat at low speed, scraping the sides of the bowl often until well mixed. It will be crumbly.

Remove crust from oven and spread evenly with jam while crust is still hot, almost to the edges. Sprinkle topping mixture over jam. Return pan to the oven and bake an additional 18 to 20 minutes, or until top is lightly browned. Allow bars to cool completely in the pan on a wire rack before cutting into squares.

Makes 15 to 24 bars, depending on size. Serve warm with ice cream or cooled with whipped topping.

CHAPTER 2

A fter reading the letter three times, Sadie texted Pete that she was coming over, and although he replied to ask her what was wrong, she simply told him she'd explain when she got there. What she needed to talk about wasn't text-message material.

The porch light was on when she pulled into the driveway, and upon reaching his front door with a plate of jam bars in hand, she took a breath and knocked three times. The decision to come at all hadn't been an entirely conscious one; she'd just known she needed to talk to him, needed his advice and support, and so here she was, banging on his door long after the sun had set.

A night breeze made the realty sign planted in Pete's front yard sway back and forth, adding a creaking sound to the chirp of crickets that accompanied the summer night. Both Pete and Sadie had put their homes up for sale a week earlier with the idea that they would buy something new together—a symbol of their new start. Potential buyers had even come through both homes—one for Sadie and three for Pete, who had a two-car garage *and* double ovens—but no offers had been made on either home so far.

The click of the lock drew Sadie's attention, and she straightened as Pete pulled the door open, shrugging his shoulder into a flannel shirt; he had on a T-shirt underneath. His salt-and-pepper hair was mussed, as though he'd already been in bed. His beard was perfectly trimmed, and his hazel eyes were clear and searching. She felt exposed beneath his gaze. Sadie's hair had a little more pepper than his did and was currently styled in a sleek A-line stacked bob that showed off the different shades of gray she'd come to terms with.

"I brought you some jam bars," she said, holding out the plastic-covered plate while he began buttoning up his shirt. There had been twelve bars on the plate when she left home, but it was a seven-minute drive to his house, and Sadie had managed to eat two in that time. She'd need to vacuum her car tomorrow; jam bars were crumbly and not the kind of treat one should typically eat while driving.

Pete stepped onto the porch and closed the door behind him, watching her closely as he took the plate. "You didn't come over to give me cookies."

Sadie attempted a smile but knew it looked false when Pete pulled his eyebrows together.

"Sadie," he said with a mixture of reprimand, fatigue, and concern. "What's going on?"

Sadie held his eyes, relieved that he knew her so well. Why she couldn't come clean on her own, she didn't know, but this situation had become a blur of emotion and frozen feelings. Wishes and remembrances were twisted together like those parasitical vines that choked entire trees to death in the rain forests.

She reached into the back pocket of her jeans and withdrew the folded envelope. She held it out to him, and he transferred the plate of cookies to one hand so he could take the letter with the other. Sadie turned and sat on the top step of Pete's porch, looking out across the darkened neighborhood and wrapping her arms around herself.

Pete sat next to her, placing the plate behind them. She didn't watch but knew each motion he made due to the swish of the papers as he unfolded them. The minutes, which couldn't have been more than two, stretched into the night as she waited for him to finish. She knew he was done reading when she heard him refolding the papers.

"You've never told me much about your sister," Pete commented. His tone was casual but Sadie knew better. He seemed to be avoiding a direct question regarding her out-of-character actions tonight, and she sensed it was because he was leaving the direction of the conversation up to her. If she said "Never mind, good night," he would probably let her leave. She appreciated the consideration but needed to talk about this; she should have told him about Wendy before now. She rubbed her upper arms, though it wasn't cold, and then, unable to find the words to explain, she shrugged as though it was perfectly acceptable not to talk about someone who shared your DNA to the person you were about to marry.

"But Jack did."

Sadie whipped her head around to look at Pete. "What?"

"I'd asked you about her a couple of times but you always managed to change the subject, so when Jack and I went fishing last summer up at Big T, I asked him to fill me in."

Sadie looked across the neighborhood again, smoothing her hair behind her ear and unsure whether she was annoyed that Pete had gone behind her back to learn about this part of her life—though she did that kind of thing all the time—or relieved that he already knew. "What did Jack tell you?"

"That she was terrible to you, well, to everyone in your family, but you especially."

Me especially, Sadie thought. Her chest tightened. *Me especially.* For Pete's benefit she nodded to make sure he knew she'd heard him. "I'm sure she was mentally ill," Sadie said after a few more seconds of silence ate up more of the night. "Borderline personality disorder, possibly, though I wouldn't rule out bipolar, schizophrenic, and maybe histrionic as well."

"Diagnosed?"

Sadie shook her head. "I've read enough and met enough people with similarities to her that I've made my armchair-psychiatrist determinations. It helps me feel a bit more peace with how she treated me—us—to know she had limitations."

"Jack said she left home young."

"She was seventeen; I was twelve." Sadie appreciated the cautious push of Pete's questions that allowed her to remain as unemotional as possible. As a former police detective, Pete was well-trained in gathering information, and she was glad for the almost formal feel of the conversation—it made it easier for her somehow, kept things distant.

A car turned down Pete's street, and they both raised their hands to wave at whomever was returning home.

Sadie wrapped her arms around herself again and continued, "I never asked what the final fight was about. It happened when I was at school, and Mom was still crying when I got home. I was *so* relieved that Wendy was gone, though it took almost a year for me to believe she wasn't coming back."

"Jack said your parents wouldn't let you talk badly about her."

Sadie shook her head. "She was still their daughter, and they didn't want us creating an air of negativity about her while she was gone in case she came back. Since we didn't discuss the *hard* parts about Wendy, we simply didn't talk about her at all. When she did come up, we spoke of her the way you might talk about a great-aunt who lives too far away to visit."

"Did your parents know how she treated you?" Pete asked. "Jack said he'd never been sure, probably because, like you said, no one talked about her much."

"They knew some of the things she did and suspected other things that no one could prove." An owl hooted in the distance, and the sound made her shiver. Or maybe she just wanted Pete to put his arm around her shoulders, which he did. Sadie leaned into him, comforted by his warmth and the now-familiar, lingering scent of his cologne. "They tried to keep the two of us separate as much as possible. It helped, I think."

"Any idea why she singled you out?"

"She was my parent's first child, and the only one for five years. My parents didn't think they'd have any other children due to some complications of Wendy's birth. From what I've heard, Wendy was always difficult, even as an infant. She had digestive issues that required hospital stays and things—not that any of that is her fault, but it made her early years difficult ones and her temperament, as my mother described it, was one of perpetual discomfort. Then I came along—a surprise child my parents never thought they'd have. I was a good baby." She shrugged, hating how braggy she felt but, well, it was what had happened. "I was healthy and smiled a lot. I slept through the night after six weeks, and as I got older, I liked to make people happy."

"Everything she didn't do," Pete said.

"I guess so," Sadie said, feeling guilty all over again, as though it was her fault that adults had doted on her, that she was affectionate and precocious and obedient while Wendy was combative and intolerant and whiney. Sadie joined Brownies when she was seven and earned badges faster than most girls in her troop. She'd loved to learn and accomplish goals, which equated to her excelling at most things she put her mind to. She sang solos in church, won art contests at school, was a good softball player on her pony league team, and always had a lot of friends.

Every triumph of her childhood, however, was punctuated with the memories of Wendy's retaliation: paint in her shoes, shredded homework, a dozen cupcakes she'd baked thrown against the kitchen wall. One time, Wendy had "accidentally" spilled hot wax from a candle on Sadie's leg, resulting in second-degree burns that prevented Sadie from going on a camping trip with their church youth group. Another time, she slammed the car door on Sadie's foot the day before Sadie's softball tournament.

Wendy never accepted responsibility—she either denied she'd done those things or explained them away as accidents—but she took a dark kind of satisfaction in seeing Sadie hurt, embarrassed, scared, or upset and was quite skilled at creating those situations.

"It was such a relief when she left home," Sadie admitted quietly, as though her parents could still overhear and remind her not to dwell on things that couldn't be changed. "I don't like to think about her."

"I can see why," Pete said, rubbing his hand against her arm, which had broken out in goose bumps. "She didn't treat Jack the same way?"

Sadie shook her head slowly. "I've never been sure why not. Maybe because he was the youngest or because he was a boy, or maybe as a girl I was more threatening to her position or something, but she didn't target him the way she did me, though she wasn't nice to him either." There was a time when Sadie had been jealous of the way Jack seemed to exist below Wendy's radar. It made her wonder what was wrong with *her*, why Wendy hated her so much. But she was also grateful that Jack hadn't been through the same things she'd endured.

Sadie waited for Pete to say something more, ask her a question or lead the conversation, but he remained silent. After several seconds had passed, she said, "I know I should go to San Francisco and help her son, but I really don't want to."

"Why not? She won't be there."

Sadie knew he'd meant to give her some kind of comfort, perhaps help her acknowledge that going to San Francisco wouldn't put her at risk. Wendy was *dead*. But crossing into Wendy's world made Sadie feel the same vulnerability she remembered from her childhood. "But your family is coming in for the Fourth of July, and I still have cookies to make for the bake sale and wedding plans to finalize and a house to sell and . . . a lot of things to do."

She liked the normalcy of her life right now; she liked her relationship with Pete, which had started when Sadie's neighbor had been found dead behind her home and Sadie had involved herself in finding answers. They'd been through a lot since then and had found this good, comfortable, and assuring place together. Sadie looked forward to becoming Pete's wife. Wendy's interference with that happiness was unwelcome, though Sadie felt guilty for feeling that way too. Shouldn't Sadie feel so terrible about Wendy's death that she would want to do right by her? Or at least by her son?

"Then don't go," Pete said. "This Jee or Jye or however you say his name said he'd understand if you didn't want to help. Did you know about her son?"

Another wave of guilt washed over her. "We were never certain if he was real or not. She didn't tell my parents about him until he was three. She claimed he'd been bitten by a neighbor's dog, and she needed money for the medical bills. My parents gave her five thousand dollars and asked if they could come out and help. She said she'd let them know, but then she didn't call for two years until she was behind on her rent and she and her son would be evicted if my parents didn't help her out again. Once again they sent money and extracted a promise that Wendy would bring him to visit. She'd called him Eddie though."

"His letter said his middle name was Edward," Pete commented.

Sadie nodded; she'd noticed that too. "She didn't come and the number she'd given my parents was disconnected soon after that. The next time we heard from her she said Eddie was living with his father—his father is Vietnamese or Chinese or something. She never sent pictures, and in time I became all but convinced that he was something she'd made up."

Pete nodded as though he understood, but Sadie wondered how that could even be possible. She wasn't sure *she* understood. "You could send her son money to help with the funeral costs and be done with it. You'd still be doing something to help, and it sounds like the financial situation is a concern for him. It's probably the main reason he contacted you, for help with the expenses."

Sadie was quiet. She *could* just send money and explain that was all she could do; the idea had certainly crossed her mind. But . . . "He's reaching out to me, and he *is* family. My parents would want me to at least try to establish a relationship with him. Wendy never gave them the chance to have one."

"And maybe helping pack up her apartment will help you find some understanding for Wendy's behavior. You've lived with a child's impression of a cruel person, and maybe seeing her through her things and talking to the people in her life will give you a new grown-up perspective."

Sadie had gotten so good at living in the moment after her first husband had died two decades ago and left her a widow with years of life to recalculate that she rarely allowed the past to overwhelm her like it was doing tonight. She was surprised that even decades after Wendy's abuse, the memories were still so raw. She appreciated everything Pete was saying, but didn't think he understood the level of trauma Wendy had brought into Sadie's childhood.

"When I was four years old, Wendy tricked me into eating some laxatives by telling me they were candy. I ended up in the hospital for almost a week with severe dehydration and an intestinal block-age. It's one of my earliest memories—being alone in a dark hospital room, wishing my mother was there while worrying that when she came the next day she'd bring Wendy with her. I was really little, but I understood that Wendy could have killed me. To this day I'm not sure if that was her goal, but in the back of my mind it seems as though it was."

Pete pulled Sadie closer and kissed the top of her head. "She sounds like a nightmare."

"She was certainly the source of a lot of them."

They sat in silence for nearly a minute, Sadie reliving the many fears Wendy had induced, things Sadie hadn't thought about for years and wished she wasn't thinking about now.

Pete's voice broke through the quiet. "It also sounds like her life after she left your family wasn't a happy one, and it ended dramati-cally."

For a moment Sadie wasn't sure what he meant, then remem-bered the heading of the article: WOMAN FOUND DEAD IN MISSION DISTRICT APARTMENT. "I didn't read the whole article," she admitted, leaving out the part about how her eyes wouldn't focus on the words. "Did it say how she died?"

"It said the police were considering a variety of possibilities. Her body was lit on fire several weeks after she died, though, which is strange. The article was written a couple of days after her body was discovered and didn't have much conclusive information. Maybe the police have established cause of death by now."

Sadie shuddered at the grisly details. "Nobody deserves anything like that." *Had Wendy been murdered?* she wondered. She'd been involved in too many murder investigations not to consider the possibility. Burning the body could have been about destroying evidence.

"I bet there are follow-up articles we could look at. And maybe we can talk to the detectives working on the case in San Francisco—I might have an in with the department that could get us some additional information. Her body was discovered just over a week ago, so forensics ought to have more information by now."

Sadie *would* like to know more about what had happened, but did she have to go to San Francisco to get that information? Couldn't she stay right here, in her own world, and gather information online and over the phone while Wendy's son closed out her life? Sadie could send money to help with expenses and fulfill her familial obligation that way.

"If you decide to go, I'll come with you," Pete said.

Sadie looked up at him. "You would?"

He smiled and tucked the same strand of hair she'd been fussing with behind her ear. "Of course I would." He brushed the backs of his fingers along her jawline, initiating a new round of goose bumps. "We could take in some of the sights while we're there. It's a great city even if the reason we're going isn't a happy one. We could make the best of it, and you could meet your nephew."

"What about the holiday? Cancelling at the last minute isn't going to win me any points with your girls." It had been a slow process building a relationship with Pete's daughters, both of whom lived about an hour away. Their mother, Pat, had died five years ago, and Sadie's life must look disturbingly dramatic from where they stood, only seeing bits and pieces of it as Pete hurried from one situation to another helping Sadie out of several dangerous events. It had to be even more difficult for them to see their father in love with someone other than their mother. They were trying, though, and Sadie was grateful for that. She hated the idea that Wendy would be the reason she would cancel their plans at the last minute.

"We could go after the Fourth." Pete lifted the letter he still held. "I'm sure . . . Eddie wants to spend the holiday with his family too. If we left on the fifth, for instance, there'd still be plenty of time for us to get things taken care of before the deadline he talks about in his letter. Maybe Jack will come too."

Sadie looked at the envelope in his hand. The thought of entering Wendy's world, even without her in it, was still overwhelming. But she could do it with Pete there beside her. Jack would make it even better.

"Sadie, she can't hurt you anymore," Pete whispered.

She looked away from those penetrating eyes and watched the realty sign sway in the breeze. Even after all these years, and evidence of Wendy's death in black and white, Sadie wasn't sure she believed him.

CHAPTER 3

It was almost midnight before Sadie got home. She was exhausted and went to bed, but she didn't sleep well. It was a relief when the sun came up, giving her an excuse to stop trying to sleep and start the day instead.

Because Wendy's son lived in California, she felt it was only polite to wait until 10:00 a.m. before she called him—9:00 his time. While she waited for the clock to strike that magic hour, she cleaned out her fridge, vacuumed the entire house, reorganized her spice cupboard, went to the post office and mailed the invitations, and ordered a new set of dish towels online.

When she finished those tasks, she read all the online articles she could find about Wendy's death. They were all so impersonal, and there wasn't any significant information other than the exact time the fire was called in—1:21 in the morning on June 25—and that several personal items were missing from the apartment.

At exactly 10:01, Sadie sat down at her kitchen table ready to dial the number Wendy's son had included at the bottom of his letter. She had already punched in the area code when she remembered Jack. How could she forget to tell Jack what had happened?

Dismayed to have not already called him, she canceled the call and dialed her brother's number instead.

"Hey, Sadie," he said cheerily into the phone when he answered. "How are ya?"

The effect of his words on the fractured feelings left over from last night was powerful, and Sadie had to blink back tears to keep from becoming emotional. His greeting seemed to offer proof that she was loved and that she wouldn't be alone in the conflict she was feeling over the death of their sister.

"Hey, Jack," she replied, glad her voice didn't shake. "Do you have a minute?" When he said he did, she explained all that had happened in the last twelve hours, then waited as he digested the information through a long pause. It was against her nature to let such pauses stretch very long, but with Jack it was different. The two of them had always bonded together in the wake of the difficulties Wendy had brought into their lives. Jack—though the younger brother—had often stuck up for Sadie and had even physically protected her from Wendy. She'd often wondered if, without Jack's loyalty, she'd have taken more of the blame for Wendy's treatment.

"Wow," Jack finally said, reverent and thoughtful.

"I know," Sadie said, nodding even though he couldn't see her. While they'd talked, she'd drawn a few dozen little squares on the paper in front of her. She started drawing lines between them in a dot-to-dot pattern. "Pete and I are going to go out on Thursday, and I wanted to know if you'd like to come with us to meet her son, pack up the apartment, and make funeral arrangements."

She could feel the regret within the sigh Jack let out before he spoke. "Oh, gosh, Sadie, I feel like the worst brother in the world to say I can't, but . . . I can't. I'm presenting at a seminar in Miami on

Monday, and Carrie agreed to fly out there with me on Friday morning so we can have a few days together before the seminar."

Sadie raised her eyebrows. Jack and Carrie had had a difficult few years—*very* difficult. Sadie hadn't known from one month to the next whether they were getting divorced or going to counseling or courting all over again, and she had stopped asking for fear that her questions made her baby brother uncomfortable. She *did* know that Jack was still living in an apartment across town while Carrie lived next door to Sadie, though they didn't associate with each other much—things were awkward.

"She's going with you?" Sadie repeated—it was that hard to believe.

Jack gave her an update about the state of his marriage: a breakthrough that had taken place in counseling and the support of their children toward a reconciliation. "It's like when we were dating, Sadie," Jack said, excitement and optimism thick in his words. "But better—more real. I think we're going to make this work."

"I couldn't be more happy for you," Sadie said, meaning every word. Though Carrie and Sadie had never been close, that was no reason to question the potential happiness Jack and Carrie could find together, and Sadie would never begrudge him that.

"I feel terrible leaving you to deal with this alone, though," Jack said.

"Don't," Sadie said. "Pete will be there with me."

"If it were just the seminar, I'd cancel," Jack added.

"Jack," Sadie said with a small laugh. "It's okay. And don't feel bad, alright?"

He apologized at least three more times, second-guessing and wondering out loud if he *could* change his plans, but Sadie responded each time with more insistence that his marriage was more important. He offered to help with any of Wendy's final expenses, and Sadie promised to hold him to that. They ended the call when his 10:15 appointment showed up, but only after she promised to call him with daily updates.

Sadie hung up, refusing to dwell on her disappointment at not having Jack go with her. Instead, she immediately called Wendy's son before she let her anxiety level rise any higher than it already was.

A man answered after the second ring. "Ni hao."

Hearing the Chinese greeting threw her, but just for a moment. She cleared her throat and regained her focus. "Hello, I'm calling for Gee or Jye—or maybe Eddie . . ."

"Jee," the man said. "This is me."

Ji, Sadie repeated to herself. *My nephew.* "Um, hi, my name is Sadie Hoffmiller. You wrote me a letter about my . . . about your . . . about Wendy." She hated how hard it was to talk about her sister and wished she'd asked Pete to be here when she made this call. Surely she'd feel more confident if he were here.

"Oh," Ji said, sounding equally surprised to have her on the phone. He didn't speak with an accent. "Yes. Hello."

"Hi," Sadie said simply. "Um, thank you for writing to me, and for the article. I'm so sorry. What a horrible thing to deal with."

"Yes, it is horrible."

They both remained silent, waiting for the other person to speak. Sadie decided to get to the point rather than prolong the awkwardness. "Uh, you'd asked about me coming out to help with the apartment, and I wondered if it would be okay if we came on the fifth—after the holiday."

"We?"

"Oh, my fiancé, Pete, will be coming to help as well."

"With three of us, the work should go quickly," Ji said in a businesslike tone. "I visited the apartment on Friday and got the keys from Mr. Pilings, the landlord. I don't think it will take us very long to pack everything up. I had considered giving most of her belongings to a Goodwill-type organization my friend is a part of, is that okay with you?"

"That's totally your decision," Sadie said. "But sure, it's fine with me." She imagined Wendy had lived a rather desolate life and suspected she hadn't acquired much of anything of value. Ji's plan to donate her belongings seemed to emphasize that theory.

Another awkward silence descended and though Sadie had a hundred questions to ask, Ji was reserved, and she was hesitant to be too pushy. "So, you live in San Francisco?"

"Above our restaurant, yes."

"Oh, you own a restaurant? What kind?"

"Chinese."

Duh, Sadie thought, shaking her head at her own stupidity.

Ji continued. "We're located on Sacramento Street in Chinatown. It's called Choy's."

"That's wonderful," Sadie said, trying to improve the impression she was making. "Maybe Pete and I will stop in for lunch while we're there."

"Sure," Ji said, but he didn't sound excited about it like she'd hoped he would. "Perhaps you would like the number for Detective Lopez. He's the investigator."

Sadie couldn't help but wonder if Ji was trying to get off the phone with her. She hoped they would be more comfortable with one another in person. "That would be helpful," she said. "Thank you."

He gave her the number and asked her to call him when she got into town on the fifth so they could make plans to clear the apartment. In the meantime Ji would set up a pickup time for the charity. They ended the call—it hadn't even lasted two minutes—and Sadie went online to make flight reservations before she could change her mind.

In the back of her mind was the continuing disbelief that this was happening. She was making plans to clean out the apartment where her sister—whom she hadn't seen in fifteen years—had died. It was almost too much to think about, and while she knew she would have to accept the enormity of the situation eventually, for now she decided to treat this like any other case she'd been involved in. Whatever emotional journey she needed to take because of her connection to Wendy could come later.

After she confirmed the two tickets from the Denver International Airport to Oakland on the morning of July fifth, Sadie looked at the number for Detective Lopez, reluctant to make the call for a number of reasons. She still needed to make two more batches of cookies, a potato salad, and two peach pies. Plus she needed to buy some fireworks. Not to mention figuring out what to wear tomorrow; she had multiple outfits of the patriotic variety so it could take some time to determine which one was just right this year. Pete was also coming over later to work on some minor repairs around the house that the realtor had suggested. How she wished all she had to do today was cook delicious food and hang out with Pete.

Afraid of delaying so long that she'd talk herself out of it entirely, she dialed the number, feeling anxious and tense, and then let out a breath of relief when the call went to Detective Lopez's voice mail. She left a message, explaining who she was and why she was calling, then asked that he call her back at his earliest convenience, which she secretly hoped would be two days from now. She hung up, feeling grateful for the reprieve, and then dove into her work with increased focus. She turned up the radio far louder than she usually would so as to better shield her from her own thoughts.

Pete showed up around one o'clock with lunch—sandwiches from their favorite deli in town—and his toolbox. Sadie turned down the radio after he had to shout "Hello" to get her attention. After lunch, she returned to her pie making and Pete got going on his honey-do list. He was replacing a hinge on one of the kitchen cabinets when Sadie's phone rang. Sadie glanced at the area code—San Francisco—before lifting the phone to her ear. She gave Pete a pointed look that kept his attention on her while he tightened the screws.

"Hello," she said into the phone. She continued to roll out the pie crust while holding the phone uncomfortably against her shoulder.

"Hello, this is Detective Lopez with the San Francisco Police Department. I'm calling for Katie Hoffmiller?"

"Sadie Hoffmiller," she said, correcting him. "Thank you for calling me back."

"Thank *you* for calling. I'm sorry I haven't contacted you before now. When Mr. Doang said he was going to write you a letter, I moved you further down my list of people to talk to, but I fully expected to get back to you before this much time had passed."

"It's fine," Sadie said, hoping that his not having contacted her wasn't a reflection to the attention that was being given to Wendy's case.

"What can I help you with?"

"Well, my fiancé and I will be coming to San Francisco in a couple of days, and I thought it would be good to let you know I'd be in town and also to see what the status of the case is."

"Sure," Detective Lopez said. There was a gruffness to his voice that didn't quite match the upbeat nature of his speech, and she wondered if he were a smoker. "The case is active, and we've managed to talk to the tenants in her building as well as to a few associates. We've finished going through some paperwork we took from her apartment, but nothing has stood out. I'm afraid the state of the body was quite . . . poor, and so forensics hasn't given us their final report yet."

Sadie asked about some of the details from the articles. No one had seen anything strange the night of the fire, and although the police were unsure of the exact day Wendy had died, they were guessing it was May twenty-second. That was the last day her phone and her credit card had been used. There was no note indicating suicide, and it seemed that Wendy had been taking a bath when she died. Neighbors in her building said she didn't come and go much; they suspected she'd been ill through most of the winter, though there seemed no evidence that she'd been seeking medical treatment for anything specific.

In turn, Detective Lopez asked if Sadie could add any information about her sister that might be helpful to the investigation, but she had to admit that she didn't know anything about her sister's life. Sadie put aside her rolling pin and turned so that she was leaning against the counter.

"You didn't speak to her regularly?" the detective asked.

"I didn't speak to her at all," Sadie said, feeling the sadness of that fact. "I haven't seen her since my mother's funeral fifteen years ago, and the last time I spoke to her was when our father died four years ago."

"I see," Detective Lopez said. Sadie imagined him making a note in his notebook: "estranged sister." "So you have no idea if anyone would have targeted her or wanted to harm her?"

"No," Sadie said. She vacillated as to whether or not her relationship with Wendy as a child was relevant to the case, but worried it was her discomfort in talking about it that made her hesitate. She took a breath and then told Lopez a condensed version of her childhood. She didn't go so far as to suggest that perhaps Wendy hadn't changed and someone else she'd mistreated had gotten back at her, but she felt sure that Detective Lopez picked up on the possibility.

"That's consistent with information we got from her neighbors and friends," he said, though he sounded a bit cautious. "It seems she had a lot of conflicts with people. I appreciate knowing a bit more about her history."

Pete had moved on to another cupboard in need of hinge repair, but she could feel him listening.

"I assume the apartment's been cleared by the police?" Sadie said, ready to move on to another topic. "We're okay to move her things out?" The landlord had given Ji the keys, so Sadie felt safe assuming the police were finished with their part.

"Yeah, we've cleared it as a crime scene. Other than the fire, which remained well contained, there's no evidence of a struggle or anything that would lead us to conclude that she died of anything other than natural causes."

"You said there was no sign of a struggle, but one of the articles said there was a robbery involved?"

"Yes, we can't find her purse, phone, or laptop computer, but there isn't any suspicious activity on her bank account or credit cards, so the thief likely only took whatever cash your sister might have had in her wallet—though she seemed to be a charge-card kind of girl."

"What about jewelry?" Sadie said, thinking of her mother's pieces that Wendy had taken after the funeral.

"We did find a jewelry box with several items—costume jewelry mostly—when we searched her apartment."

"It wasn't stolen?"

"No, we found it in a dresser drawer, so it wasn't immediately evident. The thief probably knew that electronics sell fast and easy. It seemed to be a pretty quick job."

"Other than the burglar taking the time to light the body on fire," Sadie added.

Detective Lopez paused and cleared his throat. "Well, yes, other than that. I'm afraid this is a unique case, and it has provided very few leads for us to follow up on. Once we get the forensics report, we hope to have more to work with."

"And when will that be?" Sadie asked.

"After the holiday. Perhaps not until next week. I'll check on how much longer we'll need to wait so I'll have more specific information for you when you get into town."

Pete nudged her shoulder, and she turned to him with a questioning look.

"Ask him if he knows Cornell Bateman," Pete whispered, waving toward the phone.

Sadie scowled at Pete throwing off her groove, but she did as he asked. "Um, Detective Lopez, do you know Cornell Bateman?"

"Corney?" Detective Lopez said with a laugh. "I absolutely do. How do you know him?"

Since Sadie had no idea who Cornell Bateman was, she handed the phone to Pete, who had a five-minute discussion with Detective Lopez about the mutual friend that Pete had attended the academy with nearly thirty years ago. He now worked vice out of Oakland.

Sadie was slightly annoyed by the good-ol'-boys discussion at first, but by the time they stopped talking about Corney, she hoped she'd get the chance to meet him sometime. He sounded like a great guy. Somehow Pete transitioned the conversation to questions about the case—more detailed questions than Sadie had thought to ask, things like procedure, document forensics, and Wendy's history with the department.

By the time they'd finished the call Detective Lopez had agreed to talk to his superior about the possibility of Pete coming into the station and talking through the case file with them after he and Sadie arrived in San Francisco. Sadie tried to hide her envy—police had never been that excited when *she* was involving herself in a case.

Pete hung up and handed her the phone, grinning with satisfaction.

"Are you sure you were really ready to retire?" Sadie asked cautiously. It had only been a couple of months since he'd turned in his badge, but talking the lingo seemed to have lit a fire inside him.

He came closer to her, putting his arms loosely around her waist. "You know I've missed it," he said, sounding meek and a little vulnerable.

Sadie nodded; she did know. She also knew that he'd put in some applications for different part-time positions within the department that would keep him involved, but not quite so obligated. She supposed she simply hadn't realized what a big part of him was still a cop. "Detective Lopez sounds pretty open to having you look around."

"Does that bother you?" Pete asked.

"No," Sadie said. "But it does sound as though you're taking the case, so to speak. You think it was a homicide?"

"The San Fran PD doesn't seem to think so—there were no

obvious signs of trauma to the body. But we know that at least two crimes were committed by someone—the theft of the missing items from her apartment and the desecration of a human body." Sadie suppressed a shudder at the clinical language, and Pete stopped. "I'm sorry," he said. "If it bothers you to—"

"No, it doesn't bother me," she said, determined not to shy away from things. "It's just that . . . with all the other cases I've worked on, it was someone else, you know? They didn't belong to me. It's just shocking when I let myself think that this was Wendy. My sister."

Pete paused, then spoke with a bit of hesitation. "You said you wanted to know more about her."

Sadie nodded. "I guess that's where my focus is—learning about her life. Thinking so much about her death is harder for me to do—heck, thinking about her *life* is hard for me. She discarded all of us so long ago."

Pete nodded his understanding. "What if I work with Lopez on the cop side of things—the death part. Then you can focus on the life she lived and the people she knew."

Sadie cocked her head to the side, considering. It did feel more comfortable to emphasize Wendy's history, but she didn't want to be left out. "If I agree, that doesn't mean you'll keep information from me, does it?"

Pete laughed. "I'll share whatever it is you want to know," he said. "And if at some point, you want to be the detective, I'll be more than happy to move out of the way."

Sadie put her arms around his neck, careful not to touch his clothes; her hands were still floury from the pie crust that was likely getting dryer by the minute. "Well, maybe just move over so there's room for both of us . . . if I decide I can handle it." Her smile faded as the reality of what they were facing moved into the confusing thoughts cycling through her mind. "I couldn't do this without you, Pete. And I do want answers."

Pete leaned in and kissed her. "We're in this together," he said quietly, pulling her half an inch closer.

Sadie nodded and kissed him back, grateful for his confidence since she was still unsure about how she felt. "Thank goodness for that."

Fresh Peach Pie

1 cup sugar
2 tablespoons cornstarch
2 cups water
1 (6-ounce) package peach-flavored gelatin
4 cups peeled and sliced fresh peaches*
Two pre-baked 9-inch pie crusts

In a medium saucepan, combine sugar, cornstarch, and water. Bring to a boil, whisking consistently until mixture becomes thick and clear. Add gelatin and mix well. Remove from heat and set aside. Allow mixture to cool, but not set—about 15 minutes.

While glaze is cooling, peel and slice the peaches. Once glaze has cooled, add peaches. Mix well. Divide filling between the two pie crusts. Cover with plastic wrap and chill until set—at least 2 hours. Garnish with whipped cream.

*You can use canned peaches in a pinch, but it isn't recommended.

Note: Breanna likes to add ½ cup of raspberries to the peaches. Delicious!

Makes two 9-inch pies.

CHAPTER 4

The flight from Denver to Oakland on Thursday landed just after ten o'clock in the morning, Pacific Daylight Time. Pete and Sadie picked up their rental car—a white Chevy Malibu—and put their carry-on luggage in the trunk. Sadie hated traveling with just a carry-on. She preferred to bring enough clothes that she was prepared for a variety of weather conditions and possible events she might need to dress for, but there was an extra baggage fee to bring a checked bag, so she'd picked four coordinating outfits that could be rearranged over seven days, though she had no expectation they would stay so long. According to her research, the temperatures were supposed to be in the low 70s, which seemed impossible for July, but she'd been sure to bring close-toed shoes, jeans, and a jacket in case the evenings were cool. Wasn't California supposed to be warm?

The GPS guided them expertly from this freeway to that belt route to this connection to that exit until they found themselves going over the San Francisco–Oakland Bay Bridge, or Bay Bridge for short. Sadie already felt dizzy from the driving portion of the trip and they weren't even in the city yet. How had people ever driven here without a GPS?

She stared out the window and tried to hold on to the good feel-ings from the holiday yesterday. Things had gone so well with Pete's daughters and their families, and each time Sadie was with them, their relationship felt a little more comfortable. Brooke, the older, had asked for the recipe for Sadie's famous potato salad and had in-vited her to attend a community theater production the next month to see her oldest son perform in an adaptation of *An American Tail*. It was the first time Brooke had specifically invited Sadie to anything, and it filled her with confidence that good things were happening within these new relationships. After the fireworks were over, *both* of Pete's daughters had initiated hugs good-bye. It had been such a fan-tastic day. But they weren't in Pete's backyard enjoying hamburgers while the kids played on a Slip 'N Slide anymore. Sadie wished like crazy that they were.

Pete used something called a FastTrak pass to get them through the toll booth. The pass had come with the rental car, but she wasn't sure what was so fast about it as they seemed to move as slowly across the enormous structure as every other car. While they crept forward a few feet at a time, Sadie took in her first sight of a city that didn't seem as though it could possibly fit on the small patch of land ahead of them.

"It's too early to check into the hotel," Pete said, "but we could have the concierge hold our bags while we grab lunch at Ji's restau-rant. It's just a few blocks from the hotel."

"Um, sure," Sadie said, internally acknowledging her hesitation at meeting her nephew. He'd asked her to call when they got into town. Showing up at his restaurant was as good as calling, right? She didn't want their relationship to start off badly; he'd been so formal on the phone that she worried he might not like her changing the initial contact. But she didn't want to overanalyze things either. Pete obviously wanted to go, so she kept her concerns to herself.

Over the last few days Sadie had attempted to sort through her feelings about stepping into Wendy's life. Everything weighing her down created a jumble of thoughts and emotions that meant she felt more introspective than usual. Pete allowed her the uncharacteristic silence, for which Sadie was grateful.

She thought back to what Pete had said on his porch two nights ago: "She can't hurt you anymore." Sadie knew what he meant, was even sure it was true, but the pain that she feared was not physical. Some childish part of herself—a remnant of the little girl she'd been when Wendy had embodied all of Sadie's fears—wished she could simply hide like she used to.

The automated voice of the GPS instructed Pete to exit the freeway at Fourth Street. "Or we could park at the square and worry about the hotel when it gets closer to check-in time," Pete mused while merging toward the off-ramp.

"It doesn't matter to me," Sadie replied. "What's the square?"

"Portsmouth Square," Pete said, glancing at her quickly. "It's in Chinatown. It's kind of a park with a playground and some benches, sort of a local hangout with underground public parking." He transitioned smoothly to a four-lane road with rail cables stretched above and across it and a landscaped divider running down the center. The blocks were small—a hundred yards or less—and there were people everywhere.

The sun went behind the clouds, but when Sadie craned her neck to look at the sky through the passenger window, she found herself looking up at enormous buildings, some of which disappeared into a blanket of fog that hovered in the air. It was eleven o'clock in the morning—shouldn't the fog have burned off by now?

Sadie sat back in her seat and looked at Pete. "I know you said you'd been to San Francisco before, but you seem awfully familiar with it."

"I love this city," Pete said with a wistful tone.

Sadie turned her full attention to her fiancé. She had no idea he felt so strongly about a city she had always avoided. Her daughter, Breanna, had done an internship at the San Francisco Zoo the summer after high school, and Sadie hadn't even gone to visit. Sadie's father had been sick at the time—and she was his primary caregiver—but she knew she could have arranged a trip if she'd really wanted to.

Pete continued, "It was one of Pat's favorite places to visit. Mine too. If we'd ever wanted to be urban dwellers, this is where we'd have done it." He stopped for a red light and glanced at Sadie. "You've really never been here?"

Sadie shook her head and swallowed the envy that sprang up at the realization that he'd shared this city with his first wife. It was silly to be jealous, though, and she worried that she was trying to find something to transfer her negative feelings to instead of thinking about Wendy. "How often have you visited?"

"At least half a dozen times." He looked straight ahead, a nostalgic expression on his face. "Pat and I honeymooned here and then came back on anniversaries when we could. There are so many things to see and do in this town, and it has such a rich sense of character. When the kids were teenagers, we came out for an entire week and never ran out of things to do. It was a great trip."

"That's wonderful," Sadie said, hoping her voice sounded upbeat. They'd both talked openly about their late spouses and understood they'd lived plenty of life before they met each other. But something about her fragile emotions regarding this situation, added to the realization that this city was full of memories of Pete's first wife, and the fact that they were supposed to be taking a honeymoon of their own in three weeks, blended together to create a pit in the middle of Sadie's stomach.

As they continued past the high-rise buildings and crowded sidewalks that banked the narrow streets, Pete remained silent. Perhaps he was experiencing some uncomfortable feelings, too.

There were restaurants and boutiques and cell phone stores on the ground level of the towering buildings all built side by side. Pete slowed down and pulled into the underground parking structure beneath Portsmouth Square, and they exited on foot a few minutes later to join the throngs of people enjoying the Chinatown district. The square itself had light posts painted red with lantern tops. Older Asian people and smatterings of tourists occupied the benches and checkerboard tables, relaxing and talking beneath the trees. Children laughed and squealed as they played on a slide and chased one another through the relatively small, grassless park.

"I think Choy's is just down here," Pete said, pointing. He took Sadie's hand; his touch went a long way to relieve her growing insecurities, though she worried that she held on a little tight. Whether it was some attempt to remind him that he was making new memories here with Sadie or because she was becoming increasingly anxious about meeting her nephew, she couldn't be sure.

Bright Chinese lanterns were strung across the streets, and Asians dressed in bright silk tunics handed out coupons and advertisements. Stone statues flanked doorways, and tables loaded with trinkets were set out in front of windows full of brightly colored shirts, flags, silk scarves, and jewelry. They passed a family speaking German, and a few seconds later Sadie heard someone yell at a child in what sounded like Italian. There were *so many* people.

"There it is," Pete said, increasing his pace as though they were at an amusement park and he was excited to get in line for the next ride. Sadie wasn't in nearly that kind of hurry but kept in step with him. The sign for Choy's was bright yellow with the Chinese characters to the side of the English translation written in contrasting red. In the window were posters of different foods with both the English and Chinese descriptions. The posters looked several years old, some of them more tattered and faded than others. Beside the glass front door was a green dragon statue, one paw resting on a ball. People had used the open mouth as an ashtray.

"Did you know there are both male and female dragon statues?" Pete asked, nodding to the statue, his hand on the door handle.

"I'm not sure I want to know how you can tell," Sadie replied, eyeing the statue warily.

Pete laughed. "The female dragon statues have baby dragons under their paw, and the male dragons have their paw on a ball."

"I get what baby dragons represent. What does the ball represent?"

Pete gave her a half smile and pulled open the door for her. "Because men rule the world, of course."

Sadie gave him an unimpressed look as she walked past him through the doorway. "And apparently design all the dragon statues."

Pete laughed and stepped in behind her. The fluorescent lighting buzzed overhead and made the inside of the restaurant brighter than the sky outside. Sadie had to blink a few times before her eyes adjusted. The white-walled restaurant was small—only ten tables sat close together, each with four chairs. Two Chinese men occupied one table, drinking coffee out of teacups and reading newspapers.

There was an artificial ficus tree in one corner that even from this distance Sadie could see was coated with dust, which was likely locked onto the plastic leaves by the cooking grease from the kitchen behind the red door on the far wall. Near the front door was a glass case upon which sat the cash register and what looked like a small Buddhist shrine—Sadie had seen a similar display at the nail salon where she got pedicures in Garrison.

Brightly colored Chinese lanterns hung from the ceiling but the strands weren't spaced properly and therefore didn't create the eye-pleasing pattern Sadie thought they should. The floor was faded black-and-white checkered linoleum and the chrome-legged Formica tables were likely original to whenever this establishment had been opened. Sadie hadn't been expecting anything fancy, but this wasn't anything like the restaurants she usually went to. However, it smelled wonderful and Sadie was suddenly hungry.

"Hole-in-the-wall places like this always have the best food," Pete said, barely containing his excitement as he took everything in.

Sadie agreed but couldn't come up with any good reason not to spruce things up a little. A restaurant didn't *have* to look run down to be good, did it? She'd been to plenty of restaurants that had amazing food *and* nice décor.

"Two?"

Sadie saw a small Chinese woman dressed in black slacks and an oversized black T-shirt coming toward them. Sadie smiled politely, noting the woman's porcelain skin, big brown eyes, and rosebud mouth. Her sleek black hair was pulled into a bun on the top of her head and shone beneath the too-bright lights. Sadie guessed she was in her early thirties, more from her commanding and confident attitude than from her actual looks that disguised her age. She was beautiful, and Sadie wondered if this were Ji's wife. Maybe she ran the front portion of their restaurant.

"Yes," Pete answered, since Sadie was so deeply entrenched in her study of this woman.

The woman nodded and waved them toward the table farthest away from the two men, who had yet to speak to one another. After they were seated, the woman set down two plastic-covered menus and then left without saying a word. Pete took his reading glasses out of the front pocket of his shirt and put them on to peruse the menu.

"Mmm, they have cheong fun."

Sadie didn't recognize many items on the menu. "Is cheong fun good?"

Pete looked up at her over his glasses. "Did Sadie Hoffmiller just ask me a question regarding culinary quality?"

Sadie gave him a bemused smile. "I'm afraid my experience with Chinese food is inferior to most of my culinary genius—I like beef and broccoli and fried rice, but I've never had anything this . . . authentic." She left out that things like chicken feet and bird's nest soup had encouraged her to keep a bit of a distance from traditional Chinese foods. Jack had gone to China once on business; he said most of the food he ate consisted of unidentifiable meat-stuffs dipped in gray broth. They didn't even have much rice. Sadie had at that point checked China off of her list of places she wanted to visit since food was one of the most motivating factors when choosing a travel destination.

"Really," Pete said, genuinely surprised. "Have you had dim sum before?"

"I've seen it in movies," she said, thinking of the finger foods loaded onto carts that were navigated through the tables. Sadie didn't see any carts here, though. "But I've never tried it myself." She put her menu down. "Will you order for me? I don't know what's good but I trust your judgment."

The front door opened and two more men came in and sat down without waiting for the waitress to seat them. Regulars, Sadie assumed. The door had no more than closed behind them before a group of four women pulled it open again. These ones had the stamp of tourist on them due to their numerous shopping bags and sensible shoes.

"Four?" the waitress said as she came in from the kitchen carrying a tray with two glasses of water, two teacups, and a teapot.

"Yep, just us," one of the women said.

The waitress waved them toward the last corner table in the room, then continued to Pete and Sadie's table, where she put a glass of water in front of each of them, set the metal teapot in the center of the table, and placed two handleless teacups beside it.

"Ready to order?" she said. Her words were sharp at the ends and her sentences succinct.

Pete started rattling off dishes Sadie had never heard of. The woman nodded after each item but didn't write anything down. When he finished, she returned to the kitchen without comment.

Sadie scanned the room again and found her focus settling on the wall with the kitchen door. Upon entering, Sadie had noted the white walls but now she realized that this wall, though plain white, was textured and . . . more than that, the texture made a picture.

"Do you think that's bamboo?" Sadie asked Pete, pointing toward the wall.

Pete turned in his chair and looked at it for a few seconds. "Wow, that's remarkable."

The longer Sadie stared at it, the more remarkable it was. The entire wall, a good thirty-foot expanse, looked as though it had been covered with thick white plaster, then sculpted—Sadie couldn't think of a better way to describe it—to look like a bamboo forest.

The stalks of bamboo were at different angles to one another, some from floor to ceiling, some shorter, but the texture of the plaster created the shadows that were necessary to show what was represented. "If the lighting weren't so intense, I bet you could better see what it is," Sadie commented.

Pete turned to face her. "I bet you're right, but it's beautiful."

"It is," Sadie said. The lack of small talk settled in between them. "When the waitress comes back should we ask her if Ji is here?"

"If we wait until after the meal we can compliment him on his food. Would you like some tea?"

"What kind is it?"

Pete lifted the pot, poured himself a cup, and took a sip. "I don't know what it's called, but it's good—kind of . . . flowery."

"Um, sure," Sadie said, though she was a bit hesitant to drink tea that tasted like flowers. This place didn't scream *clean* and that she was woefully ignorant of real Chinese food didn't help her feel any less out of her element. She hoped that she didn't end up with gastrointestinal distress from this meal, but maybe the tea would help calm her nerves *and* her stomach. She could only hope.

CHAPTER 5

A plate of translucent-skinned dumplings came out first, and Pete used his chopsticks to put one in his mouth. Sadie wasn't as proficient with chopsticks but managed to get one in her own mouth—after offering a quick prayer that it wouldn't make her sick. The dumpling was sticky on the outside and full of unknown flavors on the inside, but it wasn't bad.

"Good?" Pete asked when she reached for another one.

Sadie nodded and then dropped the next dumpling twice before getting it into her mouth. They had nearly finished that plate when two more plates came out.

"This is cheong fun," Pete said pointing to some kind of rolled up noodle. "And these are kind of like pot stickers—I'm sure you've had those before."

Sadie nodded, her mouth full.

"Dim sum began as something the Cantonese did but has expanded into most types of Asian cuisine," Pete said.

Sadie finished her bite and then took a sip of water. "In the movies, isn't dim sum served on carts pushed between the tables and you choose one thing at a time?"

Pete nodded and reached for another piece of cheong fun. "Some restaurants do it that way, but others do it by the plate like this." He paused and a soft smile came to his face. "Pat learned how to make gyoza—they're like pot stickers but Japanese—from a friend of ours who lived in Japan for a while. She made it every New Year's Eve."

Pat again. It wasn't as if Pete never talked about her—they'd been married for almost thirty years—but knowing he'd been to this city with her, and acknowledging that this city was likely spurring these memories, was different than the usual mentions. Stronger somehow.

Perhaps Sadie's own emotional sensitivity was playing a bigger part than she wanted to admit. She dipped the pot sticker in the vinegary sauce it had been served with while mentally giving herself a strong talking-to for being so petty and unfair.

"Sorry," Pete said, focusing on dipping his pot sticker into his own cup of sauce.

Sadie felt bad. Who was to say she and Pete wouldn't go to Yellowstone one day, where she and Neil had honeymooned? Or Virginia Beach, where they'd gone for their five-year wedding anniversary? Their room had a private balcony overlooking the ocean, and she and Neil would stay up late looking at the stars, talking of the future, and reviewing all they'd done that day. One night the moon had been full and the scent of sea had been strong, creating such a romantic mood that . . . She felt herself blush at the memory. That was something she would never tell Pete about. But remembering it helped her realize that she didn't want to take those kinds of memories away from Pete any more than she wanted to give up her own.

"Do you still have that gyoza recipe?" she asked by way of compromise.

Pete glanced at her warily. "I'm sure it's in the house somewhere. You like it?"

"A lot," Sadie said with a nod as she grabbed another one with her chopsticks, fumbled it, and tried again. Chopsticks were frustrating. Pete chuckled at her attempts and tried to help her hold the chopsticks more securely. "Hold the second stick with the base of your thumb. There you go."

Another plate came out, and Pete warned her that Chinese barbecue ribs could be a little spicy. Sadie nodded, but after her second bite of the tender meat, she realized she'd been lulled into confidence by the other dishes. Her whole face and neck were on fire. She downed the rest of her water amid Pete's chuckles.

Pete pushed his glass of water toward her, and she didn't even ask if he was sure he didn't mind. She drank most of it in a single gulp.

A few seconds later, the waitress put down a plate of what looked like doughnut holes covered in sesame seeds. Sadie threw one in her mouth before asking what it was. It was like bread but with a sweet filling. A little greasier than she'd have liked, but it did a good job of mellowing out the intense heat of the ribs.

"A *little* spicy?" she said when she finally caught her breath.

Pete leaned his elbows on the table while he finished up his third rib. "Well, I admit these are spicier than the ones I'm used to. But delicious. How did you like the jim dieu?" He nodded at the sesame seed doughnut holes.

"Not sure I really tasted it," Sadie said, grabbing another one and savoring it this time. "It's good," she said once she'd swallowed. "Is it dessert?"

"Sort of. We're still waiting on some pork buns."

"Is that everything?" asked the waitress.

Sadie opened her mouth to ask for more water, but without waiting for an answer, the waitress put a ticket on their table. "Pay at the register." She gave them a quick nod, then moved on to another table—six of the ten tables were full. Was she the only waitress working?

"I feel funny interrupting Ji when they're so busy," Sadie said after the woman disappeared into the kitchen a minute later.

"Yeah, I didn't think of that beforehand, but it does seem like we'd be imposing now, doesn't it?" Pete said.

The waitress hadn't been gone more than thirty seconds before she returned with some plates for the four women tourists, then hurried back into the kitchen again.

Pete finished off the last of the ribs, and Sadie ate the last pot sticker—even cold, it was her favorite. In fact, she'd liked everything but the ribs that had left her mouth burning. A plate of pork buns was laid on their table, and Sadie looked up expecting to see the waitress. Instead, it was a teenage girl who began gathering their empty plates, not meeting Sadie's eyes while she cleared the table. The waitress came out of the kitchen with a tray piled with more plates of food at the same time the girl headed into the back. A minute later, the girl reappeared and headed for the register.

While setting plates down for a young couple sitting in the center of the restaurant, the woman began yelling at the girl at the register in Chinese. At least it sounded like yelling, but then Sadie had always thought Asian languages sounded like yelling so she couldn't be sure. The girl answered in a softer tone, which caused Sadie to look at the waitress who waved her hand through the air in some kind of gesture Sadie didn't understand. The girl bent down behind the counter, then stood with a basket of fortune cookies she set near the register.

That must have been what the waitress had wanted because she gave a short nod and then finished serving the plates to the guests.

"Why don't we leave Ji a note instead of interrupting him," Sadie said after nodding for Pete to take the last bun. The buns were quite good, though Pete said they weren't as good as others he'd had. "Then we can walk around for a while and maybe come back when he's less busy."

Before she finished talking, she'd already started rummaging in her purse for paper and a pen. When they went to the register to pay their bill, the girl quickly slid her cell phone she'd been texting on into her pocket, then smiled at Pete and asked if they'd enjoyed their meal. Her English was perfect.

"It was delicious," Sadie and Pete said at the same time. The girl smiled shyly and took the check before punching numbers into the register.

Sadie inspected the items inside the glass case beneath the register while Pete paid the bill. There were a variety of Chinese-themed knickknacks, like painted chopsticks and paper fans. At the bottom of the case were small lacquered boxes that Sadie would have written off as more tourist trinkets if she hadn't been looking so close. However, she bent down to get a better look and could see the individual brushstrokes—tiny ones—of what seemed to be a hand-painted scene of a stream and a bridge with bamboo on one end and a row of Chinese symbols on the other.

"These boxes," Sadie said to the girl when she handed Pete his credit card receipt to sign. "Are they for sale?"

"Yes." The girl slid open the back door of the case and removed one of the boxes.

Sadie ran her hand over the paint and could feel the raised design. On closer inspection, the artwork was even more detailed and fine than she'd first assumed and the box was better crafted. There was no "Made in China" sticker anywhere.

"This is hand painted?" Sadie asked.

"Yes," the girl said as she gave Pete his receipt. "My father paints them." She tucked her straight black hair, cut bluntly at the shoulder, behind her ear. Sadie noticed a piercing at the top of her left ear. No earring, just the telltale hole.

"Your father?" Sadie said, suddenly realizing that this could very well be Ji's daughter, Wendy's . . . granddaughter. Sadie wasn't a grandmother yet, but looking at this girl and knowing she shared genes with Sadie's sister—with Sadie herself—was powerful and somewhat shocking.

Something Sadie hadn't thought about in years came to mind, and she looked at the box again. Wendy, for all her difficulties, had been very artistic. An oil painting she'd done had hung in the hallway of their parents' home for many years. It had taken second place at the county fair when Wendy had been fourteen or fifteen years old. It was because of Wendy's skill, and Sadie not wanting to compete with her, that Sadie had given up her own interest in art when she was young. She wasn't as good as Wendy, not ever, but it brought the devil out in her sister when she'd try. And now Sadie held a jewelry box, painted by Wendy's son—who also shared her blood and heritage. As did this girl standing in front of her. Sadie swallowed against the sudden thickness in her throat. "Your father painted this?" Sadie asked for a second time.

The girl answered with only a nod, but seemed to be looking at Sadie with a bit more interest than she had previously. Perhaps she sensed the emotional reaction Sadie was trying so hard to hide.

"What does this say?" Sadie asked, pointing at the Chinese symbols.

"It says 'A journey of a thousand miles begins with a single step.'"

"I've heard that quote before," Pete cut in, sliding his wallet into his back pocket. "It's a Chinese proverb, right?"

"Well, it was said by the philosopher Lao Tzu, but it has been adopted as a part of Chinese culture. It means that nothing happens if we do nothing."

She was an articulate girl, and Sadie immediately liked her. "I love it," she said, brushing her hand over the top of the box again: Ji's box. She liked to think that the journey toward forming a relationship with Ji was also beginning. "How much?"

"Sixty-five dollars. It's entirely handcrafted. A man here in Chinatown makes the boxes, and my father paints them."

Sadie reached into her purse for her wallet, but Pete touched her wrist gently and shook his head. He pulled his own wallet out of his pocket for a second time. Sadie would have argued, but she loved the chivalry, so she thanked him instead.

The girl removed a brown paper sack from beneath the counter and began carefully wrapping up the box. As Sadie watched her, she felt the questions bubbling and couldn't resist asking at least one. "Is your father Ji Doang?"

The girl looked up at her and nodded.

Sadie couldn't help but smile. She put her hand to her chest. "My name is Sadie Hoffmiller. My sister was your grandmother, Wendy."

The girl's face fell, and her eyes went wide, causing Sadie's smile to falter. This wasn't happy news? She remembered Ji had said he and Wendy hadn't been close, and she wondered if perhaps Ji's daughter didn't know what had happened to her grandmother. Or perhaps she did know, and Sadie mentioning it had caused this girl some pain. Sadie swallowed and struggled to find a way to save this situation while the girl looked at her with cautious surprise.

Gyoza

4 cups finely chopped cabbage, boiled until soft, drained
1 pound ground hamburger or pork (cooked or uncooked—your preference)
½ cup green onion, finely chopped
2 cloves garlic, finely chopped
½- to 1-inch fresh ginger, grated
Salt and pepper, to taste
1 tablespoon sesame oil
1 package gyoza wrappers (round or square)*
¼ cup water

In a large bowl, combine all ingredients except wrappers and sesame oil. Mix well.

Place a tablespoon of the mixture in the center of a wrapper. Wet one edge of the wrapper, then fold in half and pinch shut around the filling.

Heat sesame oil in large skillet over medium heat until hot. Brown filled gyozas on both sides. Add ¼ cup water to skillet and cover with a tight-fitting lid. Steam until water is gone (about two minutes), shaking the skillet every 20 seconds or so to prevent gyozas from sticking to the bottom of the pan. Remove gyozas to a plate and repeat cooking instructions for remaining gyozas.

Makes approximately 50 servings.

*You can find these in some grocery stores as well as all Asian markets.

Note: You can make and fold gyozas, then flash freeze them and cook at a later date. Store in airtight container.

Gyoza Sauce

¼ cup rice wine vinegar
¼ cup soy sauce
¼ teaspoon red pepper flakes
1 to 2 tablespoons sugar (start small and add more to taste)
1 clove garlic, diced or pressed
¼ teaspoon grated ginger root
¼ cup green onion, finely chopped
1 teaspoon sesame oil

Mix everything together in a small saucepan. Bring to a boil and then simmer for approximately five minutes (to cook out some of the vinegar flavor). Sauce will be thin, so if you prefer a thicker sauce, mix in 1 tablespoon cornstarch.

Store leftovers in refrigerator.

CHAPTER 6

Afraid she'd inadvertently crossed a line she hadn't considered, Sadie attempted to repair her smile. "Um, is your father here?"

The girl finally blinked, but the tension of her reaction didn't soften much. "He's cooking."

The waitress came up behind them and said something in Chinese. The girl looked past Sadie and answered her, also in Chinese, then pointed to Sadie.

Sadie and Pete turned toward the waitress, who was balancing a tray of food on one hand. Sadie kept her smile in place but felt increasingly uncomfortable. Why hadn't she expected anything but a warm welcome when she met Ji and his family?

The woman came to a stop and looked between them for a few seconds before continuing toward the table she'd come out to serve. Once her tray was empty, she came back to them, the tray tucked under her arm. "Ji is very busy right now. It's lunchtime. Please find another time to come see him."

It was the most words the woman had said to them, and Sadie realized that she didn't have a Chinese accent at all—rather she spoke a kind of formal English, even though the short sentences she'd used up to this point sounded like the halting English of someone not raised to speak the language. Was that some kind of game she played with the tourist customers? Pretending not to know English very well?

"When would be a good time to come back?" Pete asked.

"Wait here. I'll ask him."

She headed for the kitchen, and Sadie reviewed her experience so far at Choy's. The food was good, but the dining area was run-down, the lighting too bright, the service efficient but lacking in warmth or attentiveness to things like keeping her water glass full and welcoming the customers. Sadie didn't like to be judgmental, but she almost couldn't help it. It was also disappointing that Ji's daughter didn't seem to know Sadie was coming, and this woman who Sadie suspected might also be a relation didn't seem the least bit excited to meet them. Did that reflect Ji's feelings as well?

"Ma'am?"

Sadie turned back to the register where the girl was holding out the paper-wrapped jewelry box. She continued to avoid eye contact with Sadie, obviously uncomfortable.

"Thank you," Sadie said as she took the box.

"Don't forget your fortune cookie. Thank you for coming to Choy's." She gave a little bow.

The old men who had been seated when Sadie and Pete arrived came up behind them at the register, so Sadie and Pete took their fortune cookies from the bowl and stepped aside, waiting for the waitress to return. The men said something to the girl in Chinese, and she responded with something that made the men laugh. They said something else, and she shook her head, trying to hide a smile. Her interaction with them made Sadie feel like even more of an outsider. She didn't belong here. Why had she come?

The kitchen door swished open, and the waitress came toward them again. She held out her closed hand as though she were going to give Sadie something. When Sadie extended her free hand, the waitress dropped a key ring with two keys into her open palm. Sadie knew instantly what they were: keys to Wendy's apartment.

"The larger key is for the building, the smaller one for the apartment," the woman said. "The complex is on the corner of Mission and 22nd Street. Wendy's apartment is number five on the third floor. Ji will join you there this afternoon after he has finished the lunch rush. He said that he is sorry not to meet you now and hopes that you understand."

"I understand," Sadie said with a conciliatory smile. "Tell him I look forward to meeting him. I'm Sadie, by the way. This is my fiancé, Pete. Are you by chance Ji's wife?"

"Lin Yang," she said with a slight nod of her head at both of them. "I am pleased to meet you."

Sadie wasn't sure she believed her, but maybe it was a cultural disconnect that gave that impression. She hoped that's all it was.

"And is this your daughter?" Pete asked, waving toward the girl who looked at them quickly before turning her attention back to the register.

"Min," Lin Yang said. "Our oldest."

"Wonderful to meet you," Pete said to Min. The girl glanced at him quickly and then nodded, her head still down.

The front door opened, and Lin Yang looked past them toward whoever had entered. "Three?" she said in that clipped way she had. She stepped forward, silently dismissing Pete and Sadie as she did so.

The four lady tourists began scooting away from their table, which meant the tiny front corner by the register was about to get crowded.

"We better go," Sadie said. Pete nodded and held the door for her. Once on the loud and busy sidewalk, Sadie opened her hand and looked at the keys that would take her further into Wendy's world. Butterflies erupted all over again.

"You have a deep appreciation for art and music."

Sadie turned to look at Pete. "What?"

He held up a strip of paper. "My fortune—I apparently have a deep appreciation for art and music." He smiled. "Since I have neither, I'm guessing this is a bum batch of cookies." He popped the cookie into his mouth and waved to the cookie in Sadie's other hand. She put the keys in her pocket and opened the plastic package, broke her cookie in half, and pulled out the paper.

It is time to get moving.

Sadie read it out loud, and Pete lifted his eyebrows while he continued chewing. She looked at the fortune again and felt a strange tingly sensation, not that she believed that fortunes meant anything at all. Still, she could use the extra motivation.

"I guess there's no sense in waiting," she said, tucking the fortune into the front pocket of her purse. Despite the lack of warmth she'd felt when meeting Lin Yang and Ji's daughter Min, seeing them had expanded Sadie's list of reasons for being here. From past experience, Sadie knew that the moment things became about people rather than ideas or possibilities, she was hooked. She wanted to get to know Ji and his family so that future meetings would be more comfortable than this one had been; she also wanted his family to know that Sadie was nothing like her sister.

There was no sense in procrastinating any longer now that she'd crossed the threshold and gotten a glimpse of the life Wendy's son lived. He was a family man, an artist, and a hard worker—and he needed her help. They were family, regardless of whether his wife and daughter knew she existed, and Sadie and Pete had come to help.

She looked up and met Pete's eyes. He'd been watching her as she'd mentally talked to herself, worked things out, and lined things up. She couldn't help but wonder if he'd seen the thoughts she hadn't verbalized play out on her face.

"You're ready to do this?" Pete asked.

"It's real now," she said, summing up the mental conclusion she'd reached. "I'm ready."

Pete smiled and nodded, and then they fell in step beside one another as they headed toward the parking garage. Pete reached for her hand and gave it a squeeze. She smiled up at him; how could she have done any of this without him? They were here. Together. To learn and discover and make a connection. It *was* time to get moving, and Sadie was ready.

CHAPTER 7

It was still too early to check into the hotel, so they went directly to Wendy's apartment instead. On the way, Pete told Sadie several little-known facts about San Francisco, such as how the actor Benjamin Bratt had lived in Alcatraz during the Native American occupation in 1969 and that the cable cars were purchased from all over the world as different countries stopped using them. Each car had a placard explaining where it originally came from. He didn't talk about Pat, but now and then he went quiet, and Sadie wondered if he were catching himself just in time.

After driving longer than it seemed it should have taken to cover the distance shown on the GPS map, he slowed the car and pointed out the yellow brick building on the corner. Black letters attached to the exterior read "22nd Street Condominiums." Sadie felt a tremor run through her as she looked over the building. Wendy had *lived* here.

There were shops at street level and two floors of apartments above, everything compact and efficient-looking. A beautiful gothic cornice, painted bright white, wrapped around the roofline of the building, with the fire escape railings arcing over the top. The windows were long and narrow, but bayed from the otherwise flat façade, giving texture and detail.

The high-rise buildings of the financial district where their hotel was located didn't exist here. Instead, most buildings weren't more than three or four stories high, but built together as though all part of the same structure. There weren't many flower gardens or sitting areas, and the continued cloud cover emphasized the urban feel of the neighborhood. Sadie's expectations of Wendy's lifestyle had been low, but this building was much nicer than she'd anticipated it would be. The neighborhood was cleaner and, though she wouldn't call it upscale, it was a vast improvement over some of the more run-down areas they'd passed through to get here.

It took nearly five minutes to find a parking spot on a narrow street two blocks away, and then it was a five-minute walk to the building. Pete went into a convenience store they passed on their way and asked if they had any boxes while Sadie texted Jack to tell him she'd arrived and was heading to Wendy's apartment. She promised him an update later and put the phone back into her purse when Pete came out with a stack of empty boxes they could use for packing Wendy's things and a package of heavy-duty garbage sacks he'd purchased as backup.

When they reached the outside door of the apartment building, located between two storefronts, Pete put down his boxes in order to unlock the door with the keys Lin Yang had given them. He then held the door for Sadie. They walked down an empty hallway to a foyer that was rectangular, small, and empty. On the wall to the left was a door marked EXIT and a panel of six mailboxes. On the wall to the right were two doors she assumed led to the street-level shops. Further down the hallway were the doors for apartments 1 and 2.

There was little character or color in this space, but the elevator straight ahead of them was fabulous. It was one of the gated kinds that made Sadie think of Audrey Hepburn and New York City. A spiral staircase wrapped around the elevator shaft, and Sadie followed it with her eyes until it disappeared somewhere above them. Pete pulled back the diamond-patterned grate of the elevator so they could enter, then closed it and secured it with a latch. Sadie pushed the button for level three. It was an old-fashioned knob-style button and depressed an entire half an inch when she pushed it, which made Sadie smile.

"This is awesome," Pete said in a reverent tone as the cables jerked and the pulley began its job of hoisting them up the shaft. "I feel like Cary Grant in *Charade*—though I'm glad this elevator is a little bigger than that one, but seriously, it even has the same kind of staircase."

"Or the one in the Hotel Priscilla for Single Women," Sadie said. "Though I'm glad it works without us having to tap dance."

"Oh yeah," Pete said, looking up as the elevator continued to the third floor. "Is that the hotel from the movie where Carol Channing does that jazz number?" The second-floor foyer passed before them, looking very much like the first-floor foyer but without the mailboxes. The doors to apartments 3 and 4 stood sentry, side by side.

"Yes," Sadie said, impressed that he remembered the scene from *Thoroughly Modern Millie*. Musicals were one topic on which they didn't much agree, and though he hadn't said out loud that he didn't like musicals, Sadie suspected it was to protect her feelings.

"I didn't like that film," Pete said with a shake of his head. "The story line was unrealistic."

Sadie made a huffing sound as the elevator came to a grinding stop when it was flush with the third floor. Pete went about opening the door and then closing it again after they'd both stepped out.

They scanned the sparse foyer—there wasn't anything to it other than hardwood floors in need of refinishing and two doors set into the wall across from them, fifteen feet apart. Sadie stared at the number 5 attached to the center of the door on the left. That was Wendy's apartment. It's where she'd lived . . . and where she'd died.

The thought of such an atrocious thing happening on the other side of that door made Sadie's stomach clench. *Had* Wendy died of natural causes? How would burning the body later factor into that possibility? What were they going to see—and smell—once they went inside? Sadie shivered at the thought of it.

Pete put down the boxes and used the smaller key to unlock the apartment door. He gave Sadie a quick glance before pushing open the door. Sadie braced herself for the smell, but while there was a trace of smoke, and maybe something more than that, it was bleach and paint and . . . vinegar that made the strongest impression.

"It doesn't stink?" she asked as she tentatively stepped into the darkened apartment. The shades were closed and the lights off, giving it an eerie grayness in the middle of the day.

"I wondered if it would," Pete said, coming in behind her. "Seeing as how she was in a bathtub—a nonporous surface—and Lopez had mentioned that the bathroom appeared to be well-contained and with good ventilation. CSI must have put out the vinegar—it's the best thing for decomposition—and they've already painted with an odor-blocking primer, I'll bet."

Sadie stared at him, both impressed and disgusted that he knew so much about this, but then again he'd spent his career dealing with this kind of thing. Sadie's experience with death and murder was relatively recent, and she'd never been involved in the cleanup process. Pete met her eye and smiled sheepishly. "Hopefully that's not too much information." He reached out and touched her arm. "Are you okay?"

"I'm fine," she said, reaching for the light switch. She'd been prepared for chaos and disarray—Wendy's entire existence exemplified disorder to Sadie—but the light came on and showed her that the apartment was . . . normal. Clean and stylish even. The main space they'd entered served as a kitchen, dining room, and living room. Sadie could call it a great room, but it didn't seem big enough to call *great* unless you were trying to be funny, and Sadie wasn't in the mood for humor.

On the kitchen counter were two document storage boxes. Were they the returned files the police had gone through? There was also a plastic bag that, once she walked over to it, she realized was the jewelry box the police had mentioned having found in a dresser drawer. It felt strange undoing the staples that held the bag closed, but she was eager to see if the pieces that had once belonged to her mother were still there.

She pulled out the box, opened it, and sifted through the items until she found a gold ring with a large aquamarine stone in the center. She felt a wave of relief. She slid the ring on her finger and noted that, just as had always been the case, it was a little too big.

"Your mother's?" Pete said, startling her. She'd felt as though she'd been alone for a moment, but as soon as she realized he was behind her, she felt immediate comfort in his presence.

"Yes—and her mother's before that," Sadie said, admiring the ring. She kept it on her finger and went back to the box. Within a few seconds she found the flowered brooch her mother had worn to church on Sundays, a strand of pearls, and one of the two diamond earrings her father had given their mother on their twenty-fifth wedding anniversary.

"She lost one of the earrings," Sadie said after taking every other item out of the box to make sure the missing earring wasn't hiding in a corner. The rest of the jewelry was gaudy and bright—costume jewelry like Detective Lopez had said. "But considering that I thought I would never see them again, I'm thrilled that she still has these things."

Sadie put her mother's jewelry into the zippered pocket of her purse, then closed the jewelry box, realizing as she did so that it was very similar to the one she'd just bought from Choy's, though this box was painted red, not black. She ran her hand across the painting on the top: a crane flying over a pond of bulrushes. There was Chinese writing along the top, and Sadie wondered what it said.

Had Ji given Wendy this box? The idea created a tender spot in her heart to think that although Ji said he and Wendy weren't close, there was a connection between them. She put her purse on one of the bar stools and had a sudden pang of conscience. All of Wendy's things now rightly belonged to Ji. The idea of parting with her mother's jewelry *again* filled her with regret. But Ji was Wendy's child and had the legal claim to all of Wendy's belongings. Sadie reminded herself that they were just things; she'd given herself the same argument when she'd first realized Wendy had taken the jewelry fifteen years earlier.

"This is a really nice place," Pete said as he walked toward the large bay window at the front of the long room. He twisted the wand for the wooden blinds of the middle window and the natural light poured in. Pete commented on the view, but Sadie was still processing the apartment.

The furnishings were angular and compact but fit well in the narrow room, which was only about twelve feet wide. There was a two-person table in the dining area and a large mirror on the wall over a buffet table painted bright red and decorated with coordinating pottery. The kitchen area divided the dining area from the living room, where a small sectional couch and a large shag rug, red with orange swirls, squared off that space. A flat-screen television was on one wall with five square canvas paintings on the wall opposite.

Sadie could see areas where light gray graphite was used by the investigators to dust for prints on the wall and on the furniture, but it was minimal and the overall look of the apartment was clean, appealing, and . . . *normal.* How could it be so normal when Wendy was so *not* normal?

"Is this her?" Pete asked from where he stood in the middle of the living room, staring at the canvases.

Sadie joined him and looked at the oil paintings prominently displayed. It had been so long since Sadie had seen her sister that she couldn't say for sure that it was Wendy depicted in the paintings, but she suspected that it was.

The center canvas was a portrait of a middle-aged woman giving a speculative look, her fingers pointed beneath her chin and her long, tight blonde curls wild around her face. The other canvases were like a puzzle piece of that first painting: the fingers, an eye, the mouth, a section of curl, each with a different color of emphasis—green, blue, red, and yellow.

"I wonder if she painted them herself," Sadie said, finding it rather narcissistic that Wendy had decorated her home with self-portraits. Wendy's face staring back at her was disturbing, and she couldn't help but wonder about the idea of ghosts. Sadie was very aware that she hadn't been welcomed into Wendy's space when Wendy was alive.

"She was an artist?" Pete asked, saving Sadie from her thoughts.

Sadie turned away from the portraits and nodded. "She first left home to go to art school, and my parents sent her tuition for a while. I don't know if she ever finished." She looked back at the jewelry box Ji had painted. What did he think about the talent he and his mother shared?

"She's very good," Pete said.

She was very good, Sadie clarified in her mind. She moved to the windows and opened the other two blinds. She could feel Pete watching her for a few moments, then he turned his attention to a cardboard box on one end of the couch full of magazines and books.

"It looks like Ji already started packing things up." Pete picked up a stack of magazines and shuffled through them.

The kitchen drew Sadie to it, and she noted the dishes in the sink—a coffee mug, a bowl with what looked like petrified cereal bits in it, and a small plate with a smear of solidified jam. Had those been the last dishes Wendy had used? The thought gave her chills.

The counters were clear, the cupboards organized, and the fridge full of food that was beginning to smell sour after five weeks of neglect.

"Let's check the rest of the apartment," Pete said.

Sadie shut the fridge and looked between the two doors that led off the main space, one on the left wall and one directly across from it on the right. Both closed doors were on the living room end.

Sadie stood on the invisible boundary between the living room and kitchen as Pete twisted the knob of the door to the right. Tension seeped into her shoulders and chest. The door could lead to the bathroom—the room where Wendy had died.

Pete opened the door slowly as though he were thinking the same thing, then paused, flipped on the light, and opened the door all the way. "It's an office," he said as he stepped inside.

"An office?" Sadie was spurred into motion by the surprising answer; she hadn't expected anything other than a bedroom since there were only two doors leading off the living room area and one *had* to be the bathroom, right?

Sadie entered the room and Pete stepped aside. The door opened into the back of the room, which was about twelve feet wide and fifteen feet long. A desk sat against the wall opposite the door while bookshelves stacked with books, knickknacks, and miscellaneous, semi-organized minutiae flanked the doorway.

A closet gave away the fact that this room was a second bedroom by design, but obviously not used as such. Wendy having a home office was further evidence of the idea that Wendy's life might not be so different from Sadie's. It was an incredibly uncomfortable thought.

After observing the space, Pete stepped past Sadie into the living room and crossed to the other closed door. He wasn't as slow opening the second door, and this time Sadie was right behind him. The door opened inward and blocked the back portion of the room.

It was a bedroom with a large queen-sized bed set near the bay windows and a chest of drawers a few feet past the footboard, set against the shared wall of the living room. Across from the doorway where Pete and Sadie stood was a closet twice the size of the one in the office.

Pete stepped into the room and Sadie followed so that he could close the bedroom door, revealing another door. Was *that* the bathroom? Accessed through the bedroom?

The paint smell was stronger here, thankfully blocking out any other scents that might be in this portion of the apartment. Pete opened the final door, and Sadie tensed even as she stepped forward to look over Pete's shoulder. She relaxed when she realized that the bathroom had been completely gutted.

There was no toilet, tub, or sink—just pipes sticking out of freshly painted walls. Big sections of drywall were missing, exposing the wooden framework coated with a green substance, perhaps some kind of chemical. On the far wall, above where the tub would be, Sadie assumed, was a small window, no more than eighteen inches square. It had a handle that when turned opened the window a few inches—Sadie's parents' home had had the same type of windows.

Pete stepped over the threshold onto naked subflooring. "They took everything out." He pointed up at the bathroom fan in the ceiling, still whirring. "I wonder if that was on the whole time she was here? If the window was open and the fan on, it might explain why no one smelled anything and why the smell didn't seep into the apartment too much."

Sadie nodded to confirm she'd heard the morbid observation and looked at the thick rubber strip nailed to the bottom of the door. It would create a good seal when it was closed. Was that coincidence or design?

"If the fan vents to the roof," Pete said, still looking up at the ceiling, "it'd also help explain why no one noticed the smell. This bathroom is on an exterior wall of the building and as far from the other tenant on this floor as it could possibly be." Pete looked around. "But that doesn't explain why no one would miss her or check up on her."

One of the newspaper articles Sadie had read about Wendy's death pointed out that no one had reported Wendy missing. Didn't she have any friends? Anyone she interacted with on a regular basis?

Maybe it wasn't just family Wendy had pushed out of her life.

Sadie turned back to the bedroom and her eye caught the enormous painting hung across from Wendy's bed and above the chest of drawers. She immediately felt herself blushing, then glanced at

Pete to see that he, too, was avoiding looking at the painting. Like the canvases in the living room, it was unadorned with a frame. She took a breath and looked again in order to confirm that the nude portrait was indeed of her sister, though she was a young woman in the picture.

"Maybe we could take that down," she said.

Pete nodded, and between the two of them, they were able to lift it off the wall and lean it against the footboard of the bed. Why on earth would Wendy want to stare at herself naked? Especially a younger version of herself? It served as a reminder that there were things about Wendy that Sadie would never understand.

"Well, I guess we might as well get to work, huh?" she said to break the awkwardness that had descended. She crossed to the bedroom windows and twisted open the blinds to let in the natural light. Her breath caught in her throat as the view from the window commanded her attention. The living room window had mostly showed the buildings across the street, but this perspective was magnificent. She could see over the tops of several buildings, across the city, and out to the ocean. Even though the fog cover was still apparent, the view was relatively clear. She heard Pete come up behind her.

"Wow," he whispered, putting a hand on her shoulder. "That is spectacular."

Sadie nodded. It really was breathtaking, and for a moment she forgot why she was there and just took in the beauty of the place. Perhaps she even gained a small sense of what it was Wendy loved about this city—and what Pete loved, too. His arms came around Sadie's waist, and she hugged them to her. They stood in silence for a few seconds before Pete kissed the side of her neck, sending a shimmer of heat down her spine and causing her to close her eyes to better focus on the feel of him so close, the smell of his cologne, the comfort of his affection. In just a few weeks, Pete would be her husband. She could scarcely believe it, and yet she wondered how she could not have known from the moment she met him that they would live out the rest of their lives together?

The sound of a vibrating cell phone interrupted the moment, and Pete pulled away before reaching into his pocket. He gave the phone a quick look before sliding his thumb across the screen to answer it and putting it to his ear. "Pete Cunningham," he said into the phone, then paused a moment before giving Sadie a quick smile and turning toward the doorway of the bedroom. "Yes, Detective Lopez. We made it safe and sound." He pulled open the bedroom door and disappeared into the common area, leaving Sadie alone in Wendy's bedroom. She turned to the window again. *This is the view Wendy saw every day,* Sadie thought to herself and felt a tiny glimmer of connection.

And yet how much connection could there be to a sister who had shut Sadie out of her life completely? Sadie had always assumed that Wendy had such limitations that she couldn't live a normal life. What if the real answer was that she simply didn't want anything to do with her family? The idea that there could be something about them that Wendy hated wasn't completely foreign—Sadie had thought it before—but it raised her defenses, and she felt the sentimentality pass through her as whatever connection she'd reached for faded away. She wanted to know why Wendy was the way she was, something solid and diagnosed. It was harder to justify Wendy's actions when Sadie was presented with such a convincing defense of normalcy.

She took a deep breath of the paint-scented air. This is where Wendy lived, yes, but she didn't live here anymore. These things had once been hers, but now they were just stuff. She hadn't taken her stylish apartment or nice furniture or self-portraits with her, and the things she could have had—relationships, love—had not factored into her priorities. She'd died alone, perhaps tragically. What a horrible end.

Sadie couldn't push away the emotion completely, but neither was she willing to let it take over. She needed to distract herself with work and headed out of the room, giving one ear to Pete's side of the conversation while she picked up a couple of the boxes they'd brought and put them in the office. She took the other boxes and the garbage bags—they would work for the clothes—into the bedroom while determining where to start. Sadie had expected that Wendy's apartment would be full of things easily thrown out and given away but that wasn't the case. Did Ji really not want any of these things? He'd been here, so he knew the quality of Wendy's belongings when he said he wanted to arrange to donate them.

" . . . you bet. Thank you for making time for me."

Pete ended the call and leaned against the kitchen counter.

"You're going to meet with Detective Lopez?" she asked.

"Yeah, he has some time in about an hour. Want to come?"

Sadie absolutely wanted to go with him—well, rather she absolutely didn't want to stay here—but Ji would be coming at some point and the work wasn't going to get done if she didn't buckle down and do it. "I better get started here."

Pete frowned. "I don't like the idea of you being here alone."

All it took was him to act protective to trigger Sadie's feelings of self-sufficiency. "I'm perfectly fine here."

"Sadie," he said in a concerned tone. "We don't know exactly how Wendy died, but someone came in last week and lit her remains on *fire*."

"I'll lock the door after you leave, and Ji will be here eventually.

I'll be fine." She considered reminding him of her self-defense training—something that had saved her life in the past—but worried it would come across as argumentative.

"You're sure?" Pete asked, still looking skeptical.

Sadie crossed the room to him and put her arms around his neck. She gave him a quick peck on the lips. "Ask your new police buddies where you should take your fiancée for dinner in this town. I will be just fine."

Pete relaxed and kissed her back, though it was far more exciting than the chaste kiss she'd given him a moment earlier. "I'll call you when I'm on my way back."

They kissed once more—maybe three more times—and then Sadie locked the apartment door behind him, took a deep breath, and did what she always did—jumped in with both feet. There was work to do, and it was time to get moving.

CHAPTER 8

It was nearly three o'clock when a buzzing sound made Sadie jump
from where she was packing up dishes in the kitchen. She looked
around in alarm and saw a speaker with buttons near the door to
the apartment. Remembering a similar speaker by the outside door
of the building, she hurried toward it, took a moment to figure out
which button did what, and then pushed the button labeled TALK.

"Hello?" she said.

"It's Ji," the voice said. "Can you buzz me in?"

"I think so," Sadie said. She let go of the TALK button and
pressed the UNLOCK button, hoping it would open the exterior door
of the building. She held it for ten seconds, assuming that would be
enough time for him to enter, then let go. Anxiety washed over her
as she waited for Ji to come up.

When he knocked on the apartment door a minute later, she
took a deep breath and put on a wide smile, ready to meet her
nephew for the first time. She pulled open the door to reveal a handsome man, almost six feet tall. His Chinese heritage was obvious in
his coloring, but his resemblance to Sadie's brother, Jack, was there

too in his strong jaw and wide forehead, which made him seem familiar. He had light brown eyes and dark hair, cut short.

She held out her hand. "I'm Sadie," she said, refraining from referring to herself as Aunt Sadie because it felt presumptuous.

He took her hand and shook it once before dropping it. "Nice to meet you. I'm sorry it took me so long to get away. We stayed pretty busy today."

"I'm just glad you were able to come," Sadie said and stood to the side of the doorway so that he could enter.

He walked past her into the apartment before coming to a stop and sniffing the air. "It smells better than it did when I was here last week."

Sadie grimaced. "Was it horrible?"

"Not as bad as I expected it to be, but, yeah, you could tell stuff had happened. I'm glad it's better now, though. I was worried about you coming into that."

Sadie was touched by his concern. He turned away from her and his eye caught Wendy's jewelry box still on the counter. He paused and his eyebrows pulled together as he took a few steps toward it. He picked it up, regarded it for a few moments, and then looked up at her. "You bought this at the restaurant today?"

"No," Sadie said, shaking her head. "I did buy one—you're very talented—but it's in the car." She waved toward the box in his hands. "This was Wendy's. Didn't you give it to her?"

"No," Ji said, sounding confused.

"Maybe she bought it," Sadie suggested.

"She hasn't been to my restaurant in years," Ji said, shaking his head and putting the box back on the counter.

"Did you come *here*? To Wendy's apartment?"

"No," Ji said simply.

"But you both lived right here in San Francisco?"

"Yes."

"Oh," Sadie said, not wanting to be pushy but confused all the same.

Ji faced her and blessedly gave her more information. "If either of us had wanted to see the other, we could have. The landlord told me she'd lived here for twelve years. I had no idea. As it was, we were two people amid 800,000 who live in this city; it's easy to avoid people if you wish. I live in Chinatown. I work and raise my children there. She always knew where I was. When she wanted to find me she did, but it was rare that she would come by, and when she did, it would be because she needed money—which I never gave her. I had no interest in pursuing a relationship with her. She stayed in her community; I stayed in mine. It wasn't as though we would accidentally meet."

"That makes sense," Sadie said, focusing on the logistics he'd mentioned rather than the sadness of their relationship. Wendy didn't have a car, so it stood to reason that she'd stay close to home. "It seems most neighborhoods around here are quite self-sufficient, with grocery stores and restaurants that are accessible to those who live there."

"Exactly," Ji said.

He let his eyes run along the apartment again before they met Sadie's. "So, what would you like me to do?" he asked. "I'd started on the stuff in the living room, but then the detective showed up with those boxes"—he waved toward the document boxes still on the counter—"and I answered his questions until I had to get back to the restaurant."

Sadie nodded. "Well, I've packed up most of the cabinets in the kitchen. She has some really nice sets of dishes, and I wondered if you wanted to keep them. One is from Williams-Sonoma and—"

"I don't want anything," Ji cut in, his voice brisk.

"Nothing?" Sadie asked, glancing at the TV on the wall. It was a really nice TV, and she figured that if he wanted anything at all, he'd want that. She also wondered why the robbers hadn't taken it. Maybe because it was too big to get out easily?

"She gave me nothing while she was alive, and I won't take anything now."

Sadie was struck by the intensity of his words and by the obviously deep-seated pain he still felt about his mother. "We could probably sell some of this. She has some very nice things."

He shook his head again. "I want nothing from her."

Sadie nodded sadly. "I'm sorry for all the hurt she caused you, Ji."

He simply looked at her, and she wondered if his distrust for his mother had spread to include Sadie too. She'd sensed it when she talked to him on the phone but hoped meeting him in person would change things. She wanted him to see her as an ally, even if accepting her as family was too difficult right now. He finally looked away, scanning the apartment again.

"My friend works with a charity organization that helps new immigrants get settled here in San Francisco. He said he can send a truck tomorrow afternoon. Do you think we can get everything packed up before then? They'll take everything—furniture, kitchen supplies, and clothes. They'll even take nonperishable food and cleaning supplies."

"That's wonderful," Sadie said with a smile she hoped communicated that she was trying to understand how he was feeling about all of this. "I think we could get everything packed up if we worked hard at it. Pete, my fiancé, will be back in a little while, and between the three of us, I think we can make really good progress." She was as eager as Ji seemed to be to get this job over with, but suddenly wondered why either of them was here if neither of them wanted to be. Surely the police had dealt with other murder victims who had no one to claim their things; there had to be a procedure for what to do in that situation.

"She never told me she had a sister." Ji's flat tone caught Sadie off guard, but he continued before she could comment. "She never talked about any of her family. I assumed she didn't have anyone, let alone anyone like you."

Like me? Sadie repeated in her mind. Did he mean that in a good way or a bad way?

"How did you find my address to contact me?"

"I looked through her desk and found an envelope with your return address. Your father's obituary was inside, which is how I made the connection."

"She hadn't come to his funeral so I'd sent her the clipping. She kept it?" Sadie felt a wisp of gratitude that she'd sent it even though she'd been frustrated with Wendy for not acknowledging their father's death. That Wendy had kept it all these years meant something, didn't it?

Ji's expression showed a hint of regret that caused Sadie to brace herself. "It hadn't been opened when I found it," he said.

Wendy never even opened the letter Sadie had sent? She'd never even read the final tribute to their father? Sadie swallowed the hurt and reminded herself that this detail was in perfect accordance with the Wendy Sadie *did* know. A nice apartment and beautiful things hadn't apparently changed her much.

"Wendy cut us out of her life entirely," Sadie explained. "But I'm glad she kept the letter if only so that you could find me. I'm glad you contacted me."

"When did my mother cut you off?"

Sadie gave him a brief version of the history and ended with, "It was very hard on my parents."

"But not on you," Ji added, picking through the subtleties of what she'd said.

If not for having already promised herself to be honest with him when the hard questions came up, she'd have lied. There was obvious difficulty between Ji and his mother, and Sadie felt guilty adding to it with her own negative experience. But she wouldn't lie to him. If this man deserved anything from her, he deserved the truth. Still, she proceeded with caution, not wanting to give more than he wanted to hear. "Wendy didn't treat me well when we were young, and we never had a chance to form a bond later in life."

"What do you mean she didn't treat you well?"

It was easier to tell Ji than it had been to tell Pete, maybe because she'd had practice, or maybe because she'd had a few days to relive the experiences and reaffirm to herself that she hadn't been to blame for Wendy's bad behavior. Or maybe because she sensed that Ji hadn't been treated well by Wendy either. Those things didn't make the telling of it painless, however.

"I forgave her a long time ago," Sadie said after divulging the details of her childhood experiences. "I believe she was mentally ill and didn't always understand what she was doing."

"Perhaps you give her too much credit. Perhaps she was just a bad person and always had been."

His dark sentiment surprised her, but she was careful not to react. She had no idea what his life with Wendy had been like and didn't want to come across as dismissive or judgmental. "I'm not sure

I believe that people are just *bad.*" Yet even as she said it, she thought of some of the people she'd met in recent years who could fit that description.

Ji looked away from her to the canvas prints of Wendy on the living room wall. Sadie watched him, wondering what he felt when he looked at the portraits of his mother and wondering what Wendy had done to cause such disdain in her only child.

Several seconds passed before he looked back at her. "Did you know about me?"

Sadie had been dreading that question but took a deep breath before she answered. "My parents begged for contact when she told us about you; she called you Eddie."

Ji nodded but didn't comment.

Sadie continued. "They sent money when Wendy faced different crises and asked for help. More than once, they sent money specifically to pay for the two of you to come out and visit, but she never came. She would go for months and sometimes years between contacting Mom and Dad. And then at some point she said you were living with your dad."

"None of you ever looked for me," Ji said matter-of-factly.

There was a question in his statement, a *"Why didn't you find me?"*

"When my parents gave her money it was their expectation that they were helping you." Even as she said it, though, she wondered why they hadn't tried harder to find him. Why not hire a private investigator? Why had Sadie followed the passive lead of her parents instead of doing something herself? She tried to explain about the uncertainty of whether or not Ji had existed because Wendy seemed to have used him only as an excuse to get money from her parents, but he cut her off.

"You knew she wasn't well—you said so yourself. Did you consider that she wasn't well enough to be a mother? Knowing she might have a child should have spurred you to at least try." His expression was hardening, and Sadie felt herself tensing in response.

"We worried about that all the time, even when we weren't sure if you were real or not. When we learned you were with your father—"

"My father is a drunk. I was ten years old when Wendy dropped me off at his nasty apartment and told him he could be the parent for the next ten years. I didn't see her for almost five years. By then, I was living with Lin Yang's family and working at their restaurant so that I could eat and stay in school. I had nowhere else to go."

"I'm so sorry," Sadie said softly, feeling terrible about all he'd gone through. "We had no idea."

"And you didn't check," Ji said. His eyes and expression were cold and stony. He turned away and took a breath. "Before she took me to my dad's, we lived all over Southern California. She'd shack up with someone for a few months, then after he'd kick her out for stealing, we'd live with another friend of hers. One time we lived in our car for an entire summer. I panhandled on the beach so we could eat at the end of the day. Growing up with her was a nightmare, and all along you guys . . ." He stopped himself and took another breath, a deeper one. "Never mind," he suddenly said, straightening his shoulders. "I'm going to get started in the bedroom." He crossed the room and shut the door behind him.

Sadie blinked, trying to keep the tears down while swallowing the lump in her throat. Why hadn't they tried harder to confirm Ji's existence? Couldn't she have done something to help him? Was there anything she could do now to make it right? She pictured him as a little boy, begging for money, and had to close her eyes against the image that made her physically sick.

After several seconds, she went back to packing the kitchen, heartsick and wishing she could say something to ease Ji's hurt. The hopes she had of having a relationship with him after they finished closing out Wendy's life seemed slim, and yet she couldn't hold it against him. If she'd been in that situation and learned that there were people who could have helped her but didn't, she wasn't sure she could forgive them either.

She also wondered, as she wrapped a crystal bowl in newspaper before putting it in a box, how Wendy had gone from the woman Ji had just told her about to someone with crystal bowls and Williams-Sonoma dish sets. What had happened between then and now? Did it even matter?

CHAPTER 9

When the buzzer sounded for the second time that day, Sadie was startled all over again. It was Pete this time. She buzzed him up, then opened the apartment door and waited in the doorway for him, relieved that he was back. Ji stayed in the bedroom, allowing Sadie to give Pete a whispered update of what had happened in his absence. She heard the pleading tone in her voice and was glad when Pete said he'd try to talk to Ji. She didn't notice the white paper bag until he handed it to her and said they'd eat the "treats" in a little while.

He kissed her quickly before disappearing into the bedroom. She heard him introduce himself and immediately begin asking about Ji's work and family. Pete was a master with people, and Sadie was glad when she heard Ji answering Pete's questions. The bag Pete had handed her was from Ghirardelli Chocolate Company, and there were cookies inside. Sadie's stomach was too twisted to be tempted at the moment, so she set the bag aside and went back to work packing up the kitchen.

Half an hour later, the last of the kitchen items were boxed up, and she shifted her attention to the office. She scanned the room from the doorway and looked over her shoulder at the document boxes still sitting on the kitchen counter filled with personal papers, contracts, and other remnants of Wendy's life. She was tempted to start reading through those files first but talked herself out of it; it was more important to get the apartment packed. The files were already boxed—she could look through them another time—but there was a deadline for everything else.

Sadie picked up an empty box while eyeing the bookshelf. Pete laughed in the other room, and she wondered what on earth they could be talking about that had him laughing, but then she forced herself to move again. It was Ji's chuckle that stopped her in her tracks the second time. She hated feeling left out but took comfort in the fact that if Pete was building a bridge with Ji, she might be able to cross it later.

She started with packing the books—interior design, mostly, and a few racy romance novels she *may* have read a couple pages from before remembering the task at hand. She'd finished the top shelf and had moved on to the second when she pulled out what she thought was a book only to realize it was a box of stationery. The box was black and stored between a book about Audrey Hepburn and *Feng Shui for Dummies*.

Sadie moved the box to the desk, where she lifted off the lid. Half of the box was filled with pale pink envelopes and the other half held stationery of the same color, half-sheet size. It was a disappointing discovery—she'd hoped for something more personal—and was going to put the top back on when she realized that the envelope on top of the stack was sealed.

She set the top of the box back down on the desk, picked up the sealed envelope, and turned it over. Nothing was written on the front. It was obvious, however, that there was something inside.

Sadie considered her options for .03 seconds, before sliding her finger beneath the seal and tearing it open. Inside was a piece of the pink stationery. She pulled it out and unfolded it. The words were written in large, flowery letters with looping circles—artistic and dramatic.

He came again last night. Ecstasy!

Sadie read the words again and felt her cheeks heat up in embarrassment. It wasn't hard to guess what this note was in regards to. She looked for a date or a signature, something to give these six words some context or chronology, but found nothing. She refolded the letter and put it back in the envelope, which she then took into the kitchen and slid under the lid of one of the file boxes. She wondered what it meant *exactly*, why it was written but not sent, and who it was intended for as she continued packing up the office.

After another forty minutes—and far too much obsessive thinking—her stomach growled, and although she didn't necessarily want to stop her momentum, she could swear those cookies were beginning to call her name from the kitchen.

She set a goal to finish packing the last of the bookshelf—full of office supplies—before she allowed herself to return to the kitchen. She looked in on the cookies again and then shut the bag and pushed it away. Pete had purchased them and had not yet issued her an invitation to have one. Besides, she felt anxious enough that she worried that if she ate one, she'd end up eating all six without a second thought. It wouldn't be the first time. Better not tempt such possibilities.

However, when she breathed in the scent of the cookies she would swear had been baked fresh that morning, the rich chocolate compelled her to consider her options, which then further compelled her to poke her head into the bedroom. Both Pete and Ji looked up from where they were emptying out the dresser contents into garbage sacks. The room looked quite different than it had earlier: the closet was empty, and the bed stripped. Even the curtains were taken down.

Sadie noted that the earlier hardness in Ji's face was gone, but she still didn't make eye contact with him, embarrassed by their earlier exchange.

"Hey," Pete said, holding a bag open while Ji used his hand to scoop out what looked like underthings from a drawer. Pink, black, lacy, and completely impractical things Sadie was embarrassed for him to see let alone touch. She should have thought about that when she was alone in the apartment and saved them all from the awkwardness.

The picture Sadie and Pete had taken down had been moved to lean against the wall, and Sadie hoped Ji hadn't seen it. The only thing worse than seeing your sister naked had to be seeing your mother that way.

"I was going to run to that little market on the street and get some milk to go with the cookies. Can I get you guys anything else?"

"I'm good," Pete said, then turned toward Ji.

"A Coke would be nice," he said.

Sadie liked that Ji was letting her do something for him and nodded with a cautious smile in his direction. He wasn't looking at her, so she didn't know if he saw it. "Okay. I'll be right back."

It took about ten minutes before Sadie returned with a quart of milk and a Coke. On the way back, she took the stairs and loved the romance of it, even though her quads were burning by the time she got to the top.

The men were in the kitchen when she returned. Ji sat on one of the two bar stools tucked under the lip of the counter, and Pete stood between the counter and the sink, telling Ji about the deep-sea fishing trip he'd taken a couple weeks earlier.

Sadie entered the kitchen, hopeful that sharing some yummy cookies would make some headway toward building a better relationship with Ji. Food had that power sometimes. She tore some paper towels from the roll she'd left out for cleaning purposes and passed them out before realizing that she'd packed up all the cups and glasses. "I'll go down and get some paper ones from the store," Sadie said, turning toward the door.

"I don't need any milk," Ji said, waving toward the carton Pete was already opening. "You two can share it."

For a moment Sadie didn't know what he meant, then Pete took a swig from the carton before setting it down in front of her. Sadie pursed her lips together and got a teasing smile in return. She was not a drink-from-the-carton kind of girl.

Pete handed her a chocolate cookie with what looked like big sugar crystals on top. She took it, but was still considering the idea of going back to the market and getting an individually sized bottle of milk.

"I was telling Ji about my visit with Detective Lopez. Maybe you'd like an update too. The forensics report came in."

In an instant, Sadie knew she wasn't going to leave to buy more milk.

CHAPTER 10

"Really?" Sadie asked. "What did it say?"

"It's more what it *didn't* say," Pete said, giving each of them a serious look. "It ruled cause of death as inconclusive. The . . ." He paused to look at Ji, a small furrow showing between his eyebrows. "Are you sure you're okay hearing about these details? Sadie's used to it, but this is your mother."

"I'm okay," Ji said. He attempted a smile, though it didn't look natural on his face. "When I get off work and can't sleep, I watch reruns of *CSI.*"

"So do I," Sadie said, the connection overriding her caution. "Do you like Vegas best? Because I find the Vegas series to be the most interesting."

Ji gave her a strange look, making her aware of how overeager she'd sounded. "Sorry," she said, looking down at the counter and brushing away imaginary crumbs.

"Ji, are you sure?" Pete asked again.

"I'm sure, Pete," Ji said as though they were old friends. "If it becomes too much for me, I'll say so."

"Okay," Pete said. "The body was so badly decomposed that the police were unable to determine cause of death. They were able to conclusively rule out traumatic injury—there was nothing like broken bones or evidence of a weapon being used—and tissue samples were clear of things like toxins or drugs."

"Like from a poisoning?" Ji said.

Pete nodded. "But they can't be certain of how she died. Possibly a heart attack or stroke, or maybe drowning. Because there's nothing that specifically indicates foul play, she *could* have died of natural causes."

"Really?" Sadie said, trying to determine why this was so surprising to her. Probably because so many of the cases she'd worked had been homicide and the circumstances with Wendy's death were so bizarre.

"Every indication seems to point to the probability that she was taking a bath at the time of her death, and nothing within that part of the investigation indicates foul play."

"It's a relief to think she wasn't murdered," Ji said. "How do they explain the . . . fire?"

"Well, they can't really explain that part. At least they can't explain the motive for it or the delay in time between her death and the fire itself. Up until the forensics report came in, it seemed likely to assume that Wendy *was* killed and the killer returned four weeks later, but now there's nothing that suggests homicide as cause of death. The fire didn't cause any serious damage to the apartment, and the anonymous phone call was probably made within minutes of the fire being set; the police think that perhaps the lack of damage could have been intentional and the anonymous caller was the person who'd set the fire."

"Why would the arsonist call the fire department?" Sadie asked.

Pete shrugged. "Maybe they didn't want to burn down the whole building. Maybe they had second thoughts—the department doesn't have any really great theories either. The fire *did* further compromise the condition of the body, so perhaps the intent was to compound confusion of cause of death."

Sadie pondered that information.

"Where did the person call from?" Ji asked.

"A pay phone a couple of blocks west of here. The caller said they saw smoke from an apartment at the corner of Mission and 22nd Street, then hung up. A first responder was at the building within four minutes and saw smoke coming from the open bathroom window. The fire was already smoldering by the time they got into Wendy's apartment, which was unlocked. Nothing in the bathroom had caught fire . . . well, except Wendy. The body had been doused with some kind of accelerant, which is why it burned at all. The fan in the bathroom was also on, like we thought, and it drafted most of the smoke out of the building, leaving minimal damage behind."

"That's why the apartment didn't reek of smoke," Sadie said. "Do they know if the fan was on in the weeks between Wendy's death and the fire?"

"They only know that it was on at the time of the fire," Pete said. "But they agreed that if it had been left on it would account for the lack of other . . . smells."

Sadie furrowed her brow for a moment as she considered all the odd details. "Could they tell from the 911 call if it was a male or female caller?"

"Female."

"Maybe someone killed Wendy, thought the body would be found sooner, and when it wasn't, they had to speed up the process," Sadie suggested.

"If it was just discovery they were worried about, why light the fire rather than just call in about the body?" Pete asked.

"And if they had reason to want to destroy evidence," Ji added, "why wait a month to do it?"

"Exactly," Pete said, nodding toward Ji.

Sadie tried not to feel jealous of their friendliness as she pressed on. "And how is it that no one reported her missing or thought to check up on her until that fire? A month is such a long time."

"From all accounts, she had harassed everyone in the building to the point where everyone avoided her," Pete said.

Sadie nodded. Lopez had pretty much told her that during their first phone call.

Pete continued, "The police think that she rarely went any-where the last year or so. She had a laundry service and grocery delivery that came about once a week. Most of the tenants hadn't seen Wendy for weeks before she died so they didn't notice when she wasn't around."

"But an entire month? What about the apartment next door?"

Ji chimed in. "Mr. Pilings told me that the tenant in number six moved out in May—before Wendy died. Wendy was the only person on the floor."

"And if she wasn't coming and going much, someone on her floor would be the only person really aware of her," Pete said, nod-ding. "One of her downstairs neighbors put a cardboard box under her mail slot to hold the excess when it was no longer fitting in her slot. They went to great lengths to avoid having to deal with her."

"Which brings us back to why someone would light her on fire," Sadie said. "It's in the murderer's best interest to let as much time go by as possible before an investigation begins, so why would they return and, in essence, alert the police?"

"Why is it in their best interest to let more time go by?" Ji asked.

"Details get forgotten by witnesses," Pete said. "Especially if they don't realize they witnessed anything related to a crime. Evidence breaks down; video camera footage is erased." Pete looked at Sadie and then Ji. "The police are checking pawnshops for the items missing from the apartment. If they were pawned prior to her body being discovered, it could indicate that a robbery had occurred closer to her time of death. But the prevailing theory is that the robbery is probably connected to the fire, not Wendy's death."

"But they ruled the death to have been natural causes," Sadie reminded him, trying to keep everything straight.

"Inconclusive," Pete said. "But still suspicious."

Sadie furrowed her brow again, trying to make the pieces fit. However, they *didn't* fit. If whoever killed Wendy was afraid of being discovered, why not destroy the evidence immediately? If, on the other hand, Wendy's death and the fire were somehow separate, then . . . well, what possible reason was there to burn the body unless it was to alert the police or destroy evidence?

"Huh," Sadie said, glancing at Ji, who seemed to be just as deep in thought. He took another bite of his cookie, reminding Sadie that she hadn't even tried hers.

Sadie took a bite, expecting a basic chocolate cookie with Ghirardelli chips in it, but froze when the level of chocolate contained in this cookie exploded into something far different than she'd anticipated. She pulled the cookie back to look at it and then chewed ever so slowly, ever so deliberately. It was rich like a brownie, chewy like a cookie, but it also melted in her mouth like a truffle. The crystals on top weren't sugar, but salt, amplifying the flavor even more. She swallowed the bite with a satisfied sigh before remembering that she wasn't alone. She looked up at Pete and Ji, both of whom were looking at her with smiles on their faces, though Ji's was more guarded.

Pete glanced at Ji. "Told ya," he said softly. Ji's smile widened slightly.

"Told him what?" Sadie demanded.

"That these cookies were going to make you cry."

"I didn't cry." Her attention was captured by the rest of the cookie in her hand. She took another bite, managing to keep from making any more appreciative sounds out loud, but just barely. By the time she finished her first cookie, she was eyeing the milk and trying to ignore Pete's knowing smirk. She wouldn't cave and drink from the carton. She would be strong!

She picked up her second cookie, even though the first one was rich enough that she was satisfied. What if the cookies didn't keep well? It was her duty as a food connoisseur to ensure that none of this deliciousness went to waste.

After the first bite, however, she *needed* milk. The cookie was so rich. Pete laughed when he caught her trying to sneak some milk without him noticing, but he turned his attention back to Ji. That she didn't care how trashy it was to drink right out of the carton said more about the quality of the cookie than anything else could. She wondered if she could find the recipe online. It was one she'd definitely put in her Little Black Recipe Book if she could recreate such magnificence!

"That was amazing," Sadie said after she finished the second cookie and drank from the carton again. It took another moment before she realized she'd interrupted their conversation. "Sorry, what were we talking about?"

"Ji was telling me about Wendy's ex-husbands—I was asking him about one of them."

"She had more than one ex-husband?"

"She had four," Ji said.

Sadie lifted her eyebrows. "Four?"

Ji explained that Wendy had technically been married when she met Ji's father, Kai, though she hadn't seen her husband in a couple of years—Ji called it a "hippie thing." Her divorce was final in time for Kai and Wendy to get married a month before Ji was born, but before Ji was even two, Wendy left Kai for someone named Dan or Darin or Darryl. Ji barely remembered Husband Number Three; they divorced when Ji was four.

"She had a few boyfriends over the next several years, but she left me with my dad in order to marry her fourth husband, Rodger."

She left me, Sadie repeated in her mind. She didn't ask him to elaborate and simply nodded her understanding. Woven within his account were the other things Ji had told her about his childhood: living with friends, panhandling at the beach. What a sad childhood.

"The police talked to Rodger Penrose, the last husband, and cleared him as a suspect. They said that he and Wendy had remained on good terms, and that he had an alibi," Pete said. "They haven't located the other husbands yet."

"My dad was sent back to Hong Kong a few years ago. His papers were fake, so when immigration laws started being more heavily enforced, he was found out," Ji said without much emotion. "I think the first husband's dead, and the guy whose name starts with a D could be anywhere. I told all this to the police."

Pete nodded. "They said as much."

"So, where are things with the investigation now that the forensics are back?" Sadie asked, worried that without solid leads to follow—which they didn't seem to have—the police wouldn't keep working the case.

"Well," Pete began, "they did give it a solid week of investigation—interviews, timelines, crime scene, that kind of thing. Nothing led anywhere concrete, though, and they're discouraged by the forensics report. I think the reason they're willing to give me so much information is in hopes that we'll find some new leads for them to follow. It's hard for them to justify a lot of manpower when there's been such little success. The department is kept really busy in this city, and there isn't much extra time to spare."

It was a good choice for Pete to take the police portions of this situation, Sadie thought to herself. He obviously knew how to talk to them for them to be so open with him about the case.

"Do you think they'll find who did it?" Ji asked. He'd finished his cookies and was halfway through his bottle of Coke. Sadie didn't know how he could stand the sweetness of the soda mixed with the richness of the cookie. It made her stomach hurt to even think about.

"A month is a long time, and a victim who seems to have secluded herself from other people gives them very little to work with." He looked at Sadie. "Did you find anything interesting in the office? The police cleared out her nightstand drawers"—he nodded toward the boxes on the counter—"so we didn't find much in the way of personal items."

Sadie thought about the weird letter she'd found and glanced at Ji before deciding to tell them both about it; she'd promised to be honest with him and she would be. She fished the letter out of the file box where she'd put it earlier and handed it to Ji. She noticed his expression harden slightly before he handed it back to her. He might know his mother was flawed, but he still didn't like to be reminded of it.

"Huh," Pete said into the uncomfortable silence that followed after Sadie returned the letter to the envelope. "It makes sense to conclude it was from Wendy, but I'm not sure we can be sure about that."

"She's an artist, so she could do that fancy script," Sadie said. "And she lived here alone, so I think it's a safe assumption to say she wrote it. But it could have been done ten years ago."

"Or two months ago," Ji said. "She liked to . . . bother people; I don't know how else to explain it. For example, for six months she would take our neighbor's newspaper, then swear she hadn't when he asked her about it. She didn't read it, she just threw it away. I don't even know why she did it in the first place—she probably got this weird power trip off of it. And then I had a teacher in the third grade that she just despised, so she would send anonymous complaints to the school, accusing him of hitting the kids and swearing at us—things like that." Ji shook his head, then nodded toward the letter. "I would bet that letter is part of something like that. She was probably tormenting someone who had made her mad."

"But she hadn't sent it," Sadie said.

"Or at least she hadn't sent that one," Ji pointed out.

Sadie put the envelope back in the box. "I hope it was from a long time ago. Or maybe she thought better about it after she wrote it."

"Or maybe it was true," Ji said, a challenge in his expression. "Maybe she was having an affair with someone's husband and wanted to torment them with it."

Sadie made a face. Did people have affairs when they were sixty-three years old? She was growing increasingly uncomfortable with the conversation and decided to change the subject. "I thought I'd take the boxes from the police back to the hotel tonight and go through them there. Or I could ship them home if needs be. That way I can look through each file on its own and see if we can learn anything from it without taking time away from getting everything here packed up."

"That's a good idea," Pete said.

Sadie opened the fridge to store the milk. The too-sweet smell of food made her aware of another task she needed to complete. "Right now, however, I need to get this fridge cleaned out."

Pete crumpled up his napkin. "Let me know when you're ready for me to take the garbage out for you."

"And we're almost done with the clothes and things," Ji said, putting the cap back on his Coke and standing up from the bar stool. "I need to leave for the restaurant soon, but I can be back in the morning."

"That'd be great," Sadie said, glad that things seemed softer between them. Or maybe she was just misinterpreting simple politeness.

"Do you think we could get that bed taken apart before you go?" Pete asked Ji.

"Sure, I've got time for that."

The men disappeared into the bedroom, and Sadie armed herself with a garbage sack and kitchen cleaner. There wasn't much in the fridge—moldy takeout, withering fruit, a partial bottle of wine, and condiments. Just in case, she took pictures of everything. It probably wasn't important, but you never could be too sure.

When she finished, Pete took the bag of stinky food downstairs to the Dumpster, leaving Sadie and Ji alone in the apartment, though they were in different rooms.

Sadie moved into the living room and opened the cabinet below the TV while Ji brought bag after bag of clothes and bedding from the bedroom and stacked them near the door of the apartment.

"I'm sorry about earlier," said Ji.

She looked up to see him standing just outside the bedroom door and noted the regret in his expression.

"I understand why you didn't find me. It wasn't your responsibility."

His words were soothing, in a way, but Sadie lowered her eyes as the guilt rushed back in. "I try to justify it, but it was a selfish choice. We should have found a way to see if you needed help."

"She probably wouldn't have let you, since she worked so hard to keep me away from you."

"There's no way to be sure she would have kept us out if we'd tried harder," Sadie said. "After you were with your dad, we wouldn't have needed her help anyway."

"My father *certainly* wouldn't have let you into my life. He was very suspicious of whites, and Wendy didn't help his opinion."

Ghirardelli Truffle Cookies with Sea Salt

1 (10-ounce) bag Ghirardelli 60% cocoa bittersweet baking chips, divided

2 tablespoons butter

2 eggs

½ cup sugar

1 teaspoon vanilla

¼ cup flour

¼ teaspoon baking powder

¼ teaspoon salt

2 to 3 tablespoons coarse sea salt

Set aside ⅓ cup baking chips for later use. In a medium-sized heatproof bowl over a double boiler, melt the remaining chocolate chips and butter until smooth. Turn off the stove and let melted chocolate sit over warm water.*

In a separate bowl, whisk together eggs and sugar, mixing until well combined. Remove chocolate from the double boiler. Slowly add egg mixture to the warm chocolate, whisking constantly. Add vanilla. Mix well. Add flour, baking powder, and salt. Mix well and let batter cool for a few minutes. Add reserved ⅓ cup of baking chips. (If batter is too warm, chocolate chips will melt.)

Chill batter in fridge for 30 minutes. Preheat oven to 350 degrees.

After batter has chilled and thickened slightly, drop batter by rounded tablespoons on greased cookie sheet. Sprinkle each cookie lightly with a pinch of sea salt. Bake for approximately 8 to 10 minutes until the outside edge looks slightly cracked, but centers are soft and gooey. Cool cookies for four minutes on cookie sheet before transferring to cooling rack.

*To melt chocolate in microwave: Heat chocolate in a microwave-safe container at medium power (50%) for 1 minute. Stir until bowl no longer feels warm. Continue heating at 20-second intervals, stirring after each heating until mixture is smooth.

Note: For a delicious twist, add one of the following before baking: ¾ cup toasted pecans or pistachios, ¼ cup chopped candied ginger, or ⅓ cup sweetened coconut.

Note: For a slightly sweeter cookie, use semisweet chocolate chips.

Note: This recipe was adapted from one found on www.ghirardelli .com.

Makes about two dozen cookies.

CHAPTER 11

It was somewhat of a relief to hear that Sadie's family wouldn't have been allowed into Ji's life even if they had tried to be a part of it, but the realization did little to ease her regret. If nothing else—even if Ji's father had refused contact—Sadie should have been able to tell Ji that she'd tried. But she hadn't tried, and she hated the fact that she couldn't go back and change it. Still, regret aside, she was grateful that Ji was reaching out to her even though he was completely justified in not doing anything of the sort. He'd put her firmly in her place earlier, and she wasn't convinced that she didn't belong there.

"Did your father take better care of you than Wendy did?" Sadie asked. Ji had said his father was a drunk, but maybe he was a functional alcoholic, someone who could hold a job and take care of his family, just not as well as he should.

"Not really." Ji shrugged in a vain attempt to make the answer seem casual. "He lost apartments and jobs on a regular basis. It wasn't that different than living with Wendy had been, except that in Chinatown I was part of the Chinese community, and they looked out for me when my father didn't."

"You said you lived with Lin Yang's family?"

Ji nodded. "Her father hired me to work in the restaurant when I was thirteen. When he learned I was sleeping on the couch of my father's new girlfriend, he let me stay in a room in the back of the restaurant. After a while, they invited me to live in their home."

"They were good to you?"

"Very good. I was a part of a family for the first time, and it shaped what kind of man I wanted to be."

"And then you and Lin Yang fell in love?" She smiled softly at the sentiment, but Ji didn't.

He looked past Sadie's head at the window behind her. "By the time I was nineteen, I was running the restaurant side by side with Lin Yang's father. He'd worked the shipyards for years before opening the restaurant, and it had aged him. He wanted me to take over the business, but he wanted it to stay in the family, too. It's not unusual in Chinese culture to make that type of arrangement. He passed away a few years ago, and the ownership of the restaurant moved to Lin Yang, her sister, and me equally. He was a very good man, and it's an honor to continue his legacy."

It took a few beats for Sadie to realize what Ji was saying. "An arranged marriage?" The idea made her sad. She was so grateful to have loved Neil, and so excited to share a life with Pete. She couldn't imagine marrying for any reason *but* love. And yet, Ji had—to honor Lin Yang's father and the trust he'd put in Ji, and perhaps to ensure Ji's own security after so many years of having so little of it in his life.

That he had told Sadie at all said even more. Had he not fallen in love with Lin Yang in the years since their arrangement? If he had, Sadie expected that he'd have said as much—been a bit embarrassed by the circumstances of the start of their marriage. Instead, he'd chosen to communicate that this marriage had been, in a sense, a business decision, and Sadie felt that his motivation in pointing it out was because it still was a marriage of convenience.

"I have a good life," Ji continued. "And I suppose I can thank my mother for that in a way. If she hadn't brought me to my father, I wouldn't have my family or my restaurant. My children are smart and hardworking. The restaurant is successful and supports not only my family, but almost a dozen employees, blessing their lives in much the same way it blesses mine. I reconnected with my heritage, which brings a great deal of peace and purpose into my life."

"Did you start going by Ji instead of Eddie when you came to Chinatown?"

He nodded proudly. "My father had always called me by my Chinese name, which was his father's name too. When I moved in with him, it was the only name anyone knew me by and, I suppose, it served as a reminder of the different person I was after that. It suits me, I think."

"I agree," Sadie said with a smile. That he'd risen above such difficult circumstances was remarkable. "How many children do you have?" She'd met Min, whom Lin Yang had pointed out to be the eldest.

"I have three daughters," Ji said with a slight smile. His shoulders squared just enough for Sadie to notice, an outward reflection of the pride he felt for them. "And while I know many think that's unlucky, I am quite pleased with all of them. Min—you met her today—starts her second year at San Francisco State soon. She's in the engineering program there. Sonia is thirteen, and Pengma is eleven. They attend the Chinese-American International School."

"Is that a private school?"

Ji nodded. "Not many restaurant owners can send their children to schools like that, but Lin Yang and I work hard for them to have the best education. We're very proud of them."

"There is nothing quite so fulfilling as children, is there?" Sadie said, thinking of her own children, who didn't even know she'd come to San Francisco. She wasn't sure whether she wanted to tell them now or wait until it was all over. Wendy was a difficult subject for her to talk about, even to them, and they were both particularly busy right now—Breanna was recently married and living in England, and Shawn was finishing his last two college classes in Michigan.

"My children are my greatest blessings," Ji said, inclining his head slightly.

"Did Min graduate from high school early? You said she's in her second year of college?"

"She turned twenty years old in March."

"Oh, she looks so much younger than that," Sadie said, surprised. "And she's still living at home?"

"Of course," he said with a sharp tone. "She needs to focus on her education. She'll leave our home when she is fully prepared to run her own."

Sadie was reminded that Chinese culture was different from what she was used to. It wasn't all that unusual for a college student to live at home, but she was just surprised at the fervor of Ji's explanation; her impression was that Min's dependence was his choice rather than hers. "You're obviously a good husband and father."

"I try to be," he said with a humble nod.

"And a talented artist." His expression became instantly uncomfortable, and he looked at the floor, shoving his hands into the pockets of his jeans. "Did you do the sculpting on the wall of your restaurant?"

He shrugged. "Many years ago, but I am a business owner now. There's no time for hobbies anymore. The boxes still for sale in the restaurant are the last of them."

"A hobby?" Sadie repeated. "The level of skill on that wall and on your jewelry boxes speaks of more than a hobby. Have you ever thought of pursuing art commercially?"

Ji glanced at her quickly, but Sadie couldn't read his expression. "It's not a practical industry. I went to school for a few years, but the restaurant needed more attention, and I realized it's just as well. The restaurant is successful only when it is managed correctly and, as Lin Yang's father's health declined, the responsibility came to me. I won't dishonor his efforts by not being as focused as he was for all the years he owned it. I work seven days a week to ensure its success and, therefore, my family's well-being."

Sadie raised her eyebrows. "Seven days a week?"

Ji nodded at the same time Pete came through the apartment door, which he'd left ajar when he'd taken out the trash . . . several minutes ago. Sadie hadn't thought until now about how long he'd been gone. Before she had a chance to ask, he answered her unasked questions.

"I met the woman from downstairs." He closed the door behind him. "Her name is Shasta, and she has a pink poodle."

"A pink poodle?" Ji repeated, his eyebrows lifted.

Pete explained that the neighbor had been dressed in a pink jogging suit and had a pink poodle on a rhinestone-studded leash. Near the Dumpsters behind the building was a strip of "pet grass" as Shasta had called it, though she had assured Pete that she paid a child from the neighboring building to clean up after her dog's "business."

Shasta had been appalled that something so tragic as Wendy's death could happen in the building, but her phone had rung before Pete could ask her more about her relationship with Wendy or her experience with the fire.

"I'd like to put together some questions to ask her later," he said. "I know the police talked to her already, but I'd love to get her account firsthand. She seemed talkative and would no doubt be entertaining."

"She sounds fascinating," Sadie said, wishing she'd been there to meet her, but not at the expense of the conversation she'd just shared with Ji. She felt such relief at having had the chance to become better acquainted with him and dared to think they might be able to create a positive relationship after all.

Sadie had cleared out the TV stand while she and Ji talked. There were a few DVDs for old black-and-white movies, the instruction manual for the TV and the DVD player, and some other magazines Sadie set aside. She brushed the dust off her hands when she finished.

A chime sounded from Ji's cell phone. "I need to get back to the restaurant," he said after checking the text message. "The dinner rush will be starting soon. How much longer will you be here?"

Pete turned toward Sadie. "Do you want to stay longer?"

Sadie looked around and shook her head. They'd been there for several hours, and she was both tired and impressed with how much they'd done. The bedroom and kitchen were completely packed up, and she'd made good progress on both the living room and the office. Besides, she planned to go through the file boxes once they got back to the hotel so she still had work to do; she just didn't have to do it here. Pete and Ji each carried a box to the street.

"Oh, Ji," Sadie said, twisting her purse so it hung in front of her.

"I had meant to give these to you. They were in the jewelry box the police returned."

She kept her feelings about the pieces to herself as she removed her mother's jewelry from her purse and held them out to Ji. He took them but seemed confused.

"They're part of Wendy's estate," Sadie explained. "As is the jewelry box and everything in it. We should have grabbed it so you could take it home with you."

Ji looked at her with an inquisitive set to his brow. "Why did you separate these items from the others?"

"Well," Sadie said, looking at the items in Ji's hand, "they had belonged to my mother, but they're yours now. Your daughters and your wife would probably—"

Ji closed his fingers around the items, turned his hand over and reached toward her, shaking his head. "I don't want these."

"But they're yours," Sadie said, not taking them right away but very much wanting to.

"They're yours," Ji said, shaking his hand slightly. "I told you, I want nothing from my mother. Please take these, and take the box with everything else. I don't want it."

"You're sure?" Sadie said.

Ji seemed on the edge of getting angry and nodded sharply.

"Take them," Pete said quietly.

Sadie opened her hand and looked at the ring, brooch, necklace, and the single earring sparkling back at her, a warm sense of satisfaction coursing through her chest. She appreciated his generosity, even if that wasn't his intent. "Thank you," she said. "I think my daughter would love that jewelry box."

"Good," Ji said sharply, then looked at his watch. "I really need to go."

They parted ways with Ji amid handshakes and promises to see each other around 9:00 the next morning. Sadie waited on the curb with the file boxes while Pete went to get the car. She wanted to go get Wendy's jewelry box right that minute, but she couldn't leave the boxes unattended, and there wouldn't be time for her to run up once Pete pulled up to the curb—traffic was unreal and barely moving. She left the task for tomorrow and simply made good use of her people-watching skills. One homeless-looking man muttered to himself about rebels, and a young woman with green hair walked three large dogs who barked and nipped at each other but ignored the press of people around them. Sadie wondered if Wendy had known any of the people Sadie now watched.

Pete pulled to the curb and quickly put the boxes in the trunk of the car while Sadie got into the passenger seat. After Pete got back into the driver's seat, they fastened their seat belts. Pete looked behind him before quickly pulling into traffic; there was no place for meek driving in this city.

"How did things go with Ji while I was taking out the trash?" Pete asked after a minute of silence. "The two of you seemed to be on better terms when I came back up."

Sadie nodded, reliving the relief she'd felt at having cleared the air between them. "He apologized and we talked a little more. He doesn't seem so angry with me and my family, and I learned a lot about him. I think we made some progress."

"I'm really glad," Pete said, slowing down for a cable car to cross in front of them. Tourists hung off the edges, and a teenage girl had her arm extended to take a picture of herself.

"The two of you seemed to get along really well," Sadie said, remembering the pang of jealousy she'd felt when she'd heard the two of them laughing together. "What were you guys talking about?"

Pete chuckled. "I told him about this situation Pat and I had in Chinatown several years ago involving a cart of squash and these little kids and . . . Anyway, he knew the guy who owned that cart." Pete smiled, obviously remembering the incident fondly. "I guess he sets up that scenario when business is slow. Pat and I totally fell for it. We ended up buying a bag of squash and a whole pack of postcards by the time we left, feeling terrible about the trouble we thought we'd caused with that cart."

Sadie felt another wave of jealously, but this one was toward Pat. She made a bland comment, and they drove in silence for several seconds. Sadie worried Pete suspected the reason for her sudden quiet and so she searched for another topic. Not for the first time, it was food that saved her.

"Did you know that chicken tetrazzini was invented right here in San Francisco?" Sadie made a really great chicken tetrazzini, but hadn't known until only five or six years ago that it was invented in the city where her sister lived.

"I didn't know that, but I'm not the least bit surprised that you do."

Sadie, optimistic at the change of mood her talk of food had inspired, was preparing her next bit of trivia when Pete's phone rang. She hurried to grab the earpiece of his Bluetooth device from the middle console and hand it to him. Talking on a cell phone while driving in California was illegal, and if the cops here were as dedicated to that law as the cops in Oregon had been when Sadie visited, she didn't want to take any chances.

Pete put the Bluetooth over his ear and pushed the button on his phone to answer the call. Luckily traffic was basically at a standstill so the maneuvering didn't throw off his driving. "This is Pete Cunningham. . . . Hi, Stan, how are you?"

Sadie perked up. Stan Harlesden was the realtor handling the sales of their homes.

"Oh, wow, that's great. . . . Uh-huh . . . right . . . I agree. . . . We'll talk about it tonight. Can we have forty-eight hours to decide? . . . Great. . . . Yeah, I'll let you know."

Pete said good-bye and reached for the button on his earpiece that would end the call. Sadie was so excited about what she'd ascertained from his side of the conversation that it took her a few moments to realize that Pete's expression wasn't reflecting the same exuberance. At best his expression could be described as blank, at worst it was disappointed.

"Aren't you excited?" she asked after giving him ample time to explain himself without her prodding.

"Yeah," Pete said, giving her a fake smile before looking ahead again.

"Tell me about the offer. How much?"

"Full price, but they want me to pay the closing costs." He spoke flatly despite it being a full-price offer, which was better than they'd hoped for. They'd both listed their homes higher than they'd be willing to sell for, in order to get a feel for the market. Sadie had listened to his tone as much as his words, though, and heard something very different from what he was saying out loud.

"You don't seem excited," Sadie said.

"No, I am. It's just so . . . fast, I guess."

"Isn't that a good thing?"

"Yes, of course it is." He still sounded flat. "We've got two days to accept or counter or whatever, so there's no rush. Let's think about it but not let it distract us too much."

"Sure." Inside, however, Sadie was concerned by Pete's lack of enthusiasm. When they'd listed their homes on the same day, with the same realtor, they'd been excited at the step they were making toward sharing their lives. It had been a promise of sorts, a representation of the commitment they were making and the exciting changes ahead. If Sadie hadn't been there that day, feeling those feelings right alongside him, the heavy expression on Pete's face right now would make her question it had ever happened.

They drove in relative silence for another minute, being passed by multiple bicyclists who were making far better time than they were.

"Are you ready for dinner?" Pete said, a false lightness in his voice. "They have some of the best restaurants I've ever eaten at in this city."

"Oh, good," Sadie said with equally false enthusiasm as she tried not to obsess about his change in mood. "I'm ready to be wowed."

"Maybe we can find some chicken tetrazzini?" Pete suggested, giving her a more natural smile this time.

Sadie decided to fully embrace his attempts at changing the subject and the mood. "Well, as I was saying, chicken tetrazzini was named after an opera singer who loved to come and perform in San Francisco in the early 1900s. A chef at the Palace Hotel created the dish in her honor. I wonder if it's still on the menu?" She turned to him, feeling her excitement rise. "Could we go there for dinner? I've heard great things about that hotel."

"Sure," Pete said—flat, *again*. No excitement at all—not even the fake kind. "Whatever you want."

Sadie looked at him another moment, then faced forward. Why the sudden shift in mood again? Had she said something wrong, or was Sadie just paranoid now?

Chicken Tetrazzini

1 pound boneless, skinless chicken breasts
¼ cup diced onion
¼ cup diced celery
1½ teaspoon salt, divided
1 quart water
8 ounces uncooked spaghetti noodles
4 tablespoons butter, divided
1 tablespoon lemon juice
2 tablespoons flour
½ teaspoon pepper
¼ teaspoon paprika
⅛ teaspoon nutmeg
1 cup whipping cream (could use half-and-half or coconut milk
   instead)
⅔ cup Parmesan cheese

In a two-quart saucepan on medium-high heat, combine chicken, onion, celery, 1 teaspoon of the salt, and water. Boil until chicken is done, about 15 minutes. Remove chicken from pan with a slotted spoon, retaining the stock in saucepan.

Bring stock to a boil and add spaghetti noodles. Cook according to package directions until al dente. If needed, add additional water, one cup at a time, to cover noodles.

While pasta is cooking, shred or cut chicken into pieces. Set aside. Preheat oven to 400 degrees F.

When spaghetti is done, drain (retaining whatever veggies you can) and put noodles and vegetables in the bottom of a 9x13-inch or 11x7-inch baking dish.

In a skillet, heat 2 tablespoons butter, lemon juice, and ½ teaspoon salt until butter is melted. Pour mixture over cooked spaghetti and toss lightly.

In same skillet, slowly heat the remaining 2 tablespoons butter, flour, pepper, paprika, and nutmeg, stirring constantly until smooth and thick. Remove from heat. Add whipping cream and stir until smooth. Add chicken and stir. Spoon chicken mixture over the spaghetti and top with grated Parmesan cheese.

Cover with aluminum foil and bake for 25 minutes.

Makes approximately 8 servings.

Note: Adding 1 cup of mushrooms and 1 to 2 tablespoons pimentos sautéed in the lemon-butter sauce prior to tossing with pasta gives additional flavor and color to the dish.

Note: This recipe is perfect to assemble the night before and refrigerate until ready to bake.

Family Notes: Shawn always requests that I double the sauce. Breanna likes to add ½ a red pepper, diced, to the sauce for color. This was Neil's favorite dish for using up leftover turkey after Thanksgiving.

CHAPTER 12

Pete and Sadie decided to check into their hotel before dinner, unload the boxes from the car, and grab jackets. Though the day had been warm enough, it was decidedly cool by the time they reached the hotel. Sadie was glad she'd checked the forecast before she'd come, otherwise she'd have never guessed it would get this cold.

Sadie set the painted box she'd purchased earlier on the dresser, glad to have a memento of Ji to take home with her. She wondered about the box in Wendy's apartment. Ji had seemed confused by it being there and said Wendy hadn't been to the restaurant in years. Had Ji been selling them back then? If not, how had Wendy come to own it? Perhaps Sadie could explore the topic with Ji tomorrow.

Once they'd freshened up in their respective rooms—Sadie was on the third floor and Pete on the fifth—they walked through the towering buildings and crowded streets of the financial district to the Palace Hotel, a landmark of San Francisco. The hotel featured two famous restaurants: The Garden Court, which served breakfast, lunch, and afternoon tea, and The Pied Piper Bar and Grill, which was open for lunch and dinner.

Sadie couldn't deny her disappointment that they wouldn't get to eat in the elaborate dining room of the Garden Court, though they did peek in at the ornate columns and glass ceiling. Amazing. Pete suggested they try to come back for the breakfast buffet, and Sadie agreed to such a fabulous plan.

The Pied Piper Bar and Grill was nothing to sneeze at either, however, with its rich wood paneling, dark color palette, and painted mural behind the bar. The overall atmosphere was one of class and elegance, which made Sadie worry they were underdressed. A quick glance at their fellow diners eased her mind, however. Everyone was dressed just like they were—jeans and sweatshirts—with perhaps an occasional skirt or suit mixed in.

Pete ordered the pork chops without reading through most of the menu, and Sadie went with the salmon. She always ordered seafood when she was in coastal locations. As much as she enjoyed the "Fresh Daily" offerings at her local supermarket in landlocked Colorado, fish really did taste better when an ocean was within ten miles. Never mind that salmon wasn't found in local waters.

While they waited for their meals, Sadie showed off a bit more of her foodie knowledge by telling Pete about the *other* recipe invented at the Palace: Green Goddess salad dressing, a tribute to anchovy paste and fresh herbs. She finished off with the riveting history of Lobster Newberg, which had been originally called Lobster Wenberg in tribute to Ben Wenberg, a sea captain at the turn of the twentieth century. When the chef who had created the dish had a falling out with Ben Wenberg, he changed the letters of his signature dish around in retribution.

Pete tried to trump her trivia with the fact that fortune cookies weren't really Chinese, but rather a gimmick created as a draw for tourists to come to Chinatown when the neighborhood was trying to lose their red-light district reputation.

"Everyone knows that," Sadie said with a wave of her hand, dismissing his attempts to best her and glad that the mood had improved since the call from the realtor.

"I'd visited this city three times before I learned that," Pete said with a slight whine in his voice. "I was quite disappointed to learn it hadn't been an ancient Chinese secret."

Their meals arrived, and for a few minutes they enjoyed their food and only said things like "Pass the salt" and "This is really great."

Halfway through her meal, Sadie noticed that Pete was eating a little slower than usual. She glanced at Pete's face and after a couple more glances admitted that it wasn't her imagination that he seemed a little subdued. Something was wrong, and with all the other stress and pressure going on around them, she didn't want to add to her own anxieties by ignoring it.

She took a delectable bite of her salmon to prepare herself, then set her fork down on the edge of her plate. "Are you okay, Pete?"

"I'm fine," he said, concentrating on cutting another bite of his pork.

"Can I propose a theory on why you're not 'fine'?"

He looked up at her but said nothing. She took it as an agreement to hear her out.

"I'm guessing that being here in San Francisco has brought a lot of memories of Pat to the surface and—"

Pete put down his fork as well. "Sadie—"

"I'm not done," she cut in, though she smiled so he would know she wasn't angry. "And then you learn that there's someone interested in buying the house you shared with your wife. All of that piled together has got to be a lot to process."

Pete looked down at his food and said nothing.

"Did I get it about right?"

He took a breath. "Pretty much." He smiled at her, but it was a sad one, apologetic.

Sadie picked up her fork and took another bite in order to avoid looking into his face. His expression was making it harder and harder for her to retain her objective stance. She spoke without looking at him. "Mourning doesn't happen in a week or a month, Pete. I understand that as well as anyone. Did you and Pat eat here?" He'd known exactly where to find the restaurant upon entering the front doors of the hotel, and he'd been familiar with the menu. It wasn't rocket science.

He went back to his meal as well. Now they were both avoiding looking at one another. "Yeah, we ate here a few times."

"Is it hard for you to be here with me?"

He didn't answer for a few seconds, and Sadie looked up at him. "I'm asking as a friend, not your fiancée." Even as she said it, though, she wondered if it were true. Could she separate those roles enough to truly be objective? She hoped so. Pete needed a friend right now. She would put everything she had toward filling that role and hope it would be enough.

He cut another bite. "I didn't think it would be this hard, but there's just so many memories of her in this city—of experiencing new things together and enjoying old favorites. We stayed here at the Palace a few different times, including the last time we came."

Sadie tightened her grip on her fork. "I didn't know."

"I know that."

She allowed another silence for as long as she could stand it, which was about thirteen seconds. It was rather masochistic to continue this conversation, but maybe talking about it would help her work through her complicated feelings as well as help him make peace with his thoughts, too. "When did you guys last visit?"

Pete took a sip of his water and cast a quick glance in Sadie's direction before scanning the room as though looking for a distraction. There was plenty of distraction amid the décor, but he eventually looked back at his plate and cut a sliver of meat from the edge of his pork chop.

"We came for our thirtieth wedding anniversary. She was diagnosed a couple of months later."

Sadie's heart hitched in her chest. She didn't know what to say. No wonder the memories were so heavy for him now. She already knew that Pat had died less than a year after her cancer had been discovered. It had been too far advanced for anything other than treatments to postpone the inevitable.

Sadie imagined Pete sitting across from the auburn-haired and elegant woman Sadie had only seen in photographs, reflecting on three decades of marriage, memories, trials, children, grandchildren. Sadie suddenly felt like an intruder and wished she'd never brought it up. How had she chosen this restaurant amid the hundreds, perhaps thousands, that existed in this city? What lousy luck. Though if Pete had communicated the significance, she'd have gladly made another suggestion. Even without having traveled here before, she was aware of two or three other acclaimed restaurants in this city which could have offered not only a great meal, but far less discomfort than had come included with this one.

"Did you and Neil travel?" Pete asked when Sadie said nothing in response.

She sensed he was trying to even the score somehow by bringing

Neil into the conversation, but she was game to try it. "Not a lot. We always said we'd travel later, when the kids were grown." The pall that had been cast by talking about Pat only got heavier thanks to Sadie's answer. Neil had died when their children were little. They never had the freedom they'd planned on when their kids grew up. Prior to adopting their two children, they'd been focused on *having* that family to the point where there was little time or money for extras. "I traveled with the kids quite a bit though," Sadie added, hoping to shift the focus from their dead spouses.

"Where was your favorite place to go?" Pete asked.

They talked for a few minutes about different places Sadie had visited with her kids. San Diego and Yellowstone were at the top of her list. "How about you? Did you travel a lot when your family was young?"

"Actually, other than camping trips, we didn't do a lot of family vacations. We went back to New Mexico a fair amount, I guess. We both had family there." The tension fell like another blanket over the table. So San Francisco was really the only destination place he'd visited? And, from what he'd said earlier, he'd only gone with his family one time. Every other trip had been just him and Pat. "We used to talk about retiring on a sailboat and anchoring it at one of the piers."

Fabulous. Sadie cut another bite and wondered if Pete regretted having encouraged her to come to this city. He was obviously taken by surprise by the impact his memories were making on the trip.

"I'm really excited for Costa Rica, though," Pete said, referring to their chosen honeymoon destination and pasting a smile on his face. "I've heard great things about it."

"Me too," Sadie agreed, glad they'd chosen a place neither of them had been to before. The mood, however, was not saved entirely, and they both returned to their dinner.

The streets were as packed as ever on their way back to their hotel, but Sadie admired the way the people and traffic seemed to respect each other, ebbing and flowing appropriately and always respecting the road signs. Without such cooperation this city could never work.

"So, what's on the agenda for tomorrow?" Pete asked.

Sadie turned her thoughts to the next day and all that it might hold. "We'll meet Ji at the apartment in the morning and finish packing. Then Ji's friend is coming in the afternoon to pick everything up for his organization, though I'm not sure what time."

"Are you going to give them the painting from Wendy's room?"

"Oh, gosh," Sadie said, shaking her head. "I don't know what to do about that. It should probably go into the Dumpster, but what if someone finds it? The idea of anyone seeing it again horrifies me."

Pete genuinely laughed, and Sadie smiled at the sound. She pulled one hand out of her pocket in order to loop it through his arm. "How are you doing with all of this?" he asked after his laughter had died out. "Was it hard to talk about the forensics and the investigation earlier?"

"No," Sadie said with a shake of her head as she watched the sidewalk at their feet. "I'm glad to know more about what happened, and it makes me want to fill in the rest of the blanks."

"Detective Lopez said he'd check in with me sometime tomorrow," Pete said. "He'd sent some questions back to the medical examiner about things he wanted clarified, and he's hoping to get their response in the morning." They stopped at another light, and a dozen people quickly lined up behind them. "He also mentioned that with the autopsy complete, we need to choose a funeral home.

I wasn't sure if you or Ji would want to head that up, which is why I didn't mention it when Ji was there."

"A funeral home," Sadie said, feeling the finality of that step and yet finding irony in it as well. The light turned green, and the crowd surged across the intersection. Sadie raised her voice a little to be heard. "No one even noticed she was gone. No one thought to check on her or see what was wrong. Who would come to a funeral?"

"You don't have to hold an actual funeral. The point is that the police are finished with their part, and so you or Ji need to make arrangements for whatever comes next. You could have her cremated; it's more cost-effective."

Cremation seemed so . . . Sadie couldn't even complete the thought. So, what? Impersonal? Removed? Morbid? She couldn't help but think that someone had already tried to cremate Wendy's body. Yuck. "I'll talk to Ji about it tomorrow," she said. They turned a corner, and Sadie realized she knew where they were—no small feat in this city that felt like a labyrinth with all its one-way streets and skyscrapers.

"You did a great job choosing this hotel," Sadie said as the black awning came into view. There was a storefront a few doors down advertising a soup restaurant inside. Maybe she and Pete would eat there on another day. San Francisco, with its cooler temperatures and continual fog, seemed like a perfect place to enjoy a bowl of soup. She wasn't hungry right now, though, and tuned back to the topic of the hotel Pete had found for them. "I'm glad you got rooms at a local hotel rather than a chain. It makes it more of an experience."

"I've never stayed here before," Pete said. Sadie wondered if what he was trying to tell her was that he and Pat had never stayed there before. "But it had good reviews online."

They walked a few more steps in silence. Sadie pushed her hands deeper into the pockets of her jacket. She'd noticed that a lot of people on the street wore jackets embroidered with San Francisco. They must not have checked the weather like she had. The tourist shops likely paid their rent through sweatshirt and hoodie sales alone.

Pete pulled open the front door of the hotel for her, and she entered, grateful for the warm interior. Her nose tingled from the cold.

"Would you like to do anything else tonight?" Pete asked once they were in the elevator. It was still early enough for them to take an evening trip to the Wharf like she and Pete had talked about on the plane, but the mood didn't feel light enough to go sightseeing tonight. Besides, the fact that he'd waited until they were on their way to their rooms seemed to imply that it was an afterthought—otherwise why not bring it up sooner?

"I think I'd just like to go through those file boxes," Sadie said truthfully. "Did *you* want to do something else?" She suspected his request was only meant to be polite, so she was careful not to sound too hopeful. If, however, he *did* want to do something else, she was agreeable to that too.

He didn't look at her as he considered her question. They reached the third floor, where Sadie's room was located, and stepped out into the hallway once the elevator doors opened. "I was thinking about going to Golden Gate Park," Pete said with an odd hesitation in his voice.

The way he said it communicated that he was familiar with Golden Gate Park, which meant it held memories for him. He'd also said "I was thinking about going," not "I was thinking *we* could go." Sadie took a breath and chose to be his friend again instead of the woman he was about to marry. It took a second to shove her jealousy into a far corner, but she did it and managed to keep her expression impassive. "You should go," she said with a nod, leading the way to her room and looking for her key in her purse.

"You don't want to come?"

There was no need to read into his tone of voice that time. Sadie had already made her decision. They reached the door of her room, and she turned to face him. "I think *you* should go," she said with a kind smile. She dropped her voice to barely more than a whisper, which could be interpreted as intimate though that wasn't her intent. "Thanks for making this trip happen." She reached for his hand. He intertwined his fingers with hers, and she gave his hand a slight squeeze. "It's good that I came, and I wouldn't have done it without your encouragement. I promise to do my best not to get in the way of the hard things you're having to face."

"You're not in the way," Pete said, his eyebrows drawing closer together. "I don't—"

Sadie leaned in and kissed him quickly on the lips. "If it were my house that sold first, I'd probably be panicking too. It's a component of this that neither one of us has thought about, and we're both going to have to face it. Go enjoy the park. Feel what you need to feel." She unlocked the door to her room. They had already made a rule about entering each other's bedrooms, so Pete stayed at the threshold. She pushed the door open a few inches and planted one foot to keep it from closing.

"Are you sure? I—"

She cut him off with another kiss, in part to keep him from arguing, but also to keep things light. She held his eyes and his face relaxed.

"I'll text you when I get back."

Sadie nodded. "That would be great."

Green Goddess Dressing

½ cup mayonnaise
½ cup sour cream (for a thinner dressing, substitute with ⅓ cup
  buttermilk)
1 clove garlic, minced
¼ cup snipped fresh chives or minced scallions
¼ cup minced fresh parsley
1 tablespoon fresh tarragon, or ¼ teaspoon dried
1 tablespoon fresh lemon juice
1 tablespoon white wine vinegar
3 anchovy fillets, rinsed, patted dry, and minced, or 2 teaspoons
  anchovy paste (less to taste, if desired)
Salt and freshly ground pepper, to taste

Stir all the ingredients together in a small bowl until well blended, or in a blender for a smoother texture. Taste and adjust the seasonings. Use immediately or cover and refrigerate for up to one week.

Makes about 1¼ cups of dressing.

Note: When this recipe was developed, there was often limited access to fresh produce, so the dressing was served with shredded iceberg lettuce, canned vegetables, and a choice of chicken, shrimp, or crab. Over the years, the Green Goddess Salad has evolved. Today, the salad is referred to as "The Garden Court Crab Salad" and features farm-fresh, mixed baby greens, locally grown California vegetables, and a generous portion of Dungeness crab meat. The salad is offered with a choice of dressings, one of which is, of course, the famous Green Goddess. The dressing also makes a great dip for meats and fresh veggies.

Note: For a creamier texture, add ½ an avocado.

CHAPTER 13

I f not for the files from Wendy's office, Sadie might have obsessed over not being with Pete, but burrowing in to the remnants of Wendy's life seemed to be exactly the distraction she needed.

After taking in the general organization of the files and looking through a few different folders, she began to be bothered by the fact that the police had been through everything already. If there was anything of importance here, they'd already found it and possibly talked to Pete about it, making Sadie the last person to arrive at the proverbial party. She tried to take confidence in the fact that she could still learn more about Wendy—but what did utilities bills and credit card agreements and coupons really tell her about her dead sister?

That the police had likely organized everything made it that much more impersonal. Wendy wouldn't have created a file for "Junk mail" or "Grocery store receipts." At least Sadie didn't think she would, but there was no way to know now that someone else had decided how to categorize things.

Sadie thought back to her experiences with archeology when she was working undercover on a case. The company she worked for had emphasized the importance of finding things *in situ*, which meant finding an artifact exactly as it had been left or discarded. You could get a sense of what caused someone to leave a place by whether or not a pot had been hidden, wrapped in cloth, tipped on its side, or any other number of factors. The "situation" created context. The perspective was totally different once that situation was removed; ownership and context were immediately lost.

These files felt like that. Had the utility bills been found this way: organized in chronological order and paper-clipped together? Had the coupons been found sorted alphabetically by brand name or had they been scattered all over the apartment, stuck in books and shoved in pockets of old coats? If all these papers had been in this hyper-organized state when the police found them, it would say something very different about Wendy than if they had been scattered and piled and ignored.

As her frustrations mounted, Sadie discarded her idea to start reading at the beginning of the files; instead, she looked through the file topics for something that seemed interesting. She pulled out the file for "Bank Statements" and found them in chronological order for the past twenty-two months, though last January's statement was missing. She shuffled through to last month's statement, June, which showed an automatic payment to Netflix and a larger payment to what Sadie assumed was a health insurance company as the only debits that month.

There was a single deposit for $7,000, made on the fifth. She looked through the other statements and confirmed that the same amount was deposited on the same day each month. When the fifth was on a Saturday or Sunday, the amount was deposited the prior Friday. An automatic payment, Sadie suspected. But for what? Once again, there was no context.

Detective Lopez had told her that the last charges to Wendy's account—other than the automatic payments—had been made on May 22. There were two charges, actually. One to the grocery service Pete had told her about, and the other to a business called Wild Plum.

Sadie looked up Wild Plum on her laptop computer and found out it was an online boutique based in Chicago. She wondered what Wendy had bought for $123.33 and went back to the box of files. In a file labeled "Wild Plum," she found four different receipts, one of them dated May 24; the boutique must not have processed her order immediately. Reviewing the line items, Sadie saw that Wendy had purchased a set of bamboo pajamas.

Back at her computer, she looked up the item and studied the finer details of the pajamas—royal blue with tiny white polka dots and red piping at the cuffs. Not the worst pajamas ever made, but certainly not worth $123.33, in Sadie's opinion. Where were those pajamas now? At the police station? It was such a silly thing, those pajamas, and yet it gave Sadie a better sense of her sister than most things in the box had.

She went back to the bank statements and scanned a few months' worth. She wondered again where the $7,000 came from each month and what Wendy bought with her weekly grocery store orders. She also noticed that up through September of last year, Wendy blew through her income every month. There were numerous transactions to stores and restaurants, QVC and Amazon.com.

Starting in October, however, there were fewer and fewer charges and her monthly bills, like her power and phone, were no longer consistent. Sadie cross-checked the statements with specific utility files and found that all of them had correspondence about missing payments, shut-off notices, and threats of discontinued service if balances were not paid in full. In each case, a payment was made before the eleventh hour, but the pattern was chaotic and unorganized, whereas in the months prior, Wendy's bills were generally paid on time and never skipped altogether. Only her rent was consistent, always paid during the last week of the month.

Sadie went to the bank statements from the year before and noticed a similar pattern in regard to less-frequent spending and more missed bills during the winter months. It wasn't as severe as the more recent season, but it did seem to denote a pattern. Sadie thought back to something she'd read about bipolar disorder—or manic depressive disorder, as Sadie had first learned to call it years earlier.

The disorder was often characterized by alternating cycles of depression and mania that could be seen in a patterned history of the patient. Phases of mania could include shopping sprees and heightened socialization, while the depression cycle could result in isolation, paranoia, and inconsistency. Is that what Sadie was seeing here? Had Wendy entered a depressive episode last fall that was more severe than the others? Or, at least, more severe than the one she'd had the year before? Was her depression tied to the seasons? She looked at the boxed files and thought of all they weren't telling her about her sister.

Sadie turned her attention to Wendy's phone bill—the proof that she did have people she communicated with. Out of the last two years' worth of bills—which seemed to be as far back as any of the utilities went—January, March, and April of this year were missing. Where Wendy's spending went down in the months before her death, her phone calls seemed to pick up, and several numbers were called multiple times in a month. It was easy to identify the calls to the laundry service and the grocery store because they were called early in the week, every week.

There was another number, however, that stood out, not because of its pattern, but because of its lack of one. Wendy had called the same number once in October, three times in November, seven times in December, fourteen in February, and nineteen in May. After May 22 there were no more calls made from Wendy's phone at all. A quick check of the calendar on Sadie's phone confirmed that the calls had only been made during the week and during regular business hours.

Sadie typed the mystery phone number into the search field on Google's homepage. She clicked on the first credible-looking link and furrowed her brow as a stylish website for a modeling agency loaded onto her screen. Next Faces was the name of the company. Sadie didn't imagine Wendy, at sixty-three years old, was working as an actual model, yet half of the phone calls she'd made in the month of February were to this number.

Sadie retrieved a highlighter from her purse and marked the numbers in every statement in the folder. Sometimes the number hadn't been called at all, and even through last winter, it had only been called once or twice, but in the six months before Wendy's death the frequency picked up.

To be fair, Sadie flagged every other repeated number as well and looked them up online too—to confirm that they did, in fact, belong to the laundry and grocery services Wendy had been using. She wondered what Pete would make of these phone calls. Would he think she was on to something, or would he think it a waste of her energy to be so focused on such an inconsequential detail? The police had already seen this, after all, and as far as Sadie knew, they hadn't mentioned it to Pete.

Sadie glanced at the clock. It was after 9:00, and Pete hadn't texted her yet to tell her he was back at the hotel. Rather than let herself dwell on that, she turned back to the Next Faces website and read up on the mission statement and what services they offered—portfolios, classes, representation, and networking. They had a listing of all the actors they represented. Sadie looked for Wendy among the smiling faces but didn't find her. Did Wendy have a friend who worked there, perhaps? Why would she call the business and not a personal number?

Sadie clicked on the "About Us" page and her eyes were immediately drawn to the name *Rodger Penrose*. Could he be Wendy's fourth ex-husband? After the initial surprise of seeing his name, Sadie read through the information about the company's founder and president, then looked at his picture. Assuming it was recent, he looked to be in his fifties—younger than Wendy and quite attractive, with a confident, jovial air about him. Was Wendy calling *him* several times a month?

Sadie tried to remember what else Pete and Ji had said about Rodger earlier today. Hadn't Pete said that Rodger claimed he and Wendy had remained on good terms? Had he explained about the calls in his statement to the police? Surely they had asked about it.

A surge of frustration bubbled up again at being the one on the outside of the information, and she questioned her decision to let Pete be the one creating relationships with the police. She looked at the box of homogenized files, pre-evaluated and considered. *It isn't enough,* she thought. It didn't help her know Wendy any better because there were still so many holes in her sister's story.

Sadie hated feeling like she knew less about her sister than anyone else involved in this case, hated the idea that she'd spent the last two hours pondering on things that had probably already been figured out. There could even be things the police had kept in their official file that Sadie would know nothing about. She didn't know enough about anything to know if something were missing.

Though Sadie had considered doing a background report on Wendy before coming out here, she had preferred the idea of getting to know her sister through her life instead of from her public record. But the discoveries she'd made tonight shifted her motivation. Sadie needed to learn about her sister through any and all information available to her, and she wanted to know her at least as well as the police already did.

Because of her prior experience with background checks she'd done on suspects in other cases and for clients who'd hired her when she was running her official investigation firm, Sadie knew right where to go to get access to the public aspects of Wendy's history. She logged onto her favorite records site and began entering information into the search fields, choosing county, state, and federal records for the database search and easily regurgitating information like date of birth, place of birth, parents, associates, and known counties of habitation.

While Sadie waited for the results, which she knew could take several minutes, she opened a word processing document and began writing notes of all that had happened that day. There was a lot to record, and she kept having to scroll up and down in the document as she remembered details; she wanted to keep things in chronological order.

Once the results began coming in from the preliminary database search, Sadie opened up other Internet tabs and cross-checked details, drilling down for more information on certain aspects and losing herself in the search. This was her element—this impersonal look through records and listings. It gave a kind of ironic anonymity to the person she was learning about and, although this case was different from anything else she'd ever worked on, gathering this information was not.

More than two hours later, Sadie rubbed her eyes, which burned after such a long day and too much time in front of the computer. She leaned back and stretched her arms over her head. What she had found didn't surprise her, but there was limited satisfaction in it. Wendy had been arrested half a dozen times for check fraud, though that had been several years ago. More recently, she had some public intoxication charges and one embezzlement charge from a former employer who accused her of stealing more than ten thousand dollars. She'd been married twice since 1985, which was as far back at the site went without accessing the archives. Both marriages ended in divorce; the last marriage had been to Rodger Penrose.

Wendy had never gone to college, despite Sadie's parents sending her money for tuition, and her job history was spotty at best—a secretary, a cashier, and, for a time in the late 80s, a model at Next Faces. That was probably how she and Rodger met.

Her life had definitely improved after she married Rodger. There were no more arrests and her only work was through Next Faces. There weren't a lot of photos of the two of them together, but Sadie found enough to confirm that Wendy had played the role of trophy wife quite well. She'd been blonde, busty, confident, and expertly dressed—a far cry from the car-living, single mom she'd been when Ji was young.

Wendy and Rodger divorced after eight years, and Wendy had never held a job again. Sadie suspected more than ever that the $7,000 worth of income Wendy received each month was alimony from Rodger, who by all accounts was still doing quite well for himself. It seemed like a generous settlement when compared to the kind of money she'd made at her dead-end jobs, and Sadie wondered what had led to the end of their marriage.

She updated her notes and reviewed the information, knowing that she could keep herself busy for a few more hours if she chose to delve deeper into each particular detail of Wendy's past. But the day *was* catching up with her, and what she'd wanted from the outset was a better view of her sister. She had that now, and she'd made progress toward catching up with what the police already knew. Tomorrow she would ask more questions and perhaps insert herself more into the police part of the investigation. Pete had said he'd make room for her if she wanted a more official position; she trusted that he meant it.

It was after eleven o'clock when she closed her computer, exhausted on more levels than one. She checked her phone to see if Pete had texted her, frowning when there was no message. She took off her earrings and stored them in the jewelry box Ji had painted, running her hand over the lid after she closed it.

Ji had been surprised that Wendy had owned one of his jewelry boxes. Was he also pleased by it? Sadie hoped so. From what she'd seen through her packing today, the jewelry box might be the only connection Wendy had kept of her relationship to Ji. There had been no pictures of her son in her home and nothing that, unless someone knew she had a son, showed it. Nothing but that jewelry box that Ji didn't even know she'd bought.

Sadie wanted to wait up for Pete, but she knew it would increase her anxiety now that she was tired and out of things to keep her brain occupied. Instead, she texted to tell him she was turning in. He texted back to tell her good night and that he was on his way back to the hotel. Immediately following that text he sent another one:

I love you. See you in the morning.

She read the text three times, letting the words seep into her bones. Then she turned off the light and crawled into bed. Amazing what three little words could do sometimes.

CHAPTER 14

Sadie awoke the next morning determined to live above any tension that might be left over from the night before. She couldn't help but wonder if Pete had decided the same thing since he seemed lighter and brighter when they met in the lobby. They had breakfast at a little Scottish-themed pub up the street from their hotel. Sadie had Nutella-stuffed French toast with strawberries and bananas—divine and easy to replicate at home—though she thought a strawberry syrup would make it even more delicious. Pete had a salmon and spinach omelet, and when he offered her a bite, she couldn't refuse it. It was also delicious. Neither of them brought up their conversation from the night before or that their time to accept, counter, or refuse the offer on Pete's house was ticking away.

Instead, Sadie told Pete about the files she'd gone through and, specifically, about the bank statements and phone bills that had helped her establish a pattern of behavior. The papers were in her purse in case Pete wanted to see them for himself, but she was glad he didn't ask for them over breakfast.

"Lopez didn't say anything about the repetitive calls to Rodger's business, just that, according to Rodger, the two of them had maintained a good relationship. Lopez did mention that Wendy hadn't been paying her bills regularly, despite having plenty of money in the bank."

Sadie nodded her understanding and then went on to explain the background check and timeline she'd put together of Wendy's life. Some of the information Pete already knew, but other parts were new. Sadie felt validated in doing the work, and her confidence increased.

After breakfast they drove to the Mission District and found a parking spot about a block from Wendy's apartment. As they walked to the building, Sadie wondered where the people who lived around here parked—surely not blocks away from their apartments. Maybe, like Wendy, they didn't have cars either.

They stopped at a nearby market for some more boxes. The only ones available were for Wild Turkey Whiskey, and Sadie tried not to feel self-conscious as she walked the last half of a block to the exterior door of Wendy's building. After a few feet, however, she realized no one was even looking at her. Instead the other people were talking on phones, texting, or moving too fast to notice. Maybe it wasn't so surprising that Wendy had been dead for a month without anyone noticing—people moved so fast in this city that maybe there wasn't time to pay attention to anyone else's business.

Pete unlocked the exterior door and held it open for Sadie. A minute later, the elevator clanged as the pulley lifted them to the third floor.

When they entered Wendy's apartment, they were brought up short by the sound of Latino music. They looked at one another, and then Pete walked inside first and put down his boxes. Sadie followed. There was a drop cloth on the floor of the living room area and a miter saw placed on a metal table in the center of it. The air smelled like drywall and dust.

"Hello?" Pete called out.

"Hola?" a voice called back from the direction of the bathroom. The music was turned down and, a minute later, a short, middle-aged Hispanic man came out of the bedroom. He smiled and explained in a heavily accented voice that he was working on the bathroom. Pete responded in Spanish, reminding Sadie that he spoke the language.

The Hispanic man relaxed and introduced himself as Mario—Sadie caught that much—and smiled when Pete introduced her. Mario motioned them to follow him to the bathroom. He pointed at the new Sheetrock in place on what had been exposed framework when they'd left yesterday afternoon. Some of the mudding and taping was done as well. Pete asked Mario a question.

"Sí, sí, mañana." That was as much as Sadie understood.

Pete turned to translate their conversation for Sadie. "He's the maintenance man for the building and came in after we left last night. He plans on finishing up the walls today. Tomorrow and Friday he'll work on the tile and install the new fixtures. Saturday he'll paint."

"The landlord told Ji we had until the tenth to get Wendy's things out." Sadie looked over her shoulder at the thin layer of plaster dust that now coated the furniture still in the bedroom. It was unsettling to feel as though they were being pushed out sooner than expected. Plus Mario was making a mess.

"Apparently the new tenant wants to move in as soon as possible so the landlord asked Mario to fix up the bathroom while we move out," Pete explained. He turned back to Mario; they talked for another minute before Pete pointed toward the office and explained something to Mario. Mario nodded and smiled before going back to work.

Pete headed back to the common area of the apartment and Sadie followed. She shut the bedroom door behind them, which muted the music and would hopefully prevent the fine particle dust from infiltrating the rest of the apartment. Would Mario clean up his mess or was that Sadie's responsibility? On the heels of that thought was wondering why any of this was Sadie's responsibility. It's not as though they were going to get a cleaning deposit back, and yet it went against Sadie's nature to leave a mess behind.

Pete flipped on the light in the office, and they surveyed the room, much of it already boxed up from yesterday.

"I'll finish up the bookshelves and desk," Sadie said, then scanned the walls, where a variety of different artwork and a rather dark poem by D. H. Lawrence hung. "And clear off the walls."

Pete had walked to the closet and pulled back the door, revealing even more clothes. Sadie had seen the charges from different high-end department stores in the file box last night, so it didn't surprise her to find that her shopaholic sister had an overflow closet in addition to the large one Ji and Pete had cleared out yesterday. Even from where Sadie stood, she could see the tags hanging off a couple of the sleeves—clothes bought but never worn. What a waste.

"I can work on that when I finish the other things," Sadie said, waving toward the closet to emphasize how easy that job would be. "Can you move as much of the stuff as you can from the bedroom into the common area? It will make it easier for Ji's friend to pick up if we can contain everything to one part of the apartment."

"I can do that," Pete agreed. He gave her a quick kiss but hadn't made it ten feet out of the room before his phone rang. "Good morning, detective . . ." His voice trailed off as he disappeared into the living room area, which meant Sadie couldn't overhear his side of the conversation.

She grabbed a box and began emptying the contents of the desk into it. She thought about her plan from last night to become more involved with the police side of things, but in the light of day she reconsidered it. Did she want to get caught up in the procedures and reports of police work? Would it satisfy her frustrations if she took on that role alongside Pete?

The two file drawers of the desk were empty, but the other two drawers were brimming with miscellaneous office supplies. Sadie dumped everything into the box, then sifted through the contents to make sure there wasn't anything personal mixed in with the generic supplies. There wasn't anything of interest, so Sadie finished filling the box with other office items. Surely there would be some new immigrants who needed paper clips and Post-it Notes. She was replacing the now-empty drawer back into the desk when Pete appeared in the doorway.

"The morning is off to a good start. The police know what accelerant was used on the body—that's what Lopez was trying to clarify yesterday afternoon."

"Really? What was it?"

"A synthetic kerosene. Unfortunately, it's a common fuel and easy to buy."

Sadie shuddered at the thought of someone pouring kerosene over Wendy's body and quickly pushed the image out of her mind.

Pete continued, "But still, it's a new lead. And his sergeant agreed to let me go over the official file."

"That's great," Sadie said.

"Would you like to come with me to the station this time?"

Ji would be coming soon, and they had to get the apartment packed up before his friend from the charity arrived. Plus, she no longer felt the same need as she had last night. "I better stay," she said. "But will you talk to them about the calls to Rodger and find out what his explanation was?"

"Sure," Pete said. "You're okay here alone?"

Sadie gave him an exaggerated look. "I was fine yesterday, and I'll be fine again today. Besides, Ji should be here any time. I'll feel a lot better once we have this place packed up."

Pete accepted her confidence without further argument and left her with a kiss and a promise to call if he learned anything new. Last night seemed to be behind them, and Sadie got back to work feeling centered and calm about things, for the most part.

She finished packing the contents of the bookshelf and the desk, noting that Wendy didn't own a single book that Sadie had ever read—yet another difference between them—and then took everything down from the walls. She set aside one of the paintings, a landscape scene that looked a lot like the view from their grandparents' cabin in southern Colorado, and took a minute to try to understand the Lawrence poem. Finally she rolled her eyes and put it in the box. It had a nice frame; hopefully that would have value for someone.

As for the painting, she took it into the living room and set it against the wall, away from the items waiting to be hauled out by the charity. She wasn't sure if she wanted it or not. Did she want a reminder of Wendy to hang on her wall at home? Would that bring her joy or remind her of all the negativity associated with her sister?

She set aside the decision and turned her attention to the closet—the last task in the packing process. It had sliding mirrored doors, with full hanging racks on both sides—and a set of shelves in the middle as well as a long shelf on top. There were numerous storage containers and boxes on the different shelves.

Sadie started emptying the closet by pulling out all the boxes.

She worked top to bottom, finally sliding a Rubbermaid box from the floor of the closet at the very end. She wanted to determine the contents of each box before sorting them—nothing was labeled. One box was full of art supplies, mostly paints that had separated out and paintbrushes that hadn't been properly cleaned and were now petrified. Another box was full of Christmas decorations. One was full of old tax records and checkbooks.

Then she opened a box slightly bigger than a shoebox and was surprised to find it full of pictures. Sadie settled herself onto the floor, unable to resist looking through Wendy's life chronicled in photos. She thought she recognized Rodger Penrose in several pictures, and she found a few pictures of Ji as a child—he had the same serious expression then as he did now—but mostly the photos were of Wendy with numerous strangers who must have been friends at some point in Wendy's life.

In some pictures Wendy was laughing; in others she was holding up a drink or looking flirtatiously at the camera. She had been very pretty well into her forties, if Sadie were correctly determining her age in the photos, with a careless air that perhaps made her that much more attractive. But she didn't age particularly well once she entered her fifties; her lifestyle showed on her face even as she tried to cover it with more makeup and brighter clothes. There didn't seem to be any photos of the last decade or so.

When Sadie realized that half an hour had passed while she'd looked through the pictures, she reluctantly reminded herself that she could look through them another time. She put the lid back on and moved the box to the living room, where she placed it next to the landscape painting. She put the box of tax records with it, too; she would need to see about having such personal records shredded.

She returned to the office and finished going through the boxes.

There was nothing of any value or significance, just storage that Wendy herself likely had little use for, so she put them against the wall. The last box standing was the large Rubbermaid container Sadie had slid from the floor of the closet.

She popped the lid off and was surprised to find it full of papers. She lifted some from the top and identified a letter regarding changes to Wendy's health insurance, a store mailer, and a letter from the Department of Building Inspection in San Francisco. She scanned the correspondence—apparently Wendy had filed a complaint against her landlord, Stephen Pilings, in early May for not repairing the water heater in her apartment. The letter Sadie held was a confirmation of the department having received her claim and a promise that she would receive a response within forty-five days as to whether or not the department would pursue the matter.

Sadie looked back at the jumbled contents of the box, then at the floor of the closet where she'd found it. This was a recent letter; the date was just weeks before Wendy died. Why was it in a box in the closet?

In the next instant she realized that whatever was in this box hadn't been organized by the police. They probably didn't even know it existed. Unlike the boxes the police had sterilized, this box was exactly as Wendy had left it. Chaotic. Disorganized. Representative of Wendy herself?

Sadie felt a naughty kind of rebellion take hold of her as she anticipated learning things from the contents of this box that the police didn't know about. She immediately cast aside every other task as the anticipation of beating the police to some information took hold of her completely. She pulled the box in front of the desk chair, then settled herself into it—eager to get started, but perhaps even more eager to finish.

Nutella-Stuffed French Toast

3 eggs
1⅓ cups milk
½ teaspoon vanilla
Dash of cinnamon (optional)
Dash of nutmeg (optional)
Dash of cloves (optional)
Bread
1 jar Nutella
1 cup strawberry jam (heated to a thick syrup)
2 bananas, sliced

Heat griddle to medium heat. In a blender, mix eggs, milk, vanilla, and spices. Pour egg mixture into a pie tin or other shallow dish. Dip bread into egg mixture, making sure both sides are coated. (Adjust soaking time to your personal taste.) Cook bread on griddle, 2 to 3 minutes, or until browned. Turn and cook an additional 1 to 2 minutes.

When all bread slices are cooked, spread a tablespoon or so of Nutella between two slices and make a sandwich. Cut sandwich in half diagonally and top with strawberry jam and bananas.

Serves 6, depending on the density of the bread and how long you soak it in the egg mixture.

CHAPTER 15

By 10 a.m. Sadie had found all the missing phone bills except January's in the box. She also really wanted to talk to Rodger Penrose after confirming seventeen phone calls to him in March and twenty-one in April. She considered asking Pete his opinion but then wondered why she felt like she needed his permission. She was Wendy's sister, after all. She didn't need police authority to call and talk to her ex-brother-in-law, did she? Assuming it was him Wendy was talking to when she made those calls.

She wasn't nervous to call, not even anxious, just eager to learn more about Wendy. The line rang three times before going to voice mail, where a female voice thanked her for calling Next Faces and asked her to leave a message after the tone so that one of their representatives could get in touch for them. "Reach for the stars," the girl said before the message ended and a tone sounded.

"Hi, my name is Sadie Hoffmiller. I'm calling in regards to my sister, Wendy Penrose. I would appreciate a call back at your earliest convenience. I have some questions I want to ask whomever it was she was communicating with at your office." She left her cell phone number and ended the call, hoping someone would call her back. The sooner the better.

Disappointed not to have been able to talk to a real person, but glad to have planted the seed, Sadie returned to the box full of papers and began sorting once more, using the desk for all the different piles she was making.

After half an hour, Sadie had to stand up and take a short walk around the apartment. Deciding what to throw out and what to keep was so much harder than she'd expected. There was history amid the credit card receipts and confirmations, and those things might mean . . . something.

For instance, Wendy had flown to Las Vegas two years ago. Why? With whom? There was a receipt from a café dated over a year ago that showed two meals—with whom had Wendy eaten and why had she picked up the tab? There was a letter from a refugee organization thanking her for her donation. Did Wendy give donations on a regular basis? What criteria did she look for in a charity, and how much money had she given? Thinking of Wendy as a charitable person was another layer Sadie had to add to her sister's disjointed persona. She felt confused about what she was really looking for—a connection to her sister, or an aspect of her history that might explain her death? Both? Neither?

The task was giving Sadie a headache because she argued with herself over the significance of almost everything. In the end, she'd set aside far more than she'd thrown out, and it frustrated her to know that everything she kept would have to be looked at again, considered again, stressed over *again*. And what if she'd thrown away something that ended up being important? Maybe having had the police go through everything first *was* better than being the one who had to decide. Had the police thrown things away too, she wondered, or had they filed everything they gathered?

Sadie retrieved some Tylenol from her purse and looked at the clock. It was eleven o'clock. No one from Next Faces had returned her call, and Ji hadn't arrived either. Would it seem impertinent of her to call him to see if he were still coming? Why would he have changed his plans and not told her? She didn't want to do anything that interfered with the progress they'd made so far.

She decided to call Jack, but caught him in the security line at the airport. He sounded upbeat, and she imagined Carrie with him, both of them nervous about this step they were taking. Not wanting to interrupt what the two of them were building, Sadie gave him a basic overview and informed him that Wendy had money to cover her own final expenses. Jack was relieved, thanked her and Pete for all they were doing, and apologized again for not helping. Sadie didn't even let him finish that final thought and ended the phone call soon after.

Talking to Jack had eased some of her tension, and perhaps the Tylenol had kicked in too because she felt ready to go back to the sorting. She knew she'd feel a lot better once this task was finished. Twenty minutes later, Ji buzzed from downstairs, and Sadie ate a granola bar from her purse while waiting for him to come up the elevator, grateful she hadn't called him prematurely.

"Good morning," Sadie said as she let him into the apartment.

Ji looked at the miter saw in the middle of the living room floor, and she explained about the ongoing bathroom remodel. Mario had come and gone a few times today along with another man who had helped him bring up a new tub and a vanity, but the bedroom door was currently shut, muting the sounds of music, voices, and construction.

"I can't say I love how eager the landlord is to rent out the apartment, but I'm glad we haven't gotten in each other's way." She headed toward the office, glad to have Ji's help even though he was two hours late. Maybe he would take over the paper sorting for her. Even as she considered it, however, she realized that despite how much she disliked the task, she didn't want anyone else doing it. The idea that Ji might throw something away that she would deem important was a risk she wasn't willing to take.

Ji followed her into the office and leaned against the doorframe. "When I came by for the keys to Wendy's apartment, Mr. Pilings asked me for half a month's rent for July."

Sadie settled into the desk chair. "Are we obligated to pay it?" It seemed rather heartless, considering the circumstances. Mr. Pilings had obvious conflicts with Wendy, was quick to move in the next tenant, and was pushing for rent even though Wendy had been dead for several weeks? Pretty callous. Sadie made a note to ask Pete for more details regarding the conversations the police had had with the landlord. She also wanted to talk to him about the letter she'd found about the claim Wendy had filed against the landlord. Since the police hadn't found the letter, they might not know anything about it.

Ji shrugged. "I don't have the money to pay her rent."

"I don't think we're obligated to pay it, though we can ask the detectives about it. If so, Wendy had quite a bit of money in her account," Sadie assured him.

"She did?" Ji asked, obviously surprised.

Sadie nodded. "I'm not sure what it will take for us to be able to access it, but Detective Lopez might know." She thought about how she and Ji needed to make some decisions regarding Wendy's burial, but it didn't feel like the right time. Though they'd ended yesterday at a better place, there was still a fragility between them. Talking about Wendy's desecrated body could wait until they found a better groove with each other.

Sadie explained how Pete had moved everything from the bedroom into the common area. "It was wonderful that the two of you were able to finish that room yesterday," she added. "It puts us into the homestretch in regard to finishing up."

"So, we're just left with the office," Ji said, scanning the room.

"And I think we're almost done with that," Sadie said, looking at the clothes still on hangers and the boxes stacked on the floor of the room. "I'm afraid I've gotten a little distracted sorting through this box." She waved toward the storage container that was still halfway full and picked up some random papers. "It seems as though she was really organized in some ways, but completely scattered in others. This whole box of papers was in the closet, but it's recent bills and things. I can't figure out what it was doing in there."

Ji crossed his arms over his chest. "When I was little, she'd have times when she cleaned obsessively, was always on the go, hanging out with friends, buying new stuff, and then she'd crash and spend weeks in bed, not shower, not answer her phone, not make me go to school."

Sadie hated to admit a tiny bit of self-recognition in his description. Though she was much more even-keeled, the obsessive way in which she'd focused on the different investigations over the last few years and the way she'd then crashed after what had happened in Boston were similar in some ways to Wendy's behavior. She also thought of the assessment she'd made regarding the cycles of Wendy's life she'd seen reflected in the different statements. *It's not the same,* she told herself, but it made her uncomfortable anyway.

"That must have been hard to cope with," Sadie said out loud.

Ji shrugged. "I remember trying to wait things out until she got happy again. But then she was pretty unpredictable when she was feeling good, and she'd be gone a lot. It was hard to know what to wish for."

Sadie resisted apologizing again for not having been a part of his life. If she'd had any idea . . . But she *had* wondered. She'd just chosen to keep things out of sight and out of mind. It made her feel terrible now that she knew the truth, but apologizing again didn't seem as though it would help.

"Do you, by chance, remember if certain times of the year were worse than others?"

"Summer was always good," Ji said with a nod. "And it seems like the worst times were when I was supposed to be in school. I was really far behind when I moved in with my dad. I wasn't caught up with my age group until I was in junior high."

She made a note to do a bit more online research to verify her suspicions of Wendy's mental illness. "You're obviously very smart, in addition to being talented."

He looked away, shy and embarrassed. "Anyway . . . Sorry I was so late. My brother-in-law was supposed to open for me, but he confused the date. I've got double coverage until 5:30 though so I can be here when Shots comes around four."

"Shots?"

"Oh, that's my friend who's going to pick everything up for the Chinese Share House. He was able to get a truck for this afternoon and has some extra guys coming to help him. It's not the best time of day to be on the streets, so he wants to get it done quick—before the weekend." He looked around the room. "Should I start with the closet?"

"That would be great," Sadie said with a smile.

Ji nodded and went into the kitchen to get the garbage sacks.

He returned and unceremoniously began taking things out of the closet and stuffing them into the bags, only taking time to remove the hangers, which he threw into a pile in the middle of the floor.

Sadie continued sorting through the messy box. Had Wendy kept every piece of mail she'd received in the last two years? After a few minutes she thought of something that Ji might be able to help her clarify. "What do you know about Wendy's relationship with Rodger after the divorce?"

"Not a thing," Ji said, still stuffing bags full with clothes. "I never met Rodger. I think she didn't want me to know how much better she was living with him, and the newest man in her life was never a topic I pushed."

"Didn't she ever send you any money? Child support?"

Ji shook his head. "My father is first-generation Chinese-American. He didn't understand child support any more than he understood filing taxes or labor laws."

Sadie swallowed another lump of regret regarding Ji's growing up years. "You said something yesterday about your mom leaving you for Rodger—is that what happened?"

Ji shrugged. "It seemed that way." A new tension had entered his movements, making Sadie suspect that her questions were bothering him. She didn't want to make this any harder for him than it already was. She focused on the papers again.

After a few minutes, she looked up and caught sight of something Ji was stuffing in a garbage sack.

"Wait!" she said, jumping to her feet.

Ji startled and turned to look at her as she crossed the room in three steps.

"What?" he said.

Sadie knelt down and reverently reached into the bag. She felt around, found what she was seeking, and pulled it out, cradling the object in both hands as though it were a baby animal.

She looked up at Ji. "This is a Louboutin."

"That is a *shoe*."

Sadie turned back to the garbage sack in search of the mate. Louboutins? Really? *Oh please, let me and Wendy wear the same shoe size.*

CHAPTER 16

Sadie found the other shoe—a glossy black with the trademark red sole—and returned to the office chair after asking Ji to set all shoes aside. He gave her a look but did as she asked, throwing all the shoes into a pile in the middle of the room. Sadie had only ever seen Louboutin shoes on TV and in windows of high-end stores, but she knew that this single pair of shoes likely retailed for two thousand dollars. They also looked brand new. And they were kept in the *overflow* closet?

"Did you pack up any shoes from the other closet?" Sadie asked Ji.

"Yeah."

"Where did you put them?"

"In one of the bags for the share house."

Thank goodness Shots hadn't come for the pick-up yet!

Twenty minutes later, Sadie stood back from the kitchen table where she'd laid out fifteen pairs of name-brand shoes she'd dug out of two different bags. There were more Louboutins, as well as a pair of Jimmy Choo boots, a few pairs of Prada, and some Louis Vuittons. Though Sadie wasn't a fashionista, a rough calculation told her that there was more money on that table than in Wendy's bank account.

Ji came out of the office carrying two bags of clothes. "You're going to keep the shoes?" he asked, watching her watch the gleaming leather.

"No," Sadie said, though it was perhaps the hardest word she'd ever said out loud. Refusing the shoes was nearly as difficult to do as it had been to realize yesterday that her mother's jewelry rightfully belonged to Ji. The shoes were gorgeous, and they fit her perfectly; she'd tried on each pair and nearly drooled over the idea of keeping them for herself. But she couldn't imagine wearing them any more than she could imagine feeling comfortable in Wendy's clothes. Ji had said that since Wendy had given him nothing when she was alive, he wanted nothing from her now, and although Sadie's practical side said that was ridiculous, her emotional side agreed completely, now that she had the opportunity to in some way benefit from Wendy's untimely death.

She didn't tell Ji her intentions—to sell them on eBay in order to have more money for Wendy's expenses; who knew how long it would take to get the bank to release her funds—and instead looked at him and pointed at the shoes.

"There's close to twenty thousand dollars' worth of shoes here."

"A new grill for the restaurant costs twenty thousand dollars." He made no attempt to disguise the disgust in his voice, and Sadie didn't blame him.

Wendy hadn't paid child support, she'd had no contact with her son who worked seven days a week to support his family, but she had twenty thousand dollars' worth of shoes?

Ji returned to the office, leaving Sadie alone. After a few more minutes of admiring the shoes—and taking a picture of them that she sent to her friend Gayle—Sadie retrieved a box and carefully packed up the shoes, wrapping some of the heels in newspaper to keep from damaging any of the others. She put the boxes by the photos, taxes, and landscape painting to ensure that they didn't accidentally get loaded with the items intended for the thrift store, then she picked up the box of photos and returned to the office where Ji was still working on the closet.

"I found a box of pictures earlier," Sadie said, holding it out to him. "There are some of you as a child in here."

When Ji didn't move, Sadie took off the lid and placed the box on the corner of the desk. He pulled a sweater off a hanger and stuffed it into the bag before crossing the room to her. He reached into the box and pulled out a photo of him hanging from some kind of pull-up bar, his shirt hiked up to show his skinny little-boy stomach. Sadie thought he almost smiled, but then he threw the picture back into the box. "You can have them if you want," he said. "They're of no value to me."

Sadie chose not to argue with him as he returned to the closet. Instead, she replaced the lid and took the box back into the living room with the other things to take back to the hotel. When she did take the time to go through all the pictures, she'd set aside the ones of Ji and see if he, or maybe Lin Yang, wanted them. Maybe once the intensity of all of this wore off, he'd change his mind.

Sadie returned to the office, and while Ji finished emptying the closet, she continued the monotonous sorting. They worked in relative silence for another ten minutes before Sadie's phone rang. It was an unfamiliar number that showed up on her Caller ID, though local, and Sadie immediately thought about the message she'd left for Next Faces.

"This is Sadie."

"Ms. Hoffmiller?"

"Yes."

"This is Rodger Penrose. You left a message."

Sadie sat up straighter and felt her heart trill in her chest as her brain snapped into position for this discussion. It wasn't some receptionist returning Sadie's call, it was Rodger Penrose himself. "Yes, I did. Thank you for calling me back."

"You're Wendy's sister?" His voice was soft and cultured, charming, which unsettled her since she'd been building him up in her mind to be some kind of derelict. She remained focused, however.

"Yes, I'm Wendy's younger sister."

"I didn't realize she had a sister."

It hurt to hear yet one more person not know about Sadie's existence, but she pushed it aside. She hadn't told Pete much about Wendy either, after all. "She didn't talk about her family much, then?"

"No, I'm afraid she didn't. What can I help you with? I assume you're calling in regard to her unfortunate death."

"I'm here in San Francisco to clear out her apartment," Sadie said.

"I'm very sorry for your loss. It's been a horrendous situation."

"Yes, it has been. Did the police contact you about it after the fire?"

"I've talked to them twice, and I followed the story on the news and in the paper, though it's pretty much disappeared by now. Have they made any progress in determining what happened?"

Was he fishing for information? "Not really," Sadie lied, keeping the news about the inconclusive cause of death to herself. "They're starting to get forensic information back, though. It's all so shocking."

"I agree, it's truly tragic. Of course I was little help to their case. Wendy and I have been divorced for almost fourteen years."

Sadie thought about the highlighted phone bill and, with her free hand, pulled the pile of bills in front of her. Part of Wendy's day-to-day life consisted of calling Rodger's business, but he seemed to be positioning himself as being distanced from Wendy, which seemed silly since he had to know there would be a record.

"Is there any way I could talk with you in person?" Sadie asked, choosing her direction in the exact moment she thought of it. "I'm only in town for a few days and have been estranged from my sister for many years. I'm trying to get a feel for her life, and I would love the chance to sit down with you and talk about her."

"Oh, well, I don't know that I would be of much help. Like I said we were divorced a long time ago." He said it with a hint of a chuckle in his voice that on another day might have made her feel silly for asking. Today it didn't.

"But even your impressions of her from fourteen years ago would be helpful. I have very little to work with."

He paused a moment and when he spoke again, his voice wasn't as honeyed. "I'm afraid I have a very busy day and . . ."

"Please," Sadie said in her best pleading tone, which was at least half sincere. "I know Wendy was far from perfect, and I'm sure she caused you some heartache, but all I have left of her is her history and you were obviously an important part of that. Can I *please* come and talk to you? Maybe we could meet for lunch? Or I could come to your office?"

"Perhaps the phone would be—"

"I would prefer a face-to-face meeting if there is *any* way you can make it work. I know it's asking a lot but, please, Mr. Penrose, it's all I have left of my sister."

He paused again, and she held her breath. Plan B would be going to his office and weaseling her way into a meeting without his invitation. If it came to that, then she could talk to his office staff as well and see what they knew. But although she would take full advantage of plan B if she needed to, she would appreciate a willing conversation on Rodger's part. Hostile witnesses were tricky.

"Well, I *was* just about to head out for lunch," he said in surrender. "I work in the financial district, so I'm not sure if you can get here in time—"

"My hotel is in the financial district," Sadie said eagerly. Not that she was in the financial district at the moment, but being even a tiny bit familiar with anywhere in this city gave her confidence. "There's a soup restaurant near my hotel," she said, thinking of the sign she'd seen yesterday. It was the only eating establishment, other than Choy's, that she could think of off the top of her head. "San Francisco Soup Company. Do you know it?"

"The one in the Galleria?"

"Um, yes," Sadie said. She'd look it up on her phone to make sure, but since her hotel was called Galleria Park, and the mall where the restaurant was located was right next to it, it seemed likely they were talking about the same place. "I've heard good things about it." Which was totally untrue, but Sadie did love soup.

"I can meet you there in about twenty minutes, but I only have forty minutes after that. I have a very busy schedule."

By the time she finished the call, Sadie was mildly panicked. She didn't have a car and, while she knew the area she was going to, she had no idea how to get there. She turned to Ji, who had listened to her side of the conversation while he gathered up the hangers and put them in their own box. "Is there any way you can drive me?" she asked.

"I didn't bring a car, but you can get a taxi or take the muni. That's how I got here, and it's faster than driving, anyway."

Sadie had no idea what the muni was. "Taxi," she said with a nod. "Do I need to call one or can I just hail one from the street?"

"I'll help you get one."

"That would be great." Sadie pulled out her phone to text Pete about the change of plans.

"Why is it so important to have lunch with Rodger?" Ji asked while he stuffed more hangers into the box.

"I think he's hiding something," Sadie said bluntly. She finished the text and then opened the Internet browser on her phone, searching for "Soup Kitchen Galleria San Francisco."

"What do you mean?" Ji asked.

Sadie looked up, realizing how cryptic she sounded. "If someone killed Wendy, they had to have a motive to do it." A list of links came up on her phone, and she clicked on a map that showed her how to get to the restaurant. "And whatever that motive is will be something whoever killed her doesn't want anyone to know. Rodger said Wendy wasn't in his life, but she called his office twenty-one times in April. I want to know why."

Ji frowned. "You think *Rodger* might have killed her? Even the police can't say for sure that she was murdered."

"And, so far, they can't say that she *wasn't*, but I think circumstances are strange enough to keep that possibility open."

Ji went back to the hangers, but he looked thoughtful—the heavy kind of thinking—about what she'd said.

She tried to explain it better so it would be less upsetting to Ji, who wasn't as familiar as she was with cases like these. "If someone killed her, they deserve to be accountable for it. I'm good at talking to people, and I want to make my own assessment of Rodger Penrose to see if he might have a motive for murder. If nothing else, maybe he was tired of paying the alimony—but maybe there's another mo-tive in there somewhere, too."

Ji seemed to accept that, but he remained thoughtful as he picked up the last of the hangers. "Are you ready to get a taxi?"

Sadie nodded and followed him to the common area, said good-bye to Mario, who was measuring out some baseboard on the kitchen counter, and exited the apartment. She'd seen plenty of the brightly colored cars that seemed to make up the majority of the taxi fleet scurrying around the city, but of course there were none read-ily available once they reached the curb. She had less than fifteen minutes to get to the Galleria, and although the map she'd pulled up on her phone confirmed that the restaurant wasn't geographically far away, she had low expectations of the traffic in this city. Hopefully a cab driver would know a shortcut.

Ji stepped off the curb and waved his hand until the lime green taxi coming their direction changed lanes towards them. The car pulled to the curb a few seconds later.

"Thank you for your help," Sadie said. She moved toward the taxi but then turned back to Ji. "Oh, you'll need the keys to get back in." She reached into her purse and dug around for the keys to the apartment. The taxi honked at her, and she held up her index fin-ger, indicating she needed a minute. She found the keys and handed them to Ji. When he took them, she gave his hand a little squeeze. "Wish me luck."

Ji smiled, at least as much as he ever did. "Luck."

CHAPTER 17

Sadie's nerves relaxed somewhat during the taxi ride to the restaurant as she mentally listed what she wanted to learn from Wendy's ex-husband. Besides the official questions regarding their relationship and Wendy's death, Sadie hoped she would learn something redeeming about her sister. That Rodger and Wendy were divorced didn't seem to encourage her to think that he would have a lot of good to say, but if they had been talking every day, Sadie was willing to entertain the possibility. He seemed to be the only person with whom Wendy had had regular contact.

The cab driver dropped her off around the corner from her hotel—at least she thought that was where she was—and she headed into the entrance of the small shopping mall called the Galleria.

The San Francisco Soup Company turned out to be more like a sandwich shop than the restaurant she was expecting, but it smelled delicious. She took in the bright colors and big windows as she pulled open the glass door and scanned the patrons for Rodger. There were two men sitting by themselves—the one in the green polo shirt was far too young, mid-thirties was Sadie's guess, and the second man looked way too old until Sadie did a double take. She realized the photo of Rodger on his website was apparently out of date by at least ten years. And possibly Photoshopped.

Rodger had a full head of salt-and-pepper hair, rather than the sandy blond from the photo, and shoulders that confirmed that, although he had to be in his mid-sixties, he obviously made it a priority to stay fit. He was an attractive man and exuded a level of class and professionalism. Once again, it was another spot of normal in Wendy's life that Sadie had always assumed to be anything but.

Sadie headed in his direction, and when he looked up at her, she saw recognition in the frozen moment before he stood. Sadie hadn't thought much about whether she and Wendy looked alike, but from the expression on Rodger's face suspected that they shared at least some features.

"You must be Sadie," he said, giving her a firm handshake once she reached the table. "You and Wendy have the same eyes."

It was strange to hear that. They had the same eyes? Really? She cleared her throat and smiled. "Thank you for meeting with me. I really appreciate it."

His teeth were amazingly white when he smiled, his eyebrows perfectly shaped, and his hands soft. Rodger Penrose was a man who could afford luxuries. "What good is being the boss if you can't sneak in a lunch break now and then?" His eyes crinkled as his smile deepened. He motioned toward the cafeteria-style counter. "I haven't ordered yet—shall we?"

Sadie followed him to the counter, where he ordered a bowl of chicken corn chowder in a sourdough bread bowl. Chowder sounded good, but Sadie skipped the bread—she had a wedding dress to think of. Besides, she had a super easy cheater sourdough recipe she could make after the wedding pictures. Sometimes the only way she could accept missing out on something delicious was to promise it to herself later.

They picked up the plastic trays holding their bowls of soup at the end of the counter, but when Sadie tried to pay for hers, Rodger waved her off. She thanked him, and he told her it was his pleasure. Charming indeed. Her eagerness to learn about Wendy from his perspective was growing, and she hoped they wouldn't waste too much time with small talk. As it was, she hadn't expected him to be so open and gracious.

They returned to the table and got their meals situated. Rodger smiled at her over their steaming bowls of soup and asked her what it was she hoped to learn from him. Sadie took his directness at face value.

"Mostly I'm just trying to rebuild my sister's history," she said. "She left home when she very young and pretty much cut us off. I know so little about her life after that—and then it ended so tragically. I'd appreciate anything you can tell me about her."

Rodger accepted her explanation with a nod. "Well, she and I met back in, oh boy, the mid-80s, I guess, when she contracted with my modeling agency."

"She worked as a model?" Sadie already knew this, of course, but asking questions she already knew the answers to would help her determine if he were being honest with her. You could never be too careful.

Rodger nodded. "Local advertisers mostly. She was in her thirties and did a lot of what we call mom-spots. We'd really hoped to get her into some TV, but it never quite worked out. When things didn't stay consistent enough, we hired her to help in the office. After a little while, she and I started dating. She was a real spitfire; we had a great time together."

Sadie found it both sad and ironic that Wendy could play the mom in advertisements but couldn't do it in real life.

"When did the two of you get married?"

"In 1989. We'd been living together for a year or so and decided to make it official." He took a bite of his soup, reminding Sadie of her own, which she stirred.

"And how long were you married?"

"Eight years."

"Can I ask why you split up?"

His smile faltered, and he looked into his soup for a moment before meeting Sadie's eyes. "I'm not sure how much you want to know about Wendy. I have no desire to sully her memory."

"I want to know the truth," Sadie said with sincerity. "I know she wasn't what you would call *well*."

He seemed to relax slightly once he knew she wasn't expecting a pretty story. She still hoped for something good, however.

"No, Wendy wasn't *well*, though I didn't realize the extent of things until after we were married. I found out later she'd been on medication that had evened her out up until then, but then she stopped taking it after we'd been together for a while. She said she didn't like the side effects, but without those meds . . ." He looked at his soup again and took a breath. "Well, we had some pretty intense moments."

Rodger went on to describe Wendy's mood swings, out-of-control spending, and arguments that would sometimes last for days on end. "There was this one night, a few years into our marriage, when we'd had some friends over for dinner. She was in one of her moods, sulky and drinking way too much. Eventually, she started picking a fight with me. Our friends were there but she wouldn't let off.

"She started bringing up things from our past, issues I thought we had resolved a long time ago, and no matter what I said to try to deflect her, she kept going and going and going. Finally, she ran upstairs and locked herself in our room. I was so embarrassed and made apologies to our friends while assuring everyone we were okay.

"After our guests left, I went upstairs to talk to her and found that she had taken a nail file and destroyed every piece of art we had upstairs—which was a substantial collection and even included some of her own work—then gone to bed as though it were any other night. I woke her up and she freaked out over the damage, acting as though she knew nothing about it. I told her I knew she'd done it, and she broke into tears, pointing out that she would never destroy her own paintings. She swore up and down that it wasn't her, that it must have been one of the people at the party. She used it as an excuse to remind me how much she'd always hated my friends.

"I think about it now and wonder why I didn't leave her right that minute, but the more we talked about it, the more confused I was, until I finally just called my insurance adjuster and went with her story—someone had gone upstairs during a party and ruined the art. They did an investigation and everything, but I didn't share my suspicions and they couldn't prove anything specific. She never did fess up to it."

He talked about other instances where their fighting had resulted in the cops coming to their home in Pacific Heights and threatening them both with arrest. "It's not something I'm proud of, and I take my share of accountability for setting her off on occasion, but she could bring out the devil in me like no one else I've ever known." He looked into his soup as he filled his spoon with the next bite.

"You put up with it for eight years before you left?"

His eyes snapped to meet Sadie's. "I didn't leave—she did."

Sadie pulled her eyebrows together. "She left *you?*" An attractive, financially stable, *normal* man?

"I loved Wendy, and I took our vows seriously—in sickness and in health and all that. I set her up with a therapist on more than one occasion, and she cycled through some different medications now and then, but she eventually admitted that she liked the level of feelings she had and didn't want to take the medications anymore. She enjoyed the high times enough to deal with the dark spots, and she didn't really care what kind of impact that made on anyone else."

"So she did receive a diagnosis?" Sadie asked, eager to have her suspicions confirmed.

Rodger shrugged. "One doctor said she was manic depressive, another said it was a personality disorder, and another one said it was due to low thyroid." He shrugged. "She didn't agree with any of them, and although I wasn't sure if I could handle a lifetime of her chaos, I was willing to try. Then she met someone else and just like that moved across town, hired an absolute *shark* of a divorce attorney, and informed me that she'd only ever married me for my money and she didn't have to have *me* to get it. It wasn't until she was gone that I realized how twisted things had become between us." He paused. "Maybe the sickest part is that I still miss her sometimes."

Sadie was too surprised to comment. Why would anyone miss that kind of dysfunction?

Rodger took another bite of soup and seemed to notice Sadie's silence. "Wendy was intense, but a lot of the time it was a good kind of intense. She had such an energy about her. Don't get me wrong, I know she was a disaster and us splitting up was the best thing that could have happened to me, but the point I guess I'm trying to make is that ending our marriage was her idea, not mine."

"But the two of you remained on good terms?" Sadie asked, thinking of the phone calls Wendy had placed to him.

"Yeah, sure," he said as though it were completely normal for a couple with so much drama to be friends after a messy divorce.

"May I ask why? I mean, you knew she had all kinds of problems and believed she'd married you for your money—so why stay connected to her?"

"Because she didn't have anyone else," Rodger said. He held her eyes, and Sadie felt sure he was making the point that since her *family* wasn't helping, he'd had to step up.

"She left us too, just like she left you," Sadie couldn't keep from saying. "My parents tried to keep in contact with her."

"Well, sure, but you can hardly blame her for not inviting them back into her life. Not after the way they treated her."

Sadie blinked and felt her chest fill with heat. "What are you talking about?"

"I mean, your dad's alcoholism and your mother's depression; you have to know that her problems stemmed a great deal from the abuse she suffered as a child. It left some pretty deep scars."

The heat in Sadie's chest got stronger and hotter. She forced herself to take a deep breath. "It wasn't like that," she said as calmly as she possibly could. She wanted to ask *exactly* what Wendy had said, get details and facts she could dispute, but she worried it would take the conversation off track. Still, she felt she owed it to her parents to say something in their defense. "Wendy was the source of chaos in our home. My parents were kind and loving. She wasn't mistreated."

Rodger nodded, as though pretending to believe her. "You should try the soup before it's cold. It's really quite good."

Sadie didn't like his blatant dismissal but decided to take a few moments in order to rein in her emotions and regain her focus. The soup *was* good and tasted like it was made with fresh corn, just like her own corn chowder recipe. She'd have to try her chowder with chicken some time; she liked the density it added to the soup. After a few bites, and some substantial calming on her part, she got back to the point of the discussion.

"What happened to the relationship Wendy left you for?"

Sadie worried she was being *too* pointed—she hadn't expected them to talk in so much personal detail—but he wasn't putting a stop to it. This man had loved Wendy, perhaps still did, which made the potential scope of information he could give Sadie very important.

"I don't know what happened with the guy she left me for. We didn't keep in contact those first couple of years after the divorce; in fact, I didn't hear from her until she was working on getting her own place."

"Why did she get in touch after all that time?"

"She needed first and last month's rent. She was lousy with money and asked if I would help her out."

"Did you?"

"I wanted her to be stable, and I thought that her getting a place of her own was a good sign that she was becoming more independent. I'd come to realize by then that Wendy always seemed to have a man in her life. For the first time, she didn't, and I wanted that to work out."

He was certainly generous. Too generous? "I assume that's the same apartment she died in," Sadie said after doing the math in her head. Ji had said Wendy had lived in the same apartment for twelve years.

Rodger nodded, his expression remorseful.

"How did you feel when you heard about her death?"

"Terrible, of course. But not that surprised. It was like Wendy to go out with some drama."

"Do you think she was murdered?"

Rodger furrowed his eyebrows. "Is that what the police think?"

"I'm not sure what the police think," Sadie hedged, "but I know it's a consideration."

"I told them I thought it was far more likely that she committed suicide and the robbery was connected to the fire."

"Really?" Sadie asked, surprised. She thought of the new pajamas Wendy had purchased two days before the estimated day of her death. It was a small thing to be sure—pajamas were just pajamas, after all—but it seemed to indicate an expected continuation of her life, right? Plus, the police didn't suspect suicide.

Rodger continued. "Seems the most likely scenario to me. Like I said, she had highs and lows, and she was definitely in a low spot— had been for months."

"Doesn't it seem odd, though, that the robbery and fire could be purely coincidental? Regardless of how Wendy died, what are the chances that a burglar chose a third-level apartment in a locked building that just happened to have a dead body in it, and, instead of just robbing the place and getting out of there, lit the body on fire and placed an anonymous call alerting the police about it?"

"The tip was from the burglar?"

"No," Sadie said, worried she'd said too much. "I mean, the police don't know who made the call, that's just one way of looking at it—but it makes the assumptions about it all being coincidental feel far-fetched, don't you think?"

"That kind of thing does happen, though. The drug culture is rampant all over the city. There are some neighborhoods where people would kill their own grandmothers if it meant ensuring another week's worth of hits."

"And they break into third-level apartments in locked buildings? Wouldn't they go for an easier target?"

"I guess I hadn't thought about that," Rodger said. "I was under the impression that the police weren't putting their money on foul play, so I'm surprised that you seem so convinced otherwise."

Sadie worried she'd betrayed too much of her true motivation in talking to Rodger and focused her attention on her bowl of soup. "I'm just trying to consider all the angles. It was shocking to hear what happened to her and then realize how long she'd been dead before the fire was set. I'm trying to make sense of it in my own mind, if nothing else."

"I can imagine this has been very difficult," Rodger said sympathetically. "Wendy had drug issues in the past, and I wouldn't be surprised if she had gotten back into that lifestyle. But I sure hope the police can confirm that her hard living had simply caught up with her, and then a seemingly empty apartment had attracted a burglar who panicked when he found her and tried to burn the place down." He tore off a piece of his bread bowl. "I don't think anyone had it out for Wendy."

"She didn't have many friends."

Rodger shook his head in agreement. "No, she didn't, but she wasn't a bad person. Just not entirely well."

Sadie took another bite of soup while determining how she wanted to address the next topic. Head-on or round about? She decided on the head-on approach; the clock was ticking on the time Rodger had allotted for them to visit. "I understand she was calling your office nearly every day in the months before she died."

A flicker of guilt crossed his expression. "She needed someone to talk to. Like I said, I was about the only friend she had."

"What did you talk about?"

"I don't know—stuff. I was trying to get her to see a doctor; it seemed obvious that things were getting worse. But she didn't want to go and so mostly we talked about day-to-day stuff."

"What kind of day-to-day stuff?" Other than laundry service and grocery delivery, what day-to-day stuff did Wendy have going on?

He looked annoyed for the first time, and Sadie wondered if she was being too pushy. "Like telemarketers and TV shows and things we'd done together years earlier." He paused for a breath. "Look, I was with her long enough to know that whatever was off balance in her brain was worse from about Christmastime until the spring. She was getting older and didn't have people to support her through the bad times. She was too volatile for long-term relationships with most people, but I've always had a soft spot for Wendy and I truly wanted to help her. So, I told my secretary to put her through when she called. I talked to her about her day, commiserated about the hard things, and told her to hang in there. I was her friend—quite possibly the only one she had. We would talk for a few minutes and that seemed to be enough for her."

"And when she stopped calling?" Sadie asked. "What did you think of that?"

"I was out of town the last two weeks of May. I had told her I was leaving, and she left me seven messages from the sixteenth through the twenty-second expressing her annoyance at my not being in town. When I got back, I thought she might start calling again but she didn't. Then again, it was spring, and she usually improved in the spring. She wasn't stable but she could be relatively predictable."

He looked at his watch and straightened. "I need to be getting back to the office. Is there anything else I can do for you?"

Sadie's mind whirred through the possibilities, hating that their conversation was ending. She'd thought he was hiding something when she'd spoken to him on the phone, but now she wondered if it was simply the complexities of his relationship with Wendy that had given her that impression. What else could she learn from him?

"Oh, yes, there's one last thing," she said. "What about her son? Did you ever meet him?"

"Oh right," Rodger said with a nod. "The police told me about him—crazy that she'd never once told me she had a son."

Chicken Corn Chowder

2 tablespoons olive oil
¼ cup diced onion (about ½ a medium onion)
2 cloves garlic, diced or pressed
32 ounces chicken broth
12 ounces skinless, boneless chicken breast halves
4 ears fresh sweet corn (canned corn may be used, if desired)
1 bay leaf
½ cup chopped small green, sweet red, or orange pepper, divided
1 cup milk
1¼ cup instant mashed potato flakes
Crushed red pepper flakes (optional)
Salt and pepper, to taste

Heat oil in a large soup pan with a lid (3-quart or larger) on medium-high heat. When oil is hot, sauté onion until translucent. Add garlic and sauté 30 seconds, being careful to not scorch it. Add broth, chicken, corn, and bay leaf. (Add extra broth if liquid does not cover corn.) Cover pan, increase heat to high and bring to a boil.

Reduce heat and simmer 12 minutes or until chicken is no longer pink. Remove chicken and corn to cutting board, leaving the broth in the pan and reducing the temperature to medium-high.

Add ¼ cup chopped pepper to stock. Stir in milk and potato flakes. Shred chicken and return to pan. Using a towel, fork, or corn holder to hold hot corn, cut kernels from cobs. Add red pepper flakes and corn kernels to soup; heat through. Season to taste with salt and pepper.

Garnish servings with remaining chopped pepper.

Makes 6 servings.

Cheater Sourdough Bread

6½ cups all-purpose flour
1½ tablespoons instant yeast (Traditional yeast may be used. Simply add it with the water after allowing it to proof.)
1½ tablespoons salt
3 cups warm water (hot, but not so hot you can't keep your finger in it for 10 seconds)

In a large bowl, mix flour, yeast, and salt. Add water and stir with a wooden spoon for a couple of minutes or until a very soft dough (or thick batter) forms. There should be no patches of flour but it won't be smooth. It should be soft enough to conform to the shape of the bowl.

Cover the bowl and ignore for 2 to 5 hours; it doesn't matter if the dough falls.

To properly store the dough, put dough in a lidded container, with the lid cracked so that it's not airtight. A 1-gallon ice cream bucket works great with the lid set on top. Put in fridge and ignore for a week.

When you are ready to bake, remove however much dough you want to bake, but don't make loaves any bigger than ½ of the original amount. (A grapefruit-sized portion will feed three people.)

Sprinkle dough portion with enough flour so it won't stick to your hands. Pat and shape dough into a ball, pulling edges underneath to achieve a smooth top surface. Place shaped loaf on baking tray and cover with a dishtowel. (A layer of semolina flour or corn meal can prevent sticking to the pan, otherwise use a nonstick spray.)

Set a timer for 30 minutes.

After 30 minutes, preheat oven to 450 degrees F. Place a broiler pan or baking dish on lower rack of oven. (You will add water to this later.) Set your timer for 20 minutes.

When the timer goes off, even if oven isn't completely preheated, remove cover from loaf and dust top lightly with flour. Using a sharp knife, cut three slits about ½-inch deep in the top of the loaf.

Add 1 to 2 cups of hot tap water to the broiler pan or baking dish placed on the lower rack and put loaf in oven on the middle rack. Close oven door quickly to trap the steam. (The steam gives the bread a flakier crust.) Bake about 30 minutes, until bread smells wonderful and crust is brown. Larger loaves will take longer to cook than smaller ones.

Remove bread from oven and allow to cool 10 minutes before slicing.

Store the remaining dough in a container without the lid sealed for up to another week. The longer it stays in the fridge, the more sourdough flavor it will take on.

Note: This bread is delicious fresh, but does not make great leftovers, so only bake what you'll eat.

Note: If using a pizza stone, do not put the water dish directly beneath the pan—move it to the side of the rack—as the steam could split your pan.

Family Notes: Breanna prefers this fresh rather than sourdough-ed. Shawn will eat several slices in one sitting.

Makes 12 servings.

CHAPTER 18

Sadie still had half a bowl of soup when Rodger stood to go back to the office. She thanked him for his time and then finished her soup while writing down everything she could remember from their conversation in the notebook she kept in her purse. The information he'd shared fit into the growing picture of Wendy as a mentally ill, manipulative, smart, and selfish woman. And yet there was something admirable in the fact that Rodger had loved Wendy despite those things. Even if Sadie didn't understand why he did, she was grateful for it all the same.

The two hardest parts of the conversation had been learning what Wendy had said about Sadie's parents and what she *hadn't* said about Ji. It was unreal that Rodger hadn't known about him until the police asked last week, yet Sadie could find no reason to doubt Rodger's assertion of ignorance. At one point, she asked him why he thought Wendy wouldn't tell him about her son, and he'd answered honestly: he'd never wanted children. He'd told Wendy that when they first began dating.

Sadie's heart was heavy with that information, and she hoped that she could tell Ji about this meeting without having to divulge to him that Wendy had spent ten years with a man who never knew of Ji's existence.

She finished her notes and took the last bites of her soup—cold but still good—before heading out of the restaurant. Her hotel was around the corner, and she'd seen lots of taxis pick up and drop off near the entrance, so it seemed a natural place to find one that would take her back to Wendy's apartment.

Her phone chimed with a text message, and she moved closer to the building so she wouldn't be in anyone else's way. The sidewalks always seemed to be packed. In the process of trying to fish her phone from her purse, she dropped her notebook. She bent down to pick it up and caught sight of a man stepping quickly into a parking garage exit. Another woman on the street glanced toward where he disappeared, then continued walking toward Sadie, passing her without a smile or a greeting.

There was something familiar about the man—though Sadie had only seen a flash of him. And why had he jumped into the parking lot exit? He'd moved as though getting out of the way. Or hiding. She continued searching for her phone, keeping an eye on the area where the man had disappeared. Had she seen him before, or was her imagination running wild?

The text message was from Ji. He was needed at the restaurant and would call her later. He'd left the building keys with the man who lived in apartment two. Sadie typed her response slowly, asking if everything was okay, her attention still focused on the parking garage.

A few seconds later, the man stepped out from his hiding place. Sadie noted the hitch in his step that happened when he saw her still leaning against the building, but she didn't acknowledge him.

Instead, she pretended to send another text, forcing the man to do something—they couldn't both just stand there.

He began walking in her direction but didn't look at her. When he passed her, she casually fell into step behind him, studying his back until recognition dawned. He was the man from the soup café—the only person, other than Rodger—who had been sitting alone when she entered. Mid-thirties in a green polo shirt. Was he following her? Not now, of course. She was the one doing the following now. But had he been following her from the restaurant?

He continued up Sutter Street with Sadie a couple of yards behind him. When they reached Powell—one of the roads that had a cable car track down the middle—he crossed at the light and entered a Walgreens. He didn't glance toward her even though she was certain he knew she was there.

Sadie didn't follow him inside, but turned and hurried back across Powell before the light changed, and then ducked into the Starbucks on the corner. She could watch the door of the Walgreens through the window. If Mr. Green Shirt *was* following her, he wouldn't wait long to come out once he realized she was no longer behind him.

He didn't disappoint, and when he came out onto the street and looked around, she stepped back to make sure he wouldn't see her through the glass. After a few more seconds, he seemed to curse, then pulled a phone out of his pocket. He *had* been following her, and now he was calling whoever it was he was in league with to tell them he'd lost her.

She pulled out her phone and took a picture of him, ignoring the confused look of patrons in the coffee shop who had picked up on the fact that she wasn't there to order anything. She enlarged the picture on her phone, but it made his face blurry.

He was still talking on the phone when the crosswalk signal flashed and, along with a dozen other people, he crossed Powell, heading back the way he'd come.

Sadie moved toward the front door and, after he passed, slipped out the door and hurried to catch up. One benefit of being in such a crowded city was that he didn't seem to notice anything odd about the fact that someone was following close enough behind him to hear at least part of what he said.

"—see what I can find out, but I lost her after just a few blocks. . . . Older, not particularly attractive."

Sadie tried to ignore her offense at what must be a description of her.

"I got some pictures. . . . Wasn't spicy. . . . Okay . . ."

His legs were longer than Sadie's, and she was jogging a couple of steps to keep up when he suddenly turned his head and saw her. She came to a stop as he startled and pulled his phone from his ear. Sadie wasn't prepared to be discovered, but she had enough experience with lack of preparation to react quickly. She lifted her phone, which was still open to the camera, and snapped a picture of his shocked expression, then turned and headed up Sutter in a quick walk, dodging between people in hopes of losing him.

Several people were talking outside a small café, creating a kind of shield. Once she passed the group, she ducked behind them, through the front door of the café, and then stepped to the side of the door while Mr. Green Shirt hurried past. She wondered what his intention was if he caught up with her. Destroy the camera? Something worse?

"Hello?"

Sadie looked at a woman dressed in a starched white shirt with a name tag that said Naomi.

"Can I help you?"

"Um, yes, do you have a back door, Naomi?"

"Do you mean the patio? It's a bit cool today—are you sure?"

Sadie smiled. "Yes, the patio would be perfect."

The hostess showed her outside, and though Sadie had intended to use the patio as an escape, it was fully enclosed by surrounding buildings and wooden trellis meant to disguise the urban setting. Not wanting to run into the man who'd been following her, and unwilling to climb the trellis in order to find another way out, she sat down and accepted the menu Naomi handed her. It *was* too cool outside to be comfortable—the sun was covered in fog, again—but Sadie didn't feel she had much of a choice except to wait this out.

"Our specials today are the bleu cheese mahi-mahi sandwich, the pumpkin and mushroom bisque, and our hot apple streusel cake. I'll be right back with a water. Would you like anything else to drink?"

"Water will be fine," Sadie said as she skimmed the menu and tried to calm her racing heart. What would happen if Mr. Green Shirt found her back here, alone and with no way out? She refused to give into the dramatic possibilities. If he'd known she'd entered the restaurant, he'd have followed her immediately, right?

The waitress arrived and asked for Sadie's order. She wasn't hungry but ordered the hot streusel cake all the same. She hadn't had a dessert for two days and nothing else sounded good. Plus it was *hot*, which meant it might warm her up a bit. She didn't want to go back onto the street until she was certain Mr. Green Shirt was gone.

Once her breathing had returned to normal, and the waitress had returned inside, she texted Pete the picture she'd taken and an explanation.

Her phone rang mere seconds after the text went through.

"What do you mean you were followed?"

Sadie filled him in on the details, waiting for him to express concern for her safety or insist that she stay put until he could come to her. But he didn't. Instead he asked question after question. As the conversation progressed, rather than be hurt by his focus on the event and not her feelings, an unexpected sense of accomplishment settled over her. She kind of liked that he was more concerned about the implications of her being followed than the fear that she couldn't take care of herself.

"If he was there before you arrived, was he with Rodger?" Pete asked.

"Maybe," Sadie said. "Can the police identify the photo?"

"I'll ask them about it when I get off the phone. Do you feel safe?"

"I'm fine." The waitress brought the cake, and Sadie transferred her phone to the other ear so she could talk and eat at the same time. "I'm taking some time for him to disappear before I go back out. He knows I got his picture." She took a bite—it was *really* good and deliciously warm. Could it have bananas in it? She couldn't taste any but it would account for the smooth and moist texture. She'd have to see if she could find a similar recipe—or perhaps adapt the one in her Little Black Recipe Book and see how the banana affected the texture of her recipe, which was delicious but, in all honesty, a touch on the dry side.

"And what exactly did he say in the part of the phone call you overheard?"

Sadie hurried to swallow and stay tuned into the conversation. "Well, he, uh, commented on my looks."

"What do you mean? Like comparing you to Wendy? Maybe someone's watching her apartment."

"How would they know where I was going and then beat me there?" She didn't expound on the phone call because she didn't want to admit to Mr. Green Shirt's assessment.

"True," Pete said thoughtfully. "If he was describing you, though, then it seems unlikely he's connected to Rodger since you'd just sat across the table from him."

"Good point," Sadie said between bites. When she remembered her wedding dress, she ate slower.

"Well done, though," Pete said. "You handled yourself perfectly."

Sadie smiled at the sincere compliment. "Did you talk to the police about all the calls to Rodger's business?"

"They said that he claimed she was having a difficult time, that she often struggled with depression in the winter months, and that he was just chatting with her as a friend."

"That's what he told me too," Sadie said, almost disappointed but feeling uncharitable about it.

"Lopez is letting me read over official statements and other documentation in the file," Pete said. "I haven't found anything remarkable, but I'm still looking. I'll be sure to read up on Rodger's statement. More specific information is supposed to come through this afternoon regarding the synthetic kerosene—they're hoping to determine the brand. I'm kind of hanging around in hopes of being here when that comes in. I want to stay in the thick of things."

Pete was also going to lunch with Detective Lopez, so they said their good-byes. After Sadie hung up, she remembered Ji's text. She checked her phone but he hadn't responded to her question about whether or not everything was okay. Did that mean things *weren't* okay? When he'd arrived at Wendy's apartment he'd said he had double coverage at Choy's until 5:30. Was he planning to come back? She let the questions flow freely through her brain while she finished the cake—leaving a few bites on the plate though it was hard to do—before composing another text message for Ji.

Will you be coming back?

She was pulling cash out of her wallet to pay the bill when Ji's response came in.

Ji: I'm not sure.

Sadie: What about the share house?

Ji: I moved most of the stuff to the main area.

What about me? Sadie wondered. Ji had been the one doing all the coordinating, and Shots was Chinese, right? Would she even be able to communicate with him?

It would be great if you could come back for that.

Ji didn't respond in the time it took her to go back to the street, assure herself that Mr. Green Shirt wasn't waiting for her, and wave down a taxi. She gave the cab driver the address of Wendy's apartment building and settled back against the seat, only then considering the wisdom of her plan. If Mr. Green Shirt *was* linked to Wendy, wouldn't he go there next? And yet Pete hadn't expressed any concern about her returning to the apartment, and it was the middle of the day.

She opened her notebook in order to write down notes on her encounter with Mr. Green Shirt—maybe she could assess his threat level, which, off the top of her head, she didn't feel was very high. He'd seemed to be simply observing her, not trying to hurt her or anything like that. He'd said "Nothing spicy," on the phone, and in all honesty she'd thought of the soup first, but couldn't it mean that the encounter Rodger had had with Sadie wasn't romantic?

If "Nothing spicy" was related to the romance level and Sadie's physical appearance was important to whomever Mr. Green Shirt had reported to, then perhaps it was *Rodger* who'd been followed, and Sadie had been a secondary target. The only person who would be jealous enough to send someone to spy on Rodger during lunch was either a girlfriend or a wife. Sadie had no idea which of those partnerships Rodger currently had as he hadn't offered the information at lunch. Perhaps she should have asked.

"This it?"

Sadie looked up and realized that the taxi driver had pulled up in front of Wendy's building. "Yes, thank you." She paid him and stepped out onto the curb around the corner from the entrance. After the taxi pulled away, she headed for the door and consulted Ji's text about having left the keys with the tenant from apartment two—an odd thing for him to do since Ji hadn't met anyone who lived in the building as far as Sadie knew. There seemed to be something covert in the way he'd left the apartment, and yet she felt paranoid thinking that. If she wanted a relationship with him, she needed to take him at his word and accept that there was a problem with his business without trying to read too much into it or take it too personally. She only wished that giving people the benefit of the doubt was easier for her to do.

She pushed the button for apartment two and waited a few seconds before a man's voice crackled over the speaker. "Yes?"

She leaned in to make sure he'd hear her; she'd never been on this end of the intercom system. "This is Sadie Hoffmiller, Wendy Penrose's sister. I understand her son left the keys to her apartment with you."

"He sure did," the man responded. "I'll buzz you in and meet you in the foyer." The intercom clicked off a moment before the buzz indicated that the exterior door had been unlocked. Sadie pulled it open, walked down the hallway, and stepped into the foyer area at the same time the apartment door across from her opened. She smiled at the young man with dark hair and glasses as they met between the mailboxes and the elevator.

He reached into his pocket, pulling out the key ring and handing it to her. "I'm sure sorry about what happened to Wendy," he said with a sympathetic frown. "Lousy deal, that."

"Thank you," Sadie acknowledged with a nod as she slid the keys into her purse. "Did you know my sister?"

"Well," he said with a cautious tone. "It's not a large complex."

The discomfort of his answer spurred Sadie forward, though she tried to keep from sounding too nosy. "I wasn't close to my sister, but I understand she could be difficult to deal with. The police said she had a lot of conflicts with her neighbors."

He cast a sidelong, sympathetic look at her. "Still, everything that happened was just terrible."

"It was," Sadie said, wishing he would be a bit more forthcoming but sensing his hesitation was an attempt to spare her feelings. That would be very sweet if it were her feelings she was worried about. "Were you here the night of the fire?" she asked, trying a different track.

He put his hands in the pockets of his khaki pants and rocked back on the heels of his Tom's. "Yeah—it was intense when the fire department was banging on the door at one a.m. The fire didn't even trigger the smoke alarm. We were evacuated as a precaution and allowed back in pretty quickly. I didn't know about . . . Wendy until the next morning when the police came by asking questions," he said with a frown. "I'm Jason, by the way." He put out his hand and Sadie shook it.

"I'm Sadie. What did the police ask you about?"

"How well I knew Wendy, when I'd last seen her, if I'd seen anything suspicious around the building—that kind of thing. I didn't have much to tell them."

"You didn't know Wendy, then?" Sadie asked as casually as she could.

"Well, I knew her, but we didn't socialize or anything. All of us keep to ourselves for the most part. We wave at each other in the halls and stuff, but we don't really know one another." He paused and turned his head slightly. "I think Wendy and Shasta were pretty good friends at one point, though. Have you talked to Shasta?"

"Not yet," Sadie said with a shake of her head. She was encouraged by the information that Shasta and Wendy had a closer connection than Jason did. "But my fiancé met her briefly last night. He said she likes the color pink."

Jason laughed out loud, his wide grin filling his face. "She told me once that a big-time movie producer back in the sixties told her that pink was her color. She's an heiress and an actress, in that order. I'm not sure he meant to imply it was her *only* color, but she took it to mean that it was part of her identity or something."

"She sounds fascinating," Sadie said. "How long has she lived in the building?"

"A while," Jason said, nodding. "Ten years, maybe? They were both here when I moved in."

"And they were friends?"

"Oh no," Jason said with emphasis. "But Shasta mentioned that they *used* to be friends. They had some kind of falling out. I didn't ask what about."

"And how long have you lived here?"

"Going on four years. I work just a few blocks away." He gestured toward the west, or at least the direction Sadie thought was west. She was still rather turned around in this town. "The location couldn't be more perfect for me."

"It's a beautiful location," Sadie said. "But I understand Wendy had some complaints against the landlord. Were there ongoing issues with the building?"

Jason shook his head. "That was between her and Mr. Pilings. I never jumped on board with her crusades against him."

"I understand. I was just curious when I saw the complaint in her files. Did she try to get other tenants to join her?"

Jason nodded. "Uh, I don't know how much I should be saying."

Sadie gave her best trust-me smile. "I don't mean to make you uncomfortable," she said as though backing off from her questions. "I'm sure I'll find out about it later. I'm trying to get through *tons* of paperwork and files." She sighed heavily to indicate how much work it all was. "It sounds like she was a troublemaker, though."

Jason seemed to vacillate between not wanting to gossip and feeling sympathy for Sadie's search for information. She was gratified when she saw his resistance soften. "I don't know all the specifics, just that she'd filed a lot of complaints against Mr. Pilings."

"Do you know what the complaints were for?" Sadie asked. "The letter I found was about a water heater."

"Ah," Jason said, nodding. "Each apartment has their own heater, so that complaint would have only affected her. But sometimes the Dumpster is full a few days before the disposal company comes for it, and now and then the elevator's down for a day or two—which I admit doesn't affect me as much as the tenants on the upper floors—but those are the kinds of things she'd try to get the rest of us to throw in with her on. Like, she'd come around as soon as something went wrong, wanting us to jump on it before Mr. Pilings even had a chance to resolve it. It was weird."

"And did you ever join her in the complaints?"

Jason shook his head. "The last time she came by our place—which was last summer—I told her that if she hated it so bad, she should move. She said it was her calling to make Mr. Pilings live up to his commitment and that if I wasn't part of the solution I was part of the problem. I told her I would never sign any of her petitions so she might as well leave me out of it. After that she wouldn't acknowledge me when we passed in the foyer."

"I'm sorry," Sadie said, embarrassed by her sister's actions.

"It wasn't a big deal," Jason said with humility. "I just don't get caught up in all the drama, ya know?" He checked his watch. "Um, is that all?"

Sadie got the hint; she'd taken enough of his time. "Yes. Thank you so much for holding onto the keys, and for helping me better understand what Wendy had been doing. I appreciate it very much."

"No problem," Jason said before turning and heading back to his apartment.

Sadie moved to the elevator and pushed the button for level three. The elevator groaned and began descending from the second floor, which seemed to be its default location. Sadie wondered if people were open to talking about Wendy because they felt sympathy for Sadie or because they hadn't liked Wendy in the first place and therefore didn't feel any loyalty. People weren't usually so accommodating, but, regardless of their reasons, she was grateful for their openness.

Mario's music was still playing when Sadie arrived at the apartment, and she scowled at the fine layer of drywall dust that had escaped the confines of the bathroom. She decided to keep her purse with her—no point in getting it dusty. She was disappointed that Ji wasn't there, but he had indeed moved everything to the main part of the apartment. Only the desk, chair, and Rubbermaid box full of papers were still in the office.

Sadie closed the office door behind her and sat down in the chair, wondering how much longer Pete would be, and picked up a handful of papers from the box. She glanced over the piles on the top of the desk that she'd already sorted and did a double take when she saw January's phone bill on top of the other phone bills. It had been the only one she'd been missing when she left. A quick scan of the other papers revealed that an additional power bill had been added to that pile too. She looked into the box and realized that Ji must have taken over sorting the box after he'd finished his other tasks. He hadn't finished, and hadn't done much, but the box wasn't quite as full as it had been when she left.

Sadie picked up the January phone bill and counted the calls made to Rodger that month—fourteen calls total. It proved that the increased calls had started in January. Sadie reviewed her lunch conversation with Rodger and asked herself if she believed what he'd told her. Was it conceivable that he had kept in contact with Wendy because she had no one else? Was his version of events realistic? Who was Mr. Green Shirt connected to?

The questions frustrated her. She'd learned a lot about why people behaved in certain ways and how to read between the lines, but when it came to Wendy and the people connected to her, those skills didn't seem to be all that effective. The things Wendy had done didn't make sense to her, so how could she reason them out? Maybe if Sadie had a degree in psychology, or had her own adult interactions with Wendy to draw understanding from, she could feel more settled, but as it was, she was learning about a stranger who did strange things for as yet unknown reasons. Which, Sadie realized, was pretty much like every other case she'd investigated, except that it seemed as though this one should be different. Maybe there was no way to make sense of that.

But there were still papers to sort.

Sadie thought of her fortune from Choy's yesterday: *It's time to get moving.* She didn't have all the answers—heck, she didn't feel like she had *any* of the answers—but she did have work to do and perhaps that would lead her somewhere important.

Apple Streusel Cake

Crumb Topping
½ cup flour
¼ cup brown sugar
¼ cup sugar
1 teaspoon cinnamon
¼ teaspoon ground ginger
¼ teaspoon allspice
¼ teaspoon cloves
4 tablespoons butter

Cake
1 banana (the riper the better)
1 to 1½ teaspoon vanilla extract, to taste
1 teaspoon almond extract
½ cup milk (or almond milk, if desired)
4 tablespoons butter, melted
1½ cups flour
¾ cup sugar
2 teaspoons baking powder
½ teaspoon salt
4 apples, peeled and sliced or 1 (16-ounce) can canned apples, drained*

Preheat oven to 350 degrees. Grease an 8x8 glass baking dish, a 9-inch pie dish, or 12 medium-sized muffin tins.

To make the crumb topping, mix all topping ingredients together (except butter) in a medium-sized mixing bowl. Add butter and cut together with dry ingredients until mixture is crumbly. Set aside.

To make the cake, in a large mixing bowl, mash banana with a fork. Mix in vanilla, almond extract, milk, and butter; mix well. Add in dry ingredients and mix until just combined.

Spread half of the batter in the bottom of the greased pan. Arrange apple slices on top of batter, then cover with dollops of remaining batter, smoothing as well as possible over the apples. Sprinkle the crumb topping evenly over the top.

Bake 40 minutes. Remove from oven and allow to cool at least 15 minutes before serving. Serve warm or cold, with or without vanilla ice cream.

*If using apple pie filling in place of apples, decrease sugar in the cake to ⅓ cup.

Note: For more flavor in the cake itself, sprinkle ½ cup of crumb topping over the apples before adding the second layer of cake batter.

Makes 6 servings (or about a dozen muffins).

CHAPTER 19

It was nearly an hour later before Pete buzzed to be let into the building. Mario had left for a late lunch with his helper so the apartment was quiet when Pete arrived.

"Where's Ji?" Pete asked as he followed Sadie from the kitchen to the office.

Sadie hadn't realized that he didn't know, so she told him about Ji's texts and the information she'd gotten from Jason regarding Wendy and her troublemaking. "I'd sure like to talk to the landlord," she said. "It sounds like Wendy was making a lot of trouble for him."

"I read Stephen Pilings's statement in the file, and he mentioned some claims and things she'd filed, but he owns several apartment complexes and said that she wasn't the most frustrating tenant he dealt with. It seemed as though he was taking it in stride."

"Do the police know more about the specific claims she filed against him?" Sadie asked. "I didn't run into any files about it in the boxes they returned but I wasn't looking."

"I didn't see anything about them, but I can ask Lopez."

"And I'll check the files when we get back to the hotel," Sadie said.

"What's that?" Pete asked, pointing at the box on the floor.

Sadie looked at the box—he didn't know about that either? She explained it to him, and he came over and looked at the sorted stacks of paper on the desk.

"We'll want to take this to the PD," Pete said after picking up the letter of confirmation for the claim Wendy had made against her landlord in May. "And it was all just stuffed into this box that was in the closet?"

"Yeah," Sadie said, shrugging to show her own confusion. "And some of it is recent, like that letter that had been sent just weeks before she died, but there were other things dated almost a year ago. Did anyone say if her office was organized or not? It looks to me like the police filed all the things they gave back to us."

"They said there were a few files, but most of the papers had been shoved into drawers and things—kind of an 'out of sight, out of mind' thing. One of the desk officers filed everything to make it easier for the detectives to look through."

Sadie nodded. "So, Wendy just put papers away rather than organizing them, and at some point after early May she shoved a bunch of papers into a plastic bin and stored it in her closet?"

"It's like bipolar organization," Pete said offhandedly.

"Yeah, that's about the fifteenth thing that seems to confirm that bipolar was at least part of her problem." She paused, thinking on that for a few moments before she looked up at Pete. "I've always told myself she was mentally ill, and I think she was, but there are plenty of mentally ill people who still function, have relationships with their families, and treat people decently. She lied, manipulated, abandoned her child, caused problems in the building, and who knows what else—is it fair to blame that all on her mental chemistries?"

"There's comfort in diagnosis," Pete said.

Sadie looked back at the box. There *was* comfort in diagnosis, at least she assumed there would be, but there wasn't really a diagnosis here. It was guessing and conjecture. Would that ever be enough to get the closure she wanted? Closure. She really disliked that word, but it had fallen back into her vocabulary with this situation. But, as she had amid prior ponderings on the idea, she found herself questioning if closure existed at all. Would learning more about her sister really make her feel better? So far it hadn't. And yet the desire for closure *was* motivating.

"Sadie?"

She looked at Pete, realizing she'd gotten lost for a minute. She smiled. "Sorry. Too many thoughts in my head."

"A penny for them?" Pete asked.

Sadie shook her head. "Nothing you haven't heard before. I'm just repeating the tape in my head and hoping I can understand it better the thirty-fifth time I play it. Anyway, how did things go at the station after we talked? Did you learn anything new from the case file?"

"Yeah, I think I did," he said with a proud grin.

"Really? What?"

"The tenant from apartment 5 was tricky for the police to track down. She'd moved to Florida at the end of May. Anyway, they finally caught up with her after the holiday weekend and talked to her on the phone. Everything she said fit with everyone else: she had no idea Wendy was dead, hadn't seen anything out of place, and hadn't seen Wendy much in the months leading up to her death. This girl—Rebecca—had a couple weird situations with Wendy when she first moved into the building a couple of years ago so she'd learned to keep her distance."

"Everyone kept their distance."

Pete nodded but didn't break stride with what he was saying. "So, anyway, there wasn't much new information except that back in February, Rebecca rode the elevator up to the third floor with an Asian girl who said she was Wendy's granddaughter."

Sadie felt a tremor go through her. "I had the impression that Wendy didn't have a relationship with Ji's children."

"She didn't," Pete said with a sharp nod, holding Sadie's eyes to further emphasize the contradiction. "When Ji and I were talking yesterday he said that Wendy had never even met his daughters."

"Did this Rebecca give any additional details that would help us determine which daughter it was? Age? Appearance?" Sadie thought about Min, the daughter who had rung them up yesterday.

"No, the statement was transcribed from a phone conversation, and the mystery granddaughter wasn't an item they expanded on, though it was flagged as something to pursue in a follow-up call— which they haven't made yet. I talked to Lopez and he said he's going to see if he can get me cleared to talk to her directly. I'm wondering if anyone else in the building saw an Asian girl. Lopez gave me the green light to ask the tenants."

That thrill of excitement rushed through Sadie at having the police department's permission to dig a little deeper. There was also a sense of hesitation linked to this lead, however, hampering her enthusiasm and eagerness. "Pete, if Ji's daughter had a relationship with Wendy that Ji didn't know about . . ."

"I know," Pete said with an understanding expression. "None of us want any of what happened with Wendy linked back to Ji's family. But we can't *not* look into this. *Anyone* who visited Wendy in those final months—a time when she'd isolated herself—could have information the police need to clarify what's happened here. Regardless of who that source of information is, we have to follow up."

"But what if she had something to do with it?" Sadie said, feeling the burden of discovery that had accompanied so many of her other cases. The truth didn't always set people free—sometimes it clutched at them with iron chains. And yet Sadie believed that truth was still worth pursuing and that in the end doing what was right was better for everyone.

Pete took a step toward her and rubbed her arm. "That's a really big leap, and we can't let the worst-case scenario keep us from looking into it. She's not a suspect, just a source of information we didn't know about until now."

Pete was right, and Sadie knew it, but it still settled like a rock in her chest. She thought about all the pain Wendy had caused Ji in his life. What would he think about Wendy having had a relationship with one of his daughters?

Her earlier thoughts about Ji leaving while she was at lunch came to mind, and what had seemed worrisome then, suddenly felt suspect. "Ji was sorting through this box while I was at lunch with Rodger—the sort piles were different when I got back—and he left suddenly."

Pete pulled his eyebrows together as he considered the implications.

Sadie hurried to further explain where her thoughts were taking her. "Maybe I'm looking too much for a connection, but what if he found something"—she shook the side of the box closest to her for emphasis—"that proved what we just discovered—that Wendy and one of his daughters had a relationship? It might explain why he left."

"That could certainly explain why he left unexpectedly," Pete said. They both were silent for a few moments. "But he could have found any number of things that might be upsetting enough for him to call it quits. He puts on a good front, but I think he's quite fragile where his mother is concerned."

Sadie told Pete about Rodger not knowing Ji existed, and Pete shook his head with the same disappointment Sadie had felt when she'd learned it. "So what do we do about this?" Sadie asked. "Do we ask Ji? Talk to his daughters?"

"I would like to talk to the neighbors first and see if anyone else saw the girl. The more details and confirmations we have, the better. I'm leaning toward it being the oldest daughter, though. The other two are pretty young, aren't they?"

"Thirteen and eleven," Sadie confirmed. "Min is twenty, and I'm guessing she has a bit of a rebellious streak."

"Really? Ji made it sound like he and his wife run a pretty tight ship."

"She has a piercing," Sadie said, then pointed to the top of her own ear to show him where. "No earring, but when I glanced at it, she hid it behind her hair. I know it's not much—lots of kids have piercings—but if her parents are that controlling—and they seem to be just that—it might be an indicator that there's more going on under the surface with her."

Pete nodded his agreement. "It would take a certain level of rebellion for Min to have a relationship with Wendy behind her parents' backs, so you're probably right. Either way, we need to find out for sure who it was and what they might know."

Sadie agreed but feared talking to all the tenants could take a long time. "What if I called Ji and just asked him if everything was okay in the meantime? Maybe he'll tell me why he left."

"Just be careful about leading him too much, or forcing an answer. It's better for him to think we know something than for us to accuse him of anything."

"I understand," Sadie said.

Pete smiled and clapped his hands together. "Ji mentioned that the landlord said there was a dolly around here for the tenants to use. I bet Ji's friends would find it helpful, and I can use looking for it as an excuse to chat with some neighbors."

"I need to finish sorting this box," Sadie said, feeling the urgency, "but I really want to talk to Ji."

"We've got at least an hour before Ji's friend shows up. There's time to do both."

Sadie appreciated the vote of confidence. Pete left to find the dolly, and Sadie decided to call Ji and see what she could learn from him before she turned her attention to the box. Ji didn't answer his phone so she looked up the number to his restaurant.

"Choy's, is this for take-out?" It was a woman's voice on the phone, but it didn't sound like Lin Yang. Younger, perhaps, with a more American cadence. Could it be the daughter who'd been seen visiting Wendy?

"Um, I'm calling for Ji Doang," Sadie said, maintaining her focus.

"One moment." The woman or girl moved the phone away, but Sadie heard her call out *"Ba ba"* over the kitchen sounds in the background. Did *Ba ba* mean "Dad" in Chinese?

"Ni hao," Ji said a few seconds later.

"Ji, it's Sadie." She had decided to open with a question about how things would go with the share house in hopes that it would set the stage better than if she launched into what she really wanted to know. She asked her question and then awaited his response. Did he sound relieved that she was only calling in regard to the donations?

"He'll park on the street and have a few guys to help him load things," Ji answered. "He does this all the time so it won't take long. Pete and I took the bed apart yesterday, so it's really only the dresser, desk, and couches that will be any kind of challenge."

"Will I need to sign any kind of paperwork or anything? Can I do that or do you need to do it as next of kin?"

"If he needs you to sign anything, you're fine to do so. It will all go very smooth, I'm sure. I'm sorry I couldn't be there."

Sadie took a breath and then a chance. "Is everything okay?" she asked. "I keep wondering if something happened while I was at lunch with Rodger—you left so suddenly."

He was quiet again, but she remembered Pete's advice about not pushing him and waited for him to speak on his own. "I'm sorry, Sadie, I know you came all the way out here to help me, but I just can't do this anymore. I have a family, a life, and my mother was never a part of it. I can't make her a part of it now. With Shots coming for the contents of her apartment, it's pretty much done anyway, but I can't help anymore. I need to stay focused on my own family right now."

Focused on his family. Did he mean attentive to one of his daughters who had a relationship with Wendy that he didn't approve of? And was he stepping out of dealing with Wendy's estate *completely*?

Sadie hadn't missed that amid his explanation there was no answer to her question of what had happened while she was at lunch. "I have great respect for the care you take of your family, Ji, and while I realize that you don't know me very well, I didn't come to San Francisco to just go through Wendy's apartment. I had hoped to connect with you, and something changed while I was at lunch. I noticed you were going through the box of papers I'd found before you left, and I can't help but wonder if you came across something . . . upsetting. Whatever it is, we can talk about it. I want to—"

"I really need to get back to work, Sadie, I'm sorry." The surprising softness in his voice—rather than annoyance, which would have been warranted—was laced with regret. The fact that he'd still sidestepped her question pretty much convinced her that he *had* discovered something while she was at lunch, but she also realized that she didn't want to push any harder. Not like this. Not until there was more certainty.

"I understand. I'm sorry to have interrupted," she said with the same level of humility he'd shown in his tone. "Thanks for everything."

"Thank you, too," Ji responded.

She wanted some kind of commitment that they would speak again or see each other before she left, but it felt out of place for her to ask. She also thought about the funeral arrangements they had never discussed, but that felt even more out of place to bring up in light of him stepping away.

"Bye," Ji said a moment before the line went dead.

She hung up and looked at Pete, who was leaning against the wall with his arms crossed over his chest. She hadn't noticed him come in, but saw past him to a dolly now parked just outside the office doorway.

"No luck?" Pete asked.

"No," Sadie said, putting the phone on the desk. "But I'm more certain than ever that something other than the restaurant is what motivated Ji to leave. Maybe it was something in this box or maybe it was something else, but I asked him about it twice and he didn't admit or deny anything, just ignored the questions."

"Not quite a confession," Pete reminded her.

"No, but an *indication*," Sadie replied. "I see you found the dolly." Pete glanced over his shoulder as though to confirm the dolly was still there. "Jason in apartment two let me into a supply closet on the second floor. He also saw an Asian girl a few times between Christmas and April but never spoke to her; he'd assumed she was from one of the services Wendy had hired. She carried a black messenger bag and wore well-worn black Converse sneakers. Do you remember the shoes Ji's daughters were wearing yesterday?"

Sadie shook her head a split-second before a knock on the apartment door interrupted them. Pete pushed off from the wall to answer it. Sadie assumed that Shots and his crew must have arrived early but then realized Ji's friends would need to be buzzed in.

"Well, hello again," Pete said.

Sadie sat up a little straighter, then stood and headed into the common area.

A woman with pink hair and an equally pink kimono breezed past him in the doorway, giving him a coy smile in the process. This must be Shasta Winterberg, the pink lady of the 22nd Street condos.

"Hello there, Mr. Wonderful."

Sadie stepped more fully into the kitchen area so she could get a better look at this tenant she'd heard so much about. Her position gave her a clear view of the long wink the woman gave Pete before seeing Sadie and crossing to her. She held a pink poodle in her arms—pink! Even though Pete had told Sadie about the dog, it was startling all the same. How did you turn a dog pink? Were there such things as dog colorists? Sadie looked from the dog to the woman's heavily made-up face that did not disguise her years and smiled politely.

"Um, hi," Sadie said, putting out her hand. "I'm Sadie."

"Wendy's sister, right?" the woman said, putting out her hand—complete with bright pink nails—and barely squeezing Sadie's before petting her dog, which looked around the room with the same casual attitude this woman had. "I'm Shasta Winterberg."

"It's very nice to meet you."

"You too," Shasta said, still scoping out the apartment. Her eyes settled on the saw in the middle of the floor before moving on to the boxes and bags stacked against the wall. "I met this boy toy of yours yesterday, " she said to Sadie while waving toward Pete, who lifted his eyebrows in pleased surprise. "I've decided, out of respect for your sister's passing, not to try to steal him away, though I'm quite sure I could." She gave Pete another wink.

Pete smiled back, then, when she looked away, he sent Sadie a look that seemed to ask whether he should play this up or not—but clearly he was having fun.

Sadie wasn't sure how to answer. "Oh, well, thanks for not taking him away from me," she said to Shasta, uncertain if this woman was joking or not.

Without asking permission, Shasta walked into the bedroom. Sadie and Pete exchanged a look before following her. Shasta stood in the doorway of the bathroom, surveying the unfinished room—though it was coming along nicely—while petting her dog, then looked at Sadie. "Do you know when Mario plans to be finished with this?"

"We have until the tenth to have the apartment cleared," Sadie said, trying not to sound defensive. Everyone was in such a hurry to move on.

Shasta drew her mouth down into a pout, causing her chin to wrinkle in a way that showed why most women refrained from making such a face in the first place. "That long? I was hoping it would be done sooner."

"*You* were hoping?" Sadie repeated. "Why?"

Shasta turned her frown into a wide smile that showed high quality dentures. "This is the biggest apartment in the building— *two* bedrooms." She looked around the bedroom again. "She's had all this room to herself for far too long."

Sadie was confused, but she felt a picture coming together in her mind. "What do you mean 'far too long'?" If Sadie repeated the phrase too many times in her mind, it sounded like motive.

Shasta flashed her another Polident smile. "Didn't Stephen tell you? I'm moving in just as soon as you guys clear out and I can get my painters in to spruce it up." She stepped past Sadie and Pete, who were standing just outside the bedroom door, and walked to the large bay windows of the living room—the bedroom view was better, but this one was nice too. "Just look at that, Annie," she said in a wistful tone, petting the dog again. "Can you believe it's finally ours?" She turned away from the window, the fabric of her kimono swishing with the movement. She gave Pete another flirty smile. "You sure you don't want to stay here with me, Mr. Wonderful? There's room enough for two, you know."

CHAPTER 20

*I*s *this woman seriously hitting on my fiancé right in front of me?* Sadie thought before trying to focus on the fact that Shasta was the new tenant moving in.

Pete laughed, and Sadie turned to him in surprise until realizing that he had likely decided to play along with the flirtation. In terms of the investigation, Sadie could see it was probably the right move, but that didn't mean she liked it.

"Careful, Shasta," Pete said playfully. "I might call your bluff."

"Oh, I'm not bluffing."

Sadie cleared her throat, casting a reproachful look at Pete, who raised one eyebrow at her as though in challenge. He didn't have to play along *that* well.

"So, um, you've wanted this apartment for a while?" Sadie asked, her head tingling for multiple reasons.

"The first and second floor only have one-bedroom apartments, but the top floor has this one—the only two-bedroom—and number six is a studio." Shasta waved her hand through the air for what seemed to be no particular reason other than to keep Pete and Sadie's attention. "I moved in just a year or so after Wendy did, with

196

the promise that as soon as she moved out I would have first dibs on this place. I had no idea I'd have to wait this long. Her type rarely stays in one place very long, you know."

"Her type?" Pete asked before Sadie could say it herself.

Shasta gave another knowing smile. "Bohemian."

"What do you mean by that, exactly?" Pete folded his arms across his chest before leaning against the counter. Was it just Sadie's imagination or was he holding his shoulders a little higher than usual? He cocked his head slightly to the side and had a casual look of curiosity on his face. Sadie looked between him and Shasta, who was walking toward him and looking very pleased by his attention.

"She was flighty but had lived well enough to want nice things. I know she'd relied on men for her security, but upon losing her looks she was being forced to settle down and stake a claim. I felt sure she'd spend whatever money she'd managed to squirrel away soon enough and, without a new sugar daddy, she'd have to scramble over the bridge to Sausalito for something more *affordable*." She said "affordable" under her breath, like it was a dirty word. She twirled her hand through the air again. "But like I said, she surprised all of us. I couldn't believe Stephen didn't force her out with increases in rent, but then I learned about the addendum to her contract. What a fool he made himself out to be with that."

"A rental addendum?" Pete said. "What kind?"

"Oh, it is so ridiculous." Shasta rolled her eyes and scratched her dog's head again. Sadie felt sure the dog was medicated; it was too tranquil. "He agreed to raise her rent only one-half a percent a year, regardless of how long she stayed in the apartment." She let out a disgusted sigh and shook her head before eyeing the kitchen with a disapproving expression.

"But that wasn't the same agreement the rest of you had?" Pete asked.

"The rest of us have whatever the allowable increase is from year to year—assessed on the anniversary of our move-in month. From my calculations, Wendy was paying nearly eight hundred dollars *less* a month for her two-bedroom than I was for my single." Shasta huffed through her nose and shook her head indignantly. "Ridiculous."

Pete stole her attention back. "Why would the landlord make a different agreement with her than with anyone else?"

"He said it was because the apartment had been hard to rent—housing was in a slump at the time or something like that. However, I'm sure he learned his lesson and will never do that again, seeing as how ungracious Wendy was about his accommodations and how long she stayed."

Shasta wandered into the kitchen, running her hand over the tiled countertop. From her frown, there was something about it she didn't approve of. Or maybe it was a reaction to the drywall dust covering everything. She rubbed her manicured fingers together.

"Can I ask how you knew about the rental agreement?" Pete said, confirming to Sadie that he was absolutely playing a role in order to garner new information. Sadie had told him that Jason claimed Shasta and Wendy had been friends at some point. Pete was playing up his ignorance of that in order to build trust and make Shasta feel important. No way Stephen Pilings told Shasta about that deal—though she'd obviously confronted him about it at some point. The only other person who could have told her about the agreement was Wendy herself.

Shasta didn't respond right away. Instead, she let her eyes travel up the wall as though measuring its height. "Well, there was a time when you could have said that Wendy and I were friends, but, well, in time I simply couldn't abide it any longer. We're of a different class of people, she and I." She glanced at Sadie. "No offense."

Sadie smiled to imply that she wasn't offended, even though she was.

"And it was during that time that she told you about the agreement?" Pete asked, keeping them all on track.

Shasta nodded.

"What brought your friendship to an end?" Pete asked.

Shasta shrugged. "I'm sure I can't remember the final straw. She tended to make petty comments about people and things; she criticized my sense of style and taste in art more than once. Sometimes we'd get lunch or go to a show; other times she'd stand me up for an event and then act put out when I asked her why she hadn't bothered to tell me. Eventually I came to realize that the root of Wendy's problems was that she simply hated people. She didn't care how she made people feel, and she didn't mind when she inconvenienced them. I was a matter of convenience to her, that's all. Like everyone else in her life, I suppose."

Pete lifted his eyebrows, and Sadie shuddered at the idea of the people in Wendy's life being matters of convenience. It was an interesting way to say it, but Sadie could see the truth of it—hadn't Wendy discarded everyone once they were no longer convenient for her to have close by?

"Well, she hated dogs too," Shasta added, dropping her head to kiss her pink poodle's fluffy pompadour. She looked up again. "She told Stephen that my Annie piddled in the hallway, which was a complete fabrication, of course. Tried to get a no-pet policy in the building until she realized that I would be grandfathered in regardless of whether the rest of the building agreed to her petition. Then she left chocolate bars out on the grass strip—knowing that chocolate would make my Annie sick if she ate any of it. Basically, she was a nightmare." She looked toward Sadie and gave another of her insulting grins. "No offense, dear."

"Oh, Sadie didn't have anything to do with her sister," Pete said casually. "She understands better than most how hard she was to deal with."

"Oh, really?" Shasta said, appraising Sadie in a new way. "I can't say I'm surprised. Like I said, she hated everyone—and it seems I was right that *everyone* hated her back." She turned to take another look out the front windows and bent down to whisper something to her dog in the process.

With the woman's back turned, Sadie narrowed her eyes at Pete as playfully as she could before jumping back into the conversation.

"Did Wendy ever have any visitors that you know of?" Sadie asked.

Shasta turned and lifted one penciled-in eyebrow. "I did not keep track of who came and went from her place." There was a touch of indignation in her voice, as though the idea of knowing who came to visit Wendy was beneath her.

Pete was unfazed by her response and pushed forward with a question of his own. "The prior tenant in number six saw a Chinese girl coming to see Wendy a few times. Do you know anything about that?"

"A Chinese girl coming to see Wendy? Was she bringing take-out?" Shasta laughed at her own joke, and Sadie and Pete both kept their smiles on, though Sadie could tell that Pete's enjoyment of this conversation was waning, too.

"So you didn't see her?" Sadie asked.

Shasta scratched her dog's head. "I may have," she said, look-ing thoughtful. "Like I said, I'm not one to track the comings and goings of the other people in this building. Not like Wendy, who loved to keep track of people so she could cause trouble, like her terrible treatment of my Annie." She nuzzled the dog's head again.

"You must have been excited when the apartment became available." Pete asked, surprising Sadie with his candid question and the fact that he wasn't pursuing the Chinese granddaughter angle a bit longer.

"Oh my, yes," Shasta said with a smile, lifting her chin. "After exercising such patience for so long, I finally attained my goal. Two bedrooms is hard to come by, did I mention that already?"

"It doesn't bother you that Wendy died here?" Sadie couldn't help but ask.

Shasta blinked at her, leading Sadie to believe that she was just now thinking about that. "Well, of course, that is unfortunate, but, well, no one lives forever."

"She may have been murdered," Sadie added, ignoring the look Pete shot at her. "Does that bother you?"

"Murdered? No, no, no," Shasta said emphatically, shaking her head so that her baby pink hair shifted slightly, but not much. Hairspray. "She died of natural causes."

"And what do you think of the fire?" Sadie asked. "Seems an odd coincidence, doesn't it?"

Shasta looked away from them, but took her time formulating an answer, which made Sadie wonder if she were looking for the perfect words. "The police said it was a burglary. The robbers must have found her in the tub and thought they'd get blamed for that, right? So they tried to burn the whole building down. It's a wonder we all didn't go up in smoke." She shuddered and stroked her dog again. "It was absolutely terrifying."

"I'll bet," Pete said while Sadie clenched her jaw to keep from saying something rude. This was all about Shasta; no consideration for Wendy's death. "Did you see anything out of the ordinary the night of the fire?"

"I didn't see anything or anyone," she said, then let out a dramatic sigh. "The police asked me all about that already, you know. Whoever did it was in and out before the rest of us even knew what was happening."

Mario returned from lunch and quickly ducked into the bedroom after they all exchanged hellos—except for Shasta, who just watched him as though suspicious of his being there. He closed the bedroom door behind him.

Sadie's phone chimed a text message, and she was surprised at how relieved she felt to have an excuse to leave the room. She made her apologies and returned to the office. The text was from Jack, asking how things were going.

She replied simply that things were fine, and she'd give him a call later that night with a more detailed update, but that she could use his help in deciding what to do about Wendy's body. He said he'd look into some funeral homes in the area, and they could talk about it that night. Sadie was relieved to have at least one thing taken off her list and thanked him for the help.

After finishing the texted conversation, Sadie turned back to the box still in need of being sorted but only stared into it for minute, increasingly annoyed that no one had noticed Wendy was gone. No one cared enough to check on her and, though Sadie had cycled through those thoughts a dozen times, they still bothered her—redundant or not. Rodger had been relieved that Wendy wasn't calling anymore. Shasta was excited to get the bigger apartment. Surely Mr. Pilings was relieved to not have to deal with Wendy's complaints.

And Sadie? Was Sadie also relieved not to worry about what she could do to have a relationship with her sister? In the back of her mind she'd always hoped to have a relationship with Wendy—maybe through resolving some personality defect in herself or discovering some kind of support she could offer to open the possibility of having a *real* sister. Was she relieved that she no longer had to wonder what she could do because any chance of progress was no longer possible? Sadie hated that thought, hated how true it might be. And yet she wasn't feeling relieved about anything right now. She was as steeped in the stress caused by her sister as she'd ever been.

She shook herself out of yet another train of convoluted thought and forced herself to focus on the new information they'd learned from Shasta: the rental addendum. She wished she had the police files here so she could verify the terms, but since the files *weren't* here, she had to add it to a growing mental list of all she would need to look into back at the hotel.

She began sorting the final contents of the box and could see the bottom of the tub in some places when Pete finished talking to Shasta and showed her out.

"She is somethin'," Pete said when he came into the office.

"Something as in 'something awesome' or 'something weird'?" Sadie asked.

Pete laughed. "I don't think there's room in Shasta's life for a relationship with anyone other than Annie. But she's interesting to talk to all the same."

"Did you learn anything new?"

"Only that Shasta is indeed an heiress. Her grandfather held stock in the company that became Xerox, and she receives payments from a trust. She's quite proud of the fact that she's never worked a day in her life, other than some movie sets she worked on when she was younger. 'Glorious days,' she called them. 'Magnificent!'"

Sadie shook her head and picked up another stack of paper. "That woman epitomizes the word *diva*."

"Yes, she does," Pete said. "How are things going?"

"I'm almost done here," Sadie said. "There's really nothing left to do other than clean it up." She threw some more junk mail into the garbage but added a charge card receipt from Neiman Marcus to the stack of them she'd been growing. That's probably where Wendy bought all those fantastic shoes that part of Sadie still wanted to keep for herself. "Oh, we might want to bring the boxes I stacked by the living room window in here so they don't accidentally get donated. They're items I want to take back to the hotel."

"Okay," Pete said. A chime from his pocket indicated that he'd received a text message. He busied himself with his phone while Sadie finished sorting the last of the papers in the bin: a grocery store receipt, a magazine advertisement for a pair of boots, and a partially completed credit card application. Sadie looked at her sister's handwriting for a few seconds—she had beautiful penmanship—then put the application on a stack of other miscellaneous financials. Pete continued his text conversation while Sadie paper clipped the different stacks of paper together, then put them in a whiskey box.

Pete slid the phone into his pocket at the same moment that Sadie closed the top of the box. She brushed her hand across the cardboard and scanned the nearly empty room. "I can't quite wrap my head around the fact that I've just managed to condense someone's entire life into half a dozen boxes. Her whole life—sixty-odd years—and this is what's left. It feels so wrong."

Sadie looked up to see a pained expression cross Pete's face, confusing her. "What's wrong?"

"Nothing," he said, but then he turned and walked out of the room.

Sadie paused a moment before following him into the kitchen. She put a hand on his arm, and he stopped, then looked at her over his shoulder.

"What did I say?" she asked. She recognized this tension—it was very similar to what she'd felt from him last night in regard to his memories of Pat and the hesitation about selling his house.

"Nothing, really. No big deal." Pete took a breath, but when Sadie didn't let him off the hook, his shoulders slumped slightly and he explained his reaction. "I told Brooke about the offer on the house, and she's kind of upset about it."

"Upset as in angry?" Sadie dropped her hand but kept looking at him.

"No," Pete said, shaking his head. "Just . . . sad, I guess. She understands why I'm selling it, but her mother took her final breaths in that house and then . . ." He glanced past Sadie into the office, and she put two and two together.

"And then I commented on boxing up someone's life." If they accepted the offer on Pete's house, everything left of Pat's life would be packed up and stored, or given or thrown away.

Pete glanced at Sadie, then at the floor as he pushed his hands into his pockets. "I don't know why this is getting so hard now."

"For Brooke or for you?" Sadie tried not to let her hurt feelings show in her tone. She understood why he felt this way—she really did—but she hated it. She wanted to think about the future—*their* future—and he continued to get into the past—*his* past.

He didn't answer her right away, but she waited him out. "Things are changing," he said, as though it were that simple.

"In big ways," she added. When he didn't comment, she pushed forward, watching him closely as she spoke. "Do you want to talk about it?"

He gave her a questioning look. "Is this really something we can discuss?"

Sadie thought about that and, though she wanted to say yes, was she really prepared to talk to him about his dead wife, about how much he missed her, and how conflicted he was feeling about moving on with his life in a way he never imagined?

He'd told Sadie before that he'd had no expectation of dating or marrying again after Pat died; he was almost sixty years old at the time and could not imagine a life with anyone but her. Sadie was the first and only woman he'd felt attracted to or connected to since Pat's death, and he was surprised by how natural and right everything had felt between them. Up until this trip, that was the singular impression Sadie had of Pete's thoughts on the matter: he hadn't expected to love again and was happy to have been wrong.

But now they were in this city and someone wanted to buy the last home he'd shared with Pat. Sadie couldn't lie—to Pete or to herself—about the fact that this was uncomfortable or that she might even feel threatened, as much as she hated the idea that she could be. Pete needed a friend, he needed to talk things out, and though she wanted to be everything for him—could she be? Could she handle it?

They held each other's gaze, and Sadie saw the growing look of disappointed understanding take over Pete's expression. Though she'd said nothing out loud, just as he'd tried to keep his thoughts to himself, both of their internal processes were loud enough for the other to hear. He was struggling with memories of his wife. Sadie was unprepared to help him deal with them. They found themselves at a proverbial impasse that brought with it a river's worth of insecurity and a thimble's worth of resolution.

The intercom buzzed; Sadie was the first to break eye contact and accept the fortuitous change of topic. She lightened her tone as further indication that they were talking about something new as she moved toward the intercom. "That must be Ji's friend. His name is Shots, can you believe that?" She said hello through the speaker.

It was indeed the Chinese share house that would clear out the last of Wendy's things. She buzzed them in, then turned back to Pete, who, she could tell, was trying to find an explanation that would make her feel better about what he'd just admitted. She wasn't sure which of them she was rescuing by not allowing him to attempt it. "Will you help me move the boxes I want to keep into the office?"

Pete looked at her, regret in his eyes, but finally turned away and looked at the boxes still by the window. "Sure."

Sadie was already heading toward the boxes of shoes and photographs. She picked up the top box and turned toward the office. "I'll label everything so we know what's what. I have a Sharpie in my purse for just this type of situation." Pete grabbed another box and followed her into the office, where they put the boxes down on the far end of the room, near the window. Sadie began labeling the top and sides while Pete moved the rest of the boxes and the landscape painting Sadie was still unsure about.

"I'm going to move Mario's saw out of the way," Pete said when he finished, leaving Sadie alone with her internal pity party.

Wasn't it enough that she was clearing out her sister's apartment? Wasn't it enough that she had discovered very few positive things about this sister she'd never really known? Was it fair that she had to figure out how to navigate through Pete's complex feelings, too?

Sadie let herself feel sorry for herself until the boxes were labeled and Shots came in—with perfect English and a playful grin. Three Chinese men of various ages came in behind him. Pete introduced

Sadie and himself, pointed out the boxes in the office that the men weren't supposed to take, and then turned them loose.

As soon as the men had left the apartment for their first trip down, Sadie remembered the nude painting of Wendy. She went into the bedroom and looked at it only long enough to determine how she was going to get it to the Dumpster. She angled the canvas against the dresser and brought her foot down on the inner frame, snapping it in the middle. She snapped the other side, folded the painted sides together, and then carried it down the stairs. She felt bad for having destroyed Wendy's work, but she didn't want anyone else to stare at her naked sister. She felt better once it was in the Dumpster and she was on her way back upstairs.

Forty-five minutes later, two of the men carried the last piece of Wendy's furniture—the desk from the office—from the place Wendy had called home for the last twelve years of her life. Pete and Shots had taken down the headboard as well, and hadn't come back yet. The small elevator had turned out to be a struggle for some of the larger pieces, but they'd eventually made everything fit.

Mario's music was playing in the bathroom, reminding Sadie of how soon the remodel would be done. Once the apartment was painted to Shasta's tastes, Wendy would be entirely removed from this building—not even a nail hole left behind to tell the world she was ever here. Sadie looked around the empty rooms, finding it impossible not to give into the heartache she felt at the completion of this task. Maybe *this* feeling was exactly what Pete was afraid of in regard to selling his house—the emptiness, the proof that someone who once mattered was no longer there. Maybe Sadie understood it better than she thought. Better than she wanted to.

CHAPTER 21

Sadie heard Pete enter the apartment, and before he said anything, she cut him off. She didn't want another apology. "You said you read the statement from Mr. Pilings earlier?" she asked.

He paused for a beat before shaking his head. "It wasn't really a statement, just the notes about the conversation the police had with him when he showed up after the fire and then in a follow-up phone call."

"Did he say anything about the rental addendum Shasta mentioned?"

Pete shook his head again.

"Someone ought to ask him why he left that out," Sadie said, then let out a breath and felt her shoulders fall. Her mind moved on to the next unsettled item. "What do we do about Ji's daughter?"

"I was thinking about that and wondered if we ought to go to his restaurant tonight. His daughters were working yesterday, so maybe they're there again. We might be able to determine which daughter it was, and then maybe we can figure out how to ask Ji about it. Maybe us being there will coax more information from him. We have to remember that he doesn't have a lot of reason to trust people associated with his mother."

Sadie considered that and then nodded. She didn't want to upset Ji with direct questions unless she was sure, but going to his restaurant for dinner was a good cover for learning a bit more about his daughters. "Maybe talking to him in his own space would make him more comfortable," she said. Plus, she'd liked the dim sum, and she and Pete had been in a good place—relationship-wise—when they'd eaten there yesterday. "But on the phone he made it sound as though he didn't really want to see me again."

"If something happened while you were gone today, there might be an explanation for him giving that impression. I think if we act as though nothing has changed, he'll go along with it—or perhaps give something away. Plus, we can see if his daughters or his wife accidentally gives us information, as well. I think it's worth the risk."

Sadie thought about that. "That makes sense. I can play that up." She smiled at him, and Pete smiled back, a slightly hesitant and vulnerable look on his face. Sadie thought he was going to say something—worried he was going to say something—and so she hurried past him to get her purse from where she'd left it in the office. She put the strap over her head and then looked at the boxes still waiting to be taken to the hotel. She felt her shoulders slump. She wanted to be done.

She heard Pete come into the room behind her. "We need to take these with us," she said without looking at him. He was so close that she could lean back, just a little, and they would be touching. But she didn't lean back. She didn't know if he'd welcome it or what she'd do if he didn't.

"Why don't we take them down with the dolly? You can wait

with them while I bring the car around—like we did with the file boxes yesterday."

"That's a good idea," Sadie said, finally meeting his eyes. He held her gaze, and she could see the same hesitation she had to talk about uncomfortable things.

"We'd better get going," Pete finally said, stepping away and checking his watch. "Traffic will be a nightmare."

Choy's was busy, and Lin Yang didn't treat them as though she recognized them. Instead, she showed them to an empty table and put down the dinner menus, which were exactly like the lunch menus. She spoke in the same clipped and efficient speech she used for everyone. A younger daughter was running the cash register tonight. Min was nowhere in sight, and Sadie worried that she wasn't there. Pete and Sadie had ruled out the eleven-year-old as the possible granddaughter seen at Wendy's building, leaving just the older two as possibilities, though Sadie's money was still on Min.

The daughter working the register was wearing black ballet flats, not the Converse sneakers they were looking for. But surely she had more than one pair of shoes; it was silly to think they'd be able to identify which daughter had been there by her shoes alone.

Pete ordered for them again, some of the same things they'd had yesterday but a few different items as well; they skipped the ribs. Each time the door to the kitchen opened, Sadie tried to get a glimpse of who was working back there, in hopes of spotting Min, but the angle wasn't good. They finished their dim sum having only seen Lin Yang and the middle daughter.

When Lin Yang brought them their check, Sadie asked if her daughters were working tonight, as though she didn't see the girl at the register.

"Min is working in the back; Pengma is at my sister's. She's only here in the morning." She waved toward the register. "That is Sonia. Pay at the register."

Pete and Sadie shared a now-what look as Lin Yang moved quickly away from their table. Sadie had thought that Lin Yang would want to show off her girls, but clearly not.

"That didn't turn out, did it?" Sadie said as she set her napkin on her empty plate. She pushed away from the table before noticing someone coming toward them from the direction of the kitchen. Sadie looked up to see Ji looking sharp in an all-black chef's jacket and matching pants. He had a black cap on his head as well, making him look very official. Sadie stayed in her seat and smiled up at him.

"Your dinner was good?" he asked when he came to a stop beside their table.

"Excellent," Pete said. "Some of the best dim sum I've ever had."

"I'm glad to hear that," Ji said with a nod. He had his hands clasped behind his back, which forced him into a rather formal stance. "Shots came for everything?"

"Yes," Sadie confirmed. "He was great. Thank you for setting that up."

Pete ate the final dumpling and laid his chopsticks next to his plate.

"Now you two can return to Colorado." Ji looked between them. "The wedding is coming up quickly, isn't it?"

Sadie felt a tightness in her chest at the mention of the wedding. She knew she was overreacting to think that the tension she and Pete continued to feel on this trip meant that the wedding was off, and yet the fear was there. She looked at her engagement ring, which had always brought a zing of excitement when she caught sight of the diamond sparkling in the light. It was plenty sparkly beneath the over-bright lights of the restaurant, but the zing fizzled. She didn't know what to expect—sooner or later she and Pete would have to talk about everything again. What would come of that conversation?

"Three weeks," Pete answered for her.

"It's good the apartment was cleared out so quickly then. I'm sure you have a lot to do to get ready."

"Our flight doesn't leave until Sunday," Sadie said, wondering if he would suggest they see each other before she and Pete had to leave.

"Ah, well, then you have a day to enjoy the sights. I'm glad I was able to meet you both. Thank you for coming in so we could say good-bye."

"I hope we can stay in touch," Sadie offered. She didn't mean to sound desperate but wanted to make sure he knew she hoped their relationship would continue after she left his city.

"Certainly. Stop by if you come to San Francisco again."

Ouch. If that wasn't a "Don't call me, I'll call you" answer, Sadie didn't know what was. The door to the kitchen opened and Lin Yang came out. She looked at Ji and said something in Chinese, sounding snappish, like always. Ji looked over his shoulder and responded just as bluntly. He'd barely finished speaking when Lin Yang countered, earning a short response from Ji before he turned back to the table and attempted a polite smile, though his jaw was tight. "I need to get back to work. Your dinner is on the house tonight."

Pete lifted his eyebrows. "Oh, we fully intended to pay for—"

"I insist," he cut in, bowing slightly at the waist and taking the check Lin Yang had set down earlier. He slid it into the pocket of his jacket. "Enjoy the rest of your trip."

Sadie and Pete both thanked him, then watched him return to the kitchen. The door swung shut behind him but as it swung back, Min came out carrying a plastic tub. She came directly to their table, bowed slightly and began gathering plates, stealing glances at Sadie in the process. Sadie automatically looked at Min's shoes: worn black Converse sneakers. She caught Pete's eye before nodding toward the floor and then smiling at Min.

"How are you, Min?" Sadie asked.

"I'm good," Min said, gathering more plates. "Did you enjoy your dim sum?"

"It was excellent," Sadie said. She hurried to think of something that would keep Min talking. "Your father tells me you're going into engineering."

Min shrugged, glancing at Sadie in an appraising way. Sadie had seen the same look on Ji's and Rodger's faces when she'd met them and felt sure that Min was mentally comparing Sadie's face to Wendy's. Sadie let her look.

"You live in Colorado?" Min asked after a few seconds.

"The northern part," Sadie said. "A small town called Garrison."

"That's cool," Min said, but not as though she really thought it was cool, more in the sense of wanting to say something. She opened her mouth to say something else but was cut off by words from her mother, who was serving a group at the next table. The people she was serving jumped at the sharpness of her tone, and Min's mouth tightened the slightest bit, the only outward indication of what she was likely feeling on the inside. She bowed slightly toward Sadie and then to Pete as well. "I need to get back into the kitchen. Nice to see you again."

"You too," Pete and Sadie said at the same time as Min turned and went into the kitchen. A few dishes remained on their table, but Sadie knew Min hadn't come out to clear their table. It had been an excuse to get a final look at Sadie—her grandmother's sister.

"It's her," Sadie said under her breath.

Pete nodded.

A group of three came into the restaurant, and Lin Yang sat them at the only open table. She scowled at Pete and Sadie, giving Sadie the impression that she wanted them to leave so that their table could be available. Pete seemed to agree because he stood, putting his napkin—and a generous tip—on the table.

On their way out, Sadie glanced into the glass case, where two of Ji's jewelry boxes lay on the bottom shelf. He'd said something yesterday about not making any more. Sadie hoped he'd change his mind about that. Talents and passions were what made life worth living when the burden of existence became heavy.

"Don't forget your fortune cookie."

Sadie looked up at Ji's middle daughter, Sonia. Sadie and Pete made the slight detour to the basket of individually wrapped fortune cookies. Sadie pulled one out from the middle of the basket. "Thank you." Pete grabbed one as well.

"Thank you for coming to Choy's," the girl said. She looked more like her mother than Min did, but Sadie could still see Ji in her features as well.

Sadie smiled and carefully tore open the thin plastic wrapper.

"You guys sure do a great job here," Pete said, waving toward the restaurant and seeming in no hurry to leave. "It's some of the best dim sum I've ever had."

"Thank you," Sonia said with that same nod of her head that Ji, Min, and Lin Yang had all made at one point or another. She flickered her eyes to Sadie, but although she was obviously curious, Sadie didn't see the same comparing look on Sonia's face as she'd seen on Min's. "You're my father's aunt?" she asked. She flicked a glance toward her mother, who had her back to them as she passed out water glasses and teacups.

"Yes, my name is Sadie." She smiled in a let's-be-friends kind of way. "And you're Sonia?"

The girl nodded, seemingly pleased by the attention.

"And you're thirteen?" Sadie asked. She was aware of Pete standing back from them, opening his cookie and allowing Sadie to conduct this line of questioning.

"Fourteen in October," Sonia said proudly.

"That's wonderful. I meant to ask Min, but did you ever meet your father's mother? My sister."

Sonia glanced toward the tables again, and Sadie dared a look over her shoulder. Lin Yang must have gone into the kitchen. Sonia looked back at Sadie and shook her head.

"Did your sisters ever meet her?"

Sonia shook her head again. "*Ba ba* told us she wasn't very nice." She glanced at Sadie quickly, and her cheeks flushed pink.

"He was right, she wasn't very nice," Sadie said, smiling to show she wasn't offended. She heard the kitchen door open and suspected Lin Yang was back, but likely with plates she needed to take to customers, buying Sadie a little more time. "Did he have any pictures of her at your house?" Sadie wanted to confirm that it wasn't through a photo that Min was making her comparison. Any bit of validation would help at this point.

"No, ma'am," Sonia said. "I've never seen a picture of her." She looked past Sadie and straightened slightly before lowering her eyes demurely. "I need to get back to work, ma'am."

"Of course," Sadie said, stepping back from the counter and certain she could feel Lin Yang glaring at them. She held up her fortune cookie and smiled. "Thanks again."

"You're welcome."

Pete pushed the door open for her a few seconds later and then kept it open for a group of businessmen heading inside. One of the men asked his opinion on the restaurant. After Pete said it was excellent, the man asked for a suggestion on what to order. While Sadie waited for Pete, she broke her cookie in half and pulled out the paper.

A hunch is creativity trying to tell you something.

When Pete had finished playing doorstop and restaurant critic, he joined her near the green dragon statue. She handed him her fortune and he read it.

"Huh," he said, handing it back to her. He held up his already-read fortune with flourish and cleared his throat dramatically. "'Go take a rest. You deserve it,'" he read, then sighed. "I get the worst fortunes. Yours are pretty good, though."

Sadie read hers again.

"So what's your hunch at the moment?" Pete asked.

Sadie was a bit startled by the question, but she considered it seriously. *Did* she have a hunch at the moment? After a few seconds, she looked up at Pete. "I think Min will talk to me if I can get her alone."

Pete smiled and tucked his fortune into his shirt pocket while Sadie slid hers into the front pocket of her purse alongside her fortune from yesterday. "I think you're right."

CHAPTER 22

Pete looked up and down the street, then put his hand on Sadie's arm before heading to the left of the restaurant. "There's got to be an alley behind Choy's, right?"

"Probably," she said. "Why?"

He scanned the line of buildings ahead of them on Sacramento Street. "I can't think of anywhere else we might be able to catch her. Ji and his family live above the restaurant, so it's not like we'll catch her on her way home after her shift. But people are always coming and going in the back, right?" He met Sadie's eyes. "I saw how she looked at you; she knew Wendy—and then Sonia didn't seem to know Wendy at all."

Sadie was impressed that he'd followed what she was doing so perfectly, though she knew it shouldn't have surprised her.

They turned the corner, and Pete spied the entrance to an alley that ran behind the row of buildings. He picked up the pace, and Sadie hurried to keep up with him. The alleyway was narrow and dark—creepy—so Sadie stayed close to Pete until it opened up onto a street between the buildings that rose three or four stories.

There were laundry lines stretching between buildings and

Dumpsters lining the brick exteriors on either side. Cars were parallel parked, leaving just enough room for a garbage truck—at least, Sadie hoped there was enough room for a garbage truck. It would be a tight fit.

On the ground level, there were doors marked with Chinese characters, and sometimes English words, that indicated what business they belonged to. Several people were coming and going from different establishments. Pete told her to stand straight, don't look around too much, and try to look like they belonged there. As far as Sadie could tell, they were the only white people, but everyone was going about their business and not paying them any attention.

They found the door to Choy's, and Pete and Sadie hid on the side of a nearby Dumpster set a foot or so away from the wall. The gap gave them a good view of the doorway to Choy's, and the shadows of the building kept them well hidden. It stunk, but Sadie didn't comment about it. As far as stakeouts went, this wasn't too bad. She'd take stinky over long and boring, which is what most stakeouts were.

After nearly fifteen minutes, the door to Choy's opened, and both Sadie and Pete peeked through the space between the Dumpster and the wall, but it was just a young man throwing away a bag of garbage. They pulled back and he went inside. They remained hidden for another few minutes before the back door opened again. They only peeked long enough to identify Lin Yang talking on the phone before pulling back quickly. They listened as she spoke to someone in Chinese, her voice not as sharp as it had been when she talked to her family in the restaurant. Sadie wished she knew what Lin Yang was saying. At one point she laughed, which was a sound Sadie had never expected to hear from her. The door opened again.

Lin Yang's voice turned sharp, and a younger, softer voice conversed back and forth with her.

Pete took a turn peeking. When he came back, he mouthed "Min."

The door shut and everything went quiet. After a moment, they peeked around the side of the Dumpster to see if both women had gone back inside. Min, however, was sitting alone on a crate next to the back door, doing something on her phone. Pete and Sadie exchanged a look, and Pete nodded toward Sadie, indicating that she should go talk to her and that he would stay behind the Dumpster.

Sadie nodded—she didn't want Min to feel ambushed—and took a breath. She was just stepping out of the shadows when the back door opened again. She quickly stepped back into her hiding place, then looked at Pete with raised eyebrows when she heard Min giggle.

Together they crouched down and peered through the Dumpster-building gap again. Min had her arms up around the neck of the same boy who had taken out the trash earlier. Their foreheads were pressed together as they whispered about something. The boy's hands were at her waist, and then he leaned down and kissed her sweetly. Min looked around as though to make sure they were alone, but he pulled her closer to the wall—more in view of Sadie and Pete—and Min finally kissed him back.

Sadie moved away in order to give them some privacy, but Pete didn't until she slugged him in the shoulder. He turned to her with a goofy grin on his face, and Sadie rolled her eyes. "What do we do?" Sadie mouthed to him.

Pete shrugged, then reached for her and pulled her against him, quick and fast. Sadie pushed against his chest and shook her head.

This was not the time. They were behind a Dumpster, for heaven's sake.

The young couple continued to speak softly to each other, then went quiet for a few seconds before the door opened again. When Sadie peeked a second later, she saw that Min was alone, sitting on the crate and playing with her phone again. They hadn't missed their opportunity!

Sadie pushed away from grabby-fingers Pete and tried again—deep breath, shoulders back, step away from the Dumpster.

Min was the picture of innocence as Sadie approached and didn't look up from her phone until Sadie spoke. "Hi, Min."

The young woman startled and jumped to her feet. "Um, hi," she said. She slid the phone back into the pocket of her apron. "Uh, what are you doing here?"

"I wanted to talk to you."

"How long have you been out here?" Min asked nervously.

"What's your boyfriend's name?" Sadie had meant for the question to reflect that she was cool about the boyfriend but, at the expression on Min's face, she suspected that Min had taken the comment as a threat.

Min glanced at the door and then took a quick step toward Sadie. "Don't tell my dad," she said quickly. "Please?" The girl had more than one secret.

"He doesn't approve?"

Min let out a sigh. She shook her head and tears came to her eyes. "He wants me to marry a doctor or an engineer *after* I finish college."

"Ah," Sadie said with a sympathetic smile. "Am I to assume your boyfriend isn't on one of those professional pathways?"

Min frowned and Sadie worried she'd offended the girl. She

hurried to repair the mess she was making of this conversation. "I'm not going to tell your dad, Min," Sadie assured her. "How long have the two of you been dating?"

"We're not *dating*," Min said. Her shoulders dropped, and she let out a breath before looking past Sadie and blinking back the tears in her eyes. "My father won't allow it."

"So how long have you been sneaking kisses in the alley behind the restaurant?"

Min's cheeks turned pink, but she looked at the ground in humility. "Forever," she said quietly, the edge of tragic romance dripping from the single word that said so much. She looked up. "I'm twenty years old, you know. I can make my own decisions. My mother was only seventeen when my parents married."

Sadie was tempted to point out that Min's parents didn't seem that happily married and that was likely influencing them to want to create a different future for her. But that wasn't why she was here, and she didn't believe in forbidding kids from relationships unless that relationship was toxic, which Sadie didn't think was the case here. Not that she could really know after two minutes of observation, but still. "When you say you can make your own decisions, do you mean things like meeting your grandmother Wendy?"

Min paled in the evening light, which was quickly dimming, and when she spoke it was a shaky whisper. "You can't tell my dad about that, either."

That was a harder promise to make, but Sadie nodded all the same. She needed Min's confidence. Min sat back down on the crate and put her hands on her head, elbows on knees.

Sadie sat on a crate across from her and hoped it would support her. "Min?" she said after several seconds had passed. "I'm not here to get you in trouble, I just need to ask you a few questions, okay?"

Min looked up, tears still in her eyes. "How did you find out about Grandma Wendy?"

"Some of her neighbors saw you at her apartment building. When did you start going to see her?"

"She came into the restaurant last fall. I knew about her, but I'd never met her before." Her expression was hopeful, pleading, and slightly desperate for Sadie's understanding. "She was *so* cool."

Cool?

Min continued. "She invited me to visit her at her apartment and said she'd always wanted to know me better but that my dad was mad at her and kept her away from us. She said it would be our secret. And it was. They never found out."

They. Not just Ji.

"So, you met her here at the restaurant the first time, and then went to see her at her apartment after that?"

Min hesitated, and Sadie searched her mind for a plausible reason for these questions that Min could relate to. She settled on a version of the same excuse she'd given everyone else she'd talked to on this trip. "I didn't know my sister very well," Sadie said. "She left Colorado when she was very young and rarely came back to visit. She had a lot of problems, which is why your dad didn't want her around you guys, but she's gone now and I want to learn more about her. I'm glad she got to know you before she died." Sadie smiled sadly at the thought. "It must have made her really happy."

"It did," Min said quickly, nodding. "She loved having me come visit and help clean up the apartment. Everyone else she'd ever loved had abandoned her; even *Ba ba*—her own son—had nothing to do with her. It was so sad."

It didn't surprise Sadie that Wendy had lied to Min too. She lied to everyone, always making herself the victim, but a lie that damaged

Min's opinion of her father was a different level. "You said she came into the restaurant last fall? Do you know when, exactly?" The bank statements had showed that Wendy's spending habits changed from September to October. Sadie wanted to know on which side of that change Wendy's surprise visit to Ji's restaurant had occurred.

"It was the first part of October. My parents were at a school program for Pengma's class."

"And Wendy invited you to come to her place?"

Min nodded. "She had such a great apartment. It's on the third floor of this *awesome* building in Mission. She had really nice furniture, and you could see all the way out to the ocean through these big windows." She sighed dramatically. "She hadn't been feeling well and stuff was really messy when I first started going, but we got it cleaned up really well. Then we would talk and drink wine. She had such great insights about life."

Sadie clenched her teeth together. *Wine? Really, Wendy?* Min was twenty—almost of age—but it was still irresponsible to be seeing her behind her parents' back, never mind providing her with alcohol. "How often did you see her?"

"Every couple of weeks," Min said. "I didn't dare have her call me because my parents check my bill, so I would just stop in when I could. She was so lonely." Min frowned, making her look even younger. "I felt so bad for her and wished I could visit more often, but I couldn't risk my parents figuring things out."

Sadie considered the fact that Min had been the one keeping Wendy's apartment straightened up. "Did you by chance put a bunch of papers into a box in the closet?"

Min's cheeks pinked. "She didn't like to throw things away, but she'd let me put papers and things in the drawers of her desk or in boxes, but lots of times she'd pull everything out in between our visits. I put a bunch of stuff in that box, thinking she would forget about it and not pull it out. I guess you found it, huh? I know it was such a mess."

"You did an excellent job of taking care of her," Sadie said, wanting to reassure her that Sadie wasn't judging her for the contents of the box. She was just glad to know why it was there in the first place. "When was the last time you saw her?"

Fresh tears filled the girl's eyes. She swallowed and looked at the ground again. "She got really mad at me. I felt so bad and apologized, but when I went to see her next she wouldn't let me in the building. The next time I went she didn't even answer the buzzer. And then I found out she'd died and *then* Lok showed me an article about the fire in the paper." She wiped at her eyes and sniffled.

"What did she get mad at you for?"

Min took a breath, her shoulders rising in the process, and then let it out. "I didn't want to mail the letters anymore. But if I'd known how important it was to her I would have done it. I didn't realize what a big deal it was."

Sadie pulled her eyebrows together as the pink sealed envelope she'd found yesterday came to mind. "Letters?" she asked. "What letters?"

CHAPTER 23

Min wiped at her eyes again. "It was so dumb, I should have just kept doing it."

"Doing what? Mailing letters?"

Min nodded.

Sadie tensed in anticipation of what Min might say next. "Why did you mail letters for her? She had a mailbox in the lobby of her building."

"She said she liked them to be sent from Chinatown."

"Why?"

Min shrugged. "It was part of this thing she was doing with a friend—I didn't really get it. On the days I would go to her apartment, she'd have me take a letter back with me and I'd drop it in this mailbox by my house. This one time, though—the second to last time I saw her—I'd forgotten to put it in the mailbox right away, and my mom saw it in my bag. It really freaked me out so the next time I went, I told Wendy I couldn't mail them anymore. She got really, *really* mad and told me not to come back."

"When did this happen?"

"The first part of May. It was before my computer science project was due, and that was turned in on the twelfth."

"When did you go back to see her? The time she wouldn't let you into the building?"

"About a week later. I don't know the exact day. She answered her buzzer, but when she found out it was me, she told me to leave her alone. It was awful."

Sadie gave her a sympathetic smile. "I'm so sorry."

Min looked at the ground and tucked her hair behind her ear.

"What kind of letters were you mailing for her?" Sadie worried that if she asked if they were in pink envelopes that Min would think she knew more than she did.

"Just . . . letters."

"To whom?"

"Wendy's friend."

"What friend?"

Min shrugged but didn't answer.

"What did your mom say when she found the letter?"

"She just asked what it was," Min said, a dramatically defeated expression on her face. "I told her it was for a school project, and then I mailed it as soon as I could get out of the apartment."

"It must have stood out somehow for your mom to notice it like that. Was there something unique about it?" Sadie said, aching for confirmation.

"Well, it was pink."

Sadie had to consciously not feel too triumphant about the detail, but she enjoyed the rush of success through her chest before she moved on to the next detail. "Did the letter have Wendy's return address on it?" If it did, could Lin Yang have seen it?

"She put the same address it was being sent to as the return address," Min said. "She said it was part of the game."

On a letter to a friend? "Did your mom believe you about the project?"

"I never lie, so she had no reason to think I would," Min said, sounding miserable. "I feel terrible that I did, and then it didn't matter anyway because I only saw Wendy that one time after that—the day she got so mad and told me not to come back."

Sadie almost brought up the secret boyfriend Min had been making out with in the alley as another lie, but that didn't seem like it would work in Sadie's favor much. "Do you think your parents knew you were seeing Wendy?"

Min shook her head with confidence.

"You're sure?"

"If my parents knew, they'd have killed me."

The back door started to open, and Sadie startled, then darted to the section of wall right behind the door. It was the quickest cover she could think of. Min watched her hide, then stepped toward the door and out of Sadie's view. Sadie held her breath as the door was pushed open. She hoped whoever was coming through didn't fling the door all the way open. It was a heavy door.

Lin Yang said something in Chinese, and Sadie held her breath.

"Um, just taking my break."

Chinese again.

"Sorry, I was texting Gwen. I lost track of time." She didn't say anything else but the door started to close, fitting into the frame a second later and leaving Sadie alone with the crates and the muted sounds of the street coming from the other side of the building.

She took a breath and quickly returned to where Pete was still hiding. If he wasn't using a Dumpster as his cover, she'd have pressed her back against it and given herself a minute to gather her bearings, but instead she simply made eye contact with him. Pete nodded in silent agreement that they should go. They headed out of the alley, passing a group of men who had been smoking and talking until Pete and Sadie appeared. The men went silent and watched them. They increased their pace. The men's chatter started back up as soon as Sadie and Pete turned the corner out of the alleyway. A minute later they were back on the street.

"That was interesting," Pete said, walking fast toward their hotel. They'd had the valet park their car at the hotel for the night before walking to Choy's. The sun was setting, making Sadie wish she'd taken the time to retrieve her jacket from her hotel room, though adrenaline was keeping her pretty warm and her head was spinning. "I'd like to make a suspect list, a list of possible motives, and a list of questions we need to find answers for." She'd been taking notes all along, but making a list of suspects was different—these were actual accusations, even if no one other than she and Pete were aware of it. But they'd now met enough people and learned enough about Wendy's interactions with them that this step felt necessary.

Pete looked at her while they waited for a light to allow them to cross the street. "I think that's a good idea."

CHAPTER 24

Pete and Sadie had long ago established a rule about crossing the threshold into one another's sleeping quarters. It was too intimate and they were too unmarried. Never mind that they had the maturity to control themselves much better than your average young adult. Still, it was a good rule for two people who believed certain intimacies were to be reserved for marriage and wanted the full splendor of their wedding night. However, that was a rule that they chose to break tonight, so as not to be overheard discussing potential murderers should they have had this conversation in the hotel lobby.

They'd brought the boxes and the landscape painting up to Sadie's room and stacked them against the wall next to the boxes of files they'd gotten from the police yesterday. The room really wasn't big enough to function as a storage unit, but at least the apartment was now empty and Sadie was reasonably sure she wouldn't be adding any more boxes to the mismatched collection.

It was still weird to think that these things were all that was left of Wendy's life. She created the spreadsheet she needed for the suspect list and organized a couple of Word files that would serve for other lists and notes she would need to jot down once they began their deliberations.

Sadie sat cross-legged on the king-sized bed of the hotel room with her computer on her lap while Pete sat at the desk in her room. He had some bursitis in his knee that made sitting cross-legged uncomfortable, so she gave him the desk chair.

Sadie cleared her throat, announcing that she was ready, before launching into her nomination of suspect number one. "Shasta has wanted that apartment for years, and with Wendy dead, she's finally able to get it." She typed the information into the newly created spreadsheet as she spoke.

"Why would she let Wendy rot in the bathtub?"

Sadie startled at the bluntness, and Pete offered an apology. "It's okay," she said, waving it away. "I wanted a quick-thought discussion. I can handle it." She *hoped* she could handle it. Sometimes she was fine with the details, and other times they brought an image to her mind that shocked her. She cleared her throat. "Maybe she let Wendy . . . remain in the bathtub because she was the killer and was worried it would look suspicious if she was the one to find the body. So she had to wait for someone else."

"Maybe," he said. "But then, after a month, she ran out of patience and lit the body on fire? What if the whole building had gone up in flames?"

"Everyone's commented on how perfectly contained that fire was—and the decomposing corpse, too—I don't know why anyone thinks that was such a coincidence."

"You think Shasta would plan something like that?" Pete shook his head. "I see her as an arsenic-in-the-wine-and-watch-while-you-die-a-violent-horrible-death kind of person, petting her dog the whole time, but—"

"And maybe that's exactly how Wendy died. The police haven't been able to conclude if she'd drowned or not. I know the tox screens came back clear, but some things can be worked through the system and not show up in those tests. *And* Shasta admits that she's an actress, so maybe she's putting on a show for us and isn't the Hollywood darling she appears to be. Come next week she'll be in leather and driving a Harley down Mission Drive. Maybe she *could* have pushed Wendy under the water."

Pete gave her a half smile, cuing Sadie in that she was very close to crossing the "silly" line.

"I'm putting her on the list anyway," Sadie finished. "She had motive and opportunity and was glad Wendy was gone."

"Okay," Pete said. "Who's up next?"

"The landlord. Wendy was causing Mr. Pilings a lot of trouble, and he was making less money off of her than any other unit, even though she had more space. Getting rid of her would make his life much easier—one less headache of a tenant *and* more income. Double motive."

"But, again, why not discover her body sooner? If Wendy's body had been found within a couple of days, there would have been no need to remodel the entire bathroom, Shasta could have moved in as soon as the police cleared the crime scene, *and* Mr. Pilings would have made more money sooner. Didn't Ji say he asked for the missed rent for the time Wendy was dead in the tub? Why shoot himself in the foot by waiting all that time if his motive is money?"

"Hmm," Sadie said, looking at what she'd typed, even though she agreed with Pete's assessment. Finally she admitted it out loud, "So, both Mr. Pilings and Shasta had reason to have the body discovered sooner, *but* the body was burned in such a way so as not to cause permanent damage to the apartment building, which supports both of their interests as well."

"Maybe the fire not catching *was* a coincidence," Pete said. "Maybe the arsonist *meant* to burn down all of Mission District and something went wrong. Maybe they'd never burned a body in a bathtub before and didn't realize how it would work. If that's the case, we can rule out Shasta and the landlord. It points toward someone not associated with the building."

Sadie shook her head. "Why would they call the fire department if they wanted the whole building to burn?"

"Good point," Pete accepted with a nod. "Except that we don't know if the anonymous caller was also the firebug."

Sadie wanted to argue but Pete was right. They didn't know who placed that call, only that it was a woman and she hadn't left her name.

"So," Pete continued, "there are indicators both for and against Shasta and the landlord. Who else is on our list? Min?"

"Min did not do it," Sadie said quickly, then narrowed her eyes at the teasing grin on Pete's face. "There wasn't a hint of dishonesty in what she told me earlier."

"She lied to her mother about the letter *and* the boyfriend *and* she went to Wendy's apartment behind her parents' back for months."

"Those are very different than killing your grandmother. Min seemed very smitten with Wendy and genuinely hurt when Wendy rejected her."

"A rejection that took place a few weeks before Wendy died. Maybe she was more upset about that then she let on. Maybe *she's* taken some theater classes too."

"Stop playing devil's advocate about Min; she didn't do it and you know it." Sadie knew she was not being objective, but she couldn't make herself react with anything other than defensiveness.

"A good investigator doesn't ignore possibilities." There was a note of seriousness in his tone that Sadie disliked very much.

"Okay," she said, squaring her shoulders and deciding to play along. "So Min, who adores the grandmother she'd never met before last fall and who feels this freeing sense of rebellion against her strict parents by sneaking around to have a relationship with her, broke into the apartment she'd helped clean for months and killed her in the bathtub. Does that seem reasonable?"

"Reasonable is not a mitigating factor when looking for a killer."

"Okay, but why is Min a better possibility than Shasta, who actually had something to gain by Wendy's death?"

Pete put up his hands in surrender. "Okay, short of Min being psychotic and killing Wendy out of the rage spurred by Wendy's rejection, she probably didn't do it."

"She *didn't* do it," Sadie clarified.

Pete put down his hands. "What about Ji? Maybe he found out that Min was seeing Wendy and snapped."

Sadie wanted to be equally defensive of Ji, but Wendy had hurt him so much that she couldn't help but wonder if maybe knowing Min had met Wendy *would* push him over the edge. "I think he would have stayed clear of the apartment—and us—if he had killed her," Sadie said, though she could hear the lack of defensiveness she'd had when she'd advocated for Min. "Surely we would have seen something within his reaction to the apartment, right?"

"Probably," Pete said. "But when the police learn about Min, they'll probably question both Ji and his wife with more intensity than they did the first time around. Like Shasta and the landlord, it's not a perfect fit but it *is* motive, and they had more reason to leave the body there and then perhaps go back to try to get rid of the evidence when they realized no one was going to find the body on their own."

"Gosh, I hate thinking that."

Pete nodded his understanding. "Maybe Rodger did it," he said, changing the person of interest. "He wouldn't care that her body wasn't found for a month, and he saves a lot of money if she's gone."

Sadie considered that. "And he didn't think it was the least bit strange that she just stopped calling after having called him almost daily for months. He just assumed she was feeling better." She pointed toward her purse lying on the dresser. "Will you get the bank statements out of my purse?" she asked.

Pete complied while Sadie added Rodger to her database. Pete crossed the room and sat down on the edge of the bed next to her. "You want to check to see if the alimony was still paid, right?" he asked.

"It would be too obvious if he didn't pay it, but I just want to make sure."

Pete thumbed through the statements and pulled out several papers, handing them to her. Their fingers touched when she took the papers, and she became acutely aware of how close he was. She told herself they'd been close to one another all day. But this was different. They were in a hotel room. On a bed. She cleared her throat. "The alimony came through in June and July."

"But all that proves is that Rodger's motive wasn't saving on alimony *right away*. It doesn't change the fact that he'll be saving a lot of money from here on out. Maybe he had another motivation, like getting her to stop calling."

Sadie reviewed her conversation with Rodger—had it really

been today? "He seemed so realistic about her. He saw her weaknesses and felt compassion for them."

"You know, if you defend everyone, this won't do us any good," Pete said.

"I'm not trying to defend anyone—well, except Min and Ji—but . . . I don't know. I'm soft toward Ji because I think he loved her, and Min because—"

"You think Ji loved Wendy?" Pete said. "I sure haven't gotten that impression from him."

"I think Ji cares about her," Sadie said, wanting it to be true.

"I agree that he cared about her, but that's not the same thing as truly loving her."

Sadie wanted to argue that Wendy was his mother, that Ji had to have some love for her somewhere, but from what she'd learned about Wendy, she realized that might be overly optimistic. Of all the people Sadie had met and talked to, Ji had been the most damaged by Wendy. It was an uncomfortable point to acknowledge, but she allowed her brain to follow it. Ji *did* have motive—his mother had brought so much misery into his life, and, despite Min's assurance that her parents knew nothing about her relationship with Wendy, what if they did? She wondered how she could find out. She looked at Pete sitting beside her. "You're right that I can't just stick up for people because I don't want anything to point toward them. But I don't want Ji or Min to know we suspect them."

"I agree," Pete said, nodding.

"So, I'm thinking about how Jason had seen Min and gave a pretty good description of her, but did you ask *when* he saw her? She said she went back twice after Wendy told her not to, but never got inside the building. If Jason—or anyone else for that matter—did see her inside the building after about the twelfth of May, it would . . ."

She couldn't finish the sentence. She didn't want to say that Min being in the building would prove that she'd lied to Sadie, that she was hiding something.

"We could also ask if anyone ever saw Ji there. Didn't he tell you he'd never been to her building before he met the landlord there last week to get the keys?"

Sadie nodded.

"So if anyone saw him there prior to the first of this month, it would prove some deception on his part."

Deception. Such an ugly word. She hated thinking of Min or Ji being deceptive, and yet she felt like the deceiving one by even considering checking up on their stories. "We could talk to the tenants tomorrow," Sadie said. "Did you talk to anyone today other than Jason about Min?"

"I didn't," Pete said, shaking his head. "Also, I know Shasta said she didn't track the comings and goings of people, but she was at the top of the stairs listening to me talk to Jason, and when I ran into her that first night, she had commented that the other tenant on the second floor worked late on Thursdays and wouldn't be home until ten. I think she keeps better track than she wants to admit."

"You better conduct that interview," Sadie said. "I have a feeling you'll get better information from Shasta than I will."

"I don't know," Pete said with exaggerated concern. "She seems so distracted by my sexy manliness that my attempt to get information might just dwindle into abject admiration." He shrugged and made a face that seemed to indicate how powerless he was in regard to the eccentric woman's attraction to him.

Sadie smiled and leaned into him. "Well, she's not the only one. It's a constant battle I face when we're together." She kissed him quickly, then turned back to her computer and added "Talk to tenants about Min timeframe and if Ji was ever visiting" on her to-do list for tomorrow. She reviewed the other items on it:

- Check with PD to see if they have ID on Mr. Green Shirt
- Follow up with landlord about rental addendum
- Follow up on claims Wendy made against landlord
- Call Jack

Sadie frowned at the last item on that list. She'd told Jack that she'd call him tonight, but it was getting so late. She glanced at the clock on her computer—9:06, which made it 12:06 in Miami. Plus, it was his and Carrie's first night on vacation. An e-mail would be better.

Pete shifted on the bed so he was leaning against the headboard. It didn't move him any farther away from her, just somewhat behind her. She sat up a little straighter, suddenly mindful of her posture. Caught off guard by the instant tension—the delicious kind—that was suddenly between them, she clicked over to her list of questions and focused on the next one on her list.

"Who was Wendy sending the letters to?" she asked too loudly. "The only reason I can think of for Min to mail them for her is so that Wendy could stay anonymous. Not using her own return address supports that idea, and so does the unsigned letter I found. As for why she was sending the letters—it sounds like she was trying to convince someone that she was having a relationship with someone they care about, right?"

"Is Rodger involved with someone?" Pete asked. The touch of his fingers on her neck made her shiver, and she froze for a split second as a rush of heat filled her chest. He ran his fingers along the base of her neck, and she broke out in goose bumps, though the heat did not subside.

"H-he didn't say. But he acknowledged that he was better after they broke up, though it was devastating at the . . . what was I talking about?"

Pete turned his hand and ran his fingers beneath the collar of her shirt.

She took a deep breath, entranced by the feelings his simple touch could trigger.

"You were talking about the possibility of Rodger's wife or girlfriend being the target of those letters," Pete prompted her.

"M-maybe." She didn't dare look at him, but closed her eyes and let her thoughts move to places she rarely let them go.

Pete reached forward and with one hand closed her laptop and moved it off her lap while he kissed her neck. For an instant, Sadie remembered the ground rules they'd set and the reasons they'd set them. In the next instant, she had no memory of those boundaries and reached a hand to the side of his face as he finally kissed her on the mouth. Delicious lightning shot through her as the kiss deepened. Pete's arm around her waist pulled her closer, and they lay back on the bed together. She ran her hands over his shoulders, through his hair, down his back.

And then his phone chimed on the other end of the room, pulling the fog from her thoughts. She remembered the rules and the reasons for them and the ghost of his wife that had been haunting them for days. *Had the phone already chimed once and we'd ignored it?* Sadie wondered as they stared at each other for the space of two quick breaths. Then she worried that the passion they'd just shared would remind him of his wife for a very different reason.

Pete's smile was like the rush of a wind, clearing out the fear and restoring some of her shaken faith. "I better get that," he said, then kissed her one last time before rising from the bed and crossing the room.

Sadie smiled at the ceiling, then sat up and straightened her shirt. Her face was warm, and she put a hand on her cheeks. "Who is it?" she asked after several seconds had passed.

He didn't answer, his back to her, drawing even more of Sadie's attention.

"Pete?"

"It's just Stan." Pete's voice was flat again, just as it had been when Stan called yesterday, just as it had been after he spoke with Brooke today.

Sadie felt the mood—which had been so nice a minute ago—shift into something different. A new place, too much like some of the other uncomfortable places they'd been on this trip. She waited for more information about the text from the realtor but Pete didn't supply it. "I thought we had forty-eight hours to consider the offer?"

He didn't turn toward her. "We do. He was just checking to see if we'd made a decision."

Sadie counted five full seconds, giving him ample time to turn around and smile and say "Now, where were we?" but he said nothing at all, letting the silence lengthen between them. "*Have* we made a decision?" she asked. He knew as well as she did that "we" meant "him."

Pete didn't answer as he returned the text message, but his mood stayed heavy. She sat on the end of the bed and waited until he turned to face her. When he did, his expression was guarded and her patience was thin.

"You don't have to accept the offer," Sadie said, focusing on the business at hand. "We can live in your house and sell mine."

Pete was shaking his head before she'd finished. "I think that would be just as hard." His voice was soft enough that she could have pretended not to hear it.

There could be no pretending, however, that the words didn't cut through her, and the breath she let out was an audible one. Pete swallowed as though having just realized what he'd really said: *he doesn't want me living in Pat's house.*

He took his hands out of his pockets and let them fall to his sides. "I didn't mean it like that."

"Of course you did," Sadie said, her voice quiet as she placed her hands, palms down, on either side of her as though that would help her stability. "You never say things you don't mean." She held his eyes, silently begging him to convince her that she was wrong. Instead, he just looked apologetic and uncomfortable. And then he began walking to the door. He was going to leave it like *this?*

"I'm sorry," he said.

"Pete," Sadie said as she stood. "Wait a minute. Let's talk about this."

"I can't."

Sadie caught up to him a few feet from the door and grabbed his arm. It was the second time today she'd chased after him like this.

He stopped but didn't turn toward her.

"We have a wedding date in three weeks, Pete. If you're not ready then tell me now."

He finally turned toward her enough to meet her eyes. "It's not that, it's just . . ."

"Just what?" Sadie pushed when he didn't finish his thought. She dropped her hand from his arm. "Need more time? Need less me? Need to talk to your kids, a friend, what? It has never been my intention to corner you into something, you know that."

"Of course I know that," Pete said. He paused for a few seconds as though searching for the words to say. "I don't know how to explain it, but this isn't about . . . you."

"I know. That's the problem. If Pat is stronger in your thoughts than I am right now, then you might not be ready to become *my* husband." She couldn't believe she was saying this; the very idea of canceling the wedding made her feel as though she were about to break out in hives. But if he wasn't ready, the marriage wouldn't work. She would rather have her heart broken now than see it obliterated after he'd made promises to her that he wasn't prepared to keep.

Pete looked toward the door of the hotel room and took a breath. He didn't look at her when he spoke. "Isn't it hard for you?" he asked. "You had Neil."

His words were like ice water for the growing rage and spurred insight that wasn't entirely welcome—there was comfort in anger—but it wasn't the same. Sadie had had Neil for such a short time, far shorter than the time she'd lived without him. Perhaps because of the short duration of their marriage, or maybe because of the years she'd spent alone since his death, she'd been able to work through his absence in a different way than Pete had after he lost Pat.

"I've had twenty-two years to get used to *not* having Neil," she said quietly. "I'm not sure I could have remarried so soon after his death for the exact reasons you're struggling with now. Are you not ready for this?"

He looked back at her. The mask was gone but pain was in its place, showing the battle he was waging, the reluctance and grief and the wish for something different. Was he wishing that Pat were here or simply that he wasn't feeling this? They stared at each other for several seconds, Sadie internally pleading for him to take her in his arms and . . . what? Could he honestly reassure her? Could he say anything that would erase the last few minutes? The last few days?

When the seconds continued to tick by, Sadie backed away from him and waved toward the door. "Good night, Pete," she said, turning toward the window and looking at the building across the street from her room. For a moment she wondered if he would follow her. He did not.

"I'm sorry, Sadie," he said quietly. "I'm trying to figure this out."

She heard the door open. A moment later, the door closed behind him, and Sadie was alone with her heavy heart and darkening fears.

CHAPTER 25

It was a long night, one of the longest Sadie had had in a while.
She did not awake with any inspiration on how to ease the burden
of Pete's struggles and decided to deal with the inevitable awkwardness of the morning by running from it. She wrote a quick note to
Pete, explaining where she was going and asking him to follow up on
the leads for Mr. Green Shirt and the landlord. It made sense since
the police could help him with both of those topics.

She took the elevator to the fifth floor of the hotel and slid the
note under Pete's door a little before 8:00. She could have texted
him, but she'd said she'd give him his space and a text would be inviting a response. When he was ready to talk, he would come to her.

For her part, Sadie would focus on talking to the other tenants
of Wendy's building about Min and Ji. What she learned there would
likely direct the rest of her day. Sadie hated that she had to check
their stories—it felt like a betrayal—so she tried not to think too
much about it and hoped that, if nothing else, having plenty to do
today would help keep her mind off the events of last night.

Sadie went to the business center of the hotel; the binder in
her room had said it had a printer. Min had a Facebook page, and

though Sadie couldn't access all of her photos from the hotel's computer—privacy settings were a double-edged sword—she was able to print Min's profile picture. It was a selfie likely taken in Min's bathroom, but it was a good enough likeness to suit her purposes. Ji wasn't on Facebook, and it took her several minutes to find a photo of him, finally tracking down a mutual friend of Min's who had a picture of Ji with some people at a school function. Sadie had to download it onto her laptop, crop it, e-mail it to herself, and then print it from the hotel's computer—not simple but still doable.

Sadie folded the pictures and put them in her purse, then asked the valet to help her get a taxi since the streets and sidewalks were already full of people rushing to work. As the cab pulled away from the hotel a minute later, she admitted to herself that she'd hoped the note she'd slid under Pete's door would result in his calling her and wanting to talk about a breakthrough realization he'd had during the night. But it had been half an hour, and he hadn't called. She reminded herself that Pete needed to do whatever Pete needed to do. *Sadie* needed to do the same. Tomorrow she would fly back to Colorado and confront what may or may not be the next step in her relationship with Pete. Today, she needed to focus on what had happened to her sister.

The taxi dropped her off at Wendy's apartment building, and she let herself in. The clock on her phone showed that it wasn't yet 9:00 in the morning, and though she disliked the idea of bothering people so early, she'd already accepted that she had a better chance of finding the tenants at home at this time of day. She really needed to talk to all of them if she wanted to verify that Min and Ji had told her the truth about when they'd been to Wendy's apartment building. She approached apartment one and knocked.

A woman dressed in sweaty workout clothes pulled the door

open. Sadie could hear the voice of Tony Horton in the background, and she wondered to herself which P90X workout the woman was doing. Sadie explained who she was and that she was trying to reconstruct what had happened to her sister.

The woman—Stacey—confirmed that she hadn't been home when the fire happened, that she'd never really met Wendy, and that she had lived there for just five months. "I didn't even know her name until after the fire."

"Did you, by chance, ever see a Chinese girl around the apartment building?"

Stacey leveled her with a look that made Sadie review what she'd just said. "I believe you mean *Asian,* and there are a lot of *Asians* in this city."

Actually, Min *was* Chinese, so Sadie wasn't being politically incorrect by stating it that way, but she was embarrassed by the way the woman had interpreted the question. "This girl was seen *inside* the building—one of the tenants reported—"

Stacey put one hand on her hip. "Someone reported an *Asian* in our building?" she said with sarcastic concern. "By all means, let's call the border patrol."

"Ma'am," Sadie said, wishing her red face wasn't betraying her embarrassment. "I think you're misinterpreting me. What I'm trying to establish is if you saw her here after May twelfth—inside the building, I mean. There were a couple of times that—"

Stacey didn't let her finish. Instead, she cut off Sadie with a lecture on bigotry and ethnic stereotyping while Tony Horton yelled "Bring it!" in the background. When she finished her diatribe, she shut the door in Sadie's face.

Sadie blinked at the closed door and raised a hand to her hot cheeks. She sighed and turned toward apartment two, reviewing how she'd said things to Stacey in order to make sure she didn't give Jason the same impression. It wasn't prejudicial to point out someone's ethnicity, was it? And Stacy hadn't even answered the question about Min or given Sadie the chance to ask about Ji. The day hadn't started off very well. Sadie could feel the uncertainty of what she was doing and why she was doing it begin to creep up on her. Why had she even come to San Francisco?

The smile Jason gave her when he opened the door went a long way to calm her fraying nerves. They'd only talked one other time, but she felt as though they were friends.

"Hi again," he said.

"Hi, Jason." Sadie wished she felt comfortable enough to ask him for a hug. She could use a hug about now. "I was wondering if I could ask you a couple more questions."

"Sure. Would you like to come in?"

"Oh, I don't want to intrude," Sadie said, though she appreciated the offer. Maybe not everyone hated her. She held out Min's picture. "Pete talked to you yesterday about the girl you saw around the apartment last winter—can you verify if this is her?"

Jason looked at the picture and cocked his head to the side. "I think so," he said. "You know who she is then?"

"Yeah," Sadie said. "But I needed to be sure. Also, do you, by chance, remember if you ever saw her here after the twelfth of May?"

"Oh gosh," Jason said, making a face and shaking his head slowly. "I really can't be sure—that was almost two months ago."

Sadie frowned and put the photo back in her purse. "I know," she said, discouraged. She pulled out Ji's printed picture. "Have you ever seen him before?"

Jason's expression reflected sympathetic concern. "Um, I met him yesterday when he gave me the keys to Wendy's apartment."

"Oh yeah," Sadie said. "Um, before last week, though, had you ever seen him here in the building?"

Jason looked at the picture again, seemed to think hard about it, and then looked up at Sadie. "I didn't."

"Oh good," Sadie said, relieved as she returned the picture to her purse.

"Good?"

She glanced at Jason and realized she'd spoken out loud. "Oh, yeah, I'm trying to confirm that he'd never been here before Wendy's death."

"You think he might have had something to do with it?"

"No," Sadie said quickly. "I just want to confirm that he didn't. Does that make sense?"

"Sure," Jason said, but she had a feeling he was humoring her just a little. "Does this have anything to do with the Asian girl?" He waved toward Sadie's purse where she'd put the photo of Min.

"Yeah, well, sorta."

"Ya know, after I talked to your friend—Pete?"

Sadie nodded and Jason continued. "I asked Damon about her, and he'd seen her too—several times."

"Damon?" Sadie wondered if he was the tenant in apartment four that she hadn't met yet.

"He's my roommate," Jason explained. "He usually gets home around four o'clock in the afternoons, and he said that he'd seen her several times just as he was coming in. I'm assuming it's the same girl. Since he saw her more than I did, I wondered if that was her regular time to visit. He didn't ever talk to her, though, but he saw her coming and going by way of the stairs, so she was definitely here for someone on the higher floors."

"That's excellent information," Sadie said, glad to have another account and hoping it would work toward confirming when Min had stopped visiting Wendy. "I wonder if he would remember if he saw her after May twelfth?"

"He might, but when I talked to him, he also mentioned that he'd run into an Asian *woman* in June—not long before the fire, I guess."

For an instant time stopped, then Sadie remembered herself. "A woman?" Sadie only knew one Asian woman in this city who had ties to Wendy.

"Yeah. At first he thought it was the girl again but then realized that this lady was older."

"And he saw her in June? Before the fire?"

Jason nodded.

"Did he tell the police?"

"He said he hadn't thought about her until I asked him about the Asian girl. You know how things spark a memory sometimes."

Sadie nodded; she knew that all too well. "Did he notice anything about her that might help me figure out who she is?"

"I didn't ask him anything about that," Jason said with a frown, then pointed over his shoulder with his thumb. "I could call him real quick though."

"Really? That would be wonderful." Jason invited her in to his apartment again and this time she accepted, but she was glad he left the door open. She had no reason to suspect Jason, but it was easier to trust him with an open door at her back.

The apartment was like Wendy's but more masculine in décor. Sadie assumed it was a one-bedroom apartment since there was only one door leading off the common area. Something smelled wonderful—lots better than the stale granola bar Sadie had eaten in place of breakfast.

Jason picked up his cell phone and dialed a number. The creak of the ceiling caused Sadie to look up. Jason noticed and shrugged as though apologizing for what Sadie assumed were footsteps of the upstairs neighbor. That was something Wendy's apartment didn't have—upstairs neighbors.

When Damon answered his phone, Jason explained what Sadie was looking for and then handed the phone to her. Damon had a rich, radio-announcer-type voice with a slight effeminate drawl to it. After some quick introductions, she repeated her questions about the mystery Asian woman he'd seen.

"Uh, let's see, she had her hair up in a bun—those dancer-types, right on top of her head—but she was dressed in black slacks that didn't fit and an oversized black T-shirt. She could have rocked something a little more formfitting, if you ask me."

"You're *sure* it wasn't the same girl you'd seen before?"

"Well, I thought it was her at first, but I always saw that girl in the afternoons and this was in the morning. And then, here's the thing—" He sounded hesitant to continue as he stopped for a breath. "There's nothin' wrong with a lady getting some hair color to amp up what God gave her, ain't nobody going to get judgment from me about that, but it's got to be *maintained,* and the lady I saw coming off the elevator had a solid half an *inch* of regrowth. Not all gray, mind you, but enough that you could see the color line."

Bun.

Black slacks and oversized shirt.

It had to be Lin Yang!

Sadie's brain tried to reject the possibility—it was so . . . complex a thing to consider. "So, there's *no way* it was the same girl you and Jason had seen earlier in the year?"

"No," Damon said with a laugh. "Though, at the risk of having this sound all kinds of wrong, there was something about them that looked the same. Not just race or anything, more like . . . related. Oh, my mama would shoot me if she heard me say that!"

Sadie felt her hand tighten on the phone. "Jason said you saw her before the fire. Are you *sure* about that? And do you know when?"

"I can't remember the exact day. Maybe it was the day before the fire, maybe two. I usually have to be at the office by seven—I work East Coast hours—but I was going in late that day, so it would have been closer to 9:00. Actually . . . hold on, let me check my online calendar."

"Thank you," Sadie said while she waited for him.

"Okay, yep, here it is—it was the twenty-third, the Wednesday before the fire."

The fire had been set early on the following Friday morning—so, two days after Damon had seen her.

How had Lin Yang gotten into the building?

"Can I ask why you're so interested in this woman?" Damon asked on the phone, drawing Sadie's attention back to him. "I'd forgotten all about her until Jason asked me about the girl."

Exactly, Sadie thought to herself. Just like Pete said, evidence breaks down and people forget what they'd seen as time continues on. "I'm just trying to cover all the bases," Sadie said, choosing to be vague. "And I appreciate your help so much. Could I ask you a couple more questions?"

"Sure. What else can I help you with?"

What nice young men. Sadie asked if he could remember whether he'd seen Min after May twelfth.

"I don't think so," Damon said. "It seems like the last time I saw her was in April."

"And what about an Asian man?"

251

"The one who brings the dry cleaning?"

"Uh, I don't think so." How could she get him to see Ji's picture? She thought of her phone in her purse. "Hang on—could I send you a picture of the man I'm asking about?"

Damon agreed, and with Jason's help, Sadie texted the photo to Damon's phone.

"I think I just got it. Hold on a sec."

Sadie waited, counting slowly so as not to be too anxious. Within a few seconds Damon came back on the line. "Not him," he said. "The guy that picks up the dry cleaning is older and rounder. I've never seen this guy."

Sadie was relieved. "Thank you. I can't tell you how much I appreciate all this."

"You bet," Damon said. "I hope you find what you're looking for."

The comment was bigger than he could possibly know as Wendy, Min, Ji, and Pete came to Sadie's mind in an instant. She was looking for—or hoping for—many things regarding those four people. Would she find the answers and assurance she needed? Did they even exist? She felt unbidden tears come to her eyes, another symptom of how poorly she'd slept and how emotionally draining the last few days had been. "Thank you," she said in a soft voice.

They ended the call, and she handed the phone to Jason, who was watching her closely. "Are you okay?" he asked as he set the phone on the counter.

"I'm fine," Sadie said, embarrassed as she wiped at the tears that hadn't fallen. "I just have a lot going on right now."

Jason nodded with a sympathetic frown. "Have you had breakfast already? I made a frittata, but without Damon here to share it with me, I'll end up throwing too much of it out."

Sadie sniffled one more time. "You have a frittata? What kind?"

Frittata

6 eggs
1 ounce Parmesan cheese, grated
½ teaspoon black pepper
Pinch of salt
1 teaspoon butter
½ cup chopped roasted asparagus
½ cup chopped ham
1 tablespoon chopped parsley leaves (or ½ teaspoon dried parsley)

Preheat oven to broil setting.

In medium-sized bowl blend together eggs, Parmesan, pepper, and salt with a fork until eggs are well beaten. Heat a 12-inch, nonstick, oven-safe sauté pan over medium heat. Melt butter in pan. Add asparagus and ham and sauté for 2 to 3 minutes.

Pour egg mixture into pan and stir with rubber spatula just enough to combine eggs with the meat and veggies. Cook for 4 to 5 minutes without stirring or until the egg mixture has set on the bottom. Sprinkle with parsley.

Broil for 3 to 4 minutes, until lightly browned and fluffy. Remove from oven and, if desired, top with 2 ounces of your favorite cheese. Let cool for a few minutes before cutting into wedges. Serve immediately.

Enjoy with a variety of meats and vegetables—just avoid something that would throw off the consistency of the egg mixture, such as cream cheese or salsa.

Makes 4 servings.

Note: This is a great way to use up leftover meats and vegetables.

CHAPTER 26

J ason made a lovely asparagus and ham frittata. Sadie enjoyed it
thoroughly and thanked him over and over. After she'd insisted
on washing her own dishes, he walked her to the door and she got
that hug she'd wanted earlier. It went a long way to refuel her energy
levels. He wished her luck, and she thanked him for being just what
she'd needed this morning.

Once he closed the door behind her, she considered her next
move. She was already here at the apartment building and hadn't
talked to Shasta or the tenant in apartment four about Min and Ji.
But clearly she needed to talk to Ji—and follow up on Lin Yang.

She vacillated for a moment, then headed to the stairs and
walked up to the second floor. She couldn't decide whether she
wanted to talk to Shasta or the unknown tenant in apartment four
first but decided to start with Shasta. Maybe she could fill her in
on the neighbor Sadie hadn't met yet. She knocked and waited for
a solid twenty seconds for her to answer before she knocked again.

Disappointed but not dissuaded, she went to apartment four
and knocked. She was grateful when she felt the vibrations of footsteps coming to answer her knock, but then glanced back at Shasta's

apartment. She thought back to the footsteps she'd heard from the ceiling in Jason's apartment, which was directly beneath apartment four. Shasta's, on the other hand, was directly beneath Wendy's. Wouldn't she have noticed when there were no footsteps overhead for an entire month?

The opening of the door recaptured Sadie's attention, and she faced forward, remembered what she was doing here, and put a smile on her face. The woman was in her forties, dressed in jeans and a baggy sweater. Sadie introduced herself and explained her connection to Wendy. Carmen was a freelance writer who worked from home. She'd lived there for nearly a year and only knew Wendy through the letters of complaint Wendy had brought around.

"Mr. Pilings is what I call a corporate landlord. He prefers that we just pay the rent, without being bothered by the human lives living under the roofs he repairs only when he has to." She rolled her eyes. "I've talked to Mario about some of the response time to issues, and he told me that he's the sole person responsible for maintaining four different buildings. Four! I think that's ridiculous so, yeah, I threw in with Wendy, but we didn't hang out or anything like that."

Sadie smiled conciliatorily and launched into her questions about Ji and his family—a bit awkwardly, she thought—but the woman transitioned with her. Carmen had never seen Min before, didn't recognize Ji other than having seen him over the last weekend, and had no knowledge of an Asian woman.

"Is that all?" she asked as Sadie returned the pictures to her purse.

Sadie started to nod, but then remembered the creaking ceiling from Jason's apartment. "Uh, one last thing—there isn't anyone living above you right now, is there?"

"Nope, it's been empty since last month."

"Before, when that apartment was occupied, could you hear the tenant's footsteps when they were walking around?"

Carmen nodded. "I would have *loved* to sign one of Wendy's petitions about the squeaky floors, but of course that wasn't an issue for her so she never brought it up."

"So it's pretty loud."

"The gal that lived above me—graduate student." She rolled her eyes again. "I think she did Zumba and, man, it was ob-nox-ious. It's been very nice to have a break. I don't even have to wear my noise-canceling headphones. If it weren't a studio up there I'd probably move up there just to get away from having someone on top of me again."

Sadie thanked Carmen for her help before heading back to the main floor. She wished Shasta was home right now—she'd sure like to know why she didn't notice when the sound above her stopped—but maybe Sadie could come back later. Right now, she needed to have a conversation with Ji that wasn't the kind that could be done over the phone.

It was a relief to be able to check Min and Ji off her list of suspects though; no one had said anything that contradicted what the two of them had told Sadie about their comings and goings from the apartment. All her focus could go to Lin Yang. She wanted to call Pete and talk all of this out, but she refused to force herself into his sphere right now.

Sadie didn't want to think about how much money she'd spent on cab fare the last few days but made a mental note to stop at the next ATM she encountered to refill her cash reserves. For now, though, she told the cab driver to take her to Choy's on Sacramento Street in Chinatown, then settled back into the seat and pulled out her phone in order to give Ji a heads up. That Ji lived above the restaurant made it easy to know where to start.

On my way to Choy's. Need to talk to you.

Ji didn't respond by the time the cab driver pulled up in front of the yellow-and-red sign. The tourists were already scattered along the sidewalk even though half of the businesses wouldn't open until 10:00. Sadie scanned the front of the building that housed Choy's, her eyes traveling to the windows of the second and third floors, one of which housed Ji's apartment. How did she access the front door?

Sadie walked along the sidewalk and within a few storefronts encountered an unobtrusive door the same color as the building façade. There was a buzzer next to the door similar to the one outside of Wendy's apartment, but the names—assuming they were names at all—were written in Chinese. Plus, it was five storefronts away from Choy's, which seemed kind of far away. Sadie turned around and walked the other direction.

On the other side of Choy's was a small souvenir shop, but on the other side of *that* was another door. This one happened to have a doorway painted the same red as the doorway to Choy's, which seemed as good an indication as any that this would be the access point for Ji's apartment. It also had an intercom system. The names were still in Chinese though. Sadie bit her lip, her finger hovering over the buttons. Eeny, meeny, miny . . . she pushed the first button. A woman's voice come on a few seconds later, saying something in Chinese.

Sadie leaned toward the speaker. "I'm looking for the Doang family."

She released the button to hear the response but the line remained quiet. After a few seconds, she pushed the button again. "Hello?"

The woman's voice said something else in Chinese and, though

Sadie didn't understand any of it, the sharp tone told her that she must have the wrong apartment. Sadie nearly pushed the button to apologize but then thought better of it.

She took a breath and punched the next number. No one answered.

Another woman responded in Chinese to the third button.

"I'm looking for the Doang family."

"Number four," the woman said with a thick accent.

"Thank you," Sadie replied.

"You welcome. Bye."

Sadie pushed the button for number four. A young voice greeted her with the now-familiar Chinese greeting, "*Ni hao.*"

"Hi, is your dad home?"

The girl responded in English. "He's unavailable. Would you like to talk to my mother instead?"

"Um," Sadie said, thinking fast before making her decision. "Sure."

"Just a minute," the girl said. The speaker went quiet for a few seconds.

"Hello?" Lin Yang said from somewhere above Sadie.

Sadie pushed the button so she could speak. "Hi, Lin Yang, it's Sadie Hoffmiller. I'd like to talk to Ji. Do you know when he'll be available?" She was trying to sound both friendly and firm; she wasn't going to take no for an answer. Not with so much at stake.

Three seconds ticked by before Lin Yang answered. "Ji isn't home this morning." She still had that clip to her words that made Sadie feel like she was always angry with her.

"Is he at the restaurant already?"

"What do you need to talk to him about?"

It was Sadie's turn to pause. Talking about this over a speaker was worse than over the phone. She also didn't necessarily want to talk to Lin Yang about this without Ji, but she was equally resistant to the idea of putting this off. "Could I come up and talk to you?"

"I'll come down."

Sadie stepped away from the intercom and moved toward the souvenir shop. She didn't want to be standing front and center when Lin Yang opened the door. Thirty seconds passed before Lin Yang stepped out of the doorway and onto the sidewalk. She was wearing black cotton capris, an oversized black shirt, and bright pink flip-flops. Her hair was pulled up into her signature bun on the top of her head—like a dancer. Sadie found herself looking closely at her roots. There was no regrowth to speak of, but she could have colored her hair in the last couple of weeks.

"What is it?" Lin Yang asked.

Sadie didn't have to wonder if Lin Yang just *sounded* irritated this time. She *was* irritated, and it radiated from the set of her jaw, the lift of her chin, and the tightness of her shoulders. Sadie absorbed all this information and figured the best approach to take would be the direct one. "Have you ever been to Wendy's apartment?"

"No. Is that everything?"

The quickness of her answer threw Sadie off for a moment, but she grabbed on to her train of thought before it got away. "Are you sure?"

This time Lin Yang paused. "Why are you asking all these questions? You're bothering my family. Ji has asked you to leave us alone, and I think you should do as he says."

"Ji hasn't asked me to leave him alone," Sadie countered. At least, he hadn't asked it in so many words. "Why do you think he did?"

"Wendy is gone. You need to leave him alone."

"Wendy *is* gone, but *I'm* here, and I'm looking for answers about what happened to her. Did you know Wendy?"

Lin Yang turned her head to the side and looked into the street for a moment before looking back. "I don't want to talk to you."

She turned toward the door, and Sadie stepped forward. "Lin Yang, I know you went to her apartment and—" She grabbed Lin Yang's arm in order to keep her on the sidewalk but as soon as Sadie touched her, Lin Yang immediately twisted out of her reach, turned around, grabbed Sadie's wrist, and bent it back toward Sadie's forearm. Pain like lightning shot up Sadie's arm and into her shoulder, causing her whole body to tense up.

"Ow!" Sadie screamed, eliciting looks from a couple of tourists passing by.

Lin Yang let go, and Sadie backed up a step, cradling her aching wrist in her other hand. It had taken all of two seconds for Lin Yang to have bested her, and Sadie was reeling from it. She'd never encountered someone who knew her own moves like that, though Sadie didn't know that particular one and was disappointed in herself for not countering automatically. She hoped she wasn't losing the skills that had saved her life more than once.

Lin Yang held her eyes without flinching or attempting an apology. "I don't want to talk to you." She turned and let herself into the door.

Sadie paused for exactly one beat, then pushed the intercom button for number four.

The same young voice from earlier came on with the same Chinese greeting.

"Is Min there?" Sadie asked quickly. It had taken Lin Yang about thirty seconds to get down to the street, surely it would take her that long to get back to the apartment.

"Just a minute."

Sadie held her breath and counted: one-one-thousand, two-one-thousand, three-one-thousand, four-one-thousand, five—

"Hello?"

Sadie pushed the button so she could speak. "It's Sadie. I need to talk to you. Call me at this number as soon as you can do so privately." She rattled off her cell number then added, "Don't tell your mother." She repeated the number again then let go of the button.

"Okay," Min said quickly, then broke the connection.

Sadie took a deep breath that she hoped would calm her racing heart. She pulled her phone out of her purse and stepped underneath the souvenir shop awning so it didn't look so obvious that she was loitering outside the apartment door. Her phone vibrated.

Min: I can't talk. What's wrong?

Sadie: I need to ask you some questions. Can you meet me somewhere?

Min: I'll meet you behind the restaurant in ten minutes.

Sadie: Perfect.

Sadie headed toward the alley where she and Pete had gone the night before. She looked warily at the windows on the upper levels of the building once she was in the alley, which was empty this time of day. Could Lin Yang look down and see her? Just in case, she stayed as close to the brick wall as possible.

Sadie felt sure she knew which apartment belonged to Lin Yang when she saw three black aprons swaying on a line stretching from the top. She leaned against the door she'd met Min outside of last night and tried to prepare for what to say and how to say it. She didn't want to come between a parent and a child, but if that parent was a murderer . . . she stopped herself. Did she truly believe that? Did she think Lin Yang could have *killed* Wendy? Sadie thought of the cold expression she'd seen on Lin Yang's face when she had twisted Sadie's wrist, and Sadie shivered. Maybe Lin Yang could.

CHAPTER 27

Ten minutes came and went. Then fifteen. Sadie texted Min a single question mark. She didn't respond. After another two minutes—seventeen minutes felt like forever when heavy thoughts were swimming in her brain—she was considering what her next move should be when the back door of Choy's began to open.

She quickly stepped out of the way and Min poked her head out. She beckoned Sadie inside. Sadie was quick to comply, then blinked several times to help her eyes adjust to the darkened restaurant kitchen.

Min pulled the heavy door shut behind them. "Sorry, I had to wait long enough that it didn't seem suspicious that I came down a little early. Luckily I'm opening today, but everyone else will be here in about twenty minutes."

"Thanks for meeting with me," Sadie said.

They stood in a little alcove, a kind of enclosed porch with boxes stacked on either side. Min turned and walked toward the interior of the room; Sadie followed. There was better lighting here, and Sadie scanned the ancient-looking grills and stoves, blackened through years of use. A commercial dishwasher was in one corner, a shelf full of pans and utensils in another, and the smell of grease and spices hung heavy in the air. The room was smaller than she expected.

"What's happened?" Min asked, worried. "Why did you need to talk to me?"

Though Sadie would have liked to ease Min's nervousness, she wasn't sure that was possible. At the same time, staring into this girl's face reminded Sadie that although Min was an adult, she was still a child—Ji's child. Sadie would need to handle this with delicacy. "I just had some follow-up questions about our conversation last night." Her explanation did nothing to ease Min's expression. "Is there *any* chance that your mother knew you had met Wendy?"

Min shook her head.

"Are you *sure?*"

"My parents would have killed me if they knew."

"Is there any way your mom could have known that letter was from Wendy?" If that were the case, however, it didn't explain why Lin Yang would have gone to the apartment a couple of weeks ago, and not when she'd found that letter back in May.

"No," Min said emphatically. "There's no way my parents knew. I told you it didn't have Wendy's name or address on it. Why are you asking this?"

Sadie sidestepped the question. "What did you tell your parents you were doing during the times you saw Wendy?"

"I would stop after class on days when I wasn't scheduled to be at the restaurant right away. I never stayed long—an hour at the most. They would be working and never realized I came in late so long as I beat the dinner rush."

"You don't think they suspected anything? I get the impression they pay pretty close attention to their kids."

Min shook her head. "My parents are very busy, and I'm careful not to make those types of things a habit. They *are* very strict, though. If they'd known I was seeing her—seeing anyone without their permission—they'd have grounded me to my room for a year."

"They hated her so much?" *And trusted you so little?* but Sadie didn't say that part.

Min frowned. "My parents didn't talk about Wendy much, but when they did, it wasn't good. Once I got to know her, though, I realized that they just didn't understand her. No one did." She paused for a moment. "She was just different. Like, stuff didn't worry her and she just wanted to do whatever with her life, you know? She was a free spirit, and even though I know she wasn't a great mom when *Ba ba* was little, she felt *so* bad about that. She tried to apologize to him several times, but he wouldn't accept it. She used to travel a lot and met all these movie stars and things. She was *so* cool, and my parents are just . . . They just don't understand."

"Do you think they were trying to protect you from her?"

Min pulled back slightly. "Protect me from what? She was an old lady. It's not like she would ever hurt me or anything. And she was really sorry for not being a good mom to my dad. That day when she came into the restaurant to see him and he wasn't there, she bought one of his jewelry boxes. She said that maybe that was the only part of him she would ever have. It was so sad."

Sadie didn't allow herself to get caught up in the sentimentality. "You say she wouldn't hurt you, but she got mad at you when you said you couldn't send the letters anymore."

"Well, yeah, 'cause she had that game she was playing with her friend and I was messing it up."

"Didn't it seem strange that she didn't mail the letters from her own building? Doesn't it seem that if you were uncomfortable, she should have been okay with you not sending the letters?"

Min lifted her chin in defiance. "She was sick—like depressed and things. Like I said, no one understood her."

Except Min. Somehow Wendy had managed to create this us-against-the-world feeling between her and Min. She might have been mentally ill or just mean or whatever, but she had power over people. "Can you tell me *anything* else about the letters? Maybe who they were addressed to?"

A flicker of guilt crossed Min's face and she looked away.

"Min," Sadie pleaded. "This is really important."

Min looked back at her. "Why? Why does any of this matter? My grandmother is dead." Her eyes filled with tears. "No one loved her, no one took care of her, and my parents would never understand if they knew that I at least tried. You're supposed to help your family, and she needed help. I'm really glad I got to meet her before she died, but just because she's gone doesn't mean that everyone should talk bad about her and invade her privacy. She could write letters to whoever she wanted to."

Sadie processed everything Min said through the filter of a twenty-year-old young woman with hardworking but controlling parents. Of course she saw Wendy as a victim, especially since Wendy played up that position. And of course Min would want the same respect of privacy for Wendy that she wanted for herself. Min was an adult living in her parents' home, under their rule, their structure. Sadie needed to treat Min like the adult Min wanted to be, not the child she still was in many ways.

"I'm sorry," Sadie said, lowering her chin and softening her tone. "I respect you for wanting to protect your grandmother. I have no doubt she was also glad to meet you; it must have been a great blessing to have had your help all those months. I would like to know who she wrote the letters to so I can talk to that person and see if they know anything that might help us figure out why this happened to Wendy. I don't mean to make her out to be a villain. I just want to understand what happened. She was sending those letters to some-one and that person might know something important. By helping me, you're helping Wendy, Min."

Min's expression had changed during Sadie's explanation, and she dropped her head before taking a deep breath. Sadie hoped it was meant to give the girl extra resolve to help her. "I didn't pay at-tention to the address or anything except for the fact that it was in Nob Hill."

"Okay, that's helpful," Sadie said, even though it wasn't. She had no idea where Nob Hill was. Was it a district, like Mission and Chinatown, or a whole different city? But she could look it up later, so she didn't push for details. "Thank you. And the name?"

"That part was kinda weird."

"Kinda weird how?"

"Well, I asked her one time if it was her sister or something 'cause they had the same last name. I hadn't thought about how her last name was actually her ex-husband's until way later."

"So the last name was Penrose," Sadie concluded, another piece snapping together. "What was the first name?"

Min shrugged. "I don't remember."

"That's okay," Sadie said quickly, holding onto the fact that it must have been a woman's name for Min to have assumed it was a sister. "This is so helpful. What did she say when you asked if it was her sister?"

Min looked uncomfortable and didn't meet Sadie's eyes. "She said she didn't have a sister."

It still stung, but Sadie nodded as though it didn't.

Min continued. "Then she told me that Penrose was a pretty common name and it was no relation." Min looked past Sadie toward a clock on the wall. "The other employees will be coming in soon. You should probably go."

"Thank you, Min," Sadie said, stepping forward to give her a quick hug. "I so appreciate your help."

"And you're not going to tell my parents about any of this?"

"I'm not," Sadie said, slipping into a more motherly role. "But Wendy's neighbors saw you coming and going from her apartment. The police are going to be looking into it."

Min's eyes went wide and her face paled.

"I won't tell your parents, but they *are* going to find out you were visiting Wendy. It might go better for everyone if you take responsibility and tell them yourself."

Min looked truly terrified at the suggestion.

"Min," Sadie said, putting a hand on the girl's shoulder and giving her a quick squeeze of support and comfort. "Regardless of whether you agree with the way they show it, your parents love you. It's not easy on us parents when our kids grow up. We're scared for them, and it's hard to consider our life without them. However unfair you may think they are, know that they are doing what they believe is best out of love. Even when they know the truth they will *continue* to love you. If I can help you talk to them, just say the word."

Min looked questioning, and Sadie hurried to rescue her from her thoughts. "I realize they don't necessarily like me, but I think you're a good girl . . . uh, young woman, and *if* I can help, I will. I have two children of my own who have grown up and left home. I know how your parents are feeling, but I understand your position as well."

Min nodded and wiped at her eyes, still looking stunned by the unexpected turn. "I, uh, better show you out before anyone comes down." She stepped past Sadie toward the back door.

Sadie followed her into the semidarkness. Min pushed open the door, lighting up the alcove and the boxes lined against the walls. Most of the boxes were labeled in both Chinese and English, and the open one on top caught Sadie's eye—Fortune Cookies. Sadie thought about how helpful the other fortunes she'd read on this trip had been so far. "Could I have a cookie?"

"Sure," Min said, still holding the door open.

Sadie reached into the box and imagined that the right one would feel different than the others. After feeling around for a few seconds, however, she remembered that the employees would be there soon and grabbed a cookie. As she turned toward the door, the box beneath the cookies caught her eye. The word "chopsticks" had been crossed out and relabeled "lamps."

"Do you sell lamps?" Sadie asked, thinking of the display case at the front of the restaurant and the fact that there were no lamps in it. She opened one end of the cellophane wrapper of her cookie.

"We used to have them on the tables. I think my mom's going to sell them online or something."

"Oh, like little oil lamps then, not plug-into-the-wall lamps."

"Yeah, oil lamps. At dinnertime we'd light them and turn off some of the overhead lights. It looked really cool, kind of romantic."

Sadie thought about her first impression of those over-bright fluorescent lights in the restaurant. Lamplight would create such a different ambiance. She removed the cookie from the wrapper. "Why did you get rid of them?"

"*Ma ma* just didn't want them anymore," Min said with a shrug. "She said they were dangerous."

Sadie's fingers stilled instead of breaking open the cookie. "Dangerous?"

"Yeah, because of the kerosene. She was worried one of us girls would get burned when we blew them out and refilled them at night. I guess she didn't think about the fact that we've been filling and cleaning and lighting those lamps our entire lives." Min rolled her eyes.

Kerosene? Sadie looked at the box again. "You used kerosene in the lamps?"

"Well, a synthetic kerosene. It has a higher flash point for indoor use."

Holy cow! "When did your mother take the lamps off the tables?"

"I don't know, a couple of weeks ago maybe?" A sad expression crept over her features. "A lot of stuff happened a couple of weeks ago, didn't it?"

Sadie managed a kind of awkward laugh while thinking *I need to talk to Pete!* But she *couldn't* talk to Pete. What was her next best option? "Min, where's your dad right now?"

"I don't know. He had a meeting this morning. He said he'd be in by the time we open at 11:00 though."

Lin Yang's voice could suddenly be heard from the kitchen, talking to someone in Chinese. Min gave Sadie a quick look of fear, and Sadie hurried through the open door. Min pulled the door closed without saying good-bye, leaving Sadie alone in the alley. Ji had pretty much dismissed her twice now—once over the phone and then again after their dinner last night. Sadie hated ignoring that fact, but she *really* needed to talk to him. More than ever.

CHAPTER 28

Sadie returned to Sacramento Street and walked toward Portsmouth Square, where there were some benches. She'd forgotten about the cookie in her hand until she reached for her phone. Suddenly, the cookie was a chore instead of a pleasure; she put it back in the cellophane wrapper and then in her purse. She didn't have any room in her brain for it at this moment.

The park was full of people: tourists consulting maps, kids playing on the playground, and old Chinese men talking loudly while they played checkers. Sadie found an empty bench on the Washington side and sat down. She sent Ji a text telling him she needed to talk to him ASAP. She didn't have high expectations of him responding since he seemed to ignore her texts far more often than he answered them, but she hoped the sense of urgency would help.

While she waited for him to reply, she thought about the name and address on those letters Min had been mailing for Wendy. She opened the Internet browser on her phone and went to the Next Faces website. She didn't remember Rodger's bio on the site saying anything about his personal life the first time she read it, but she read it again to confirm that there was no mention of a wife. She needed her laptop to do a thorough hunt for information, but it was at the hotel and she didn't want to go too far for fear of missing her chance to talk to Ji.

Verifying if Rodger had a wife and then possibly finding out if she was the person who had hired Mr. Green Shirt was important. But was Sadie giving her suspicions about Lin Yang the proper attention if she could push them aside so easily? Lin Yang had something to do with either Wendy's death or the fire—or both. Topics of focus couldn't get much bigger than that. And yet until Sadie heard back from Ji, what could she do about it?

Feeling stuck reminded Sadie of the fortune cookie. That she would think of a silly cookie at a time of such serious consideration annoyed her. She was not a superstitious person, so as she fished the cookie from her purse she told herself she was simply being efficient and keeping it from getting crushed. After breaking the cookie in half, she pulled the paper out.

New people will bring you new realizations.

Sadie read the fortune a second time and then reviewed the other fortunes she'd received: one had spurred her to get to work, the other had told her to take a hunch seriously. Perhaps she would have done the same things with or without the fortunes—both of Pete's fortunes had been worthless—but silly as it was, those little words of wisdom had given Sadie a bit more confidence in moments when she needed all the confidence she could get.

Sadie pondered the implications of this newest bit of advice found within a cookie shell and the fact that Ji hadn't replied to her text, Pete hadn't contacted her, and she was currently sitting on a bench doing absolutely nothing. Without her laptop she couldn't access the investigative websites she used for background checks, but she didn't need all the fancy access her laptop provided her to do a basic search for information. She might as well do what she could.

She opened up the browser on her phone and Googled "Wife of Rodger Penrose, San Francisco, California." It took a few minutes of weeding through links and images until she found a picture of Rodger with a beautiful blonde woman who looked fifteen years his junior. Sadie followed the image to the website, which belonged to a charity organization that had hosted an event several months earlier. The caption read, "Rodger and Leann Penrose, silver tier boosters."

With a name in hand, Sadie was able to do a more refined search, and a few minutes later she was on the website for a nearby upscale boutique which was owned and operated by one Leann Penrose. Consulting a different map that showed the neighborhoods of San Francisco—or districts—confirmed that the boutique was located in the Nob Hill district, the area Min had said the letters were sent to. According to the map, the boutique was just on the other side of Chinatown, and based on a rough calculation regarding the small blocks, Sadie estimated that it was about a fifteen-minute walk.

If the one letter Sadie had found in Wendy's apartment was any indication, Wendy was likely harassing this woman. On the other side of the coin, however, was that Rodger's wife was the one person Sadie and Pete had identified as having a motivation to hire someone to follow Rodger and see who he ate lunch with. Perhaps those two details were connected.

New people will bring you new realizations.

She looked at the two halves of the cookie in her hand. She wasn't in the mood to eat them, but she'd heard that if you didn't eat the whole cookie, your fortune wouldn't come true. She read the fortune a third time and decided to pay a visit to Mrs. Rodger Penrose.

Min had said Ji would be back to the restaurant by eleven o'clock. Sadie could very well be finished interviewing Leann and back in Chinatown by then, assuming Leann was at the boutique this morning. Sadie checked her watch; it was just after ten o'clock, which was listed as the time the boutique opened Monday through Saturday. Sadie called the number listed on their website.

"*Pour Vous* boutique, this is Tia."

"Hi, is Leann in?"

"Sure. Hold on just a minute."

Sadie hung up, threw both halves of the fortune cookie in her mouth, and put the fortune in the front pocket of her purse with the other ones. She chewed with her cheeks puffed out as she consulted the map on her phone and started walking toward the Nob Hill district, trying to figure out how she would best get Leann Penrose to talk to her.

CHAPTER 29

Sadie's legs were on fire by the time she reached the boutique. The map might have showed distance, but it did *not* show the hills involved in the walk. She rested against the side of the building to catch her breath before pushing through the front door of Pour Vous. She knew the name was French, but wasn't sure what it meant. It sounded like "Poor you," which she didn't think was the kind of association anyone would want for their clothing store, but, well, Sadie had never been in retail.

The small store was packed with brightly colored purses, scarves, and jewelry. There were some clothing items as well, but the focus seemed to be on accessories. Although Sadie was in no mood to shop, her eyes were drawn to a fabulous silver shoulder bag that she knew would coordinate with practically everything she owned.

"Hello. My name is Tia. May I help you?"

The spell was broken. Sadie looked into the face of a young woman dressed in all white, with shimmery green shoes that matched her eye shadow. She had dark coloring, which made the white and green really pop. Sadie wondered if Tia was the girl she'd talked to on the phone a few minutes earlier and hoped she wouldn't recognize Sadie's voice.

"Actually, I was looking for Leann Penrose. Is she here?"

"Sure," Tia said with a smile. "I'll get her." She disappeared, and in her absence, Sadie sidled up to the silver shoulder bag. She lifted it off the rack and inspected it from every angle. It was more of a metallic gray than actual silver, and it had fun detailing that almost looked like flowers but wasn't too flamboyant.

She put it over her shoulder and noted how perfectly it held against her side. It wasn't so big as to look like luggage, but it was large enough to hold anything she could need. Sadie took it off her shoulder and looked at it again. For the last few years, she'd favored the cross-body purses that allowed her to be hands-free, but she'd admired bags like this and loved the femininity of this one in particular.

She checked the price tag and felt her eyes widen before immediately shifting into justification for the expense. She wasn't having a bridal shower, so couldn't this be a kind of wedding present for herself? But thinking of the wedding made her think of Pete and the weirdness between them that might change everything. She put the purse back.

"Hello?"

Sadie turned and found herself facing the woman she'd just looked up photos of online. Leann was dressed in royal blue skinny jeans and a gold-and-white striped shirt with an orange scarf tied around her neck. Despite the colors being so different and so bright, they all worked somehow. The girl—uh, woman—also looked to be about a size four.

Sadie wondered if anything in this store would even fit her other than the purses, scarves, and jewelry. She held out her hand. "Hi, my name is Sadie Hoffmiller, and I wondered if you had a few minutes to talk to me."

Leann's smile remained polite as she shook Sadie's hand—limply—but there was a glimmer of confusion in her green eyes. "I suppose. How can I help you?"

Sadie paused, and whatever brilliant ideas she'd had about how to approach this woman fizzled out. A customer entered the store and both Sadie and Leann glanced at her before making eye contact again. "Um, well, actually, it's a little delicate. Could we go somewhere private?"

Leann pulled her eyebrows together, but just a little. A Botox scowl for sure. She also turned her head slightly to the side as though expectant or hesitant, Sadie couldn't be sure which. Tia began talking with the new customer, leading her to the other side of the store, though that wasn't very far away.

"Delicate?" Leann repeated in a cautious tone.

"Um." Sadie took a breath. "I'm Wendy's sister."

Leann's expression turned to surprise—at least as much as it could—and she took a step back. She said nothing, leaving it up to Sadie to continue. "I'm sure I'm the last person you want to talk to, and I have no desire to make things more uncomfortable for you than Wendy has already done, but will you please talk to me?"

"I never met her," Leann said, the tiniest note of fear in her voice. "I wouldn't have anything to say to you."

"Was she sending you letters?"

Leann's nostrils flared, and she looked around as though making sure no one could overhear them. Then she closed her eyes and lifted a hand to her forehead. "Oh gosh," she said under her breath, shaking her head as though in disbelief. After a moment, she opened her eyes and looked at Sadie. "So it *was* her?"

"You didn't know?"

The bell above the door sounded. Two more young women, laughing with each other, entered the store together. They were slender and sparkly with long hair in loose curls and painted nails that caught the light; Leann's signature customer, Sadie assumed.

"This isn't a good time. I work all day today—it's the weekend." Leann clasped her hands together in front of her and began scratching one nail with the thumb of her other hand.

"I only have a few questions. We can get through them quickly." She wanted to add "if you'll cooperate," but that sounded a little too threatening. "If I *could* come back later, I would. I'm really not trying to make this hard on purpose, but I have limited time and what I need to talk to you about is *really* important. I need to understand those letters."

Leann started shaking her head in refusal, leaving Sadie no choice but to pull out the big guns.

"I had lunch with Rodger yesterday, and a man followed me out of the restaurant."

Leann stopped shaking her head as her jaw went slack. *Bingo.*

"I need answers, Leann," Sadie said in a pleading, but kind, tone. "If I can't get them from you, I'll have to ask Rodger, and—"

"No," Leann said. She bit her lip. "Did you already tell him about the man who followed you?"

Sadie shook her head, relieved that she hadn't talked to Rodger about Mr. Green Shirt. "I haven't spoken to Rodger since our lunch."

"What *did* you and Rodger talk about at lunch?" Leann asked, still anxious but no longer casting her eyes around the store with such furtive discomfort.

"I'd be happy to tell you everything Rodger and I talked about if you'll help me understand the letters."

For a moment, it looked as though Leann was vacillating, though Sadie wasn't convinced it was entirely legitimate since the look in her eye had become calculating. Leann wanted to know what Sadie and Rodger had discussed.

"Okay," she finally said, then turned toward the cash register where her employee was not disguising her curiosity very well. The three customers in the store were browsing on their own. "Tia, I'll be back as soon as I can. Watch the store."

CHAPTER 30

M aybe we could go to a café or something?" Leann suggested as
she and Sadie stepped onto the sidewalk.

"That would be perfect," Sadie said. She nearly asked if there
was a place nearby before realizing that there were a hundred places
nearby. It was just a matter of choosing one and walking a few yards
in any direction.

Leann nodded. "I could use some coffee." She led the way to the
closest Starbucks—one of an estimated six hundred or so Sadie had
seen since she'd arrived.

Leann stepped up to the counter and ordered a nonfat café latte.
No wonder she was a size four. Sadie wondered if a nonfat café latte
had any flavor at all; she preferred flavor to skinny jeans.

Sadie ordered a vanilla steamer with two percent milk instead of
the whole milk she'd have preferred and patted herself on the back
for not ordering a chocolate croissant to go with it.

They both stepped aside once they'd ordered and waited for
their names to be called when the drinks were ready.

Leann stood beside Sadie with her arms crossed over her chest, more protective than defensive. "How do you know about the letters?" she asked without looking at Sadie. "Did she keep copies?"

Sadie wished Wendy *had* kept copies, but she hadn't. "No, I didn't find any copies but I found a letter that hadn't been sent." She told Leann what the letter said, and Leann closed her eyes as though struggling to hear it. "Were they all like that?" Sadie asked.

Leann nodded but didn't say anything.

"Did you believe it?" Why else would Leann have hired a private investigator?

Leann shook her head. "Rodger and I have a good marriage," she said before letting out a breath that communicated some insecurity. "But those letters were so horrible, I couldn't help but wonder whether or not it could be true."

The barista called Leann's name, and she stepped forward to get her latte. A moment later, Sadie's name was called. The two women automatically headed back to a small table at the far end of the coffee shop. It couldn't really be called private, but it would do.

"Does Rodger know about the letters?" Sadie asked once they had sat down and stirred their drinks with the tiny straws.

Leann shook her head and took a sip of her coffee.

"Was the private investigator trying to figure out who was sending the letters?"

"Yeah," Leann said with a hint of embarrassment in her voice.

"*And* determine if Rodger was having an affair?"

Leann nodded and looked at the cup she was holding in both hands.

"Why did you suspect it was Wendy sending them?"

"One of the first letters said that the only woman he'd ever really loved was Wendy and that he'd go back to her eventually. None of the other letters gave any indication about the identity of who was sending them, but I knew Wendy was crazy enough to do something like that." She looked up, perhaps to see if Sadie was offended by the accusation, but Sadie just smiled, noting that it was getting easier to hear people tell her hard things.

"Your PI never found out it was her?"

"Not conclusively, no, but he did learn that Rodger and Wendy were talking on the phone nearly every day." There was a catch in her voice, but something was off about it; it seemed theatrical somehow. Rodger had met Wendy through his talent agency. Maybe he'd met Leann the same way. Then again, maybe it was Sadie's own cynicism that had her considering such a possibility. It was a reminder, however, for her not to take the things this woman said at face value. There may very well be an agenda that Sadie knew nothing about.

"You didn't know they were talking?" Sadie asked.

Leann looked at her in surprise. "You did?"

Sadie carefully chose what information to give her, hoping it would bring her more information in exchange. "I talked to Rodger about it at lunch yesterday, but he said he knew Wendy was mentally ill and struggled in winter months, so he talked to her when she called because she had no one else. But he didn't tell *you* that?" If they were innocent phone calls, why not talk to Leann about it over a glass of wine at the end of the day?

Leann took a sip of her drink. "Wendy is a bit of a sore subject between us."

"Why?"

Leann tapped her fingernails against her cup. "Are you married?"

"I was, once," Sadie said.

"Well, maybe you can't understand then, but I've never been married before, and I thought when Rodger and I got married that it would be him and me—that's it. Instead, he's got this ex-wife who takes his money every month, is in all these photos throughout our house, and is known by his friends and some of his associates. People talk about her all the time. She was so over-the-top and engaging, so wacky and weird, that she made an impression. I am constantly told 'Wendy' stories when I'm with Rodger's friends."

Sadie tried not to squirm amid the similarities of her own situation, with Pete's wife having such a presence in their relationship right now.

Leann continued, "And, because of her taking Rodger to the cleaners, I had to sign a prenup, which didn't seem like a big deal before we were married. But once I learned he was talking to her on the phone every day . . . If things don't work out with Rodger and me, I get nothing and Wendy keeps getting all that alimony." She took another sip of her drink and what seemed to be a calming breath. "So, yeah, Rodger telling me that he talked to her on the phone almost every day wasn't something that would have gone over very well." Leann looked down at the table, possibly so Sadie wouldn't notice that, despite her wiping at her eyes, there weren't any tears. She took a breath and looked up. "That he was talking to her and *didn't* tell me is even worse."

"Sounds like things have been hard for you guys," Sadie said, wondering why Leann had previously said that she and Rodger had a good marriage. "When did the letters start arriving?"

"December," Leann said. "Right before Christmas. In fact, the first one looked like a Christmas card except it was pink. Anyway, inside it told me that I better enjoy the holiday because Rodger would surely have left me by that time next year. It was terrible."

"I'm so sorry," Sadie said with complete sincerity. "Why didn't you tell Rodger about it?"

"Would you tell your husband and give him a chance to cover his tracks?"

I would if I didn't think it was true, Sadie thought. But obviously there was enough insecurity in Leann's marriage that she didn't have such confidence. "When did you hire the private investigator?"

"After the third letter. They came every couple of weeks so it would have been the end of January, I think. I had to get some confirmation or I was going to lose my mind."

"So you were getting the letters and then the PI you hired confirmed that Rodger was talking to Wendy on the phone every day."

"At the *office,*" Leann emphasized. "Not on his cell phone, where I might have seen the number."

"Did you know *she* was the one calling *him?*"

"Most of the time she was," Leann said. "But my PI got copies of the office phone bills and Rodger was calling her sometimes, too."

Sadie kept her surprise to herself. She only had access to the numbers Wendy had called, and Rodger had made the contact sound so one-sided that she hadn't even considered he might have initiated additional phone conversations. If he was, then it cast doubt on the explanation he'd given Sadie about simply trying to pacify Wendy during a difficult time.

"Did your PI discover proof that Rodger was being unfaithful?"

"No, he didn't."

Was Leann disappointed about that? Sadie wondered. And how jealous was she? If she was jealous enough to hire a PI for months, was she jealous enough to put a stop to the contact between Rodger and Wendy once and for all? Leann wouldn't care if the body stayed in the apartment for a month, and with Sadie's new theory that Lin Yang was the fire-starter, Leann could have killed Wendy somehow and then staged the robbery the police were assuming had happened at the time of the fire.

And yet, the main frustration Leann had communicated so far was the fact that Wendy's alimony had forced Leann to have to sign a prenup. That was only an issue if Rodger and Leann divorced, right? Something wasn't matching up, Sadie just didn't know what.

"What did you think when the phone calls and the letters stopped?"

"I was just so relieved," Leann said, stirring her coffee again.

"How did you find out about Wendy's death?" Sadie asked after considering and rejecting half a dozen other ways to ask the question.

"The police contacted Rodger. I hadn't received any letters after we returned from our anniversary cruise so when we found out she'd died during the time we were gone, it pretty much confirmed my suspicions that she was the one writing them."

"Is that where Rodger was the last part of May?" Sadie asked. He'd only told her he'd been out of town.

Leann nodded. "We take an anniversary trip every year. This year he surprised me with two weeks in the Mediterranean. We had a good time, and I felt like we were getting things back to where they'd been before the letters, you know?"

There were still a few more holes Sadie needed to fill. "So you never met Wendy?"

Leann shook her head.

"Did you know where she lived?"

"My PI found out her exact address. Before then I only knew she was in one of Steve's buildings," Leann said, shrugging one slender shoulder.

Steve? As in Stephen Pilings, the landlord? Sadie felt her proverbial antennae flip up, then noticed Leann's expression turning hesitant, suspicious. Had Sadie not schooled her expression as well as she should have?

"I really need to get back," Leann said, taking a final sip of her drink. "I hope I've been able to help."

"You've been very helpful," Sadie said, though she realized that she had told Leann very little about her conversation with Rodger yesterday, which made her wonder if there was another reason for Leann to have agreed to talk to her. Fortify her position, perhaps? "I just have a couple of more questions, then I won't bother you again."

Leann gave a tolerant smile.

"The letters weren't mailed from Wendy's zip code, right?"

"No," Leann said. "They were sent from Chinatown."

"Wendy's son lives in Chinatown—did you know that?"

Leann nodded easily, unsurprised to hear that Ji existed.

"You know about him?"

"Yes," Leann said, obviously unsure why this was important but sensing that it was.

"How?"

"My PI found out about him. We figured he was mailing the letters for his mother, or maybe that she was visiting him and mailing the letters when she was in that part of town. Is it important?"

"Well, Rodger told me yesterday that he only learned about Wendy's son from the police after her body was found."

It was just a flicker—a small and inconsequential flash behind her eyes—and it was gone too quickly for Sadie to interpret it properly. "Right," Leann said with a nod that was more animated than anything else in the conversation. "He was really surprised by it since he had no idea. Is that all? I really do need to get back."

She was totally covering for Rodger. He'd known about Ji before the police told him but pretended that he didn't. Why would he do that? Leann was watching her, and Sadie had an image of Leann calling Rodger as soon as they parted company to tell her version of this conversation. She would likely leave out several details—or maybe she wouldn't. Maybe knowing that Sadie knew about the PI would spur Leann to explain herself before the police got wind of it or before Rodger learned about the letters another way.

"One last question," Sadie asked quickly. "If you had your PI following Rodger because you were afraid that he and Wendy were having an affair, then, when all contact with her stopped over a month ago and Wendy was found dead two *weeks* ago, why did the PI follow Rodger yesterday?"

Leann's left eye twitched ever so slightly. "I feel better when I know who Rodger's spending time with, that's all."

Earlier Leann had said that she and Rodger had a good marriage. But they couldn't talk about his ex-wife, Leann had started getting letters weeks before Rodger's phone calls with Wendy had begun and didn't tell him, *and* she liked keeping a PI on the payroll to keep tabs on her husband? That wasn't anywhere near a "good" marriage in Sadie's opinion.

She took a drink of her steamer as she pondered why *else* Leann would keep paying a PI month after month. It would be expensive— and Leann had been frustrated that Rodger was still paying alimony to Wendy—and seemingly unnecessary since Leann claimed that the PI hadn't found any evidence of Rodger being unfaithful.

A couple of years back, Sadie had owned her own private investigation firm. Part of why she hadn't stuck with the business was that the majority of the work she was hired to do consisted of background checks that required hours on the computer and tedious amounts of paperwork. The next most common job she was hired for involved following spouses suspected of cheating. She had hated standing in the shadows and taking pictures of people coming and going from hotel rooms—that hadn't been why she'd wanted to become a PI.

Working those cases, however, had required her to learn a few things about prenuptial agreements and how they worked. They weren't what most people thought they were—one rich person protecting his or her assets—and they were often complex agreements with a sliding scale of settlements based on when and why the marriage fell apart.

"I really need to get back to the shop," Leann said. "The tourist traffic is going to start picking up soon."

"Right," Sadie said with a nod. "Can I ask you *one* more question?"

Leann let out a dramatic breath and gave a polite, if not tight, smile.

"I've heard that some prenuptial agreements have a stipulation that has certain settlements based on the behavior of the partners and, in California, don't both parties need to have legal representation when the agreement is entered into?"

The hardening of Leann's expression told Sadie she was on the right track.

"I can't help but wonder," Sadie continued, "if your attorney made sure there was some language regarding what would happen if *Rodger* cheated on *you,* if your marriage fell apart through no fault of your own. What kind of settlement do you get if you can prove he committed adultery?"

Leann stood abruptly, all of her pretenses gone in an instant. "I need to get back to work."

Sadie barely had time to stand herself before Leann breezed out of the coffee shop. Sadie opted not to follow her and instead sat back down and watched through the window as Leann disappeared from view.

The only conclusion Sadie could draw from the final question asked but not answered was that Leann stood to get some kind of settlement if Rodger was the unfaithful party in their relationship. Not only was Leann willing to pay someone to find out if that were true, she was pretty eager to get the information. Someone wanted out of that relationship, and Sadie didn't think it was Rodger Penrose.

Sadie hoped that by calling Leann out, she had bought herself some time before Leann would tell Rodger they'd talked. She wanted to follow up on the new questions she now had about Rodger and what he had told her at lunch yesterday. She hoped she could figure it all out; she needed all the time she could get right now.

CHAPTER 31

Sadie took a few more sips of her steamer, which was now optimally cooled, and then checked her phone. It was nearly 11:00, but Ji still hadn't texted her back—never mind that Pete hadn't contacted her either. Should she go back to Choy's and meet up with Ji there? But then she'd learned some things from Leann that she wanted to follow up on, too—like the fact that Leann knew Stephen Pilings, so Rodger probably knew the landlord, too. And Rodger might have known about Ji sooner than he claimed, which begged the question of why he would hide that knowledge. No, not hide—lie about. Very different word.

Pete might have the answers she needed, assuming he'd spent the day researching the things she'd asked him to, but she'd have to call him to find out and that could potentially undermine her "I'm confident enough to give you the distance you need" demeanor that was *killing* her to maintain.

She didn't know what to do about Pete or Ji, but she had to do something, so she opened up an Internet browser on her phone and looked up Stephen Pilings. She found a Facebook page and, after a few false starts, came across a property management company based in San Francisco. She opened up the "Properties" tab on the website, and the third photo down was Wendy's building on 22nd Street and Mission. Rodger had admitted to *financially* helping Wendy get into that building. Was it too much of a stretch to assume he might have asked a favor from a friend with an available apartment, too?

There was no bio for Stephen Pilings on the website, though his name was listed as owner. Once again, if she were in her hotel room with access to the sites she used to do background searches she could review all kinds of public records and start to build a profile of both him and Rodger Penrose. She could go to the hotel and do it now, but that would take her away from the other lead she wanted to follow: Lin Yang setting Wendy on fire.

Thinking that made her head spin all over again. Had Lin Yang really done that or was Sadie grasping at straws? What possible reason could motivate anyone to do something so horrendous? If she accused Lin Yang of setting the fire and she was wrong, her chances of a relationship with Ji were over. If she were right, though, would her chances be any better? Beyond that, was a relationship with her nephew the ultimate prize or was truth the goal she should be reaching for?

She leaned back in the metal chair and put her phone on the table. She closed her eyes and pressed her hands to her temples, trying to ward off the headache that was knocking at the base of her skull. What should she do now? Where was another fortune cookie when she needed it?

"Are you finished?"

Sadie opened her eyes to see a young woman poised to pick up Leann's cup, which was likely still half full. "Yes, thank you."

She stood up as the girl took both cups. She adjusted her purse over her shoulder and thought of the silver bag in Leann's shop.

Whatever enthusiasm she'd had for it half an hour ago was gone. There was no room in her brain for something so frivolous now.

She was almost out the door, still unsure of whether she would go to Choy's or to her hotel, when her phone alerted her to a text message. She'd never moved faster to get her phone out of her purse to see who the text was from: Ji or Pete?

Ji: I'm here now. What do you need to talk to me about?

Was this a sign that she should keep her focus on Ji and Lin Yang for the time being? She got another text.

Ji: There's something I need to talk with you about too. When can you be here? If you could beat the lunch rush, I'd appreciate it. We get hit hard after 12.

Just like that, the decision was made. A block later, Sadie stepped away from the sidewalk so as not to disrupt the flow of foot traffic. If she wasn't going to be pursuing the possible connection between Stephen Pilings and Rodger Penrose right now, she needed to share the information she had with Pete so that he could. It was silly to let her emotions get in the way of sharing information about the case. It would also be a relief to know that while she was busy with one unsavory task, progress would be made on another one.

I think Rodger P and landlord know each other. Can you follow up? Rodger P's wife, Leann, hired PI that followed me because she suspects infidelity. On my way to talk to Ji. Also Choy's has synthetic kerosene & Lin Yang was at apt days before fire.

She read it through again and then sent the text, wondering if Pete would call her in response, as he had at other times during this trip. Just in case, she debated in her mind how she should act if he did call. Professional or aloof? If he brought up the issues between them, should she discuss them or insist they focus on the case for now? She started walking and was waiting at a crosswalk when the response arrived.

Ask Ji about life insurance—PD just got a call about a claim.
I will look into Rodger/landlord angle. Lin Yang + kerosene?
Yikes. Be safe. Love you.

Sadie cleared her throat and blinked quickly to overcome the emotion the last two words of his text brought up. He did love her. Which made this all the more confusing for both of them. She thought about how Leann's jealousy of Wendy had made her an impossible topic between Rodger and Leann. Granted, there were likely other things going on in their relationship, and Wendy wasn't well, but Sadie still saw it as an example of what she didn't want between her and Pete.

But she couldn't focus on that right now. She had a very awkward conversation coming up and needed to be ready for it. As she walked toward Chinatown, and planned how she would respond to a variety of imagined scenarios once she arrived, she thought of the other information from Pete's text message. Sadie didn't remember seeing anything about a life insurance policy in the boxes of files.

But Ji had been sorting the messy box when he'd left yesterday. And a claim had been called in—had it just been this morning? Didn't Min say Ji was at a meeting this morning?

She picked up her pace and hoped she could keep all the questions straight in her mind. Now was not the time to get lost in confusion.

CHAPTER 32

Sadie reached Choy's around 11:15 and, with her hand on the door, she took a deep breath and prayed for . . . whatever she might need during this discussion. She walked in and blinked at the bright interior, just as she had the first time. The bright lights made her think of the oil lamps that had been removed from the tables for no good reason, lamps that used the same type of fuel that had been used on Wendy. The thought made her shudder.

There were some men seated around one table, although the rest of the restaurant was empty. Sadie scanned the room for Lin Yang, relieved that she wasn't there at the moment. She headed toward the red double doors of the kitchen and was just raising her hand to push them open when they pushed back at her instead. She quickly moved out of the way; she'd been hit by a door before and had no desire to repeat the experience.

Lin Yang stepped through the doors with a teapot in one hand, her fingers clutching the handle a bit tighter when she saw Sadie. They faced off for a moment before Sadie found her voice.

"I'm here to talk to Ji."

Lin Yang didn't move and her expression remained hard, which detracted significantly from her natural beauty. "Ji is busy. Only employees are allowed in the kitchen."

"He asked me to come."

"Come back another time."

Sadie stared the woman down. "He asked me to come *right now*."

A bell jingled, and Sadie and Lin Yang both looked toward the door, where a young family stood blinking in the bright lights.

"Wait for me," Lin Yang said, then stepped past Sadie. "Four?" she asked the new arrivals.

Sadie remained where she was, directly in front of the kitchen doors, and looked at the bamboo design in the plaster of the wall. She so wanted to head through those doors and find Ji, but she didn't want to make a scene at his place of business. Or did she?

She watched Lin Yang hand out menus and fill the old men's teacups before putting the pot on the table. This morning Lin Yang had been aggressive with her, but they had been alone—relatively; now Ji was in the next room, and Sadie knew even more than she'd known when she'd talked to Lin Yang earlier. In the time it took Lin Yang to return to her, Sadie had changed her goals for this meeting. She would talk to Ji, but she would also take advantage of the chance to talk to Lin Yang, too.

"As I said," Lin Yang said, "now is not a good time. The lunch rush is starting. I will have Ji call you and decide another time that the two of you can talk, if that's what you wish."

"You went to see Wendy a few days before the fire."

Lin Yang didn't react at all; instead she crossed her arms and fixed Sadie with her signature cold look. "You know nothing," she said simply.

"I also know about the lamps you took off the tables at about the same time that Wendy's body went up in smoke. The same type of fuel in those lamps was used to—"

Lin Yang suddenly kicked at Sadie's knees, throwing her off balance.

She put out her hands to catch herself, but Lin Yang grabbed one arm and twisted it behind Sadie's back so that by the time Sadie fell hard to her knees, one arm was pinned behind her and the pain radiating from her shoulder left her speechless.

The exclamations of the customers in both English and Chinese didn't drown out the hissing sound of Lin Yang's voice in her ear. "You know nothing. Get out of my restaurant and don't come back."

Sadie was ready to agree to whatever Lin Yang asked; she could barely think straight for the pain shooting up her arm, through her shoulder, and down her back. But reason took over. Lin Yang was obviously desperate to chase Sadie away, and that in and of itself communicated how much she had to hide. But Lin Yang had reacted impulsively—they weren't alone here.

"Ji!" Sadie screamed as loudly as she could, which, unfortunately, didn't come out as strong as she'd have liked.

Lin Yang pulled her arm up higher, and Sadie just screamed that time, but it was louder than her first attempt.

One of the men at the table said something, and Lin Yang turned and yelled at him in Chinese without letting go of Sadie's arm.

Sadie could barely breathe for the pain when she heard the spring-action hinge of the kitchen door and Ji's voice at the same time. "What is going on out here?"

Lin Yang answered in Chinese. Ji responded in the same language.

Sadie waited for Lin Yang to let go of her arm, but she didn't until Ji pulled her away. Sadie crumpled onto the linoleum, her torso trembling as she tried to put her arm back into a normal position. Her chest heaved for breath, and then people were helping her to her feet.

"Thank you," she said once she'd been assisted to a chair by two Chinese men.

Ji and Lin Yang were still yelling at each other, and although Sadie couldn't understand anything they said, their tone of voice and the expressions on the old men's faces let her know that the discussion was serious. One man whispered to the other, who nodded before casting a sidelong look at the fighting couple, as though not wanting them to know he was watching.

"Are you all right?"

Sadie looked into the face of the father of the family who'd been seated a minute earlier. She looked past him to the mother and two children who stood by the door, looking scared. "I'm fine now," she said. "Thank you."

The man looked between Ji and Lin Yang. "We're outta here. You should come with us."

"He's my nephew," Sadie said, waving toward Ji, who was now screaming at Lin Yang, who was screaming back. Sadie forced a smile. "He won't let anything happen to me."

The man didn't seem convinced, but a moment later he nodded and then ushered his family out of the restaurant. The Chinese men were right behind them, still whispering to each other and trying not to look at Ji and Lin Yang, who were nearly nose-to-nose. The veins in Ji's neck were bulging. Although he was more than a foot taller than his tiny wife, her ferocity balanced them out.

Sadie stayed in her seat. She wasn't sure her legs would hold her up if she tried to stand. She took a breath in anticipation of entering the foray from where she sat and then yelled, "I think Lin Yang lit Wendy on fire!"

Ji and Lin Yang snapped their heads toward Sadie. Silence. Sadie watched their reflexive expressions. Ji was shocked and confused. Lin Yang, on the other hand, was angry. She glanced at Ji and said something in a normal tone of voice, but Ji didn't even look at her. He continued to stare at Sadie.

"What?" he said after a few more moments had passed.

Sadie quickly organized the details in her mind so she could present a solid hypothesis. "I think Lin Yang went to Wendy's apartment and doused her body with the kerosene you used to use in the lamps on the tables, and then she lit Wendy's body on fire."

Ji blinked, then turned to Lin Yang and spoke to her in English. Sadie could only assume it was for her benefit. "What is she talking about?"

"She's as crazy as Wendy," Lin Yang said, sending Sadie a hateful look. "I don't know what she's talking about. I had nothing to do with Wendy."

Someone opened the front door, and they all turned to look at a young couple who stopped short just over the threshold.

"We are closed," Ji said, walking toward them.

The young man pointed toward the sign lit up in the window. "But the sign says—"

Ji marched to the sign and turned it off. "We are closed." He said it harshly enough that the potential customers backed away from him and exited without argument. Ji pulled the door closed behind them, turned the lock, and then faced Sadie, who was still sitting, rubbing her throbbing arm. Sadie had had surgery on this shoulder a couple of years ago; she hoped Lin Yang hadn't damaged it too severely.

"Lin Yang *didn't* have anything to do with Wendy," Ji said. "She only met her a few times, and I had never even been to Wendy's apartment until this week. Why would you make this kind of accusation?"

Sadie told him about Lin Yang being seen at the apartment, the lamps being removed from the tables around the same time, and the forensic tests that determined the accelerant used on Wendy's decaying corpse was synthetic kerosene.

Lin Yang cut her off in Chinese and took a step toward her husband.

He glared at her, causing her to stop. "English," Ji commanded her.

"I will not talk of this with her here." She scowled at Sadie, who held her eyes without showing the intimidation she felt.

"Oh, yes, you will," Ji said. "Or I will call the police and do nothing to help you when they arrive."

He believes me, Sadie thought, shocked at how easily he'd sided with her.

Lin Yang took a breath, and her eyes narrowed when she spoke. "I did it for you."

Ji visibly startled. "Me?"

Sadie held her breath.

"To protect you," Lin Yang said flatly.

Ji startled a second time. "Protect me from what?"

"From the police. She was an evil woman, and I would not let her ruin our family."

"What are you talking about?" Ji said, anger building with every word.

"I knew you wouldn't stand for Min seeing her. I understand why you did it—you were protecting our family, as was I."

Ji was quiet, his eyebrows furrowing, then lifting, then furrowing again as he thought through what Lin Yang had said.

Sadie watched them closely, her entire body tight in anticipation of what was unfolding before her and with anxiety about what might be coming next.

"You think I killed my mother?" Ji finally said.

"As I said, you were only doing what was best for our family. For Min."

"Min?" he said, sounding more confused than ever. "What does Min have to do with any of this?"

Sadie waited for Lin Yang to say something, but she suddenly looked confused and kept her mouth closed. Had Lin Yang thought Ji found out about Min and Wendy and had killed his mother because of it? Did Lin Yang, then, burn the body to cover for him and then place the anonymous call to the fire department?

"Min met Wendy last year," Sadie said, looking at Ji when she spoke. "Wendy had come to see you here at the restaurant but met Min instead. They struck up a friendship, and Min would go see her sometimes. You really didn't know?"

"I'd have never allowed it if I'd known," Ji said, his voice little more than a growl. "My mother was a terrible influence, but . . ." He turned to Lin Yang. "You think I would kill my mother?"

"She was horrible," Lin Yang said, her tone justifying her accusation.

"But you think I would *kill* her?" His eyebrows went up, and he took a step away from Lin Yang. "You went to her apartment? You—"

Lin Yang began to speak in Chinese again, pleading.

"English!" Ji shouted at her, causing her to jump.

Sadie watched Lin Yang's small hands clench into fists and felt herself tensing all over again in response. She knew better than to underestimate Lin Yang again. She was brutal when she wanted to be.

"I did it for you," she said in a cold voice.

"You have *never* done anything for me," Ji spat back. They glowered at one another, and Sadie took the silence as her chance to throw out another question. She looked at Lin Yang.

"Did *you* kill Wendy?"

Lin Yang waved that away as though annoyed. "She was long dead by the time I—" She caught herself mid-confession and pursed her tiny lips.

"You were seen at the apartment a few days before the fire," Sadie said. "Maybe you'd gone there a month earlier, too."

Lin Yang glared at her, and then turned to Ji as though looking for his support. He had his arms folded over his chest and stared at a spot on the floor; he said nothing. When Lin Yang realized he was not going to speak, she looked at Sadie with abject hatred in her eyes. "Of course I didn't kill her. I didn't know about Min seeing her until a few weeks ago."

"How did you find out?" Sadie asked.

Lin Yang looked between Ji and Sadie, then lifted her chin slightly. "Someone called the restaurant asking for Wendy Penrose's son. I asked to take a message. They said that they hadn't heard from Wendy for some time and wondered if Ji or our daughter had spoken to her recently. I couldn't understand why anyone would think one of our daughters would know anything about Wendy. And then I found a picture of Wendy on Min's phone."

Sadie felt her heartbeat racing. Someone had tipped off Lin Yang!

Lin Yang glanced at Ji again. "I didn't want to upset you so I went to talk to Wendy myself, to tell her to leave us alone." Sadie wondered if Lin Yang had planned to beat Wendy up too, but she didn't say as much out loud. "Wendy was already dead," Lin Yang finished.

"How did you get in the building?" Ji asked with skepticism. He wasn't convinced that Lin Yang's involvement was limited to the fire. "You have to be buzzed in."

"When she didn't answer my requests on the intercom, I waited until someone left, then caught the door before it closed. I didn't break in."

What impressive morality, Sadie thought to herself. Breaking in was wrong, but burning a corpse could be justified.

"And her apartment?" Ji asked.

"Was unlocked. When she didn't answer, I tried the door and it was open."

"Someone called you," Sadie said. "Who?"

"They did not say and I did not care. I wanted none of Wendy in our life." She made a dismissive gesture with her hand.

"Was it a man or a woman?"

Lin Yang glared at her, withholding her answer until Ji asked her the same thing.

"A woman."

A woman? Leann was the first woman to come to Sadie's mind. The *only* woman to come to mind. Sadie was so caught up trying to determine what in Leann's hidden agenda would lead to the phone call that she missed the first part of what Lin Yang said next.

" . . . and I was protecting my family." She turned a softer look on her husband, who was so tense he looked as though he were carved from stone. "I thought you had killed her, and if it were discovered, we'd have lost everything. I have no regrets." She said something else in Chinese.

Ji shot her an angry look, his jaw tight. "You had no qualms about my being a murderer?"

"She was a horrible woman," Lin Yang said.

Something was wrong with Lin Yang. Very, very wrong. Even if their marriage wasn't a happy one—and Sadie had seen nothing to convince her otherwise—their children were obviously their world, which made their family of utmost importance. Important enough for Ji to kill for, in Lin Yang's mind. Important enough for Lin Yang to destroy evidence and clean up any proof that might lead the police to Ji, too.

"Did *you* call the fire department that night?" Sadie asked.

Lin Yang looked hesitant, then down at the floor. "I thought the alarm would go off in the building, but I waited across the street for a few minutes and nothing had happened. I didn't want anyone to get hurt."

Sadie found Lin Yang's sense of humility disturbing. She was proud of setting the fire, but seemed embarrassed to have made the call.

"Did you stage the burglary?" Sadie said, determined to learn everything she could from this conversation. She was quite sure that after this, Lin Yang would never speak to her again.

"I thought that would help the police," she said, though it made no sense to Sadie. "If they thought it was for a robbery, they wouldn't look elsewhere."

Rather than consider Ji for killing his mother to prevent her from having a relationship with his daughter. Yes, something was very wrong with Lin Yang. She was impulsive and yet contemplative, logical but with distorted thinking.

Sadie was satisfied with what she'd learned about the fire and turned to look at Ji, waiting until he met her eye before she asked the question she had already asked him twice before. "Why did you leave the office yesterday, Ji? I thought it might have been because you'd discovered Min and Wendy's relationship, but that wasn't it, was it?"

Ji shook his head, then uncrossed his arms and reached into the wide front pocket of his chef's jacket. He pulled out some folded papers. "I finished all the packing I could think to do after you left and moved everything to the living room. I thought I could finish sorting the box you'd been working on, but a few minutes into that task, I found this." He unfolded the papers and held them out toward Sadie.

She stood and crossed the room toward him to retrieve them. She kept her eyes on Lin Yang's balled fists. She now understood how she herself had gained the upper hand in so many prior altercations with people much bigger and stronger than herself: they'd underestimated her, just as she'd underestimated Lin Yang. Sadie was determined not to make that mistake again.

Sadie scanned the paper enough to verify that it was a life insurance policy. She looked up at Ji. "Why didn't you tell me you'd found this?"

Ji indicated for her to turn the page, which she did, scanning the second page as he explained what she was reading. "I'm the sole beneficiary. After listening to you and Pete talk about who would have had a reason to kill Wendy, I worried you would see it as motivation."

Sadie felt her eyebrows go up when she read that the policy was for four hundred thousand dollars. She looked up at him. "You didn't know about this until yesterday?"

Lin Yang was watching, listening, but seemed as tense as ever and a little confused, leading Sadie to believe this was the first she was hearing of the insurance policy, too.

"No," Ji said. "And even after I found it, I didn't believe it. Or at least I didn't believe it was valid. I wanted to make sure it was real before I told you and Pete about it."

"Is it valid?" Sadie asked, but she already knew the answer. The insurance company had called the police that morning, and she didn't imagine they would do that unless it were an active policy.

Ji nodded but he didn't look like a man who had just inherited nearly half a million dollars. "I called the agent listed on the form and met with him this morning. He'd helped Wendy get it just over a year ago. She paid for two years' worth of premiums up front."

The kitchen doors opened, and Min stood there, her eyes red, her face wet with tears. Sadie tried to give her a compassionate look but Min hung her head in humility and wouldn't meet anyone's eyes. Sadie silently pled that her parents would be soft with her; the girl needed some kindness.

"I am so sorry, *Ba ba, Ma ma*," she said in a shaky voice, still looking at the floor.

Lin Yang began snapping in Chinese until Ji silenced her. He turned to Min, and Sadie watched him consciously relax his expression. "Tell me," he said simply.

Min sniffled and then recounted much of the same story she'd already told Sadie about meeting Wendy and going to her apartment. "I just wanted to know her, and then I wanted to help her. She was very sad. I would clean her apartment and keep things straight and organized. I thought I could help her feel better. I wanted to make her happy."

"But you couldn't, could you?" Ji said, softly enough that Sadie's breath caught in her throat. He'd wanted to help Wendy feel happy, too, and at some point in his life had had to admit that he was equally incapable.

Min shook her head.

"You were wrong to go against us," Lin Yang cut in, angry and sharp. "I am embarrassed and—"

"She's twenty years old," Sadie couldn't help but add. "Talk to her like an adult who made a choice to get to know someone she was obviously curious about. You, on the other hand, made a much more serious decision, Lin Yang. Take your own responsibility for that before you browbeat your daughter."

If Lin Yang thought she could, Sadie felt sure she'd have strangled Sadie with her bare hands right then.

Min looked at her mother, and Sadie could see the tears streaking down her cheeks. Twenty or not, she looked very much like a child. "Did you really do that, *Ma ma?*"

Lin Yang lifted her chin. "I was protecting my family."

"You burned her up?" The entire room went silent. Lin Yang stared past them at a spot on the wall, her chin still lifted in defiance and self-justification.

Ji put an arm across Min's shoulders, but it was obvious that neither of them was familiar with such physical affection. After a moment, Min turned into her father's chest and began to sob. Sadie felt the emotion catch in her throat. Min had loved Wendy, and so had Ji, at least at some point. Perhaps they understood each other better than anyone else could. Lin Yang stood there watching them, isolated and alone. Ji wrapped his arms around Min's back and patted her head somewhat awkwardly before he turned his head toward the kitchen.

"Lok," he called out over his shoulder.

Min's secret boyfriend pushed through the red doors, reminding

Sadie that the surprises for Ji and Lin Yang weren't over. Lok looked scared to death.

"We're closing for the day," Ji told him, Min still buried in his shoulder.

"We're . . . closed?" Lok said in obvious surprise. He looked at Min, and Sadie saw his concern for her. Ji and Lin Yang didn't seem to notice.

"Yes," Ji said. "You, Deming, and Fred can close up the restaurant and go home. I'll pay you for the full day."

"Will we be open tomorrow?"

"Of course," Ji said, causing Lok to nod and scurry back to the kitchen, where he began talking to the other workers. Ji looked at Sadie over Min's head. "Will you please call the police detective that Pete has spoken to and tell him we'll be in soon?"

"No," Lin Yang said, shaking her head. "I was doing what was right for my family. I will not go to the police. It was a private matter, and I did nothing wrong."

Ji turned to her, his expression tight and angry. "You lit my mother on fire!"

The words echoed in the restaurant and everyone was quiet for the space of two beats until Ji continued in a softer but controlled voice. "You will make this right with the police, and only then will we find out if it's even possible for you to make this right with *us*."

CHAPTER 33

L in Yang transitioned into Chinese after Ji's ultimatum, which meant that Sadie could only hear his side of the argument—he spoke in English—that continued until the two of them got into a taxi. Ji carried a white plastic bag the restaurant used for take-out orders with them, but inside was Wendy's purse, laptop, and phone, which Lin Yang had hidden in the storage closet of the restaurant, apparently unsure how best to dispose of them. Also in that bag were Wendy's original keys to her apartment, which Lin Yang had taken during her first visit to Wendy's apartment and then used to get into the building to actually set the fire. That Lin Yang had found Wendy dead, left her there, and then taken two days to plan the fire was mind-boggling.

Min and Sadie stood on the curb and watched the taxi disappear into traffic while people streamed past, oblivious to what had happened inside the restaurant that was now closed in the middle of the day. After the taxi was gone, Sadie turned toward Min, who looked completely overwhelmed.

"Are you okay?" Sadie asked.

Min shrugged a shoulder and took a breath. Her eyes were still red and puffy. She spoke to the sidewalk in front of them. "I can't believe my mother could do such a thing."

Sadie nodded. She didn't know how Lin Yang could have done it either. Planned it. Doused Wendy's decomposing body. Lit a match and dropped it. Sadie shuddered at the thought. She wondered if there was a way to suggest Ji insist on a psychological assessment of his wife before he decided whether or not to post bail.

But it was another woman who had called Lin Yang about Wendy in the first place. Who? Why?

"Do you think *Ma ma* killed her?" Min asked, finally looking up at Sadie, an open, scared expression on her face.

What did it feel like to suspect your own mother of murder, Sadie wondered. "I don't think so," she said, hoping she was right. "For all your mother's faults, she didn't lie about the fire. I imagine she'd be honest if she'd done more than that." Sadie suspected Lin Yang might have likely been just as pleased with herself if, in fact, she'd killed Wendy too; she certainly had taken some twisted pride in protecting her family by burning Wendy's body. "I believe her when she says that she thought she was protecting your father."

"He would never hurt anyone," Min said with sincerity. "I wish he had been more forgiving, but I know he wouldn't have hurt his mom."

"I don't think he'd hurt her either," Sadie said, looking at Wendy's granddaughter. "I hope when this is all over, you can sit down with your father and hear what it was like having Wendy as a mother. I admire your love for her and am glad you were able to help her, but please don't discount the pain your father suffered because of her choices. You had two healthy and whole parents"—well, something was wrong with Lin Yang but that was beside Sadie's point—"but your father didn't have any. He has worked hard to give you a life you might easily take for granted, though I realize it's not perfect."

Min looked sufficiently humbled. "I know that. And I thought a lot about what you said to me this morning. I need to tell them about Lok. They can't forbid me from loving him, can they?" She gave Sadie a pleading look, as though not entirely convinced and needing Sadie's help to believe it.

"You're an adult woman," she said simply. "And being honest will help your relationship in the long run, even if the short-term is hard."

Min nodded and looked toward the end of the street where the cab with her parents had disappeared a few minutes earlier. "I'm going to talk to Lok," she said, sounding assured but still nervous. "And then we're going to the police station."

"Both of you?"

Min nodded. "You're right that if I want to be treated like an adult I need to act like one. Lok and I have been seeing each other in secret for three years. I love him so much." Tears rose in her eyes, and she quickly blinked them away. "My parents did not marry for love. They don't know what it's like to feel the way I do, but maybe I can help them understand."

Sadie smiled even though she knew that Min could not anticipate how difficult the path ahead could be. Then again, Sadie couldn't predict it either. Maybe Min's parents were as ready for her to be an adult as she was. Though Lin Yang was likely going to be charged with desecrating a human body, arson, and perhaps interfering with a police investigation. Maybe with all of that going on, Min's announcement of her secret boyfriend would roll right off them.

Sadie put her arm around Min's shoulders and gave her a side hug that seemed to embarrass the girl a little bit. "I wish you the very best."

The two of them parted ways: Min inside the restaurant to help close down the kitchen, and Sadie toward her hotel room. She wasn't entirely sure what she'd do there, but she could try to verify the relationship between Rodger and Steve Pilings, or maybe learn more about Leann Penrose. When Sadie stopped at an intersection, she realized that Ji and Lin Yang were going to show up at the police station and no one would be expecting them. She pulled out her phone and sent a quick text to Pete. Her phone rang within seconds.

"Lin Yang *confessed?*" Pete asked. Even though he was only calling because of the case, she loved hearing his voice on the other end of the phone. Sadie explained what had happened with Min, Lin Yang, and Leann Penrose.

"A woman called the restaurant," Pete repeated. "But she didn't say who she was?"

"Which makes sense if she is the reason Wendy was dead in the first place."

"True," Pete said. "You're thinking it was Leann?"

Sadie reviewed the conversation she'd had with Rodger's wife. "It doesn't fit that well," she admitted. "Whoever made the call knew Min had been visiting Wendy, but how would Leann know that? Yet she's the only woman linked to . . . Wait—"

She let the thought move all the way through her brain before she expressed it out loud. "Shasta's on our list of suspects, and I realized this morning that with Wendy dead in the bathtub, Shasta wouldn't have heard any footsteps above her for a whole month." Sadie explained how the tenant in apartment four complained about how terrible the floors were. "Why would Shasta not have noticed that there were no more footsteps?"

"And she could very well have seen Min. Did you get a chance to talk to her when you were at the apartments earlier?"

"She wasn't there so I couldn't show her Min or Ji's pictures, and she was pretty evasive about things yesterday."

They both went quiet as they pondered this realization.

"And we know she pays more attention to her neighbors than she admitted to," Pete said.

"Right," Sadie said, feeling the probability growing in her mind. "And she and Wendy were friends at some point, so she would know about Ji and maybe even know the name of the restaurant. If she wanted to tip someone off, she would know where to start." She paused for a moment as her thoughts moved further ahead, or perhaps backward since now she was thinking about the potential scenario she'd laid out last night. "Maybe she *did* kill Wendy but wanted someone else to discover the body."

"And risk damaging the apartment by leaving Wendy there?"

"But there wasn't much damage," Sadie said.

"I'll tell Lopez," Pete said. "But, honestly, it might be a while before they can get to Shasta—things are happening fast over here. Between Lin Yang and Mr. Pilings—they'll have their hands full."

"What's happening with Mr. Pilings?"

"Pilings and Rodger both belong to the Presidio country club," Pete said, eager to share what he'd learned. "Wendy had lousy credit, and it's not a stretch to think she had lousy credit twelve years ago too—lousy enough to keep her from being able to get an apartment on her own. So, if Rodger knows Stephen Pilings, who owns several buildings, maybe they worked out a deal so Wendy could live in one of his units."

Sadie had thought the exact same thing. "And then she turned out to be the tenant from hell."

"Exactly," Pete said. "Lopez got right on the phone to set up interviews with both Pilings and Penrose once we figured out the connection, but we got a call from Pilings's lawyer a little bit ago— he's not talking."

"He lawyered up?" Sadie said. "Doesn't that make him look more guilty?"

"It certainly comes off as suspect. *And,* Lopez and I went down to the building inspection office and learned that Pilings was fined last year for having too many substantiated claims against him from tenants. Wendy wasn't the only tenant within the buildings he owned who had been giving him trouble, but she was the only one with multiple claims and likely the person who put him over the top of what the department considered reasonable."

"So, he had even more motive to get rid of her," Sadie summed up. "He already wasn't able to raise her rent very much, and now she was costing him both money and reputation."

"He also had opportunity—entry into the building is a moot point for the man who owns it." Pete paused. "Except he was out of town—New York to visit his son's family, I think. It was mentioned in the notes of the original conversation he had with the police after the fire."

"Rodger was out of town, too," Sadie said. "Maybe they hired someone."

"Possibly, but there's still the matter of why the body would be left in the apartment if Pilings had anything to do with it. He'd run a heck of a risk leaving it there for so long."

"Lin Yang said that Wendy's apartment door was unlocked. Maybe the door was left unsecured in hopes that someone else might find the body."

"And you think that person was Shasta?"

"Maybe."

Sadie heard a voice in the background of Pete's side of the conversation.

"Hold on a minute." The phone went quiet, other than some muffled noises, and then Pete came back on the line. "Ji and Lin Yang just showed up. I gotta go."

"What about Shasta?" Sadie asked. When she put Ji, Lin Yang, Rodger, and Stephen on one side of a teeter-totter and Shasta with her pink dog on the other, she could see why Pete's attention, as well as that of the San Francisco PD, wouldn't be captured by the Pink Lady of 22nd Street.

"Uh," Pete said. "Do you want to go talk to her?"

Sadie felt a rush of adrenaline at the implied approval in Pete's comment. "Yeah, I do."

"I'll let Lopez know. I'm sure he'll be fine with it. Will you text me the name of the guy who saw Lin Yang in the building before the fire?" Pete asked.

"Yeah," Sadie said. "I'll do that as soon as we get off the phone."

"And then come down here when you finish up with Shasta, okay? Lopez will want to talk to you too."

"Okay."

"Love you," Pete said quickly. "See you soon."

"Love you too," Sadie said, but Pete was already off the line by then. Sadie clicked the phone off, then found Damon's number— from when she'd sent him Ji's picture to identify—and forwarded the contact information to Pete. When she finished, she put her phone back in her purse and thought of the fortunes she'd had during this trip: It is time to get moving, a hunch is creativity trying to tell you something, and new people will bring you new realizations. She would put all three to work right now and see where they took her.

She lifted her chin with resolution and quick-stepped through the crowds of people zipping back and forth on the sidewalk. She put her hand up in the air, spotted a yellow cab, and waved her hand back and forth. "Taxi!"

CHAPTER 34

Saints be blessed, Shasta was home! She pulled open the door and gave Sadie the same bland look she'd bestowed on her yesterday. She then made an exaggerated look behind Sadie, as though hoping to see someone else. Annie peeked around Shasta's legs. It looked like the small dog was wearing pink plastic tips on her claws. Seriously, when was enough, enough?

"I'm afraid Pete didn't come with me today," Sadie said, smiling as though she didn't see the disappointed expression on the older woman's face. "It's just me."

"Well, it's a pleasure," Shasta said, though she obviously didn't mean it. She was wearing pink slacks, a multicolored flowing blouse, and pink pearls. Her hair was a shade darker than it had been yesterday and recently styled, leading Sadie to guess that the reason she hadn't been home that morning was because of an early appointment with her hairdresser. Maybe to impress Pete, who had ended up in the center of her pink bull's-eye. A glance past her showed a pink rug, patterned pink curtains, and a pale pink sofa at the end of the long common room. That much pink would make Sadie downright sick to her stomach if she had to look at it all day.

"What can I do for you?" Shasta asked, drawing Sadie's attention back to the woman who likely drew attention everywhere she went.

Sadie had decided on her approach during the cab ride over and pulled Min and Ji's pictures from her purse. "I was wondering if you've seen either of these people around the apartment complex."

She looked at both photos for a few seconds, then up at Sadie. "Why?"

"Some of the other tenants had seen them, and I'm talking to everyone in the building by way of confirmation. I know you don't micromanage everyone's comings and goings, but it would sure help if I had your opinion to back up everyone else's."

Shasta smiled at the thinly veiled appeal to her vanity and self-importance. She put a finger to her lips and made a "Hmm" sound, drawing out the moment for dramatic effect. She pointed to Ji's picture first. "That's Wendy's son," she said. "I haven't met him, but I saw him with Stephen last weekend when he came to inspect the apartment. Stephen told me who he was later."

She was on a first name basis with the landlord. Interesting. "You didn't see him prior to that?"

"No."

"Did you know Wendy had a son?"

"No," Shasta said just as evenly, but Sadie didn't believe her. Wendy had reason not to tell Rodger about Ji, but there was no reason she wouldn't tell a girlfriend.

"And her?" Sadie asked, pointing to Min's picture.

Shasta shifted her eyes to Min's photo. "I don't know who that girl is."

"Other tenants said they saw her in the afternoons sometimes— around four o'clock, maybe?"

"I have a *very* busy social calendar, I'm afraid, and I'm simply not here much."

Other than this morning, Shasta seemed to have been here plenty in the last three days. "Well, thank you," Sadie said, easing into the meatier portion of the interview. "You've lived here ten years, is that right?"

Shasta nodded. "And seven months."

"And you've been waiting for Wendy's apartment that whole time?"

Shasta rolled her eyes. "If someone had told me in the beginning that I would wait this long, I'm sure I'd have found somewhere else. I always felt she was on the verge of leaving, so I stayed."

"Patience is a virtue," Sadie said.

Shasta nodded. Annie whimpered, and Shasta scooped her up, settling the dog in her arms and stroking the pink afro on her head.

"I bet the construction has been frustrating for you," Sadie said while putting the pictures back in her purse.

"Oh, you have no idea!" Shasta said with more animation than she'd showed up until now. "Mario and his friends have no respect, and I've told him as much. They work late into the night—all that banging and stomping had me calling the vet about some antianxiety medication for poor Annie." She kissed the dog's head. "But at least they're almost done. My painters are coming first thing Monday, you know."

"Wonderful," Sadie said. She secured her purse closed and then looked directly at Shasta. "It must have been nice not having anyone above you for a little while."

"Oh, it was," Shasta said, smiling contentedly. "Made me that much more eager to get on the top floor. Two bedrooms *and* no one above me. Priceless, really."

She hadn't yet caught on to the nuances of Sadie's questions. "So," Sadie said in an attempt to casually segue, "at what point did you notice that you *weren't* hearing any footsteps above you?"

Shasta's hand on Annie slowed slightly and her gaze, which had been nonchalant until now, was suddenly pointed. When she spoke, however, her tone hadn't changed. "I didn't think anything of it," she said easily.

"Really?" Sadie asked. "The other tenants I've talked to have commented on the squeaky floors. Wendy's floor doesn't squeak?"

"Oh, it squeaked," Shasta said, her look still too intense for the languid tone of voice.

"Then you must have noticed when it wasn't squeaking. Wendy didn't go out much, right?"

Shasta watched her carefully, calculatingly, as she continued to pet her dog. After what seemed like far too long, she finally answered the question. "Mario told me Wendy had gone out of town, so of course I didn't think anything was out of order."

"Mario?" How had she and Pete never thought to talk to Mario? There was no way that information could have been in Shasta's statement to the police—someone would have jumped all over it. Which meant Shasta was throwing him under the bus.

"Yes," Shasta said, raising her eyebrows. "He'd come to fix a broken outlet and mentioned she was out of town when I commented on how quiet things had been up there."

By now Sadie had a hundred more questions to ask, and yet wisdom prevailed and she didn't ask a single one. Things were too precarious in light of this new information. Lin Yang was being interviewed, Stephen Pilings was being tracked down, and the police were on the scent for Rodger too. But even without asking questions, a possibility was laying itself out in Sadie's mind.

What if, after a few weeks of unusual silence, Shasta went upstairs on her own to find out what was going on with Wendy. What if she found Wendy in the tub, but rather than report it herself—how gauche and bohemian would *that* be?—chose to call Ji instead so that it would be someone else's problem. It was a weak motivation, but she *was* in line for the apartment and she'd had conflicts with Wendy in the past, or . . . maybe she was the killer.

But that didn't explain why Mario had told her that Wendy was on vacation. Unless Shasta was lying about that.

Sadie kept her polite smile in place while thinking of what to do next. The police could figure out the missing bits and pieces; Sadie had learned what she'd come for. She reached into her purse and grabbed her phone.

"I'm afraid I've got a call," she said, then held the phone to her ear. "Hi . . . Yeah, I'm just leaving. Hold on." She moved the phone away from her mouth. "I've got to go, Shasta. It was great talking to you."

"Likewise," Shasta said, still petting her dog, still looking at Sadie too sharply.

Sadie put the phone back to her ear, turned toward the elevator, and continued her pretend conversation until Shasta shut the door to her apartment.

"Bye," she said to the nonexistent caller and lowered her phone from her ear. She wished she were at the police station right now. She wanted to read Shasta's official statement, and she wanted to know if *anyone* had thought to talk to the maintenance man who had access to every room in every building of Stephen Pilings's properties.

Sadie started texting Pete as she walked toward the elevator. It was hard to condense her thoughts to an appropriate text message, and she deleted her first attempt and started a second one. The pulleys of the elevator began to creak when she was still a few feet from the elevator.

The car, which had been on the second floor, began descending to the main floor. Sadie frowned at the delay it was going to cause her in regard to getting to the police station, but she still had this text to send anyway. Whether Shasta was in league with Stephen and Rodger or acting on her own behalf, Sadie had no way of knowing, but she believed that Shasta had known Wendy was dead and called Lin Yang.

Sadie pushed the down button, then glanced down the open elevator shaft, curious to see who had beat her to it. She couldn't see much through the cables and grates. She finished the text, tapped her foot impatiently—for all its charm, the elevator was on the slow side—and then saw the stairs. Duh. She was three steps down when the elevator clunked into place below. The person who entered spoke, and Sadie halted mid-step, with one foot in the air. It was a man's voice. And he was angry and . . . sounded familiar.

"Would I be here if I didn't know better than to call his phone?"

Sadie was sure she'd heard that voice before, though not that tone. No one answered the man's angry question, which led her to believe he was on the phone. She leaned closer to the shaft, eager to hear something else or catch a glimpse of his face, but she heard the elevator door lock into place instead and then the elevator began moving, drowning out his voice.

She waited a split second before she ran back up the stairs to the second floor, crossed in front of the elevator and started on the next flight. She paused long enough to see if the elevator stopped on the second floor, but it kept going. She took the stairs more slowly now, trying to stay just barely ahead of the elevator. When it got closer to her position, she heard the voice again.

"Don't think I've forgotten who had this brilliant idea in the first place, Steve."

Sadie gasped as recognition of the voice dawned: Rodger Penrose! She ran up the rest of the steps as fast as she could, afraid he might see her. What was he doing here? And he was talking to Stephen Pilings on the phone? Holy cow!

She reached the third floor and found herself facing a serious decision. It had been a while since Sadie had purposely put herself in a questionable situation to learn new information. Pete would want her to leave but . . . the door to Wendy's apartment stood slightly ajar and the sound of Mario's music came from inside. Mario was the only person on this floor that Rodger could be here to talk to. Mario had become very important in the last two minutes.

Sadie looked behind her. The top of the elevator was nearly flush with the third floor; there was no time for second-guessing. She entered Wendy's apartment and closed the door behind her. She looked around to make sure Mario was still in the bathroom. She walked quickly on the balls of her feet into the dark office—thank goodness she'd taken the time to close the blinds last night. She stood behind the door that was open just enough for her to look through the two-inch gap between the door and the jamb and still remain hidden in the shadows. She reached into her pocket for her phone, quickly turned off the sound, and texted Pete.

Rodger's coming to Wendy's apartment and I'm listening.
I think Mario's involved.

CHAPTER 35

M ario!"
Despite knowing she was well-hidden, Sadie pulled back at the sound of Rodger's voice and pressed the phone against her thigh. A second later Rodger came into view, stopping just past the kitchen counter. He was wearing a white shirt and tie today, with slacks and shiny shoes—every part the white-collar executive.

"Mario!" he called again.

The Latin music stopped. Rodger turned toward the bedroom door. His back was to Sadie, but she assumed Mario had come out to meet him since he stopped before going into the room. She could hear the lilting accent of Mario's voice, but couldn't make out any words. She leaned a bit closer, but then Rodger turned around, facing her. She pulled back as he paced toward her, gripping his hair in his fingers and swearing over and over. She held her breath, then let it out slowly when he turned and stomped back toward Mario, who said something Sadie couldn't hear over Rodger's ranting.

"No, everything is not okay," Rodger yelled. "The police want another interview with Stephen—at the police department."

Mario came further into the room. He wore a tool belt around his waist and had his arms crossed over his chest, tucking his hands into his armpits. "The police know nothing," he said with confidence, his voice not as thickly accented as it had been the day Pete and Sadie had met him for the first time.

Sadie's stomach fluttered at the confirmation that Mario *was* in on this.

"Then why are they questioning him again?" Rodger swore a few more times.

Sadie's phone hadn't vibrated to indicate Pete responding to her text, and she felt her anxiety building with the idea that she was alone in a dangerous situation. This was not a good time for him to not be reading his text messages.

Mario said something she couldn't hear, and Rodger whipped back around and yelled in response, causing Sadie to startle slightly behind the door.

"What do you mean, she's a cop?"

"No, no, no," Mario said as though Rodger's rage was trite and juvenile. He stepped around Rodger and leaned against the kitchen counter, one ankle crossed over the other. "The sister's boyfriend is a *retired* cop. They been trying to figure things out all week."

The red of Rodger's face darkened and his eyes bulged. "What! Why didn't you tell us this?"

"I told Mr. Pilings of the things they talked about. He said it was 'under control.'" Mario cocked his head to the side. "He says that a lot." His tone had lost its playful spark.

"You know I've done everything I can to help your situation," Rodger said, his agitation humbled slightly. "I made sure the paperwork was finally filed, I paid up the attorney fees; I really went to bat for you, Mario."

"But my family is still not here," Mario said, an edge to his words. "I have waited for months. I have done everything Mr. Pilings has asked of me, and they are still not here." One arm shot out toward the bathroom. "Even after this, my family is not here, and once again he is saying that everything is under control when he does not know this is so."

Rodger glowered at the other man. "If you'd taken the body out immediately like we agreed to and staged it as a disappearance, none of this would have happened. She didn't have anyone who was going to come looking for her, and we could have—"

Mario cut him off with a humorless laugh. "*Everyone* has come looking for her."

"Because of that fire," Rodger said, his own tone rising. "Like I said, if you'd stuck to the plan then—"

"Then my family would still be waiting. I told Mr. Pilings that I would remove the body as soon as I had proof that my family's papers were complete."

Rodger shook his head and turned toward the window. "Things don't happen that fast, Mario. The red tape involved in immigration right now is insane."

"But he did nothing until he was the one in danger, did he?"

Rodger seemed to give up the argument. He took a breath and let it out, an expression of sympathy softening his face and his tone. "Steve said he'd talked to you in the beginning about what would happen if the police got too close to him. That's why I'm here—to put that plan in motion. I'm sorry."

Mario's face hardened even more. "After all of this I am to go back to Mexico?" There was a growl to his words, a low-level thunder that emphasized what he thought of the idea. Mario's chest swelled as his rage increased, the veins in his neck bulging. "I have fixed Mr. Pilings's buildings, I have played his games with the promise that he would bring my family to me, and now I have killed for him! He is the reason for all of this!" He spread his hands wide, like an umpire calling a runner "safe," but he lost none of his fervor.

Rodger's nostrils flared as he stared into Mario's rage-filled eyes, but he wisely said nothing.

Sadie's heart was pounding after the confession she'd just heard. She cautiously lifted her phone, opened up a text message, and glanced at the screen only long enough to hit REPLY to her last text. The glow of the screen worried her, so she turned to her side to block it from the gap in the doorway.

You better send help.

She was no longer hiding behind a door to overhear a curious conversation; she was ten feet away from a murderer. Mario undid his tool belt and laid it on the counter as though announcing that he was done with the remodeling project.

Rodger frowned. "I will make sure that you are treated fairly from here on out. We'll work out a monthly payment to ensure a better life for you and your family wherever you end up."

Mario grunted. "You and Mr. Pilings will stay out of prison, but I am going back to a country that is a prison for me all the same."

"At least you'll be with your family there, and you'll be taken care of financially. If the police catch up to you, none of us get that luxury."

The two men faced off, and then Rodger reached into his back pocket and pulled out his wallet. "I have two grand right now. I can have the rest for you tonight. How soon can you leave?"

"So that's it?" Mario asked.

"None of us wanted it to happen this way. Let's just hope it doesn't get worse." Rodger sounded tired as he pulled the bills from his wallet and handed them toward Mario, who put them in the back pocket of his carpenter jeans. Rodger's phone rang but he ignored it. "Find a way to contact me in a few weeks. It would be best to contact me through my business rather than my personal phone. We'll make arrangements. Be careful."

They were leaving, which was both a relief and a concern. She was anxious to get out of there with what she'd learned, but the police needed to catch Mario before he disappeared. Pete was her only resource for getting backup, and he wasn't replying. If she could text 911 she would.

"You'll call me tonight when you have the rest of the money?" Mario asked.

"I can't *call* you!" Rodger snapped, then seemed to catch himself. "Do you think I'd have dared to come here if I could *call* you? The police can't know we know each other." He stopped, took a deep breath, and let it out with puffed cheeks. Forced calm. "Okay, uh, let's meet at Pier 39 tonight, across from the wax museum. There are enough tourists that no one will remember us there. I'll have the rest of the money."

"In cash?" Mario asked.

"Of course it will be in cash," Rodger said. "Steve and I made arrangements, just in case. I just have to get it."

Mario nodded. "I will meet you at Pier 39 at eight o'clock tonight. I'll leave from there and be across the border by morning." There was a solemnity to his voice, a resigned acceptance.

Sadie wondered if he regretted having left Wendy in the tub as blackmail for the landlord or if he took some kind of satisfaction from having caused the turmoil that Rodger and Stephen now had to deal with. How did a man who could do such things think it all through?

Sadie's phone vibrated in her hand—finally!—and she lifted it closer to her face so she could read the text message.

We're coming! Hold tight.

Thank goodness. She hit REPLY and then glanced out the gap in the doorway, not connecting the light from her phone and the men's silence until she saw Mario staring right into her hiding place. She pressed the phone against her chest even though she knew it was too late.

Oh, biscuits.

CHAPTER 36

Sadie dropped her phone and then slammed her heel into the glass face when Mario's pounding footsteps started toward her. She didn't want them to know the police were coming. A moment later a hand grabbed her arm and pulled her roughly out from behind the door, throwing her toward a wall.

She stumbled in an attempt to keep her feet before catching herself. She turned to the doorway of the office, her only escape, and sank into a crouch, preparing to defend herself.

Mario's shoulder rammed her back against the wall, knocking the air from her lungs and preventing the scream which had been bubbling up. He wasn't taking any chances and, though she got a good elbow into his ribs when he threw his arm around her neck, he immediately pulled so tight that she feared he was going to snap her neck right there and then.

She gasped for air while going up on her toes, elbowing him in the side again, and scratching at his arm around her neck.

He pulled her backward, keeping her off balance and dragging her into the common area of the apartment. He threw her to the floor before she could plant her feet.

Popping lights sparked in her peripheral vision when her head hit the hard wood. She coughed for air but managed to sweep her foot against Mario's leg, knocking him off balance—but not enough.

An instant later, Mario straddled her chest, pinning her arms with his knees in the process. He slapped a hand over her mouth before she'd had the chance to get enough air to scream.

She drew deep breaths through her nose, kicked her knees into his back and squirmed beneath him, but she may as well have been wrestling stone for all the good it did her. Mario was small, but he was solid and ruthless.

Realizing she wasn't going to get away through her own physical attempts, Sadie looked to Rodger. He was standing a few feet away from them, his eyes wide and his mouth open in shock. Sadie tried to plead with her eyes—eyes that were like Wendy's—but then remembered that he was part of having Wendy killed. He hadn't killed her himself, however. Could he really watch Mario kill her, now? Was Mario really going to *kill* her?

As soon as she dared hope that wasn't his intent, she realized how much he had to lose if she survived. She'd heard the confession, she knew Rodger and Stephen were involved, and she knew that Mario's motivation in killing and leaving Wendy's body behind was because of his family. She knew too much for them to let her go. The panic that had been building began to crumble into a cacophony of fear, regret, and, scariest of all, hopelessness.

"I can't stay here," Rodger said in desperation, but his voice lacked the mercy Sadie had hoped for. She stared at him, yelling behind Mario's hand, which seemed to be pressing her harder and harder against the floor. "I shouldn't have even come."

"But you will leave *me* to do the work," Mario said over his shoulder. "Again." Sadie tried to lift her head, and he shoved it hard against the floor again, initiating more lights in her periphery. "You know why we killed your sister?" Mario suddenly yelled at her, his dark eyes boring into hers. "She was too much trouble. She did not know when to leave things alone. Just like you."

Sadie moved her eyes to Rodger again; he was her only hope. He narrowed his eyes when he spoke to her. "He's right, you know," he said. "Wendy ruined people's lives. She was writing my wife letters claiming that I was unfaithful, did you know that? At the same time she's calling me every day with this sob story about her life, she was trying to ruin my marriage. When I found out about those letters, I'd had it. And then she filed yet another complaint against Stephen. She was trying to ruin both of us, and it was working!" He looked at Mario as though tempted to reiterate Mario's role in why this had all fallen apart, but he must have chosen against it because he looked back at Sadie, glaring. "Take care of this last thing for us, Mario," he said, his voice terrifying in its sudden calmness. "Do whatever it takes, however you want to do it. I promise to take care of you and your family."

Mario looked over his shoulder at Rodger. "I will go to the police myself if either of you do not follow through on your promise."

"I understand. I'll make it work." He nodded toward Sadie. "Just take care of her."

Tears flowed down Sadie's cheeks. Could this really be happening? Was Rodger really going to abandon her to this psychopath?

Rodger turned his back on them and hurried from the apartment, the door snapping shut behind him.

Mario looked at Sadie, his face hard and his eyes glinting. She wanted to close her eyes against him, block out the sheer hatred and power she saw in his face, but she refused to give him the satisfaction of seeing her cower.

"I made some mistakes with your sister," he said in a soft and even voice. "Leaving the body was a risk, and it has not turned out good for me, but that is not the mistake I am talking about. The *first* mistake is the one I made when I chose to kill Wendy Penrose fast and without explanation."

Sadie's body shook with fear and anger, but her eyes were still focused on his face. In her mind she was seeing Wendy, the amorphous figure of her sister that had taken shape in her mind these last few days. Sadie realized that she'd never made the arrangements for Wendy's body. She'd left her there in the morgue all this time, too caught up in rebuilding Wendy's life to finalize her resting place.

"She was in the bath, her crazy hair up on her head. I pushed her under the water so hard and fast she did not even knew it was me." His expression fell. "And now I am going back to Mexico forever, and Mr. Pilings has won again. My family will never have the life I promised them. They will never know what it is to have all the luxuries that you take for granted. Because of this, you will suffer. This time, it will be long and slow and horrible."

He shifted his hand slightly, lining his thumb against the side of her nose, then he pressed his thumb toward the rest of his hand, pinching Sadie's nose closed and cutting off her ability to breathe.

Sadie's body reacted and she threw herself back and forth, screaming behind his hand and kicking the floor as hard as she could in hopes of alerting . . . who? Shasta, who'd found Wendy's body and called Lin Yang?

"You are the only one to blame for this," he said, unfazed by her attempts to get free. "Too. Much. Trouble."

The lights in her peripheral vision became a fireworks show as she tried to fight the unwinnable battle. As the oxygen was slowly depleted from her body, her legs stopped kicking. Her senses failed her, and her vision tunneled into black.

CHAPTER 37

Sadie had heard once that the most alert of the five senses when sleeping or drugged or in some other way unconscious was hearing. It's why fire alarms made noise. For her, however, it wasn't sound that awoke her. It was the smell of smoke.

As soon as Sadie's brain realized what it was she was smelling, her eyes flew open and she blinked at the smoky air. Her brain couldn't compute where she was or what was happening, but she knew something was very, very wrong. When she tried to sit up, a searing pain ripped through her side and a failed attempt to scream informed her that she was gagged. No, taped?

Mario hadn't killed her.

Yet.

She breathed through her nose and fell back into the position she'd been in when she regained consciousness: lying down but propped up slightly. She attempted to move her hands but realized that they were bound as well. Carefully, she lifted them—the motion hurt her side, too—but she needed to see what was impeding her movement.

Her hands had been taped palms together, and though her fingers were free, her thumbs were trapped under several layers of thick duct tape. She attempted to use her fingers to pull the tape off her mouth, but without her thumbs, she couldn't get a strong enough hold.

She tried to take a deep breath in hopes of clearing her mind, but the smoke brought on a coughing fit, which she feared would suffocate her again as she gagged and coughed into her nose. Her side ignited with each shudder of her body. Once she regained a steady breath, she used her fingers to lift the collar of her shirt over her nose, then she looked around. She was in a room, a small room a . . .

She faced forward and saw a shiny new faucet at her feet.

She was in a bathtub.

Just like Wendy.

A new level of dread tugged at her, and she tried to control her panic. She looked at her right side that was causing her so much pain. The blue of her shirt was purple, almost black, and a stream of her own blood trailed down the side of the brilliant white tub toward the drain. She had been stabbed, bound, and left in the bathtub. But there was also a fire.

She remembered what Mario had said to her. He wanted her to suffer; he wanted her to feel the terror of a slow and painful death. And by recreating the fire that had undone all of his plans, he would succeed.

Pete.

He'd said help was on the way, but that didn't mean he'd sent a fire truck. How long had she been unconscious? Five minutes? Ten? San Francisco took fire seriously; how long would it take for the fire department to get to the apartment?

People were probably trying to get to her right this very minute, *right?* But Sadie couldn't lay there and hope for that.

Think, she told herself, forcing herself to remain calm. *Think.*

One of the things Pete had taught her, and that her own experiences had solidified, was the importance of knowing your environment. She looked around at the newly tiled walls and stared at the small frosted window above the tub; it would be too small and too high to crawl through, and it only opened a few inches. Then she looked up at the ceiling, where she saw the grate of the bathroom fan. If she could turn that on, it would draw the smoke out better than the window would, right? It might also draw the oxygen out, but she couldn't breathe with all the smoke anyway.

Was the bathroom door open? She took a breath and held it as she forced herself to lift enough to look over the edge of the tub toward the doorway through which smoke was coming in fast. Her instinct was to try to escape this room, this apartment, this building, but the fire was between her and the way out. And could she even make it to the stairs in the condition she was in?

She whimpered behind her gag as she lowered herself back down, her whole side on fire—though not literally. Not yet. She *had* to shut that door. This room had contained the smell of Wendy decomposing; closing that door might buy her a few more minutes too. To close it, though, she would have to get out of the tub, cross the room, and push it closed. Sitting up had taken everything she had, and yet if she stayed there, she would die.

She said a pleading prayer in her mind and then moved as quickly as she could to sit up, throw her arms over the side of the tub, and pull herself over the edge. She crumpled onto the newly tiled floor, screaming in pain behind her gag and feeling tears trailing down her face, which was pressed against the floor. She'd sustained a lot of injury in recent years—far more than she'd have ever thought possible for a fifty-something-year-old woman to survive—but she'd never felt anything like this. Already blood was pooling on the tile. How much blood had she already lost?

She attempted to army crawl to the door, but the pain of using her torso for momentum was impossible. Instead, she pushed herself to her knees, gritting her teeth and crying out, though she made very little sound. There was no time to let the pain ebb away, so she braced her shoulder on the wall and used it to push up against until she was standing.

The smoke was thicker when she stood, but of course it would be. She'd taught school for twenty-five years, and her second grade students knew to crawl beneath smoke should they ever be caught in a house fire. But she couldn't crawl. Still bracing herself with the wall, she walked to the door and used her foot to slam it closed. Perhaps she should have also closed the bedroom door but maybe the fire was *in* the bedroom. She could hear crackles and pops, and the apartment wasn't big enough for the fire to be too far away, regardless of where Mario had started it.

The closed door and thick rubber strip along the bottom prevented more smoke from getting in, but the room was still filled with it, and she could barely breathe. Sadie flipped the switch for the bathroom fan. A whirring sound filled the room, and she carefully lowered herself to the floor, short of breath, sick to her stomach, and shaking from the pain in her side. She feared she would lose consciousness at any moment. Sweat dripped from her hairline and prickled beneath her skin. She knew that paper burned at a temperature of 451 degrees—thank you, Ray Bradbury—but did apartments also burn at that heat? How hot would it get before the heat alone killed her? She used her fingers to pull her shirt over her nose again.

Pete, she called out in her mind. *You're here, right? You're coming for me?*

He would know she was in the building, but he wouldn't know exactly where. Was there anything more Sadie could do? On another occasion she'd found herself locked somewhere she shouldn't have been, with no way out and few options, but there had been pipes which she'd hit over and over until someone followed the sound to find her.

With that in mind, she moved as quickly as she could to the new cupboard beneath the new sink and pulled open the door. She wondered if Mario had felt any regret destroying the work he'd done in the room. Would he have felt more regret over that than for killing her?

The pipes were plastic, but even if they'd been metal, she realized she had nothing to hit them with. There was nothing in this newly remodeled bathroom: not a plunger or a toilet paper holder or even tools left behind. She leaned against the cabinet, tempted to collapse on the floor and wait for rescue, but her experience had taught her that any form of giving up could mean the end of everything.

She scanned the bathroom again, and her eyes landed on the back of the toilet, specifically the lid covering the tank. She pushed herself to her feet—the pain was excruciating—then fit her fingers underneath the porcelain lid. She counted to three in her mind and then pulled up on the edge of the lid as hard as she could. It cartwheeled off the top of the toilet, toward the tub, and hit the knob of the faucet on the way down before it hit the tub itself and broke into three pieces.

The broken knob started spraying water. Sadie hadn't expected that—she'd just been trying to break the lid—and pulled away from the spray until she realized it was cold water. Beautifully cold. She stepped into the spray and let it drench her, hopefully buying her a little more time in the rising heat.

She hobbled toward the bathtub and picked up the smallest piece of broken porcelain, which was roughly the size of half a dinner plate. She looked around for something she could brace it with and saw the toilet bowl. After reminding herself that it was brand-new and therefore as clean as it would ever be, she dropped the piece of porcelain inside it and propped it against the side of the bowl. Then she started moving her wrists back and forth on the sharp edge, cutting through the duct tape and, too often, through her skin as well. She bit back a scream every time she cut herself, and the toilet water turned pinker and pinker. It felt like forever before she could wrestle one hand out of the tape and use it to pull off the rest.

A quick inspection showed a dozen or more cuts, some of them pretty deep, but her hands were free. She ripped the duct tape off her face, sure she'd taken a layer of skin with it, and howled with pent-up pain as she fell against the wall, breathless, dizzy, and exhausted.

She pressed her hands against her side and began crying in earnest, babbling prayers and pleadings and thinking about her children, the wedding that wouldn't happen, all the life she had left to live, and the fact that she was going to die just like her sister had. Surely the police would find a way to tie this back to Stephen Pilings—lawyer or not they would be able to prove he was part of this, right? It was little consolation if it took her life to put him away.

The heat was getting intense, and though a lot of the smoke had cleared out, it was getting harder to breathe. She backed into the spray of water again and stepped over the side of the tub before sinking into it. She plugged the drain, hoping it would help retain the cold water. She picked up one of the pieces of the toilet lid, but when she hit the faucet with it, it barely made a sound. She let it drop back into the tub that was filling up with water made pink from the blood draining out of her body. She lay down, half of her face in the rising water. She began to shiver, which she found terribly ironic, and wondered if having her side wound in the water would cause her to bleed out faster.

More thoughts came to mind, and the tears that leaked out of her eyes had nothing to do with the pain she felt almost numb to now. Would Pete ever fall in love again, now with two women to mourn? This was so unfair to him.

And then she heard something.

A voice?

"I'm here!" she shouted, and pushed herself awkwardly and painfully to her feet. She stepped out of the wet tub and felt assaulted by the heat, but moved to the door and started knocking rapidly. "I'm here!" she yelled again, feeling the heat through the door. She paused and listened. Nothing. She said it again, "I'm in here!" She banged on the door five times, listened. Nothing. Yelled, banged, listened. Nothing. Again and again and again she did it, certain she'd heard something earlier and determined that if she died in here she would be found with her hand in a fist and her mouth open in a scream. Then she heard something else. A chopping kind of tearing sound. She took a step away from the door, but is that where it had come from?

The sound continued, filling the room, confusing her as to where it was coming from until a piece of the ceiling fell into the tub. She looked up then, and backed as far against the wall as she could. They were coming from above.

Like angels.

"I'm here!" she screamed. Her chest shuddered into a sob as she looked up through the growing hole in the roof. "I'm here!"

CHAPTER 38

The nurse finished taking Sadie's vital signs and double-checked the IV bag hanging at the top of the apparatus next to Sadie's bed. Sadie thanked her and then relaxed against the pillows once the nurse left, hoping she could fall asleep again. Pete had been in the chair next to her bed the last time she'd been awakened by the nurses, but he wasn't there now. Daylight peeked through the edges of the mini-blinds on the windows of her hospital room. Perhaps he went down for breakfast, or to call their families.

The pain meds made it impossible for her to stop the tears that normally she would have avoided. But this was the first time in almost sixteen hours that she'd been alone with her thoughts. Mario had meant for her to die. He'd orchestrated it even though he wouldn't be there to see her panic. Apparently, just knowing she'd feel the true terror of her situation was enough satisfaction for him.

And Pete had saved her. He'd insisted she was still inside even after Shasta and Annie were brought out and Shasta said the building was empty. She'd confirmed that she'd heard a struggle above her prior to the fire, though she'd turned up her TV in an attempt to drown it out.

The firefighters couldn't access the third floor by then, and it was Pete who demanded they go in through the roof, which typically they wouldn't risk with an active fire still going.

Amid the drama of the evening and night, Sadie had managed to tell the police that Mario and Rodger were meeting outside the wax museum at 8:00 that night. The police had arrested the two men, and a solid force of half a dozen detectives were now collecting statements, reviewing documents, and piecing together the convoluted investigation. Stephen Pilings had been arrested; his attorney couldn't stop things now.

Justice would be done, and there was some satisfaction in that. Sadie reflected on the fact that she'd come to San Francisco to learn about her sister, and, though she'd hoped for a redemption she hadn't found, she *had* learned about the life Wendy had lived. And, ultimately, she had learned who—of the many people in Wendy's life who had reason to want her gone—had killed her. It was all so sad, and though Sadie knew she would never overcome the regret of what Wendy had done with the life she'd been given, at least she could be laid to rest. At least Sadie could say she did her best by her to the very end.

At some point last night—she wasn't sure when—Jack had called Pete. He was worried when Sadie hadn't returned his messages. With her phone broken and burned, she hadn't even known he was trying to reach her. Pete filled Jack in on what had happened and reassured him that Sadie was going to be okay.

Jack had already talked to Ji and taken over the arrangements for Wendy's body. The two of them had decided to have Wendy cremated and her ashes interred in a burial plot shared by Jack and Sadie's parents in Colorado. Sadie thought that was a fitting choice. They could visit her resting place together and continue to work through the complexities of their feelings toward their sister. Sadie had not found closure, not yet, but she was hopeful that if the concept really existed, she would find it one day.

Beyond that, Sadie knew that having Wendy close to home was precisely what her parents would have wanted. They had never stopped loving their daughter.

There was a light knock on her door, and Sadie began frantically wiping at her eyes as the door opened. She didn't want Pete to see her upset. She wasn't entirely sure where things were between the two of them, but she knew she didn't want to appear undone. It was a taller, darker man who stepped inside her room, however. Ji carried a bouquet of flowers Sadie felt sure were from the hospital gift shop.

"Ji," she said softly, smiling with sincerity as he came to her bedside and sat in the chair reserved for Pete. He looked at her with a sympathetic expression, likely looking for the injury that had kept her in the hospital, but the stab wound in her right side was bandaged beneath her hospital gown. The bruises on her arms and face, as well as the bandages on her hands, would have to do. "You're sweet to come."

Ji placed the bouquet on the bedside table. "How are you feeling?"

"Like I was stabbed," Sadie said with a smile. Her son, Shawn, could say things like that in dark moments and lighten the mood, but it didn't work as well for her, and she wished she hadn't tried it when Ji winced. "But I'll be okay."

"How long will you stay in San Francisco?"

"They said I would be in the hospital for one more day, to make sure everything's alright. Then I'll probably stay in a hotel a few more days before I travel home. Perhaps I'll still get a chance to see some of the sights."

"I wish we had room for you to stay with us while you recover, but I'm afraid our apartment is very small."

Sadie appreciated the sincerity of his offer. "You get full nephew-points for the thought."

Ji smiled.

"How are things with Lin Yang?"

His expression turned heavy. "She was released about an hour ago on bail. She'll stay with her sister for a little while."

"That might be a good idea for a number of reasons," Sadie said rather boldly.

Ji looked at her, hesitant.

She smiled to soften the rest of the words piling up in her uninhibited mind. "Arranged marriage or not, you deserve to be happy with your partner." She thought of her own situation and wondered if Pete could really be happy with her as *his* partner. Had facing his memories of Pat made him reconsider their compatibility?

Ji looked at the floor.

"Ji." Sadie waited until he looked up at her. "Do you like working at the restaurant? You said you were pursuing your art at one point but gave it up—it wasn't practical, but is it your passion?"

She saw a flicker of unease on his face, and then he scrubbed a hand over his forehead. She didn't rescue him from the answer he was obviously uncomfortable giving. Finally, he let out a breath. "The restaurant saved my life," he said quietly, looking at Sadie. "When you're thirteen years old and no one cares what you do or where you are, most of your options aren't good ones. Lin Yang's father offered me a life—a *real* life—and he entrusted me with his daughter and his legacy. I can never repay that debt."

"Is it a debt you're meant to repay? Does your unhappiness pay that kindness back to her father?"

She moved her hand so it touched his. He flinched, which made her wonder if he was used to any kind of affection or touch.

After a few seconds, Ji said, "I will admit that all of . . . this has had me thinking of things differently than I have ever dared to do." It was obviously difficult for him to say such words.

"A lot of your life has been something you didn't get to choose. If nothing else, now you have some new choices, and if you decide not to change a thing, at least *you* chose it." Sadie patted his hand and smiled, relaxing back against the pillows.

"There is something to be said for that," Ji said. "For now, I have contacted a criminal attorney to help Lin Yang."

"I hate for the life insurance to end up going to an attorney," Sadie said. "But at least—"

"I'm not taking the insurance money," Ji said, squaring his shoulders proudly.

"Why ever not?" Had she heard him correctly? She *was* heavily medicated.

"It feels like blood money," Ji said. "My mother couldn't be bothered to give me what I really wanted from her when she was alive, and her money gives me no solace now."

"Ji, that's the most ridiculous thing I've ever heard." Ji startled at her directness, but Sadie continued. "Take the money."

He shook his head. "I'm sure she only got the policy so she could use it to manipulate me into helping care for her as she got older and sicker—that's probably why she came to see me that day she met Min. It doesn't feel right to take that money."

"Of course it doesn't feel right," Sadie said. "Nothing about Wendy feels right to any of us, but she went to the effort of getting herself a life insurance policy, and she chose you to be the person to receive that settlement. Money will never make up for those things you would rather have had from her, but it is something. Perhaps it's the best she was capable of."

Ji shook his head. He really was a proud man. Too proud, in Sadie's opinion.

"Instead you'll go broke paying for an attorney?" Sadie asked rhetorically. "Will that mean your daughters no longer get to go to their schools? Does it mean you'll have to sell the restaurant? Are you willing to lose everything you've worked for because of Wendy? And stay in an unhappy marriage and career for Lin Yang's father?"

Ji clenched his jaw and looked away.

Sadie knew she'd been too harsh, and she softened her voice before she spoke again. "Ji," she said, reaching to put her hand on the side rail of her bed. "You are a good man."

He stared at the floor.

"Ji," she said stronger, then waited for him to meet her eyes. "You are a *good* man. You have taken a really lousy set of cards and built a family, a life, a future that no one—not a single person—thought you capable of doing. *You* did it. Without support from your parents. Without support from your aunt, uncle, and grandparents, who should have fought harder to be a part of your life. Those accomplishments are worthy of your pride, but don't let that pride destroy this opportunity. Life doesn't have to be something we tolerate, Ji. There is happiness to be found here. This money could help you."

"You make it sound so easy," Ji said in a tired voice. "As though there's a price that can—"

"It's not a *price*," Sadie cut in. "Money will never heal what you didn't have any more than keeping the restaurant will make Lin Yang's father more comfortable. Money will never make up for what Wendy didn't, couldn't, or wouldn't give you. But it is the one thing from Wendy—other than having created you in the first place—that can do some good."

The door opened again and Pete entered the room.

"I'd better get going," Ji said, standing up. "Let me know if I can do anything to help."

"You can take the money," Sadie said, filterlessly. "You can bless your family with it, and then you can paint me something beautiful that I can put on my wall and brag about to all my friends when they exclaim over the talent of the artist. I don't want to have to pull out those jewelry boxes every time I want to impress someone."

She was glad to see Ji's smile at her suggestion. He gave her a slight bow, chatted with Pete a few moments before saying good-bye, and left the room, pulling the door closed behind him.

"Oh, I forgot to ask him about Min," Sadie said right as the door closed.

"I talked to him last night. He said that he'd put off letting her grow up long enough. I'm not sure what that will translate into exactly, but it's got to be better than things were before."

"Good," Sadie said, but she couldn't look at him; she didn't know how to act.

With the bad guys in jail and the mystery solved, she and Pete would have to address everything that lay between them now. She looked down and smoothed the blankets across her stomach in an attempt to quell her anxiety. Too much had been happening last night for them to address their personal situation, but the crisis had passed, and Sadie knew they would be discussing it now.

In order to avoid Pete's gaze, Sadie closed her eyes, but then startled when he touched her hand. Her right forearm and hand were less cut up than her left, but she still had gauze wrapped around the thumb and across her palm.

Pete lifted her hand and kissed the inside of her wrist, just above the bandage. "I love you, Sadie," he said, so soft and sweet that her tears were impossible to hold back. She lifted her other hand to wipe at her eyes—embarrassed to have such little control over her emotions—but found it heavy with an IV, bandages, and tape. She opened her eyes to find him looking at her.

"Sadie?"

"I love you too, Pete," she said in reply, a lump in her throat. She pulled her hand away from his so she could wipe at her cheeks. She wanted him to leave and take all this intensity with him. But she also really wanted him to stay.

"I'm sorry."

"It's not your fault, Pete."

"But if I'd been paying better attention and gotten your first text, I'd have gone to the apartment immediately and none of this would have happened."

"Oh, you're talking about the attack," Sadie said, though she'd only meant to think it. Darned narcotics.

Pete pulled his eyebrows together for a moment and opened his mouth before he realized what she meant. He leaned forward, resting his elbows on his knees and looking between his feet. "The last time Pat and I came to San Francisco, she *seemed* strong and healthy and well. We walked the streets, hiked the redwoods, and tried to see all the things we'd missed on our earlier trips. By the end of that week, she was worn-out. I teased her about getting old; she said it felt like more than that and I paid it no mind. We returned home, and I went back to work. She struggled to get her strength back, but rather than make sure she went to the doctor, I told her to eat better and be more active." He paused and took a breath. "By the time she went to the doctor—almost three months later—her cancer was advanced. We opted for surgery anyway. Radiation, chemotherapy—anything to buy her more time, but I wondered how much time we'd lost because we hadn't taken her complaints more seriously—because I hadn't taken her complaints more seriously."

Tears streamed down Sadie's face again.

His forehead was all she could see until he lifted his face to look at her. "I *have* mourned her, Sadie. I have come to accept the way things are, and I know that what happened to her was not my fault and that she would not want me to be alone. Because of how strongly I know all of that, I wasn't prepared for what coming here would do to me. It took me back to that place before she was sick—or before we knew she was sick, anyway—before I felt all that pain and heartache and guilt. I missed her more than I have for a long time, and yet I *love* you. I found myself wondering what I would do if something happened to you. Could I go through all that pain again? If I had kept from falling in love again—which is precisely what I'd planned to do when Pat died—I would have prevented myself from ever feeling that kind of loss. The complexity of all those thoughts took me off guard, and I didn't handle it well. I'm sorry."

"I'm sorry, too," Sadie said, putting her hand over his. "I wish I knew how to help."

Pete smiled. "That you want to help me through this is one of the many reasons I love you like I do."

Sadie repeated the words in her mind and realized that his love for Pat was one of the reasons she loved *him* like she did as well. Despite the awkwardness of knowing he loved someone else, that he'd shared so many years of significance with his first wife, knowing that he *could* love like that was further proof of the caliber of man he was. She shifted without thinking and pain shot frontward and backward and side-to-side, causing her to gasp.

Pete stood quickly. "Are you all right?"

"Fine, just moved too fast. I'll probably do it two hundred more times before I learn my lesson." She took a breath and looked up into his handsome face. "We can put off the wedding and—"

"I accepted the offer on the house yesterday morning. My girls are going to start organizing Pat's things so that some of it will already be sorted when we get back to Garrison. Pat's sister is going to come down from Cody to help out as well."

"Are you sure you're ready?"

Pete smiled and leaned in, planting a kiss, as soft as silk, on her lips. As she'd told Ji, the past was the past—good or bad there was nothing the present could do to change it. What held power, however, were the choices they made today and the effect they could have on the future.

"I brought you something," Pete said. He reached into his shirt pocket and pulled out a paper napkin, which he unfolded to reveal a fortune cookie.

She looked at it and then at him. He smiled and nodded toward it.

She picked it up from his hand but needed his help to break it open. He held the end with the paper toward her and she slid the paper out.

No one can walk backwards into the future.

Pete smiled at her inquisitive look. "There's a little factory where you can do special orders. I think we should order some for the wedding."

"Or maybe make our own," Sadie suggested as she considered how much fun it could be to put their own fortunes inside. "I used grenadine syrup in place of some of the liquid in order to make some pink ones for a baby shower once. I bet I still have the recipe somewhere."

"Sounds a little too Shasta Winterberg for me," Pete said.

Sadie laughed.

"It's a good fortune though, isn't it?" Pete said. "That we can't hold on to the past too much."

"It's a very good fortune," she said, then raised her chin and pursed her lips, inviting him in for another kiss. He did not make her wait long.

Pete loved her. She loved him back. The past was gone. The future was wide open. What could be more healing than that?

Fortune Cookies

Note: The key to good fortune cookies is <u>patience.</u> Reading the recipe all the way through before beginning the process is also a very good idea.

3 tablespoons butter or margarine, softened
3 tablespoons sugar
1 egg white, room temperature
½ teaspoon vanilla (almond extract gives cookies a different flavor)
⅓ cup flour

Grease two cookie sheets. Preheat oven to 375 degrees and place one cookie sheet inside while the oven heats up.

In a small bowl, mix softened butter and sugar with a fork until smooth. Add egg white and vanilla and mix until well blended and smooth.

Blend in flour 1 spoonful at a time, mixing until batter is well blended and smooth.

When oven is preheated and batter is prepared, removed heated cookie sheet from oven and put the second cookie sheet inside the oven to heat while you prepare your first batch.

Dip the rim of a drinking glass (about 3 inches in diameter) in flour, and press four outlines firmly onto the hot cookie sheet. These rings will serve as your guide for the size and shape of the cookies.

Drop one teaspoon of batter into each outlined circle and use the back of a spoon to carefully spread out batter to cover the entire ring. Cookie should be quite thin. (The heated cookie sheet melts the butter in the batter, making the batter easier to smooth out.)

Put cookies in the oven and remove second heated cookie sheet. Bake 5 to 6 minutes, or until edges are lightly browned.

(It's a good idea to do just one cookie on your first pan to make sure you know the right amount of cooking time. Doing more than four cookies at a time might lead to burnt fingers as you try to hurry and shape the cookies before those remaining on the pan cool too much to be handled.)

While the first batch of cookies are baking, prepare the second batch by filling flour circles with batter on the newly heated pan.

Remove baked cookies from oven and place cookie sheet on a cooling rack. Place second pan of cookies into the oven and bake another 5 to 6 minutes.

Quickly loosen the cookies from the sheet with a spatula but don't turn them over. Working with one cookie at a time, place fortune in the center and gently fold cookie in half. Hold edges together while putting the folded side of the cookie over the edge of a mug or cup, pulling the corners down, one on the inside of the mug and one on the outside. Quickly place folded cookie in a muffin tin to keep its shape as it cools.

Repeat with remaining cookies. If cookies become too brittle to fold, return to oven briefly to soften.

Note: Food coloring can be used in batter but colors may not stay true during cooking.

Acknowledgments

This series is getting harder and harder for me. In the hope of keeping each story fresh and interesting in its own right, I have less to work with, in a sense, each time I begin a new book. I need new motives, new plotlines, and new ways for people to die. You should see the lists I have of how many horrible ways there are to kill someone—it's disturbing, to say the least.

It has also gotten harder for those people I depend on to make these books work. Namely:

My writing group: Nancy Allen (Isabelle Webb Series, Covenant, 2010–2013), Becki Clayson, Jody Durfee (*Hadley, Hadley Bensen*, Covenant, 2013), Ronda Hinrichsen (*Betrayed*, Covenant, 2014), and Jenny Moore (*Amelia and the Captain*, Covenant, 2014). They go through tedious rewrites of the early chapters over and over again and help me keep Sadie true to her character. I'd be lost without them.

Sadie's Test Kitchen: Annie, Danyelle, Laree, Lisa, Megan, Sandra, and Whit (Gyoza). They are the force behind the recipes. They share great ones with me, hone the ones posted on our private blog, and are absolutely essential to this process. I simply could not have done this series without them, and I so appreciate all the time and talents they have lent these last five years.

Shadow Mountain: Jana Erickson keeps everything going smoothly as my product director; Shauna Gibby creates the delicious covers; Malina Grigg does the typesetting, and Lisa Mangum is my editor extraordinaire. I seem to be making it a habit that each book is requiring more rewrite suggestions from her, and I am grateful beyond words for her patience, brilliance, and continual encouragement. Lisa's intern, Alannah Autrey, gave some great feedback on *Fortune Cookie* as well, playing an integral part in the final version.

My friends and family: I have come to realize that amid this journey I am on, the greatest blessing is the people I have met along the way. This includes readers, other writers, business associates, and people who would be in my journey regardless but play a part in this portion of my life as well. My sisters, Crystal White and Jenifer Johnson, beta read this book for me, as did my dear friend Jenny Moore. Lending their abilities to my endeavors is both a professional and emotional service to me, and I so appreciate all that they have done to help this book along. Margo Hovely (*The End Begins: Glimmering Light*, Covenant, 2012) unknowingly contributed the Cheater Sourdough Bread recipe, but I shall always call it the "bread of shame," though it never was that. ☺

My sweethearts: For this book, my husband, Lee, and three of our children were able to spend a weekend in San Francisco—one of my husband's very favorite cities. We ate and walked and mapped and photographed and visited and brainstormed and thoroughly enjoyed ourselves. It truly is a city of diversity, character, culture, and really great food. It was fun to experience it with them and then morph some of our experiences into this story.

The reason I have been able to develop this career is because of my husband's support and my children's patience. I have always tried to be a mom first, and while I have not always succeeded at that, I feel greatly blessed to have been able to have my family and my writing and make them all work together, but I certainly don't make it work by myself. I love these guys more than I can say, more than I can express, more than I can believe sometimes, and will always cherish them as my greatest blessings from the Father in Heaven who has given me so much.

Enjoy this sneak peek of

WEDDING CAKE

Coming Fall 2014

AUTHOR'S WARNING

Wedding Cake is the final book in the Sadie Hoffmiller Culinary Mystery series. As such, storylines and characters from earlier volumes will be revisited that may give away details of those earlier books. If you have not yet read the other books in the series, you may want to do so.

CHAPTER 1

Dead birds were the antithesis of a wedding day, which should be all about hope and goodness. That's why Sadie was making tiny tulle bags of birdseed for her wedding guests to throw instead of rice. *Two days*, she thought as she finished tying a gossamer bow on one of the favors. *Two days and I will be Mrs. Peter Cunningham.*

Sadie's phone rang and she pivoted from the kitchen counter to the kitchen table, where her phone vibrated against the lacquered tabletop.

She glanced at the caller ID before smiling and putting the phone to her ear. "Hi, sweetie."

"Hey, Mom," her daughter, Breanna, replied. There was a lot of noise in the background, and Sadie imagined her daughter—tall, dark, and beautiful—plugging one ear while standing in a corner of the Heathrow airport in London. "We're checked in and will board in about twenty minutes."

"Wonderful." Sadie allowed herself to take a break from the myriad wedding details and sat in the worn brown recliner in her living room. It was her favorite place in the house, and she settled into the squishy softness of its embrace with a sigh indicative of her long day. Forty-eight hours—well, forty-one, really—and she would be Pete's *wife*. She could hardly believe that after three years of what could only be classified as a tumultuous dating relationship, they were finally getting married. "What time do you land in Minneapolis?"

"Around four o'clock in the morning your time," Breanna said. She stifled a yawn, reminding Sadie that it was about 3:30 a.m. in London right now—8:30 p.m. here in Colorado, though. Since it was July, the sun was just setting, casting orange shadows through the big front window. The red-eye flight from London to Denver wasn't the best itinerary available—in fact, it might have been the very worst—but it had allowed Liam, Breanna's husband of only six weeks, to attend an important event that evening.

"I hope you'll be able to sleep on the plane," Sadie said.

"I'm not worried about that," Breanna said. "I'm *so* tired. The flight is nine hours, which will give me plenty of time to rest before the layover. We should be to Garrison by noon or so tomorrow."

"Wonderful," Sadie said, hoping the jet lag wouldn't be too difficult for them. "Pete swapped out the bed in your room for a queen-sized bed from his house. It's got fresh sheets and everything." Sadie liked Liam quite a lot, but he'd grown up wealthy and privileged, and she worried that her home wouldn't meet his expectations. "I even bought new towels." They matched the bedspread and the new curtains Sadie had put up; she'd been going for an English countryside look and then worried it would look pretentious.

"Don't stress too much," Breanna said with a smile in her voice. "We're looking forward to staying at the house. Shawn's there already?"

"He flew in this morning," Sadie said, smiling at the anticipation of having both her children—and Liam—under her roof at the same time. It didn't happen very often, what with Breanna living on another continent and Shawn finishing up his degree at Michigan State. "He's at Pete's bachelor party right now."

"Oh, a *bachelor* party. And you're not spying on them?"

They joked for a bit about what the men might be doing. Sadie kept to herself that she knew *exactly* what they were doing: barbecuing Omaha steaks, drinking imported beer, and playing poker until midnight at the home of one of Pete's police department buddies. It had only taken a quick scroll through Pete's text messages and eavesdropping on a couple of conversations when he thought she was occupied with something else to assure her that she had nothing to worry about on this last night of "debauchery"—not that her investigation meant she didn't trust him. It was just a habit, good or bad, depending on the circumstances of its employ.

It had been an intense few weeks: Pete preparing to move out of his home that had just sold, Sadie's house still having the realty sign in the front yard. After the honeymoon they would step up their efforts to find a new place of their own and then, maybe, she would lower the price on her home to encourage it to sell in the unpredictable market.

"Well, I better go," Breanna said on the phone. "If I use the restroom now and don't drink too much water on the flight, I might be able to avoid the horrible bathroom on the plane *and* sleep straight through."

Sadie said good-bye with a smile that stretched all the way to her toes. Sixteen hours from now she would get to hug her daughter and new son-in-law. And twenty-four hours after *that*, she'd be making vows to the man she had come to love so much. Still grinning, Sadie pushed up from the chair, then flinched slightly at the tugging pain that pulled at her right side, just below her ribs.

Three weeks ago she'd been stitched up following the most harrowing experience of her life, which was saying a lot based on the number of harrowing experiences she'd survived in recent years. She'd healed better than the doctors had expected, but she was still sore and she had to be careful about moving too quickly. Sadie credited the healing to the level of endorphins running through her bloodstream as the wedding plans had picked up speed.

Sadie moved a bit more carefully into the kitchen and finished tying up the rest of the birdseed packets. When the task was finished, she put the tiny bundles into a basket and set it next to the front door so that she'd know right where it was when she was running around crazy in the hours before the ceremony.

She scratched "birdseed favors" off her to-do list and sat down on one of the kitchen chairs, pulling the guest list she'd been meaning to get to all day in front of her. There was a purple check mark next to the guests who had responded that they would be in attendance and a black X next to those who had RSVP'd that they couldn't make it. Sadie had expected that most of her friends from out-of-state wouldn't be able to attend the ceremony, but she'd loved all the phone calls of congratulations and catching up that sending the invitations had garnered. Everyone was so happy for her and Pete, and she loved hearing their well wishes over and over again.

There were a few names unmarked on her list, including Ji, her recently discovered nephew. He wasn't sure he could get away from his restaurant but hadn't yet said he *wouldn't* be there. She still held hope that he, and perhaps his daughters, would be able to attend.

There were half a dozen other guests she hadn't heard from, and she considered whether or not she should follow up with them. She didn't want to put anyone on the spot, but what if their invitations were lost in the mail? She'd feel terrible if they learned about the wedding later and believed she hadn't included them. Or what if they'd tried to get in touch with her but called an old number, not realizing that she'd put her new number on the invitation? If they hadn't received the invitation at all, they might not have her new number.

There was still time to make a few calls—at least those on the West Coast—but was it worth the possibility of an awkward conversation? She tapped her pen on the paper—*decisions, decisions.* She needed to give Braxton's—the restaurant where they were holding the wedding luncheon—a final guest count by tomorrow at noon.

Her thoughts were interrupted when her phone chimed with a text message. She picked up the phone and noted that though the texter came up as UNKNOWN, the area code gave away that it was someone local.

> *Unknown:* Hi, Sadie.
>
> *Sadie:* Hi, who's this?
>
> *Unknown:* You don't know? I'm hurt.
>
> *Sadie:* Your name didn't come up on my contact list so you'll have to tell me. ☺
>
> *Unknown:* Think about it for a minute. Do you really not know who this is?

Sadie furrowed her brow as she remembered some advice Pete had given her almost two years ago when she'd disconnected her landline, forwarded her mail to a post office box, installed an alarm system on her home, and gotten her first private cell phone number, which she only shared with select people.

"Don't answer any calls or texts from unknown numbers,"

Pete had said. "I'll look them up, and when you know who it is, you can decide whether you want to call them back. Don't take any chances."

As time had moved forward, Sadie had bit by bit given up the protective measures that had felt so necessary at the time. She felt a little silly for thinking about Pete's advice now since she'd sent her new number out to dozens of people she'd invited to the wedding. It was surely one of them teasing her. But that didn't sit quite right. Most of the people in her life knew that she'd had some difficult times; they wouldn't play with her anxieties like this, would they?

Her phone chimed again, and she regarded the phone with increased irritation before picking it up.

You're not even going to guess? I thought you'd missed me.

Annoyed at the interruption but determined to get to the bottom of it, Sadie took the phone with her across the room where she sat down at her desk and opened her laptop. She typed the unknown phone number into the Google search bar and scrolled through the links until she found one that would give her the origination information about the owner of the phone number.

The link didn't give names, but it did tell her that the number was registered through an AT&T wireless store in Fort Collins, Colorado—the closest large city to Garrison—and that the account had been opened in 2002. Not only was the caller someone from town, it was someone who'd had the same number for more than a decade. That should give her some comfort, but it didn't give her as much as she'd have liked.

"This is ridiculous," Sadie said, standing up from the desk and heading back to the kitchen table and her to-do list for tomorrow.

She wanted to make sure it was complete before she turned in for the night.

Ridiculous or not, however, her anxiety was triggered and she felt tense. In search of a remedy, her eyes were drawn to the pan of rice pudding still on the stove; she crossed the room toward it. Shawn had requested his favorite dinner—Evil Chicken—and she'd made enough extra rice to make rice pudding for dessert. Shawn had left for the bachelor party before the rice pudding was ready, so she'd enjoyed a bowl herself and had been waiting for it to cool before she put it in the fridge. She really shouldn't have a second bowl, especially this late at night, but she knew that the creamy dessert would help her calm down and focus—good food always did.

Sadie took a bite of the still-warm perfection while expertly pushing the feelings of tension from her mind. It was all about compartmentalization, and she was not going to give the obnoxious texter more power than they deserved. Especially when so many other things needed her attention.

She scanned the to-do list to see if she'd missed anything. In fact, she had! With a smile, she wrote, "Clear out space in bathroom for Pete" and felt her stomach flip-flop at the thought of how soon they would be sharing the master bathroom. The master bedroom. Pete was still in his house, for now, but after the honeymoon he'd move in with her.

Holy moly, this is happening!

The chime of another text message shattered the glitter-tipped thoughts, and her eyes snapped to her phone, still on the desk where she'd left it. The tension returned. She looked at the clock—it was just after 9:00 p.m.—then reminded herself that this newest text could very well be from someone else. Perhaps one of the guests who hadn't yet confirmed their attendance. Or maybe it was *Pete* texting to tell her he loved her.

Sadie pushed away from the kitchen table and walked toward the phone. The screen had gone black by the time she reached it. She picked it up and slid her finger across the screen to wake it up.

Didn't I tell you that you'd never be free of me?

Jane!

Sadie's breath caught in her throat as the name came unbidden to her mind. Her heart began to race. Her tenuous optimism faded. She had become so used to not thinking of the woman who had threatened her life in Boston—it had been almost two years, after all—that it was a shock to suddenly jump to that conclusion, and she immediately tried to dismiss it.

There were several people who blamed Sadie for getting caught in a variety of criminal behavior—it could be one of them toying with her. But Jane was the only one of them who had gotten away, so to speak. And Jane *had* said those exact words: "You'll never be free of me." Wouldn't it be just like her to wait until two days before Sadie's wedding, on an evening when she would be home alone, to make good on that threat?

Sadie took a deep breath in an attempt to calm herself. Pete would want her to call him about this. She turned back toward the kitchen and began toggling to the keypad on her phone. *Did I lock the doors after Shawn had left for the party?*

She told herself, again, not to overreact. It was probably nothing. A moment later, the squeak of a floorboard froze her in place. Her head snapped up but her eyes stared blankly at the cabinets in front of her.

This is not happening two days before my wedding!

Sadie felt the warmth of another person standing behind her at the precise moment something suddenly covered her eyes. She screamed, dropped her phone, and grabbed at the hands that were blinding her, pulling her backward.

A throaty whisper in her ear nearly paralyzed her. "Guess who?"

ABOUT THE AUTHOR

J osi S. Kilpack began her first novel in 1998. Her seventh novel, *Sheep's Clothing*, won the 2007 Whitney Award for Mystery/ Suspense. *Fortune Cookie* is Josi's twentieth novel and the eleventh book in the Sadie Hoffmiller Culinary Mystery Series.

Josi currently lives in Willard, Utah, with her husband and children.

For more information about Josi, you can visit her website at www.josiskilpack.com, read her blog at www.josikilpack.blogspot .com, or contact her via e-mail at Kilpack@gmail.com.

IT'D BE A CRIME
TO MISS THE REST OF THE SERIES . . .

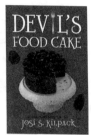

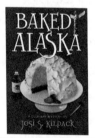